PRAISE FOR *THE GIRL FROM KRAKOW*

"Well researched and well imagined, the novel expands historical data into full, vivid scenes. Fans of historical fiction or readers looking for something new after finishing Anthony Doerr's *All the Light We Cannot See* will enjoy Rosenberg's story of reinvention, self-discovery, the power of personal connections, and the kindness of strangers."

—*Booklist*

"[*The Girl from Krakow*] is a page-turner with a focus on how ordinary people cope when trapped in totalitarian systems. With its strong characters, Rosenberg's novel is a winner."

—*Publishers Weekly*

"When a prominent philosopher like Alex Rosenberg turns his mind to writing a novel, there is reason to celebrate. With vivid, fast-paced storytelling verve, Rosenberg sweeps us across Europe during a morally fraught decade in a novel that is as sure to make you think as to feel."

—Rebecca Newberger Goldstein, author of *36 Arguments for the Existence of God: A Work of Fiction*

AUTUMN
IN OXFORD

ALSO BY ALEX ROSENBERG

THE GIRL FROM KRAKOW

AUTUMN IN OXFORD

A Novel

ALEX ROSENBERG

LAKE UNION
PUBLISHING

Published by Lake Union Publishing, Seattle

www.apub.com

Amazon, the Amazon logo, and Lake Union Publishing are trademarks of Amazon.com, Inc., or its affiliates.

ISBN-13: 9781503939073
ISBN-10: 1503939073

Cover design by Shasti O'Leary-Soudant
Photograph of couple by FPG / Getty Images
Photograph of Oxford University by Lynn James / Getty Images

Printed in the United States of America

CONTENTS

PART I

22 January 1959

No Service on the Circle Line:

Accident at Paddington

CHAPTER ONE

At 2:30 p.m. Tom Wrought left the college for London. He was to meet his lover, Liz Spencer, at the Gresham, a shabby hotel in Bloomsbury. They would spend a few hours in the room, then walk over to Charlotte Street and find a restaurant. Afterwards they would return to the hotel and continue to make love with an ardour that seemed inexhaustible.

It was a blustery day in mid-January 1959. Grey clouds still lowered, but the rain had stopped. Tom decided to walk to the Oxford railway station. He told Lloyd—the staircase "scout" or servant—to cancel his tutorial. After checking his pigeonhole at the porters' lodge, Tom came out the Trinity College gate and headed down the Broad to George Street. There the beauty of the college gave way to a hundred grim little shops, each cadging a living from undergraduates with overdrafts.

Tom carried nothing more than a toothbrush, a package of sheaths, and a book under review. He was working against a deadline, and the hour and a half to London would not be wasted. The reviewing—for the *Times Literary Supplement*, the *New Statesman*, and the Manchester *Guardian*—supplemented his meagre fellow's stipend. It also made him something of a public figure in England—the Pulitzer Prize–winning historian, blacklisted in the States, and now making things difficult for the establishment's admiration of America.

As Tom stood in the queue for a London return ticket, his eye wandered beyond the booking stall to the platform. There, a few dozen feet from the open door, was Liz's husband, Trevor Spencer, looking every inch the banker—in a black homburg and a trench coat, carrying a tightly wound umbrella. Spencer was no banker, but it suited his self-image to dress like one. His face was in a newspaper, the *Express*, which evidently absorbed him completely.

How to avoid him? Surely Spencer would not be travelling first. Tom decided to ask for first class, took his ticket, and immediately walked out of the small station back into the street. Separated from the view of the platform by the walls of the building, Tom waited. He watched the 3:05 express come in from Cheltenham. When he heard the conductor's whistle, he hastened onto the platform and found a compartment in first class. He settled himself against the plush blue velour, covered at the headrest by an antimacassar, and contemplated the printed appeal for Dr. Barnado's children's homes in a frame opposite.

His travelling companion was a taciturn woman. Tom was grateful. But he was unable to concentrate on the book he had to review and instead watched the rolling pastureland turn into the suburbs of Reading and then the industrial ring round London. Should he worry about where Trevor Spencer was going? No. It was simply an unhappy coincidence.

When the train reached Paddington he remained in his seat until Spencer passed the carriage window. Only then did Tom rise and walk slowly down the platform, allowing the distance between them to increase. He needed Trevor to buy his underground ticket and be on his way down one of the long moving staircases before Tom did so.

At the tube station booth there was no sign of Trevor and no queue for tickets either, so no reason to postpone his own descent to the trains. But as Tom stepped onto the escalator, he could see at the bottom of the long descent Trevor's black homburg just getting off and heading for the Circle line in the direction of Baker Street—where Liz worked.

Now what? Suddenly Tom's desire not to be spotted turned into a need to follow Spencer, at least until he could be sure this was no more than a coincidence. Liz had said enough about her husband's suspicions to worry him.

As Tom reached the platform, he heard a train, and looking down the tunnel he saw its headlamps. When he turned, there was Trevor well along in the middle of the platform, still reading his paper.

Then it happened. In a matter of seconds, no more. The train began to slow as it entered the station. Trevor Spencer looked up towards the train, saw Tom watching him, and dropped his newspaper. Suddenly a man darted out and pushed Trevor onto the tracks just in front of the still rapidly moving train. Trevor's assailant could not have timed it better. Too soon and Trevor might have scrambled away across the track; too late and he would have bounced off the side of the carriage. Then the man turned calmly and walked off the platform under the **WAY OUT** sign in the direction of the ascending escalators.

There were dozens of people on the platform, but no one had actually been watching or could have seen much beyond what their peripheral vision took in. Trevor Spencer's sudden, aborted cry, audible over the screech of the train, brought them all to attention. People were converging at the point of the platform from which he had been pushed, though there was nothing to see in the gap between train and platform, nothing at all. It was as if Trevor Spencer had simply vanished. But everyone knew there was a body down there on the tracks.

Tom, however, saw nothing of this. The instant after Trevor recognized him, seventy-five feet or so down the platform—the instant Trevor disappeared beneath the train, the instant the murderer calmly began walking towards the **WAY OUT** sign at the end of the platform—that was the moment Tom began to run in an urgent attempt to apprehend the man. Arriving at the base of the long upward escalator, he could see no one hurrying, and no one even resembling the killer. He turned and looked down the corridors to the other lines. There were five at the combined Paddington and Edgware Road stations, each adorned by the identical advert for Bovril. If Trevor's killer wasn't in sight, it was hopeless. *So,* Tom thought, *I need to find a policeman and tell him what I saw.*

But what had he seen? All he could describe was the colour of the man's coat, and that he wore a hat pulled down in a way that covered most of his face. That wouldn't help much. *What would you say to a policeman anyway: you knew the victim, you were conducting an affair with his wife? He might have discovered we were to meet in London and intended to confront us?* And then Tom began to feel an icy sweat. *Why don't you just tell the police you actually cooked up this very murder in your head three months ago?*

The platform was the worst place he could be. How to escape? The cramp in his stomach made rational thought difficult. He began to walk back to the Circle line platform he had come from. Before he had taken five steps, he realized that there would be no trains at that platform till the body was recovered. Instead he turned towards the Hammersmith line and began walking briskly down the passageway.

When he reached the first landing of steps, he again stopped. Wiping the cold sweat from his brow, he unbuttoned his topcoat, one that he now realized looked rather like that of Trevor's assailant, as did his hat. He loosened his tie and took a deep breath. *How can I reach Liz? Should I even try to reach her?* He looked at his watch. *Would she still be at her office? If I call, her assistant will answer. Then her assistant would know . . . know what? Know about us? She already does. She'll know something is wrong.* Tom was already thinking like a guilty man, or at least a suspect. He turned and sought the escalators. In the cold air of the pavement on Praed Street, the perspiration was still running off his forehead, stinging his eyes. He mopped his face and began looking round for a telephone box. Liz would leave the office at five and would go to the hotel. He had to leave a message for her. It would have to be guarded.

"Gresham Hotel," came the strong Irish accent of the desk clerk they both knew well by now.

"Can you take a message for Mrs. Spencer?" The room was always booked in her name. "Tell her that there has been an emergency in"—if he said Oxford, she'd think it was the children—"in London, and she should go home immediately."

"Is this Mr. . . . . Spencer?" Evidently the man had recognized Tom's voice. Liz and Tom had always used Spencer, her name, when they booked. Could he dissimulate? He had to.

"No, my name is"—Tom looked out of the call box at the gold lettering on the darkened windows of the pub across the street—"Watney, Mr. Watney, like the lager."

"Very good."

Sitting in the train back to Oxford, the cold sweat returned, along with the cramp in the stomach. His temples began to throb, his pulse to race. Tom had to get up from his seat, seek the corridor, and throw open a window. He sought to calm himself with a cigarette. And now he felt the same nemesis that had sought him out back in the Hürtgen Forest during the war. It was the thought that he might as well be dead.

The rush of nicotine to his lungs made him dizzy, and the smoke in his nostrils burned. He flung the cigarette onto the tracks. He had to face the fact that almost everything he had done in the last hour or so was wrong. When the police found out—and not if, but when—his actions would all make him appear to be guilty of Trevor's murder. There was really nothing to do but wait for the nemesis, just as he had done in combat.

You joked about doing it, that evening coming back from Paris, with Liz in the sleeper car corridor. Could you have done it, Tom? Well, you love her enough to want him . . . dead? No. Not dead. Just gone. You love her. She's unhappy. You'd do anything to put an end to that unhappiness. Yes, but my doing this wouldn't end it. Killing Trevor Spencer wouldn't be a solution to our problem. But, Trevor dead—is that a solution? No, Tom. Not the way it happened.

⟢

At 5:05 p.m. Liz Spencer found herself in front of the Baker Street tube station in a crowd. Before them was a chalked sign on a hoarding: NO SERVICE ON DISTRICT AND CIRCLE LINES—ACCIDENT AT PADDINGTON. She looked at her watch. There was no stop very nearby that could get her directly to Russell Square. In the rush hour a cab could take an hour. What to do? She sought a tube map. *Ah, Bakerloo line to Piccadilly, and Victoria up to Russell Square. Very good!* Pleased with her improvisation, she descended the steps to the ticket booth.

Liz was no more than a quarter of an hour late. Plenty of time before the dinner reservation she had made at the little Italian seafood restaurant down at the end of Charlotte Street. *And plenty of time after supper as well,* she thought, smiling to herself. It was already dark as she ascended the stair against the current of sombre office workers moving down out of the early gloom of a winter night. Liz, however, welcomed the velvet darkness of the street as a deep cloak over the intimacy she would share with Tom.

She entered the Gresham Hotel to a smile from the Irishman at the desk. "Ah, Mrs. Spencer." And then a frown came over his face. "Message for you." He wouldn't say aloud what he had written out. Bad news was better read than heard.

She looked at the paper, then back at him blankly.

"Sorry, nothing else. I thought it was Mr. Spencer, but he said not."

Liz looked at the note again. *It has to be Tom. No one else knows, except perhaps your assistant, if she suspects. She might, no, she must! But it was a man who called asking for you.*

Liz turned and left. Preoccupied by the message, she was on automatic pilot as she made her way to Russell Square for the tube up to Kings Cross and over to Paddington. By the time she was on the District line, service had returned to normal. At Paddington she had to wait an hour for an Oxford train. In the waiting room on the platform, all the way back, she couldn't help running through scenarios. She didn't want to. *Whatever it is, you'll imagine something worse. You're just working yourself up. It wouldn't help.* But anxiety drove out all control over her consciousness. The message had been from a Mr. Watney. *But I don't know anyone named Watney.* It wasn't the children. It couldn't be. They hadn't been in London, surely! *It could only be Tom. But why would he have made up a name when he called the Gresham? Why would he have told me to go back to Oxford?* There was just no way to fit the pieces together, nothing she could add that would even narrow the possibilities. She could steel herself if she knew what awaited her. Instead, she could only imagine the worst. Fumbling for a cigarette, she realized that she had seated herself in No Smoking.

<hr />

It was 9:30 p.m. by the time the train pulled into Oxford. Had Liz been in Smoking, she might have seen the two Scotland Yard detectives travelling up to Oxford in the same train. They were in a cab heading to Park Town crescent well before Liz reached the car park in front of the station.

<hr />

The au pair, Ifegenia, a young Italian girl, met her at the door. "There are two police here to see you. They've just come. In the lounge." She helped Liz off with her coat and hung it next to the two rather shabby coats she had just taken from the policemen. Then the girl disappeared into the kitchen.

"Mrs. Spencer?" It was properly interrogatory. The men had risen as Liz came to the threshold of the room and remained there. She nodded. "Chief Inspector Bennett, Scotland Yard." The man was squat and wide, with thinning hair combed over a glistening pate, five lines of deep wrinkles across his forehead, a boxer's flattened nose. He was in serious need of a shave. Liz bit her lip and waited. "This is Detective Sergeant Watkins." Bennett indicated the thin and chinless younger man beside him, with NHS glasses and heavy eyebrows below a short haircut. Watkins and his governor were both dressed in dark off-the-rack suits with unstarched shirts and plain woollen ties. They looked tired, impatient, out of sorts. But they were making an effort to be polite.

"I fear I must inform you that your husband, Trevor Spencer, has been killed, in London. A homicide, actually." The inspector looked down at his notepad. "At four ten he was standing on the District and Circle line platform at Paddington. Someone pushed him in front of an oncoming train, and then left the scene."

The older detective was continuing to speak, but Liz couldn't hear. Instead, she found herself in Trevor's place, falling to the tracks before the oncoming train. She felt that horror as a sharp pain in her abdomen, followed by a wave of nausea. She put her hand to her mouth, but the urge to vomit passed. As the enormity of what he had said washed over her, Liz began to lose balance and had to grasp the lintel. The two men reached out to steady her, but she fended them off as the blood quickly returned to her brain. She needed to sit. The men moved back towards the chesterfield, and Liz took the armchair.

Detective Bennett was silent, waiting for her to regain some composure. But Liz was still absorbing Trevor's death. The visceral dread she felt erased at a stroke all the anger, resentment, fury at Trevor that the years had accumulated. Suddenly—and permanently, she later realized—they were transformed into pity, grief, regret. When the tears came, it was Watkins, the younger policeman, who proffered a handkerchief.

Finally she searched for something to say. "Are you certain it was him?"

"I am afraid so, ma'am. Identification on the body."

"And you are confident it was murder?" Liz had to ask the question. Then she worried. Was this question appropriate as the first response from a sudden widow?

"Yes. The trainman saw the event clearly. What else might it have been, ma'am? Do you think he could have been contemplating suicide?"

"No, no . . . I only thought if it were at a tube stop, it might have been accidental."

Now Watkins intervened with an insistent tone. "He was pushed." Looking at his notes, the detective continued, "By a man of above average height in a belted trench coat wearing a hat, face not visible to the trainman."

Bennett continued, "I must ask, Mrs. Spencer, did your husband have enemies, anyone who might have profited from his death, perhaps some unstable person with a grudge?"

Liz tried to gauge how long she should appear to be thinking about this question and then said, "No one at all. Not a soul."

"Is there anyone who might have profited from his death?" Bennett was persistent.

Liz shook her head, but all she could think of was *Yes, there is someone. Two people, in fact—Tom and me*. And then she recalled the thought experiment Tom had conducted one afternoon during three days they'd managed to steal in Paris: pushing Trevor in front of a tube train at rush hour could solve all their problems. *Could Tom possibly have done such a thing? Impossible, Liz, unless you understand nothing about human character!* The thought that he might have done it momentarily frightened her, for Tom and for herself, but then she was sure. The very idea was absurd.

Thankfully Bennett was not reading her mind; instead, he was consulting his notes. He looked from them to her. "What line of work was your husband in, Mrs. Spencer?"

The answer came with evident reluctance. "He was unemployed. He'd been an estate agent and then a used car salesman. But he was discharged from both jobs and hadn't had any work recently."

"How long had he been out of work?"

"I'm not sure. He didn't tell me immediately when he lost the last job. It's been over a year since he sold anything much," she replied as evenly as she could.

Looking round at the comfortable house, Detective Bennett replied with an interrogative tone, "Private income?"

Liz flared slightly. "No, Inspector. Working wife."

"Excuse me," came the surprised apology.

The second policeman now cleared his throat. "Any idea what your husband was doing in London today?"

"None. I've never known him to go to London alone in all the years we've lived here." It was true; why shouldn't she say so?

The detective fished a business card out of his side pocket. "Does this mean anything to you?"

Liz looked at the card. Victor Mishcon, a London solicitor. "Nothing whatsoever."

"It was in his billfold." He took the card back from her. "I am sorry to have to ask, but might there have been another woman, one with a jealous husband?"

Liz's eyes widened. This was something she'd never thought of. "No, I can't imagine it, Inspector. Why do you ask?"

Pure chagrin overcame the rather sour look on the man's face. He reached into his pocket. "We also found this in his jacket." It was a neat little envelope, about one and a quarter inch square, with a flap, coloured in a light blue.

Liz made her face into an impassive mask of stolidity. "What is it?"

Bennett was still flustered. "It's an empty prophylactic packet, French in origin and not sold in Britain."

Liz recognized the brand. So, Trevor had found her out. She opened her mouth and covered it with her hand. That had to be the right thing to do.

Bennett decided that Mrs. Spencer had been hit with one shock too many. It was time to terminate the interview. "Here's my card, Mrs. Spencer, in case there is anything you need to tell me. Someone will call in a day or two about the disposition of your husband's . . . remains." He had decided not to say *body*. All three of them rose. The two policemen moved to the door, collecting their raincoats.

"May I call you a cab?" she volunteered, looking at her watch.

"No, thank you. We've troubled you enough for one night. We'll find our way to the station." Without shaking her hand, they moved sombrely out the door.

⟞⟝

Liz watched them out the lounge window as they walked down the crescent until they were out of sight. Then she moved to the telephone in the hall.

"Tom, is that you? It's Trevor. He's dead." She could hear the disbelief in her voice.

His reply staggered her. "Yes, I know. I was there when it happened."

"You were in London?" Liz took the receiver from her ear. Could Tom have had something to do with Trevor's death?

"I was on the underground platform when he was pushed."

Her worst apprehension suddenly returned. "My God. That's what your message to the hotel was about!"

"Yes. I didn't know what to do. I tried to follow the killer, but I lost him almost immediately. Then I realized that the police would have to tell you and that it would be best if you were home when they did."

"Best?" She let the word hang.

"Better to find you at home than in some seedy London hotel. The police don't need to know about us."

"It's too late for that, Tom. Two detectives were here when I got home. They told me what happened. Then they asked some questions, and they showed me two things Trevor had in his pockets: the business card of a London solicitor, and the wrapper from a sheath of the sort we've used, the ones we got in Paris." Tom was silent on the other end of the line. Into the silence Liz blurted her worst fear, "At least their only witness couldn't identify you."

"I told you. I saw the killer." His reply was tinged with anger. "What are you saying? Do you think I killed him?"

"No. It's just—" She stopped. The scenario Tom had sketched one afternoon in Paris three months before hung there silently between them. Then she began again. "No, of course not. Only that the train-man is the sole witness they could find who got a good look at what happened, and he can't place you at the scene. But there's a good chance this will unravel our secret."

"Why?"

"It's obvious, Tom. The story will make all the papers. My assistant, Beatrice Russell, will read about it. She knows about us, even knows about the Gresham Hotel. Remember when I left my diary there, and they called the office? The police will interview the solicitor. The condom wrapper will make it obvious why Trev consulted him. Then they will begin to question me. And what will I say?"

"The truth. We'll be alright."

"Tom, you're wildly gullible and dead wrong." Liz paused for him to respond. She took the silence for continued resistance. "If I tell the police about us, they'll soon find out we were in Paris at the same time. All they have to do is look at our passports. They'll put two and two together and get five. It may take them a week or so, but unless they're sloppy and lazy, there's every chance it will come out that you were on that platform. Someone will have seen you at least near it."

"What do you suggest?"

"We could leave." She gulped. "No, that's as bad as a confession. And there's the kids."

Tom added, "Besides, I really can't go back to the States, and Canada would probably extradite me if the Brits asked."

"We need a solicitor, I think, or two." Her voice sounded firm. Now, not for the first time in their relationship, Liz was completely in control. "Don't talk to the police without one, promise?"

"What will you tell the children?" She felt the anguish in his voice.

Liz was still in charge. "I have till they wake in the morning to think that through."

Tom heard the line disengage.

⟦⟧

She stood there in the hall, one hand still on the receiver. How was she going to tell her children their father was dead? Olivia was nearly ten. Ian was just seven. She would have to tell them together, but they would respond quite differently. The girl's grief would be palpable. She had only just begun to seek the attention of a father who was "distant." The boy, Ian, was already adopting the English upper-class demeanour his schoolmaster prized as "phlegm." Liz didn't want him to cope with his father's death that way.

How will you *cope? What will you tell yourself, Liz? What is it you really feel? Your husband is dead, someone you once thought you loved, still cared about, as least as your children's father. Yes, it makes things much simpler. Yes, you're now free to do as you really wish. But . . . he's dead, dead. Face yourself, Liz, and admit what you feel, at least to yourself.* She flushed. The feeling was unworthy, she knew.

And then a worse thought came back to her. *Could it have been Tom?* He'd given up a great deal for Liz already. Some position, wealth, comfort, a wife who wanted him, even if she didn't love him, not the way Liz did. *He loves you, Liz. Is it a manic emotion, one that could lead him to kill?* Liz knew well enough from her own past how overwhelming emotions could overpower.

No, he's not like that, not at all.

CHAPTER TWO

Tom woke suddenly from an unbearable dream. But the instant his eyes were open, all trace of it vanished, obliterated by what had oppressed him when he had closed his eyes the night before. How had he found sleep at all in the rush of awful scenarios that had crossed his thoughts? Well, they were all back now. He staggered to the common bathroom in the landing, thankful to be still alone. False bonhomie with the undergraduates who shared it would have been impossible.

Fellows living in college were not gregarious at breakfast. Each served himself from the sideboard. Most were absorbed in one or another of the morning papers spread on the long, wide table at which they were eating. It was a small mercy. He knew that one look at him and all would see the guilt.

Tom took his usual bowl of Weetabix, coffee, and toast, and surveyed the choice of newspapers before him. He needed a London paper today, not the Manchester *Guardian*. Picking up the *Daily Mail*, he looked at the bottom half of the front page and then began to turn the inside pages. He worked his way through from the front and then went back through the pages. If there had been a report, it was too small to find, even by someone looking for it. *Strange,* he thought. His sense of oppression lifted a little.

At eleven thirty Tom was in his study with an undergraduate droning through a rescheduled American history tutorial paper. The student's monotone made it easy for Tom's thoughts to wander repeatedly back to his predicament. The boy looked up at the end of each paragraph, expecting a reproof or a correction. Hearing none, he took up his paper and continued to read aloud. Finally he came to the end and glanced hopefully at his tutor. Tom was trying to think of something to say when there was a knock at the outer door of his rooms. He recognized the knock. It was Lloyd, his scout, who knew well enough that he was "sporting his oak"—closing the outer door as a signal that he was not to be interrupted. It had to be something urgent.

Slightly relieved at the reprieve from having to say something intelligent to the student, Tom rose and went to the door. It was indeed Lloyd, who looked over Tom's shoulder at the undergrad and whispered, "Very sorry, sir. I wouldn't have disturbed, the oak and all, but it's the police, sir." The repeated "sir" showed his discomfort. He paused, gauging Tom's reaction. "They want a word."

Tom felt the flush of heat spread up from his torso. How could they have put him together with Trevor's death so quickly? Perspiration broke out on his temples. He turned to his tutorial student. Had the boy noticed? "Sorry, Norris, we'll have to reschedule again." Then back to Lloyd. "Are they downstairs?"

"No, sir. They're at the porters' lodge. Shall I have them come along?"

"Yes."

Without really enough time to compose himself, Tom recalled Liz's advice: say nothing without a solicitor present. Three minutes later there were two uniformed Thames Valley constables at his open door, carrying their custodian police helmets at their sides.

The younger of the two spoke as if he were reading from a script, while the older one monitored his performance. "Mr. Thomas Wrought?" Tom nodded. "I have a warrant for your arrest on a charge of murdering one Trevor Spencer."

Tom was about to respond when the older policeman raised his hand to him. "Let him continue, sir."

The younger policeman did so. "You do not have to say anything, but anything you do say will be taken down and may be given in evidence."

"Very good, Kimble." The older copper turned to Tom. "If you promise to come quietly, I'll not have to restrain you, sir."

"Yes, certainly. Where are we going?"

"Police station in St. Aldate's. But the remand is to London, sir."

Why do you keep calling me sir, when you're arresting me for murder?
"Shall I take anything? A coat, a toothbrush, a book?"

"It's chilly and wet, sir. Your coat and hat."

⟢—⟣

They walked through the college, along Broad Street to the High, and then down towards St. Aldate's. Passers-by gave the three men hardly more than a nod. Tom had never noticed the police station, a rather large Georgian pile amidst the mock Tudor of the other buildings on the street. He wondered whether he should ask to see the warrant. But he said nothing. Expecting to be questioned at the station, he was disappointed to learn that he would be there only long enough to arrange transport to London. In fact, except for the offer of a cup of tea, he was left sitting unattended in a corridor facing the duty sergeant's desk for almost an hour. Tom tried to convert the anxiety cramping his stomach into anger, resentment, outrage. But everyone was being too polite, considerate, almost apologetic.

Surely he could have walked away at any time. Was there a reason for this laxness with a murder suspect? Was it the class system asserting itself, treating him like a gentleman, the fellow of an Oxford college, someone above suspicion even when under suspicion? Or was it something else? Did they *want* him to leave, to escape, to betray a sign of guilt? He would not do so.

At one thirty, two men in worn coats and rumpled suits came into the station and approached the duty sergeant's desk in front of Tom. They showed identity cards. "I'm Inspector Bennett; this is Sergeant Watkins. We're here for Wrought." The duty sergeant lifted his pen and wordlessly pointed at Tom sitting behind them, while handing them the warrant.

Bennett turned. "Mr. Wrought, are you prepared to come with us to London?"

"Do I have a choice?" Tom's tone was just barely ironic, and he brought his hands together for handcuffs.

"That won't be necessary." Bennett signalled the way out.

<hr/>

There was silence among the three men all the way to London. Tom sat in the rear of the car with Bennett, while Watkins drove. In ninety minutes the two detectives did not even engage in small talk. Were all police this taciturn? Why weren't they interested in asking him questions? Tom needed to assert his innocence. But they asked nothing. It was as if they already had his confession.

<hr/>

The police car turned from Victoria Street into New Scotland Yard, and Tom was led to a narrow hall. Here the desk sergeant at a raised desk spoke. "Turn out your pockets." Tom did so. The sergeant brought out a manila envelope and handed it to Tom, who filled and sealed it, signing his name across the flap. The sergeant spoke again. "You will be held here pending a bail hearing in the high court Monday morning, Mr."—he looked at the warrant—"Wrought."

Expecting an interrogation at last, Tom looked up at the officer. "May I make a telephone call? Can I get in touch with a solicitor?"

"Do you have one in mind, sir? We can make contact."

"I don't, Sergeant. I don't even know how to go about choosing one." *Who can you call?* he asked himself. *Who might know someone? The master of Trinity? One of your editors? The American embassy? That's what an innocent American would do, isn't it?* "I'm an American citizen. Will the embassy help me?"

"Consulate, sir. I'll call them." Tom nodded in thanks. The sergeant continued. "But this late on Friday, sir, no one will answer, not till Monday morning I fear."

Then, still without a question from the two arresting officers, he was led to a holding cell. But for his promise to Liz, Tom would have demanded to be questioned then and there.

Liz waited for a call from Tom all that Friday and Saturday. On Sunday morning a constable presented himself at Liz's door on Park Town crescent. "I'm sorry to trouble you, ma'am. But I have a warrant here"—he looked down at his paper—"to take away your passport. Material witness. You may contest this ruling before the magistrate at town hall tomorrow morning."

"Very well. I'll get it for you." In a few moments she was back, handing over her British passport. "Constable, can you tell me, was a man named Wrought arrested yesterday or this morning?"

"Shouldn't really say, ma'am. But yes. They took him to Scotland Yard Friday afternoon."

<hr />

On Monday morning Liz went into London. This time the endless morning darkness was oppressive. Riding the underground from Paddington, Liz felt caught in a cave-in so deep it was pointless to even try to move the stones that trapped her.

Snap out of it! You're no good to Tom or yourself like this!

She was at the office of Victor Mishcon before opening hours. This was the solicitor whose card her husband, Trevor, had in his billfold when he was killed. Perhaps he could shed some light. She moved aside for the secretary, who unlocked the front door, and when the woman asked if she had an appointment Liz replied, "No. My husband, Trevor Spencer, was here some time ago and saw someone. Now he's dead, and I was hoping to speak to the person he talked to."

At that moment Victor Mishcon came through into the vestibule, looked at Liz, and smiled warmly. The receptionist spoke. "Mr. Mishcon, this lady's husband was here last week, perhaps you recall, without an appointment. You spoke to him briefly."

"Yes, Miss Finch, I recall the gentleman."

Here Liz began to speak. "I'm afraid he's dead, sir. I was hoping you might be able to shed any light for me on what he consulted you about."

Mishcon handed his coat and hat to the receptionist and opened his door. "I'm so sorry. Come through, Mrs. . . ."

"Spencer. Thank you."

He motioned her to a chair, the very one Trevor must have sat in, and took a seat behind his own desk. "My condolences. Normally what is said here must be protected by attorney-client privilege." He shrugged his shoulders. "But your husband was not a client. In any case, I provided him with only the most generic information."

Deftly he walked Liz through Trevor's questions and his answers. Liz did not interrupt.

"Your husband told me that he was contemplating a divorce and needed advice. He described his situation, and I provided him a broad outline of the relevant law. I told him that if you are working and he is at home not employed, the law deems him to be the children's caregiver, and you would have to continue to support him and the children in a divorce."

Mishcon now looked slightly flustered. "I asked what grounds he contemplated, and he told me adultery. I told him in that case, his wife could well lose custody of the children." Mishcon paused, allowing Liz to absorb this information. As she did not pose any question, he took up his recollection of the interview.

"Your late husband asked specifically if in a divorce you could oblige them to move to more inexpensive lodgings. I told him the law would permit removal, but only to accommodations substantially similar and in the same area. Finally, he asked if you could take the children from Britain were you to get wind of a divorce action. I told him that he could probably secure a court order to prevent it."

When he had finished, Mishcon drew a breath. "There it is."

"I must tell you, Mr. Mishcon, my husband died under suspicious circumstances. I believe I will need a solicitor to represent me in a criminal matter." Mishcon's eyes widened. Liz saw his look. "I didn't mean to—"

The solicitor waved her apology away. "I don't suggest you did anything improper. It's just I cannot help you, Mrs. Spencer. It's not my field." He paused for a moment. "But I have a young friend who does practice criminal defence." Then the solicitor pulled open the drawer in front of him and brought out a card. "If you have no objection to a woman, that is." Liz shook her head vigorously. "Miss Alice Silverstone." He passed the card to Liz. "Her firm's offices are on the other side of Red Lion Square, number twelve."

Liz rose. "You have been more than helpful, Mr. Mishcon." As she opened the door, she could hear the receptionist on one side and Mishcon on the other.

"It's Scotland Yard, Mr. Mishcon, CID," the receptionist said. "A Detective Bennett would like a word. I told him you'd be free late this afternoon."

Liz was rather surprised that CID hadn't already interviewed Mishcon. She walked out quietly. Cutting across Red Lion Square, she found number twelve.

⬥

By Monday afternoon Tom had made attempts to eat five meals, none of which had been met with success. Much harder to deal with was the excruciating boredom, combined with complete mystification about what was happening to him. He still had not been questioned. This seemed to him very strange. There was nothing about his predicament he could put his mind to. At first he had felt no more than a vague disquiet. Was it the civility of the English police? The certainty that he was innocent? The whole experience was far less menacing than what he'd experienced in the war. But by Sunday afternoon the attempt at equanimity had been replaced by serious disquiet; Monday morning Tom awoke to cramps of anxiety in his gut.

When his lunch tray came through the Judas port, he spoke out. "Am I to have a bail hearing today?"

"Dunno, Wrought," came a voice. "But there's a solicitor here to see you. Quite a looker she is too."

A moment later the cell door opened. A young woman entered. She wore her dark hair long, and it was unevenly cut at her shoulders, a look Tom had seen in France the previous fall. Her attire was French as well, a severe blue suit, linen shirt with sparkling cuff links at the protruding sleeves. She was not tall but wore high heels and wore them well, Tom thought, admiring her legs. Her face was an olive-coloured oval, with deep-set eyes, heavy lids, a good deal of eye makeup under a strong brow line. Her nose did not come to a point but curved down in an arc over the upper lip, on which even from several feet Tom could see a fine line of nevertheless feminine hair. The woman exuded determination and energy. He rose from his bunk.

"I'm your solicitor, Mr. Wrought—Alice Silverstone." She put out her hand and grasped his with a firmness he'd last experienced in North America. "We have only a few minutes before your bail hearing."

"Who engaged you, Miss Silverstone?"

"Elizabeth Spencer. Mrs. Spencer has briefed me. For the moment I am representing her as well, so all our communication is protected. Anyway, she told me everything"—Silverstone looked into his eyes and repeated the word—"everything, at least as far as she knows it. Now, we are going up into the Central Criminal Court, the Old Bailey. I will apply for bail. The Crown will oppose. But they'll have to say why, and it will give us a start on a defence. Now, what did the police tell you when you were interviewed?"

"I wasn't." Tom's tone was emphatic, and it appeared to startle Silverstone.

"Not at all? No one asked you any questions? They had a warrant; they must have some evidence against you. You've been told nothing?"

"Only that I have been arrested for murdering Trevor Spencer."

Silverstone thought for a minute. "They must think they have a very complete case against you. They'll have to tell the judge how strong it is, but for the moment we have almost nothing to go on."

***

As he climbed the stairs into the dock at the high court, Tom chided himself for a slightly unworthy thought: *Silverstone? Probably Silverstein.* As she came into view alongside the dock, Tom decided he'd trust her. *A*

Jewish woman solicitor. She must be twice as good to survive in her profession. Let's hope so.

———————

Two hours later Tom was shuffling down the corridor of Her Majesty's Prison Brixton, where he would await trial for murder. He was wearing prison garb that was no worse than what he'd worn in the US Army. The thought passed through his mind: *How quaint, but how characteristic that inmates are issued ties and expected to wear them.* He smiled to himself. It was a fleeting distraction from persistent apprehension threatening to become panic.

The bail hearing had been a formality at which his solicitor had been able to say hardly a word. The Crown's solicitor had opposed bail, informing the judge that there were multiple witnesses to the crime and to the suspect's flight from the scene. "Milord, the defendant had not only means and opportunity, but motive, which the Crown will be able to substantiate by witnesses when the time comes." He added ominously that the defendant had been known to leave jurisdictions in the past against the wishes of authorities.

Miss Silverstone had asked for a moment with her client. Granted it, she whispered to Tom, "What was that about leaving jurisdictions against the wishes of the authorities?"

"Someone has probably told them about the US government's threats to take away my passport. I'm on a blacklist for membership in the Communist Party when I was a kid."

"Did they actually take away your passport?"

"Well, no. I managed to slip out of the US last summer before they could."

His solicitor nodded, then wondered, still in a whisper, "How did the prosecutor know?"

Tom had no answer to that.

When it came her turn, Tom's solicitor rose. "Milord," she began. The historian in Tom asked himself why it came out more like "mee laird" sans the *r*, as though every officer of the court were a Scotsman in their initial words to the judge. It was not the first time he had been diverted from his plight by some quirk of the criminal justice system in Britain. Beyond the boredom of his three days in the "nick," Tom had been repeatedly surprised by the way things were happening to him, especially the studied politeness of the screws—as the voices from other cells taught him to call the warders. It seemed reassuring in a way, as if they knew he was innocent.

Silverstone cleared her throat and repeated herself, "Milord, I have only just met my client and have had no time to prepare a case for bail. However, Mr. Wrought's standing in his profession, his status in his university, and his freedom from any previous record of arrest in the United Kingdom are, I believe, sufficient grounds, along with some amount of surety moneys, to grant him bail."

"Is that all, Miss Silverstone?" There was distaste in the judge's voice. Tom couldn't tell whether it was owing to the solicitor's sex or perhaps her religion. Or both. Tom searched the judge's face for malice, but no one else bothered to look up from their briefs. Perhaps he needed to reconsider how reassuring these institutions would be. "Bail denied. Take the defendant down."

<hr />

On Tuesday afternoon Liz Spencer was seated in Alice Silverstone's office on Red Lion Square. It was cold in the small space, and she had kept her coat on. Hardly larger than a broom closet, the office was in an advanced state of disarray—open law books everywhere, stack upon untidy stack of legal papers, many of them stained with the rings of saucerless teacups.

Looking the solicitor squarely in the face, Liz recalled the response her initial statement had produced the day before. Silverstone's look of astonishment had immediately turned to one of pleasure as she replied, "Am I to understand, Mrs. Spencer, that your husband has been murdered, and you want me to defend the man the police suspect must have killed him?" When Liz nodded, all Silverstone had said was, "Excellent." *A very strange response,* Liz couldn't avoid thinking.

Unlike the disorder of her cubbyhole-like office, the solicitor was, Liz noticed, again impeccably dressed: a grey suit this time, with a strand of pearls over a light-blue blouse, and still another pair of stiletto heels. The woman's brief bag made Liz's attaché case seem shabby by contrast. And she was not cold. Silverstone was radiating energy.

There was no ashtray on the desk, but Liz could smell the stale aroma of tobacco smoke. When she began to light up, Silverstone wagged her finger. "No smoking."

Before Liz could say anything, Silverstone began. "There are several things that trouble me about this case. They make it hard for me to know where to begin. First, the CID detectives haven't even bothered to interrogate their suspect."

Liz had to interrupt. "CID?"

"Criminal Investigation Department. Scotland Yard to everyone else." Silverstone returned to her enumeration. "Second, nothing in the papers, or almost nothing. A tiny squib on Friday about a death causing train delays the evening before. Then nothing. And here's a third oddity—the apparent motive is obvious. So, I don't understand why they have not even questioned you."

"They have taken my passport. They know where to find me."

"But if this is a murder motivated by love and the threat of disclosure or of divorce, the police should be interested in what you could tell them under caution. I think they must know already that you had nothing to do with the murder. But how could they know that?"

Liz couldn't pretend not to be relieved, but she saw the point. Silverstone was almost looking past Liz, pursuing her line of reasoning.

"The biggest mystery, however, is this: the fact that Mr. Wrought was on the platform at the time your husband was killed."

Liz interrupted. "Can we call him Tom, please?" Liz wanted a cigarette badly by now. The intensity of Silverstone's demeanour was difficult for her. She needed to humanize the interview. "I'm sure he'd want you to call him that."

"Yes, certainly. Better call me Alice, then . . . Liz?" Liz nodded, and Alice's voice resumed its slightly officious timbre. "Please do let me go on. You tell me his presence on the platform was coincidence. If we accept that, then not only did someone else kill Trevor Spencer, but they killed him for reasons that had nothing to do with Tom's presence on the platform that afternoon." She paused. "I can't believe that." Then she made eye contact with Liz. "Who would have wanted to kill your husband?"

Liz met her gaze. "Only Tom and me, I am afraid."

"Exactly. That rules out coincidence and makes the lack of police interest in questioning you very mysterious." Alice hesitated, and then continued. "Mrs. Spencer—Liz—for the moment you are my client. If you didn't kill your husband, you have nothing to fear from telling me everything. If you did and you confess it to me, I cannot tell the police. I can only withdraw as your solicitor."

"No, it's nothing like that." Liz fumbled with her cigarettes again.

"Go ahead; smoke if you must." She pulled an ashtray from a drawer. Liz offered her packet, and Alice shook her head. "I'm trying to quit."

Then Liz began to speak. "Anyway, they'll find out we had a motive, Tom and me both. Trevor knew about us. The police told me he had a prophylactic cover in his pocket when he was killed."

"First I have heard of this. Please explain." Alice was making notes.

"They think it points to Trevor's having an extramarital affair. But it came from my clothes drawer, I'm pretty sure. It's a kind you can only get in France."

"So, there is no chance the irate husband of some other woman could have done this to Trevor."

"None."

"Well, there is nothing to stop us from suggesting it to a jury, is there?"

"I suppose not, but it would just be another coincidence once they find out Tom and I went to Paris."

Alice drew an audible sigh and crossed out the words she'd been writing. "Go on. Is there more about your husband that might make you want to kill him?"

"Well, for the last few years I'd been supporting him and our kids."

"That doesn't rise to the level of motive for murder."

"But they'd say he was threatening to hold the children hostage in a divorce by painting me as a mentally ill adulteress."

Alice stared at Liz. "Are you? Mentally ill, that is? We already know about the adultery."

Liz flushed. "I'm afraid I had a serious psychotic episode sixteen years ago, when I was nineteen. Trev knew about it."

"Does anyone else know about your psychiatric history?"

"Only Tom. But there were also some police records in Toronto. I was arrested twice—the charge was soliciting and drug possession."

Alice frowned. "An assiduous Crown prosecutor could find those records in Ontario."

"I suppose so." Liz lit still another cigarette from the one she'd almost finished. Was it nerves or shame?

Alice didn't seem to notice. "Here is another remarkable thing about this case." She paused for effect. "The Crown prosecutor told the judge at the remand hearing that they had witnesses as to motive, along with means and opportunity. But I had a word with Victor Mishcon, and he told me that the police came and interviewed him about Trevor Monday afternoon, *after* the remand hearing. So they must have known about you two before they found out that Trevor consulted him about divorce."

"Yes," Liz said, "but how could they have known? My personal assistant, Beatrice Russell, is the only one who might have guessed. She'd have to tell them she suspected Tom and I were lovers. She might even know we'd meet sometimes at a hotel in Bloomsbury. But they haven't interviewed her either, not yet anyway."

Alice's voice finally acquired a touch of emotion. "So, Trevor Spencer was killed at four ten on Thursday afternoon. The police knew enough to arrest Tom Wrought for the murder by Friday morning. The CID is efficient, but that must have been a record." By now Liz could see clearly where Alice's thoughts were headed even as her words were formed. "Conclusions: first and most obvious, the police have an informer, a very well-informed informer. So well informed they didn't need to do the normal police spadework. And so reliable the police could believe him implicitly. Second, Tom's presence on the platform at the time of the killing was not coincidental. The killer—killers, probably—knew he would be there. They wanted him to be there. They needed him to be there. And third, Tom was the target, the victim. Your husband was killed by someone who wanted to pin it on Tom, perhaps even to have him hang for Trevor Spencer's murder."

"But if someone wanted to get rid of Tom, why kill Trevor? Why not just kill Tom?"

Liz's question was left hanging in the air for several seconds. They both looked up at the cloud of smoke hovering above them in the incandescent light of the windowless room.

"Yes," said Alice. "That is a puzzle."

It was exactly the sort of puzzle Alice Silverstone had been seeking for weeks now. She needed it badly. She needed a reason to go on doing what she wanted most to do—criminal defence—and in a case so interesting and so seemingly closed that prying it open would take her completely out of herself.

For weeks she had been feeling the slight twinges, the momentary cramps, the rearrangement of her insides that the oncologists had warned her about. These were the signposts showing her the coming endgame—if they were right. Their track record had been by no means perfect. She would laugh at the thought. Everyone had been optimistic after the surgery, and equally so after the radiology. This sort of uterine cancer was supposed to be a known quantity to them. The doctors had been confident what to do. But then came ominous signs, even in her first postoperative visits, queries, lab work, and reexams, and finally an interview in which she was advised to prepare for the worst.

Any family to talk to?

No, both parents dead, in a maritime accident the previous summer.

Any brothers, sisters, fiancé, friend to tell and to help you?

'Fraid not. Only child, too busy with my career for men.

No one ever talked about cancer. It was even more taboo than sex. Alice had been slightly surprised the oncologists were so direct and frank about her condition. The one thing they would not tell her about was the suffering—the intractable, searing sensations, worse than any burn, the pain that she'd feel towards the end. It required some digging and reading and questioning, but it didn't take Alice long to find out about it.

Then Alice had seated herself in the drawing room of the rather large house in St. John's Wood she had inherited when her parents had died two years before. She had poured herself a strong whiskey and soda and set herself to think through her situation. *You've got decisions to make, and you have to find ways to make them stick.* It was the kind of person she'd trained herself to be—analytical, unemotional—ever since she'd set her sights on the law. It had been hard work to train herself to focus on facts, not feelings. But now it would pay off.

It wasn't just the pain. She knew she couldn't deal with the expressions of sympathy and regret that would mask most people's real responses to fatal illness—secret gladness it was not them. She'd have to trick the world into treating her the way she'd always wanted it to: pleased to see her, but slightly surprised at her cheekiness, her drive, her success. She was going to want to treat herself the same way, right to the end. How?

She had a little money, about six hundred quid, and she could sell the house in St. John's Wood if she needed more. But what would she spend it on? Travel? Alone, with no one to share the experience? A fling? More fashionable clothes? A fast car, or a saloon driven by a chauffeur? A box at the opera? Fatuous! Frivolous! None of it would take her mind off her fate for a moment. Only one thing would. She had to keep working, right to the last day if she could. She would need a case that would be more important to her than anything else.

———⟨═⟩———

As for the pain, she'd have to find a compliant physician. And she knew where to look: the now elderly medical man who had treated her since childhood. Dr. Kalb knew her, inside and out . . . *Well, perhaps not really my insides, or he'd never have let this happen.* Despite the long acquaintance, in his consulting room, he was all business, just what she wanted.

"So, Alice." He looked up from the clinical reports. "These people say you've got about six months."

She searched his stolid face. "But are they right?"

He looked back at the X-ray and then at the report before him. "I'd say four or five months is optimistic."

"Well, I have thought about things and decided. I want to spend what's left having the most fun I can. Doing what I like doing most."

"Which is?" Kalb smiled as though he knew his patient well enough to answer his own question.

"My work, what I do best, being a solicitor. All I want is a case to sink my teeth into and see to its end."

Three days later, Liz Spencer had walked into her office with the very case she needed. By then Alice had filled the prescription for morphine and a brace of syringes that Dr. Kalb had written out.

Alice pushed her chair back from the desk, kicked off her pumps, and swivelled her chair so that she could put her feet up. She looked at her client. "Let's begin with everything you know about Tom Wrought."

At last warm, Liz stood to take off the tight-fitting bolero jacket she had worn, stretched her arms, and looked at Alice imploringly. "Please, can I smoke another?"

Alice grimaced but nodded.

How much does she want to know? Everything, she said. For eight months Liz had been unable to say anything to anyone about the most important thing in her life. And now she'd be able to tell someone everything. Suddenly the muscles in her shoulders loosened, as if she'd finally let down a two-stone rucksack.

Liz sat down, lit a Gold Leaf, and cleared her throat. "We met eighteen months ago when Tom and his wife, Barbara, moved in next door to us on Park Town crescent in Oxford. But our relationship began only last spring." *Where to start?* The night Tom took Liz to high table at Trinity College, and they decided to become lovers. "Alice, did you go to Oxford?" she asked.

"No, Cambridge."

"Still, you know about high table, dining in hall, all that rigmarole?"

Alice smiled. "I'm afraid so."

"Well, it began the second time Tom took me to high table dinner at Trinity College."

PART II

May–August 1958

Idles in the Wanton Summer Air

CHAPTER THREE

A lover may bestride the gossamers

That idles in the wanton summer air,

And yet not fall.

—William Shakespeare, *Romeo and Juliet* (Act 2, Scene 6)

At six thirty in the early evening of a day late the previous May, the sun still had two hours more to shine in an unusually blue sky—unusual for Oxford at any rate that spring.

It was guest night at Trinity. Tom Wrought finished fiddling with the French cuff and pulled on his suit coat. He couldn't pretend he wasn't anxious. *Really, there's no reason to be apprehensive.* He tried without success to convince himself.

The evening would be entirely innocent on the outside. He knew that on the inside it wouldn't be. His thoughts would be altogether different from what he could dare to say. But later he'd be able to watch high table dinner unroll in his imagination again and again. He would add it to the other memories: chilly mornings on the Thames, Liz pulling at her oars in a double scull; a golden autumn afternoon wandering through the parkland of Blenheim Castle; laughing over an indigestible haggis on a wintry Robbie Burns night; watching her face embrace the warmth of the Cotswold pub after a sodden day's tramp under scudding clouds. These were the things he'd already stored up, but not before cutting everyone out of the memories but her.

Tom Wrought had been saving images of Liz Spencer for the better part of a year. Now he was leaving Oxford, and they'd have to last.

He stepped out onto the crescent, turned left, and knocked at the very next door in the row of somewhat formal but now aging, undetached three-storey houses. Unlike the red-brick villas of North Oxford, the terraces of Park Town were clad in stone, now chipped here and there after a hundred years of English weather. Like some of their London counterparts, they faced a lovely, enclosed garden, private to local residents only. No one had even dared take the iron grillwork that surrounded it for the war. It was all still there, along with the metal fencing protecting each house even as many grander buildings in the town lacked theirs.

No answer to Tom's knock. He knocked again. *Patience! Someone will answer.* Then, the bright-blue door opened, and there was Liz Spencer, her eyes smiling through the wrinkles, the freckles catching the soft sunlight.

"Sorry, just back from London. I was settling the children down in the garden." She wore a dark suit jacket over a plain white blouse. The matching skirt was narrow and rather short. The navy blue contrasted with her very blonde hair. Elizabeth Spencer was thirty-five. She looked younger in every way except for those wrinkles around her brown eyes.

Five feet five inches in her stocking feet, and thin—just more than nine stone. *(What was that in American measure? One hundred twenty-six pounds?)* She followed his eyes as they ranged over her. "Alright for high table?" As usual, she had foregone any makeup. Her face was not the kind that needed much; naturally reddish lips and cheekbones were high enough to cast shadows towards her jawline. The eyebrows arched away as though a question were on her mind.

"Very much so. We'll match." Tom was wearing a suit of the same colour and a striped tie. He was also thin, about six feet, with a face that revealed more about him than merely his age, almost forty. Tom Wrought had seen much more than the inside of a historical archive. Furrows across his brow, even in repose, deep-set eyes, skin drawn down a long face. The nose was large, the eyebrows bushy; the hair was dark and in need of cutting. Little about him suggested his Scandinavian origins. Tom's mouth seemed permanently fixed in a slightly self-deprecating smile, a look that the twinkle in his eye seemed to belie.

She reached out and touched the tie. "Trinity College?"

"No, actually, my alma mater in New York."

"Will that be a provocation?"

"They won't ask. Everyone will pretend they know exactly which Oxford college it is. Meanwhile, they'll be wondering if I ever spent time in Cambridge."

"Shall I drive?" Liz asked. Tom had assiduously avoided driving—on the wrong side—in the year he'd been in England. "I don't think we want to cycle down dressed for a guest-night dinner." It was almost a mile along the Banbury Road to Trinity's Broad Street entry.

They moved to the curb, where a Humber Super Snipe was parked. It was her company car, a perk, a tax dodge, and a requirement for her work. The American in Tom found the vehicle quaint—no fins, hardly any chrome, one colour, less than twelve feet long, almost five feet high, and a manual choke, of all things.

Over the rumble of the rough little engine Liz inquired, "You won't get into trouble, bringing me to high table again?" Women were rare in college.

"Probably will, but not because you're coming for the second time. They won't even remember that it was you back in December." He paused. "No. I'll get stick for bringing a woman at all. But if they want me to subsidize their damn guest nights, they'll have to accept my guests. Besides, last time you charmed them all. Lunch the next day, they were full of you. I expect you'll do it again."

There was little traffic as they passed ranks of red-brick Victorian piles punctuated by the occasional mock Tudor—timber and stucco. All were resolute in their orderliness on either side of the Banbury Road. Each stood gravely behind its low red-brick wall, from which arose rhododendron in bloom. The closer to town, the larger and more opulent were the structures. Under stout elms in May leaf, the wide avenue wore a house pride that had finally recovered from the postwar austerity everyone in Britain could still remember.

Liz parked in front of Blackwell's Bookshop. There were few cars and many cycles in the road. Parking was never a problem.

Walking along Broad Street towards the Trinity gate, Tom noticed how the sun cast a soft gold over the patches of sandstone that remained unstained between the black and grey streaks of coal dusk. It was a glimpse from another time. The war had not damaged Oxford directly, but it had left its marks. Across Broad Street the soot-stained walls round the Bodleian Library still awaited replacement of the ironwork railings that had been taken for weapon-metal in 1940. How, Tom wondered, had Park Town crescent escaped this fate? *Must be a matter of class again.* Now, in 1958, after almost fifteen years of reconstruction, there still remained open spaces of neatly smooth rubble dotted across London. But for the lost ironwork, Oxford could almost pretend the war had never happened.

"Hello, Wrought." A large man in a beard passed them, nodding and smiling.

"Who was that?"

"History don at Balliol."

"Why was he smiling so broadly?"

"I expect it was because he knows my wife." No one could mistake Liz for Barbara Wrought—almost six feet tall, raven haired, with a face that reminded every art student of Rossetti's sitter, Jane Morris. Liz wore her blonde hair shoulder length, in a French style. It made Tom think of Simone Signoret in that year's most talked-about film, *Room at the Top*.

"Where is Barbara tonight, Tom?"

"Duplicate bridge tournament. She can't get enough of it." They both knew that married fellows were forbidden from bringing wives—even the wife of another college fellow—to college meals.

The ritual of guest night began with cocktails. No one in the senior common room was drinking sherry. It was a long, narrow space, lined in sandstone, with a built-in sideboard heavy with liquor bottles. The walls were momentarily painted almost peach coloured by the sun slanting through large unmullioned windows open to the warm spring air. A dozen elderly armchairs, polished smooth in places, leather cracked and peeling, were planted round the room. They were evidently too comfortable for the fellows to consider replacement. The day's broadsheet newspapers were strewn across side tables. Several of the ashtrays had not been emptied.

———

Liz saw that she was the lone woman among a dozen males. It unnerved her slightly, but she told herself, *This is the only way you'll ever see the inside of an Oxford college.* Besides, she liked Tom's company . . . really liked it. He was fun and smart, and he was interested in her opinions.

Tom was on the far side of the room, with a glass in each hand, wending his way through the cigarette smoke already settling on the room. Before he arrived, a hand proffered Liz a packet of Rothmans, while a gold Dunhill lighter hovered conspicuously in the hand's mate.

Liz looked at the man's face. *About sixty-five, very calm,* she thought, *reassuring, a rare don who put you at your ease. Rather rumpled, wearing a three-piece grey suit, prewar from the cut of it.*

"No, thank you."

The man took one himself, lit up, drew on the cigarette, and then carefully blew the smoke behind her. "Somerville, Lady Margaret Hall?" He volunteered the names of two nearby women's colleges. "History don from the States perhaps?"

"Actually, I'm in trade." The self-description was intended to provoke. It didn't.

Arriving with the drinks, Tom made an introduction. "Liz, may I present the master of the college, Sir David Lindsay Keir. Mrs. Elizabeth Spencer."

"Hope I haven't offended by accusing you of being a historian like Tom. And an American too."

"I'm not even an amateur when it comes to history. Not American either. I read maths in Canada, actually."

Before he could reply, the master of Trinity was forced to turn and greet another guest.

Liz looked back to Tom. "Still struggling with Barbara about whether to go back?"

"Same argument from her for months now: the blacklist is nothing to worry about. McCarthy's been dead for a year. It can't last forever. Besides, I won't need anyone to give me a job. She has all the money we need."

"Sounds pretty convincing."

Tom did not reply.

The dinner gong sounded. Fellows in gowns and guests lined up in pairs at the stair that ascended to the hall. Each pair looked at the seating chart as they passed. Tom knew they'd be placed well away from the centre of the table. They hung about till most of the party had filed up the six steps from the senior common room to the great hall. Taking a gown from the hooks, he touched Liz's forearm, and they went up the stairwell into the brightness. All year, each time he had mounted this stairway, Tom had felt rather like the accused coming up into the dock at the Old Bailey. *Thomas Wrought, you are accused of masquerading as an Oxford don. How do you plead?*

Below the timbered ceiling, the vast space was noisy with undergraduates at long tables. Behind them on the dark, wainscoted walls hung five hundred years of portraits—kings, nobles, but mainly former masters of the college—each lit from above by its own picture lamp. On the raised podium, the high table gleamed with sterling plates and fresh-cut flowers. All were reflected in the glass facets of the decanters coloured mauve by the claret that filled them.

As the fellows entered, the gowned undergraduates rose in a hush. All stood while the master intoned a Latin blessing in monosyllables most could repeat exactly as though it were a mantra. "*Bénedic, Dómine, nos et haec tua dona quae de tua largitate sumus sumpturi. Per Christum Dóminum nostrum.* Amen." The last sounds were swallowed by the noise of two hundred chairs scraping across flagstone echoed from the timbered ceiling and followed by the resumed din of competing conversations.

Liz and Tom sat opposite each other at the table end, flanked on only one side by two young scientists—junior fellows. They smiled when Liz said, "Don't forget, Tom, fish fork first." At the previous guest night she'd attended, Tom had been reproved by a sharp elbow when he began spearing the langouste with a meat fork.

"No worries tonight. These two won't hold me to the senior tutor's standard."

The younger men nodded and then fell to discussing chemical bonding. That suited Liz. She was eager to get back to Tom's future. "Surely you could get some teaching back in the States?"

"Nothing worth accepting. How about you? Ever think about going back to Canada?"

"Sometimes. Doesn't matter though; Trevor won't leave."

"Can't blame him. Seems to be doing well enough. I see him coming and going in the Wolseley sedan, grey flannels, regimental tie. Stood me a drink at his club last week—rather posh." Liz could not suppress a frown. He noticed. "You're alright financially, aren't you?"

Liz bridled slightly. "You mean why am I still working?" Tom began to shake his head, but Liz wouldn't be interrupted. "Trev's having a tough time. Hasn't sold a house this year, only two last, and both in Jericho to family friends who came down from Birkenhead." Jericho was where college servants and tradesmen lived.

They both fell silent. Liz put down her fork and looked at Tom for a moment, trying to decide whether to say what she was really thinking. She knew well this wasn't done. No one said the things she was thinking, not aloud. *Tom, I don't want you to leave.* Instead, she began to cover old ground again. "I don't know how much longer I can hold things together. It feels like we're in a downward spiral, circling a drain, and Trev just can't, won't swim against the tide."

They'd talked about her husband before. It was easier when they rowed a double scull along the river together and didn't have to face each other. Somehow Liz could be candid then. Not facing him, she wouldn't have to respond to the grimace that crossed his face whenever they touched on the subject of Trevor.

Trevor Spencer had insisted on moving his young family back to England after a series of setbacks in Canada he'd chalked up to prejudice against Brits. But things had not been any easier in Blighty, and he'd slipped steadily down a slope of sales jobs, for which his persona was totally unsuited. Liz couldn't even tell Tom that her husband was no longer trying to sell houses. Now he was trying to sell used cars in Cowley, with equally indifferent results.

I don't want to talk about all that again. Liz bit her lip. *Well then, say what you're really thinking. To devil with the niceties!* She put down her fork. "No, Trevor's work's not the problem. I guess I could live with a failure." It was like hesitating before a dive into icy water. *Just say it.* She gulped. "I don't love him, Tom. If I ever did, I don't anymore."

Clearly taken aback, Tom could only jest. "Marry in haste, repent at leisure?"

Liz persisted. "Marrying in haste was not my mistake. I did it with malice aforethought. I fell for a Brit accent and a nice foxtrot. We had a secret affair for almost a year. Not easy, especially in Toronto. Then when Olivia was on the way, we married." It was, she recognized, a revealing admission. What did the Americans call it? A shotgun wedding? One didn't even tell one's friends.

They were, Tom realized, at a juncture: he had to pretend she had never made so frank a disclosure, or match her candour with his own. His decision was easy. "Well, I didn't exactly marry for money. But I'm afraid I've stayed married this long because of it. And what they say is true: anyone who marries for money earns it."

"You certainly do," she said. "Earn it." She looked up as the steward removed her plate. "The way Barbara snipes at you. Sometimes I can't bear listening."

He didn't want her to feel sorry for him. And he was not going to censor himself any more than she did herself. A little too loudly, he added, "Well, at least the sex has been good." Then he realized where they were and looked furtively at their closest dinner companions. The young scientists were still absorbed in chemical bonding. Tom realized that he and Liz might as well have been alone in the vast hall.

Liz must have thought so too. She now raised the level of intimacy beyond anything polite society allowed. "I haven't slept with Trev for a year." Tom wouldn't ask why—she had already crossed lines people didn't stray beyond, even among closest friends—but she plunged on as if he had. "No imagination, no interest in his partner. Bad breath, running to fat. And all I can think of when he tries to get on top is that I am sick and tired of supporting him." She smiled bitterly at her double entendre.

"Well, you're certainly not sparing yourself supporting him. I see you leaving mornings at six fifteen, coming back at eight or nine at night, when you get back home at all."

She nodded. "I must be spending, what, a hundred nights a year on the road . . . one bloody hotel or another, all round the country. Abbey National have three hundred branches." Tom noted the plural verb. She had been in England a long time. "The turnover in tellers is endless."

"Pass the claret." The peremptory command boomed down from the senior tutor's place to the master's right at the head of the table. The cocoon round Liz and Tom was broken.

⟤⟡⟢

The din gradually subsided as more and more of the undergraduates finished their meals and left the hall. High table conversation became more general until the master stood. Carrying his napkin he led the table down to the fellows' dining room for dessert. There he commanded Liz to sit with him. College tradition required each fellow to sit with a new partner at dessert, and Tom found himself opposite a student of the seventeenth-century poet John Dryden. All Tom could think of was *The Rape of the Lock*. His interlocutor reproved him for confusing Dryden with Alexander Pope and thereafter had nothing to say.

"The master was entertaining," Liz said when she joined Tom as they reentered the senior common room for coffee, the third act of a guest-night performance. "He was actually interested in how to manage bank tellers."

48

"He's got people management problems of his own." Tom looked over his shoulder at the roomful of college fellows.

Liz lowered herself into one of the old leather chairs, and Tom brought two coffees from the sideboard. They lit cigarettes and contemplated the blue smoke between them, each trying to decide how to pick up the salacious thread they had both been tugging at over dinner. And suddenly Liz and Tom smiled with the mutual realization that both wanted to get back to this forbidden subject. Their grins became conspiratorial. But in the common room, people couldn't help overhearing. Some would be trying to, for that matter.

Before the moment evanesced, Tom had to decide. Was the intimacy of Liz's admissions a signal, an invitation? Did he dare break the unwritten but well-established proprieties? Should he risk a rebuff that would destroy the fantasies a year had stored up? Like Liz, he was poised at the edge of a pool of icy water, screwing up the courage to dive. Then he thought, *In a week I'll be gone, back to the States forever.* He dove.

"Liz, what will become of us?" The presumption in the question made him blush with emotion. Did she notice?

She replied, "I wish we could spend some time together before you leave."

"Don't see how."

"Come to London for a day. I'll skip work, and we can play tourist."

"Yes. Let's do it."

—◆—

They came down the set of stairs from the senior common room into the large quad. It was now dark but still warm, almost a soft summer night. Their pace was leisurely; both wanted the moment to linger.

Tom turned to his right. "My college rooms are over in that tower. Care to have a look?"

Liz shuddered slightly and continued to walk straight ahead.

Now you've done it, Tom thought. *An obvious enough attempt.* In silence they passed the great oak in the middle of the quad, turned into the smaller front quad, and then went along to the porters' lodge that opened onto Broad Street. "I suppose that sounded pretty blatant back there."

Liz replied, "Yes. Just for a moment I felt like I was in a scene from a film." She smiled at Tom with slight embarrassment.

"Which one?" he asked.

"That Celia Johnson-Trevor Howard one Noël Coward did years ago. After the war, the one with the score from Rachmaninoff. *Brief Encounter.*"

"Ah, where the doctor and the married woman fall in love and break it off for the sake of their families . . ."

"Yes. Remember the scene where he lures her to a friend's flat, and you want so much for them to consummate the affair . . ."

"But someone intrudes . . ."

"And she flees, ashamed. That was me for a minute there." But suddenly Liz regretted her demur, regretted it profoundly. She couldn't bring herself to say it out loud, but she put her arm through his and sought his hand. Tom understood.

Broad Street was quite deserted when they reached the car. Tom gently leaned Liz up against its side. His head came close to hers. "Now I am going to make a pass at you. But slowly enough that you can stop me if you want."

"I'd like that very much." His lips found hers, and then their tongues touched. There was an immediate sensation he had not felt for a decade. As the kiss lengthened, she threw her arms over his shoulders and showed no signs of letting go.

A bright Thursday morning three days later, they were in a second-class carriage on the down train to London. Liz spoke first.

"What did you tell Barbara?"

"Seminar at Kings College London. What did you tell the Abbey National?"

"Nothing. I'm pretty much my own master. I spend so much time travelling round the country, they don't really expect me at the home office on a schedule."

"What shall we do?" Tom asked in all innocence.

"Art galleries! The National? The Tate? Let's start at the National and do them all."

"In one day?"

"It's all we have."

Jostling against each other in an underground carriage, Liz grimaced slightly, wondering, *Should I bring this up?* "Tom, you've never said exactly why you were blacklisted."

"I was what they used to call 'a premature antifascist.' Joined the Communist Party when it was the only opposition to fascism. I never denied joining."

"You're not still a member?"

"Not for twenty years now. I quit the Communist Party the day Stalin signed the nonaggression pact with Hitler."

"But that was in 1939. You must have been, what . . . nineteen years old?"

"I was seventeen when I joined the Young Communist League."

"Whatever for?"

"Only one reason really. Racial equality. Only thing I've ever really cared about when I was growing up in New York. Still care about it. Anyway, when I joined in the thirties, the Communists were the only people in the US committed to racial equality. There was just no other way to fight Jim Crow back then." He wouldn't bore her with an American history lesson. "But when Stalin ordered the party to support his pact with Hitler, I had to quit."

"So, why the blacklist?"

"I wouldn't name names—refused to tell a congressional investigator who else I knew in the party. But the blacklist was really a pretext to stop me teaching in the States. So here I am." He moved his hand over hers. He was prepared to tell her more, much more—how he'd been foolish, how the party had betrayed its commitment to Negro equality when it became inconvenient later in the war. But they had reached Trafalgar Square, and she did not pursue the matter.

⟞⟝

Standing before Uccello's *The Battle of San Romano*, he kissed her for the first time that day. The room was momentarily empty. The guard had moved into the next gallery shadowing two children. Standing next to Tom, Liz had opened her mouth to speak. Before she could say anything, he had covered it with his. Her tongue found his until the need to breathe overtook them.

Liz mocked reproof. "Look at the painting, sir." She went on, "Like all battle pictures, it's too neat and clean."

"I'm afraid if you want real war art, you'll have to go to the Imperial War Museum."

"Spare me the tanks." She had obviously been there. Liz looked at her watch. "Time for lunch."

⟞⟝

They were sitting in the dingy snug of a pub on Long Acre just off Charing Cross, finishing the bangers and toying with the mash.

Liz put down her fork. "Tom, ever wonder why there's nothing like the blacklist in England?"

"If being a member of the British Communist Party when you were a kid was a crime, half the Labour Party front bench in Parliament would be in jail."

"What is it exactly about Britain that makes it so different from the US when it comes to red-baiting?" Her tone made the question sound rhetorical, but Tom replied.

"It's the establishment, Liz. If you are from the right people, went to the right school, finished Oxford or Cambridge with a good degree, speak without a Gordie twang, then you're really quite alright." He pronounced the last four words in a mock Mayfair accent. "Even if you were a Communist as a kid, or a Fascist for that matter, so long as your people were 'sound.'"

"I think there may be another reason the blacklist doesn't reach this far." Liz turned from the window to face him. "Rejecting the blacklist plays to the Brits' vague sense of superiority to America."

"How's that?"

"Perhaps your friends are too polite, knowing you're a Yank. But Brits don't mind talking down America among themselves. Not hard to do so, of course. McCarthyism is like segregation. Makes them feel a bit smug."

"So, my being blacklisted back in the States feeds English condescension? Never quite thought of it that way." Tom didn't like the idea.

They came out of the dank pub squinting into the bright sun pouring down onto the Charing Cross Road. "On to the Tate?" Tom inquired.

"I have a better idea. Follow me." She took his arm and led them north up the Tottenham Court Road. Soon they found themselves amidst uniform lines of red-brick, three-storey buildings, interrupted by vacant lots that German bombs had opened in the cityscape nineteen years before.

"Where are you taking me?"

"To meet some friends." She would say no more.

Deep into Bloomsbury they turned a corner and found themselves in a long, narrow, green space so quiet it could hardly be London. Woburn Square was lined with white mullioned windows staring out of red-brick Georgian mansions. Soon they stood before an imposing building with two signs at the entry, **WARBURG INSTITUTE**, and below it in smaller letters, **SLADE SCHOOL OF FINE ART**.

As they mounted the steps Tom warned, "I'm not going to buy any student pictures."

"No worries." It was all she said as she led them up a wide marble stairway into a gallery. Liz stopped, looked round, and smiled. "These are my friends . . ."

From where they stood at the entrance to the large room, Tom could recognize a Botticelli, two Fra Angelicos, and across from them the nineteenth-century impressionists. How had he missed this room in half a dozen visits to London since 1944?

"What is this place, Liz?"

"It's the Courtauld Gallery." Liz was drawing them towards a large canvas next to a window. A fine muslin drape filtered the sunlight falling on the paintings. "My best pal." She nodded at the large picture, a young woman with blonde bangs. The girl wore a tightly nipped velour jacket. Its scooped neck over a white lace collar revealed a generous bosom above a narrow waist and wide hips. Both her arms rested on the bar, which was littered with bottles. Behind the girl a wall mirror reflected the crowded café in which she was serving drinks. Beneath the large painting was a superfluous label: *A Bar at the Folies Bergère* (1883) by Edward Manet.

Liz turned to face Tom. "What will you have?"

"You." He leaned down and kissed her. This time she reached out, pulled his hand to her waist, then let it find its way beneath her sweater.

They heard the museum guard before he could see them. Separating, Liz began to pull Tom along a corridor that led from the large room. *Is she trying to get away from the guard?* Coming into a smaller gallery, she stopped. "You wouldn't have wanted to miss this room, I hope."

'Two paintings faced each other across the room. Like Buridan's ass, Tom couldn't decide which was drawing him more strongly. After a moment the Modigliani won out. Was it the frank display of pubic hair? No, the Gauguin nude was just as graphic. But Modigliani's woman was staring at him, hard. He moved towards it and made an effort to study the painting carefully. *Study the painting? Study . . . nothing.* He was losing himself in this woman's body. He looked at Liz. *What are you thinking?*

She must have read the unspoken question on his face. "Let's get out of here before I take off my clothes." Liz turned and left the room.

⊰⊱

"When do you need to be back in Oxford?" They had left the British Museum and were walking along Great Russell Street back towards Tottenham Court Road.

"Late. I told Barbara I was being taken to dinner after the seminar at King's."

"Good. We'll take the last train."

"So, dinner . . . or do we call it supper?"

Liz ignored the question. "I'm hungry."

"Well, there is only one decent restaurant in this part of London. Schmitz's on Charlotte Street." London was famous for inedible food, even in the best hotels.

"Never heard of it."

"A haven for impoverished academics. Large portions of non-English food, cheap."

A half hour later they were seated in a crowded dining room decorated in the kitschy gemütlichkeit of an Alpine Weinstube. Before them large golden-brown cutlets lapped over dining plates. Neither Tom nor Liz were eating, however.

"We're going back to the States next week. Flying into Montreal."

"Why not New York?"

"Passport problems. State Department's been threatening to take away my passport for the past few years. If we fly into Montreal, we can drive to Barbara's place in Saranac Lake without showing any papers at the US-Canadian border. They won't even know I'm back, not for a while."

"What will you do?"

"Swim, sail, run the Chris-Crafts"—these were powerful inboard motorboats. "We'll hike. It's a big Adirondack lodge, notched logs, huge porch, boathouse. Barbara bought it a few years ago to get away from summers in DC."

"No, I meant, what are *you* going to do? Your future?"

"Barbara's decided. She says the right lawyer can fix the passport thing." He said it, but he didn't believe it. Tom recalled to himself how he had spat the famous names back at his wife: "Chaplin can't go back to the US even if he wanted to. Paul Robeson hasn't had his passport for ten years. Linus Pauling couldn't get to England just to give a scientific talk. Will your lawyers be any better than theirs?"

"But if you can't teach," Liz said, "what will you do?"

"I can always write . . . for those left-wing mags that don't pay anything." That would suit Barbara Wrought. She wanted to return, wanted to cut a swath through Manhattan society with her fashionably blacklisted husband an ornament on her arm. It was true that he was a bit of a celebrity in Cambridge, Hyde Park, Morningside Heights, Berkeley, even Chapel Hill. *Maybe it wouldn't be so bad if you went back,* he tried to convince himself.

Liz frowned. "Doesn't make any sense to me, your staying with her."

"No more sense than your staying with Trevor."

"I've got children to think about."

"You're right. I'm sorry." He reached for her hand, and she proffered it, smiling. But now she was suddenly asking herself, *What are you doing here, in a restaurant in London with a man you're not married to? Allowing, encouraging him to maul you, almost in public.* Then she realized it wasn't guilt or embarrassment she was feeling. It was deepening regret. The day with Tom couldn't last much longer. The waiter was approaching. It wouldn't do. She withdrew her hand from Tom's.

Liz sighed. "We both know that staying in a marriage is always easier than leaving it, no matter how much you rub each other raw from day to day."

Tom had to nod his agreement. "It's not even a question of staying or leaving. After a few years, it's a whole web of habits that's too hard to break."

They fell silent for a long moment.

"So, you'll go back . . . to the States?" she asked at last.

"I guess so."

It was after nine o'clock, and the last Oxford train was about to depart. Liz led Tom down the platform to the farthest first-class coach, where she began searching for an empty compartment. Tom was looking dubiously back and forth from the first-class carriage to their second-class return tickets. As if to reassure him, Liz observed, "I take the late train often. They only check tickets at the barrier." She pointed to the entry gate at the top of the platform. "Trust me, this is the last train tonight. It's three-quarters empty. They won't ask for tickets on board."

It was evident to her that Tom didn't quite understand what she was doing. They were too late to buy first-class tickets, but riding in first was the only way they'd have any chance of a compartment to themselves. Could it be he didn't want to be alone with her?

No. That wasn't it. As soon as the train began to ease its way out of the station, Tom snapped off the compartment's overhead lights so they could not be seen. In the late twilight their reflections on the window disappeared, and the darkness of the track bed reached into the compartment. It made them feel invisible themselves.

Liz slid over to the corridor side of the compartment, pulled down the blinds, and locked the door. Tom was now no longer in any doubt. He moved next to her on her bench. She leaned back against the white antimacassar on the headrest and took his hand. They would have to wait through twenty-five minutes as the train called at six stations to Reading, each stop holding them hostage to the threat of unwanted companions.

Once the train passed beyond Reading, the line between sky and fields was effaced by a darkness broken only by the odd yellow road lamp. She knew there would be no stops in the last thirty-four minutes to Oxford. They felt the rhythm of the regular click of the rail gaps. At the same moment, their faces came together. Tom hesitated; Liz did not. With her right hand Liz pulled his head towards her and with her left hand guided his right beneath the sweater again. She came away from the kiss smiling and moved his hand down to the hem of her skirt and under it, sliding her thighs down the seat to give him access. Then, with her right hand still on his neck, firmly guiding his mouth back to hers, her left hand began methodically to undo the three buttons on his trousers fly. Tom couldn't help thinking, *Was this going to be harder than pulling down the zipper on an American suit pant?*

Liz was flying blind. She knew this might be the only completely intimate moment they'd ever share, and she wanted it to remember him by. So, there would be no inhibitions. It couldn't be intercourse, not in a railway compartment. Could it come close? Yes, it could. She needed to send intricate messages, ones that neither had the words for. And she had only her hands to send them.

The journey was just long enough. As the train began perceptibly to slow for the station, Liz came to a climax with a shriek and three twitching shudders, while decisively bringing Tom along with her.

They fell back in their seats. Tom reached for a handkerchief. Liz spoke first. *"La petite mort."*

"Sorry?"

"That's what the French call it. Almost a perfect name."

CHAPTER FOUR

"We're leaving Wednesday."

"In four days?"

Sitting astern of Liz, Tom watched her oar blades pull two deep strokes. It was six thirty in the morning. The June sun was making the droplets gleam as they ran off each blade when it broke free of the water. They were in a double scull. It was warm, and she was wearing a singlet that set off her androgynous shoulders. He turned to study her triceps glowing with spray as her upper arm flexed with a stroke. The dome atop Christ Church college gate loomed over Folly Bridge. It was an unavoidable focus for rowers at this spot where the Thames was called the Isis. Even with a coating of coal dust, the dome retained enough lustre that the sun still glinted off it.

"Barbara told me last night. Her father asked her to come to California. Family business. So, she booked us on the Trans-Canada Airlines flight for Wednesday morning."

"What a shame. I have to be in Exeter and the southwest the following week for four days. I thought . . . if you could find a way . . . to join me . . ."

"I'm coming back, Liz." He turned towards the bow to see her reaction.

"When term starts, next October?" She was smiling.

"No. I'm coming back the next week. If you'll meet me at Heathrow."

"But you will only have just left the week before."

"The beauty of air travel. A Lockheed Constellation makes it across the pond in about sixteen hours. My plane will land at eight in the morning next Monday. Can you pick me up on your way to Exeter?"

"What will you tell Barbara?"

"Leave that to me."

"You're mad . . . but I'll be waiting." She knew immediately that she would be. *Why, Liz? Is it just the promise of sex?* The answer came back firmly: *No. But if it were, it would be enough.* As for the guilt that might well up afterwards, she would simply have to deal with it. Life is too short. *For once you'll abandon yourself to—*she needed to find the right word to express what she wanted—*abandon yourself to pleasure, delight, so free from restraint it might even become wanton. You'll do everything you want, completely and without a qualm.* Even on the hard bench of the scull in the cold breeze straining with each stroke, she could already relish the sensations she would feel.

She repeated what she had said, louder, to make sure he understood. "A week from Monday. Yes, I'll be there." And then she began to feel disquieted. She'd felt something at least a little like this thirst before, years before. It had driven her into an abyss. Having climbed out once, she knew she'd never be able to survive a second descent.

No, Liz. This is different, Liz, quite different!

She needed to convince herself.

Coming out of customs, Tom's eyes found Liz at the same instant her eyes found him. Their smiles were so wide they hurt, laughing with delight at the trick they were playing on the world. Tom reached her. There was pleasure in his voice. "You're here!"

"I'm here."

He looked around, finally believing his eyes. Instead of leaving forever, he had been gone from England for less than a week.

"How was the flight?"

"No idea. I swallowed a Seconal as the plane took off from Montreal. Didn't wake till we stopped at Dublin a couple of hours ago."

They were in the Humber, headed down the old A303 for Exeter. "How did you do it, Tom? Didn't Barbara try to stop you?"

"Stop me? She doesn't know I'm here."

"What do you mean?"

"It was a bit tricky. I had to take her back to Montreal to fly to San Francisco. So, I packed a bag and shoved it into the trunk of the Lincoln. It was right under her own bag. She never noticed. I saw her off at her gate, went back to the car for my bag, changed in the terminal, and caught the transatlantic flight an hour later."

"But won't she call from California?"

"Ah, yes. I sent a telegram, telling her I had decided to do some wilderness camping. Said I'd be out of touch for five or six days."

"Will she believe that? Have you ever done anything like that before?"

"No, I haven't." He thought for a minute. "Will she believe it? I don't know. She certainly can't imagine I'd come back here a week after I left."

"I don't think we have to worry much about Trevor either. He's never showed much jealousy."

"Take a man's word for it. The husband who isn't jealous doesn't love his wife."

Some minutes later Tom broke the silence. "How did it happen, Liz? Why did you and Trevor ever come back to England?"

"We came in '52, once Trev decided that the austerity was really over." Briefly, she reviewed the history. Trevor Spencer had left Britain for Canada in the spring of 1939. War was coming, and he wanted no part of it. When the call-up papers followed him to Toronto, Spencer immediately enlisted in the Canadian Forces, knowing full well that there would be no Canadian conscription for overseas service. He had a boring five years, shuttling from one training barracks to another. But it was safe. With an education in a minor public school in Birkenhead, Spencer had managed to secure a commission and a certain amount of comfort, far more than his older brother, Keith, who had remained in Britain and then served in the ranks three years slogging up the Italian boot. Liz could feel the older brother's resentment of Trevor when they were together.

"How did you meet Trev?" It was a question Tom never felt he had had a right to ask before.

"In Toronto after the war. He was at uni on a government grant for vets. Like your GI Bill. Somehow he gave the impression that he was from money. My people noticed that." Tom didn't comment on Trev's deception, and she went on.

"I liked a lot about him. Good at sport, a bit older, a little more sophisticated. The accent." She laughed. "In Canada, even a Merseyside twang was considered worldly." Liz still thought Trevor Spencer attractive fifteen years later. His blond hair fell to the right of his forehead, and he kept it long enough to be noticed. His smile could be wide, though in repose his lips bent downward in a smirk. About five foot eight, he was stockier now than he'd been in his twenties. "I was in my last year, and Olivia was on the way when we married. My father got him a job selling commercial real estate. But it just didn't work. He rubbed the Yanks the wrong way, and when the Canadian vets found he'd avoided overseas service, they wouldn't do business with him."

Liz went on. "Anyway, Trevor decided the problem was sheer prejudice. Hatred of the Limey. Once he'd convinced himself of that, the only recourse was to return to Britain. It was really quite precipitate." Again Liz decided she couldn't tell Tom the whole story—not yet, anyway.

"And you agreed to come?"

She ignored the question. "Well, once we got here, Trev started facing real prejudice. The tony crowd recognized the Merseyside accent through the airs and graces. Not just the wrong regiment in the wrong army, but the middle-class origins, no Oxbridge degree, no old boy network. Maybe in Liverpool he'd have had a chance."

"Why didn't you settle there?"

"Have you been to Liverpool?" She took his silence for a no. "Very working class. Not enough ABC1s, too many C2Ds for Trev." The classifications were well known in England. As and Bs were people with educations. Below them were the C1s who still wore coats and ties. C2 and below wore coveralls and worked with their hands, or not at all. A Brit could tell whether you were A or B, C1 or C2, or worse, to a certainty, just by your accent, of course, but also by your dress, the brand of cigarette you smoked, newspaper you bought, what you drank and ate.

Tom was rueful. "Only the Brits would divide the classes six ways and give each one a precise label."

Liz nodded. "So, Trev didn't want to bring the kids up there. Then, once we decided on Oxford, he insisted on Park Town crescent."

Now Tom looked perplexed. "Why? There are cheaper places to live. North Oxford, for instance."

"Yes, but Trevor refused to live in one of those mean little villas up in Summertown. Told me he'd never be able to sell houses to the rich if we looked hard up."

"Know what you mean. Barbara didn't want to live there either. Said if we were going to have to live in Oxford, we were going to live well."

"You could afford it. I had to find work double-quick when we got here. But I was lucky. The job pays well, and frankly, I like it. It's fun."

They fell silent. Tom was absorbed by the Wiltshire landscape, the deep green of fields dotted to their horizons with sheep, long low walls formed up over the centuries from stones ploughed out of the ground and rolled to the fields' margins. There were few cars on the A303, though the occasional tractor held them up. He watched the low, flat clouds, layered over thin ribbons of blue. Their scudding revealed a strong wind coming down from the northwest that Tom could almost feel through the windscreen.

Then, suddenly there was Stonehenge, solitary, unannounced, looming out of an open field. A dozen monoliths in grey stone looking as though some giant had upended the family's tombstones and jammed them into a circle so tight no one could move between them. Apparently a few had remained after he'd finished the circle, so the giant had laid them over the largest stones as lintels.

Liz pulled into a lay-by, came to a stop, and pulled up the hand brake. Wordlessly they came out of the car and looked across the meadow towards the monoliths.

She spoke first. "I've passed these stones many times on the way to Exeter. It's time I stopped."

Almost reverentially they walked across grass resilient from recent rain. By the time they reached the stones, the tips of their shoes were covered with water stains, and their socks were wet.

As they stood there, Tom opened a packet of cigarettes and offered one. Liz shook her head. Then he spoke. "Three thousand years these stones have been here. And no one knows what the place means."

Liz surveyed the circle again. "Lots of guesses. No one any better than another. No one will ever know for sure."

Tom was thoughtful. "One thing we can be sure of. Whatever meaning it had to its builders was an illusion, though it must have been a powerful one."

Liz felt the wind strengthen. She reached up and folded the lapels of Tom's coat against his chest. "Well then, I'm going to give it a real meaning, at least for us, from now on."

"And what is that, oh high priestess of the Druids?"

"They will be mute memorials to the next four days. For the rest of our lives, every time one of us passes this way or sees a postcard or even just thinks of these stones, they will remind us of the days we'll have spent together."

"That's quite a burden of meaning for these stones to carry. Do you think they'll last long enough?"

They both laughed at that.

"Let's get to Exeter." She smiled mischievously.

⸻

Two hours later they were in the town, following signs to the cathedral. Liz evidently knew where she was headed. As they came into Magdalen Street, she pulled over and stopped. "I usually stay at the White Hart, just next to the local Abbey National branch. But we can't stay there."

"Why not?"

"Isn't it obvious? They know me. And the branch is next door to the hotel. We could easily be seen." Tom had no reply. "I've an idea." She let down the handbrake, eased up on the clutch, and moved back into traffic. Turning right they passed the cathedral in its lush green close, and a few left turns later, the car drove up to a large, white, two-storey plaster structure. Liz pulled into the small forecourt and turned off the engine.

She looked at Tom, checking for a wedding ring on his finger. "Mr. and Mrs. Wrought?" He nodded, and they entered the hotel. They were met by a plump face with a tracery of fine veins on each cheek, over a pink twin set and glasses on a beaded chain. She had bustled into the entry from a service door. Smiling brightly, the woman opened a register and proffered a hand-sharpened pencil. "Mr. and Mrs. . . . ." She invited the man to complete the phrase.

"Wrought," Tom supplied, and inscribed the registry. "Just the night. With bath."

"And breakfast in the morning?"

Tom looked at Liz, who nodded.

"One pound seven and six, please." Mrs. Twin Set was not going to remove the key from the board behind her until Tom reached for his wallet.

Tom turned the skeleton key twice, locking the world out. Then he sought Liz, who had gone into the bathroom to arrange her face. He pushed his body against hers and moved his hands to her waist. Driving them beneath the skirt top, he began moving them up under the blouse towards her breasts. Liz grabbed his hands and pushed them down.

"Sorry, I've got a job to do. I need to get to the bank." She looked at her watch. "It's two o'clock. They'll just be reopening after lunch. You need a sleep, anyway, after your flight. I'll be back at four thirty."

Before he could remonstrate, Liz had turned the key back in the lock and was gone.

Two hours later she was stroking the side of his face, slowly rousing him. Tom turned towards her and came fully awake. She whispered, "At last," and brought her face down to his.

One long kiss, and then he rose. Leaning back on the bedstead, Tom was wearing only shorts.

He looked at her. "I'd like to take your clothes off . . . very slowly."

Liz rose wordlessly and stood before the bedside. *Yes, I'll be a sybarite.* This was the very thing she'd sought, she realized. To slowly but completely have all good manners breached, every constraint waived, each norm undone, every prohibition flouted. *For once, to expose all of me to someone and have all of him exposed to me, to consent to everything and have everything consented to.* She stood there searching her mind for inhibitions to surrender, almost calculating which violation of convention would be the sweetest.

Tom moved to the edge of the bed and began undressing her. She was wearing a blue-grey Glengarry plaid blouse and matching skirt under a blue blazer, black medium-height heels, dark stockings, no jewellery. Without first removing the blazer, he carefully unbuttoned the blouse till it reached the skirt. No full slip, but a black bra that was mainly lace. "How did you know?" he asked.

"All men like black underwear."

Tom now took off the blazer, and Liz began to unbuckle the belt at her waist. "Don't help," he admonished as he pulled the belt through its loops. Then he reached to her side to unbutton the skirt. It slid to the ground, revealing a black half-slip, which Tom tugged till it was below her hips and fell freely to the floor. The panties were black too. Now he unbuttoned the cuffs at her sleeves and, walking around her, helped her out of the blouse. In a moment she would be almost as undressed as he was.

Impatient, Liz threw her arms over his head as she had done in the train ten days before and drew his mouth towards hers. Tom followed her lead and then moved his hands to her shoulders, pulling each strap of her bra down so that the tops of each cup curled over away from the flesh until they revealed, first, two dark areoles, and then two very erect nipples.

Now Tom pulled himself away, dropped to his knees, pulled down her underpants, and with hands on her thighs, moved them apart.

"What are you doing?" Her tone was quizzical, not resistant.

"Giving you pleasure," he replied as his hands moved around her thighs and his face moved below the surprisingly scant fleece between her legs.

It's the very sort of wantonness you've craved, she smiled at herself, *and yet you had not even thought of it yourself, Liz.* She was soon responding to his lips and tongue. After a few moments, Tom rose to her breasts. But after only a few kisses and nibbles there, her hands were on his shoulders, firmly pushing him back down. He moved to his knees willingly. Being led by a woman was not a new experience for him, and he'd always liked it.

They turned around so her back was to the bed. Then she fell back across it, with her feet still on the floor. "I want you . . . inside," she commanded with an explicitness that surprised her. Rising up from his knees, he obeyed. But just at his orgasm, Tom withdrew, dropping to his knees again. Then he drove his face between her legs and kept it there until Liz began to spasm. With her legs still shuddering, she pulled his face away from her body. He threw himself on the bed beside her.

"Well, you're a very considerate gentleman, Mr. Wrought. I do believe you'd even hold a door for a lady."

He smiled, unsure which act of his had occasioned this observation. "I was just brought up right."

"By whom, your wife?" Liz really was curious, not jealous, curious about what had just happened. She needed to talk about it. Most people didn't, of course, not even well-matched, long-married people. But she sensed that Tom shared her need, just for once, to get beyond the mores they'd grown up with. There they were, lying naked next to each other, spent after an act more uninhibited than she had ever imagined. Talk should now be easy. She began. "So, why did you withdraw?"

"Surely that didn't surprise you."

"With Trev when we still had sex, I had to force him to pull out. You just did it yourself, and at the last possible second."

"Well, it wasn't much of a sacrifice. I am going to have you again in a few minutes, and there won't be any need to be cautious the second time."

"Why not?"

"Never made love with a fellow twice in one night? You have a treat coming—in fact, several." He stroked her face. "Body can't replenish sperm that fast. If I come in the next twenty minutes or so, there won't be any." There was a frisson between them at the clinical explicitness of Tom's description.

"As a matter of fact, I never had sex with Trevor twice in one night, when I was still having any sex with him at all. But that other thing you did . . ." It wasn't so much that she couldn't talk about it, as that she didn't have the words to describe what they'd done.

Tom supplied it. "Cunnilingus?"

"Is that what it's called?" She thought for a moment. "Why it's practically onomatopoeia . . ."

⟨⬩⟩

"Shall we eat in the hotel?" Liz asked, but before he could answer she observed, "No point looking for a decent restaurant. This is provincial Britain. You won't even get good fish and chips in Exeter."

A few moments later they were in the dining room, contemplating the choice between fillet of plaice and kidney pie. Liz looked from her menu. "How did you manage that?"

"What?"

"Having sex that many times."

"Shh, not so loud. I don't know, but I think it may have something to do with actually being in love . . ." He reached under the table for her thigh. He wanted her to say it.

She wouldn't. "Don't mistake lust for love, Tom." Before he could reject the injunction, she went on, "Nothing wrong with lust. In fact, it's the most intoxicating cocktail there is. I haven't had nearly enough of it lately, and I am going to make up for lost time."

"We have four days." He wouldn't tell her again that he was in love.

"So long as Trev doesn't find out."

"I don't understand what you're worried about. You don't love him. You support him. In a divorce you'd keep the kids and get the house in Park Town crescent."

"I wish it were that simple." She sighed. "I've seen a solicitor, the best matrimonial causes specialist in London. First of all, since I am the breadwinner, he'd get the kids to raise, and I'd have to support him."

"No! That's absurd."

"The law, my dear, is a well-known ass!" She frowned. "Because I work, he's treated as the principal caregiver. It doesn't matter that there's live-in help." She looked at Tom. "And now he can sue me for divorce on grounds of adultery." She gulped. "Then I'd lose the kids."

"Why not just take them back to Canada? Divorce laws there are different, no?"

"Won't work. The moment he got wind I wanted to leave, he'd take the children to his parents in Birkenhead, and then put up every legal obstruction possible. I'd be mired in the courts for years. More than one solicitor has told me the same thing."

"You have studied this matter."

"I'm afraid so. The children are the reason I've stayed married to Trev. My kids are the only thing I'd never give up."

"But . . . doesn't this"—Tom looked round—"aren't we putting them at risk?"

"Very much. If Trev were to twig to . . ." She searched for the right word, but only came up with "this." She looked at her lap. "If he found out about an affair and consulted a solicitor, the first thing they'd tell him is that he could take them away from me in a divorce for adultery. That's what mine told me."

"Why did you ever consult a lawyer to begin with?"

"Once it became clear that I was going to support the family, I thought I'd better know exactly where I stood."

The fish and steamed veg arrived, and they began pushing it around their plates.

Tom's unspoken thoughts dwelt on her children. *They must mean more to you than I ever could. But then why are you here, with me, not with them?* He looked at her, no more interested in the unappealing food than she was. *I'm not going to risk losing you to find out.*

Liz was working through exactly the same problem. Why was she here risking everything for lust? It must be lust. Yes, but it was lust driven by love, made deep and rich and worth it all by love. *You're in love with this man, Liz. That's what overbears the risk, not the lust. Do I need to tell you in words too, Tom?*

<hr />

The next morning they reached the Dorset coast. Beyond Torquay, the road wound along the dark sand and shell beaches. Liz caught Tom smiling at the small palm trees planted before the tidy villas, each trying gallantly to suggest the Riviera in a wan sun. At Brixham they marvelled at the bathers' hardihood in the stiff easterly. But then as they began driving away from the headland, the wind dropped, and the sun shone with almost Mediterranean strength. They opened the windows and let a soft July breeze sweep in. The road climbed a hill between ancient stone walls protecting an orchard. Abruptly the walls began to retain rising hillsides that steepened on either side of the narrow lane, until Liz and Tom found themselves enclosed by a canopy of trees, their leaves dappling the sun and in places dividing the light into shafts picking out dust moats in the still air. The car slowed at the crest, and Liz let it quietly coast through a dark tunnel of overhanging branches, down to where the road abruptly ended at the water's edge.

To their surprise, before them was a four-car open ferry just negotiating its junction with the end of the roadway. After a moment the ferryman signalled them to drive aboard. Cranking his bus ticket machine, he came up to Liz at the driver's side. "Half a crown, please." Tom passed her the coin, and she received her ticket in return.

They got out of the car to enjoy the ride across the broad Dart River, wide here at almost its mouth on the English Channel. Looking across, Tom asked the ferryman about the large red-brick building on the brow of the hill above the town.

"Royal Naval College."

"Ah yes." Then he remembered the film from the Rattigan play. "*The Winslow Boy* and all that?"

"Don't know about no Winslow boy, but the late king and his father were cadets here." The ferryman briefly contemplated Tom and Liz, then continued, "The first time the queen met Prince Philip was up there too, when he was a cadet, so they say."

⟹⟸

Forty minutes from the ferry, a couple of hairpin turns brought them at last to a real beach, of fine sand and smooth pebbles, stretching out to the southern horizon.

"Let's go for a walk." Liz pulled into a lay-by. Opening the door, she left her shoes and strode to the beach. Tom did the same. They walked hand in hand down to the water, wishing they were in swimwear. Tom rolled up his trousers and took off his shirt. Liz pulled up her blouse, unbuttoned it, and tied it at her midriff, indifferent to the black bra now visible under it.

She pointed to a derelict hulk lying a hundred yards away at the water's edge. "That's what's left of an LST." Tom knew what an LST was—a tank-carrying landing craft—only too well. He said nothing. "This should be a famous place. But no one knows about it."

"Why?"

Liz went on without answering. "My father was here in 1944. Canadian military liaison with the US Army. Brought me once, after the war."

"Why here?" Tom persisted.

"The Yanks decided to have their dress rehearsal for D-day on this beach in April of '44, just a month or so before Normandy. It was a disaster. Killed more than a thousand GIs. And no one ever heard about it, even when the war ended."

"What happened exactly?"

"My dad said there were a dozen or so LSTs—landing ship tanks—big as freighters, headed for this beach, protected by one little corvette, what the Americans called a destroyer escort. They were attacked by German E-boats—high-speed torpedo boats. Complete cock-up. Lots of soldiers in the sinking LSTs drowned just because they didn't know how to put on their life jackets. Others died of hypothermia; the water was that cold."

"So, what did the Americans do about the fiasco?"

"Swore everyone to secrecy."

"It's all a bit like Stonehenge, then. That wreck is a monument to illusion."

"Surely not. The fight against Hitler was real and urgent."

"Yes, it was. But not to a lot of the men who died here, or at D-day, for that matter." Seeing Liz becoming visibly angry, Tom hurried to explain. "I was here. In England, with those guys. Right through the war, Americans mostly just wanted to fight the Japs. Not many of them ever cared about European 'politics.' That's what they used to call the fight against Nazism—'politics.' Most of their officers shared the racism of the Germans, if not the fanaticism of the Nazis. The men didn't have much against Krauts and no love for Yids, Frogs, Wops, or Ivans. We Americans even had our own *Untermenschen*—six million Negroes."

Liz turned towards him. "So, what you're saying is the illusion is ours. We celebrate a victory the men who died here didn't even care much about achieving?"

Tom could only nod.

She sighed. "You've got a deeply disturbing grip on the history of your country, Tom Wrought." Then Liz surprised him. "And I know why you do. I've read your book, the one that got the Pulitzer Prize—*What If the South Had Lost the Civil War?*" Tom was silent, still surveying the derelict landing craft at the shoreline.

They were finishing supper on the terrace of a surprisingly satisfactory seafood restaurant overlooking the tip of the Kingsbridge Estuary in the town of the same name. The evening had stayed warm even as the sun declined till its rays made the brackish water of the estuary glow in a pointillist foreground of flickering iridescence.

Tom lit a cigarette and offered the pack to Liz, who fished one out and leaned forwards as he lit it. His eye searched the décolletage of her summer dress unbuttoned to not very deep cleavage.

Liz dipped into her purse and drew something small from it. Then she reached across the table until she deposited what she had removed from the bag into his hand, which she closed around it. It was a flat box about an inch on either side. "Here's a little gift I bought you in Exeter this morning."

Tom didn't need to open his hand, which continued to cover the box. Only one sort of thing came in a box that size.

"You wicked girl." He smiled with pleasure as he slid the box across the table and into his jacket pocket without looking at it. "I couldn't have bought any in Saranac, still less in Montreal. They're illegal in New York, and it's practically a capital offense in Quebec to be caught with them." He wouldn't say the words that described her gift. He didn't like any of them. "I wondered why you went into that chemist's this morning in Exeter. Didn't want to ask."

"Thought I might be buying sanitary products? Men are so squeamish. We spent the entire afternoon and the last night nude and lascivious in every way we could, and you couldn't ask what I went into the chemist's for?"

Tom admired her candour. "How did you pluck up the courage to ask for them?"

"Wyvern Barracks, Royal Artillery, is right there in the middle of Exeter. So, every chemist in the town stocks French letters. They treated me like a trollop, but the chemist handed them over."

"Funny, the Brits call them 'French letters,' a lovely name, and the French return the compliment by calling them *capote anglaise*." They finished their cigarettes and rose from the table. "By the way, you're wrong . . ." He left the observation incomplete.

Liz took the bait. "About what?"

"We weren't lascivious in every way possible last night. There are several more variations we can try tonight."

Friday morning they woke early. It would be a long drive to Heathrow for Tom's return flight.

"Liz, I've been holding back asking you what you thought of my book."

Behind the wheel, she turned to him and replied archly, "I was wondering a bit whether you cared." Seeing he was serious, she went on, "Of course, the title provokes. *What If the South Had Lost . . .*" Liz emphasized the last word. "But then you start reading and find you have to unlearn so much about the post-Civil War Reconstruction you thought you knew." She thought for a moment. "Like, for example, the secret ballot. We were all brought up to think it a wonderful thing, a great reform that protects democracy. To learn it was introduced first in the South to prevent Negroes voting because they couldn't read a written ballot . . ."

"Yes. There's a great deal more of American history like that. Take the two most important reforms of Roosevelt's New Deal almost twenty-five years ago—social security and the right to unionize. They were both designed to exclude Negroes."

"What do you mean?"

"Simple. Roosevelt needed the Southern senators to pass them. They wouldn't vote for either unless they excluded agricultural workers and domestics—the two jobs Negroes were mainly limited to. So he cut them out of both."

"I see."

Tom looked at Liz. "I'm pleased you read the book."

"Months ago, Tom, and admired it."

He gave a mock bow from the waist. Tom's hand closed around her thigh. "But I'm wondering, why is a Canadian who studied math in university even interested in this stuff?"

"Well, apart from my interest in the author, why shouldn't I be? Aren't you interested in quadratic equations?"

He winced. "Not in the slightest."

※

An hour later Liz pulled up at London Heathrow East Terminal, drove her tongue deep into Tom's mouth for the last time, and pushed him out of the car. She drove off without, he noticed, looking back.

※

Five minutes after leaving Heathrow, Liz finally remembered. In four days together she'd entirely forgotten to mention the two men— Americans, by their accent—who'd come to Park Town crescent looking for Tom, only to discover he had left for the States a few days before. *Well*, she thought, *it probably wasn't important.*

CHAPTER FIVE

Once the plane had reached cruising altitude, Tom asked for a martini, lit up the last of his English cigarettes, and began to think things through.

He needed to decide what he wanted. Could he treat the problem as one of balancing credits and debits, what he was willing to give up versus what he'd receive in exchange? *Well, you could try,* he thought, looking over the Irish Sea and the lovely curve of the Constellation's wing. *Sixteen hours to Montreal should be enough time to figure things out.*

Then it overwhelmed him, the sinking feeling he'd had in a dream that came too often: suddenly you realize that you have agreed to go back to somewhere you never wanted to see again, and it's irrevocable. He'd waken with immense relief that it was only a dream. But now he was awake and oppressed by the same feeling. *Do you really want to live in Britain? For years? Forever? Little England?* A year at Trinity had deprived him of most of his anglophile illusions. Could he bear Blighty anymore?

Too often England depressed Tom, when it did not outrage him. To begin with, there was the class system that everyone bought into, even its victims.

He remembered a particular incident with special vividness. One Saturday in the spring, he'd been showing American friends around the colleges. As they turned into All Souls, the porter came out of the lodge growling, "Sorry, sir. University members only." Tom looked at him with visible disdain and said in just the right accent, "It's alright; I'm a fellow of Trinity." The porter drew back, inviting Tom and his friends to enter the precincts. No questions. Just the say-so of someone with the right accent. Did the disdain in his voice help? The deference had put Tom in a white heat for days.

Daily life in Britain was mean. Not just the plumbing—"the drains." Central heating was simply unknown. You awoke freezing and straight away reached for the shilling coin you left on the mantelpiece the previous night just to insert in the electric grate. The Harris tweeds were unbending, the trousers made Tom's thighs itch, and then there were the damn monkish gowns they made you teach in, eat in, pray in.

Once breakfast was over you couldn't look forwards to anything much worth eating all day. And the food was, as the British still said, *dear*. Within days of his arrival at Oxford, Tom could see why most fellows ate every meal they could in the hall. Younger fellows without an independent income would organize their entire lives—weekday and weekend—around college meals.

At least college rooms were sometimes warm. But the work was killing—a dozen tutorials a week, endless college committees, lectures to give. By contrast, the life of an American professor was a year-round holiday.

Barbara and Tom had lived in a relatively large home in Park Town crescent, where no college fellow without private means could live. *A large house?* Tom nearly laughed out loud. The undetached "villa" was identical to every other house in the crescent. The front door opened to a narrow hallway and a steep stairway. There was a "lounge," twelve feet by twelve feet, separated from the cramped dining room by sliders. The kitchen gave out onto a narrow strip of grass lush in the dismal rains, except when turned into a quagmire by children's games. It was weeks before someone explained the warming closet, essential in a climate where everything was always damp. Tom couldn't understand the absence of showers or the ubiquity of baths, vast porcelain tubs on lion's claw feet. Somehow they remained cold to the touch even when full of hot water.

When Tom complained about shopping, his friends would not listen. They remembered the austerity that began in 1940 and only worsened when the war ended in 1945. Sugar and meat had been rationed till 1954. It still seemed like austerity to Tom. Hardly any fresh fruit or vegetables, even in the Oxford Covered Market. No cheese but cheddar. Not even the cafés brewed coffee. The war seemed to have addicted everyone to Nescafé.

There were exactly two TV channels and no transmission after midnight. *BBC Third Program* on the "wireless" was incomparable. Tom would rise early on Sunday morning just to listen to Alistair Cooke's *Letter from America*. But radio didn't make life bearable by itself.

Tom was grateful that an educated elite was in control of the culture. But it was the class system all over again. Wherever he went, the wireless was tuned to *Radio Luxembourg*, the pirate broadcast that sounded as much like an American pop station as it could contrive. Meanwhile, everyone paid the BBC licence fee—subsidizing chamber music, countertenors, opera that the rich could perfectly well afford to pay for.

Just watching the curtain go up at a cinema made him angry: the first thing you saw was a licence from the British Board of Censors. And when the film was over, they piped in "God Save the Queen" to the backs of an audience sauntering out, thinking only whether a pub might still be open. When Brando in *The Wild One* was banned the previous winter, Tom could only laugh.

The double standard was appalling. Henry Miller's books printed in Paris by the Olympia Press circulated freely enough among the educated, but *Lady Chatterley's Lover* was comprehensively banished from the booksellers.

There is the theatre, you have to give them that, he thought. There'd be nothing like Osborne's *The Entertainer* in New York for years. Tom had been more moved by *A Taste of Honey,* written by a woman named Delaney. It was a working-class drama with a cross-racial love story. The open homosexuality of the black hero would have made the play impossible in the States, even off-Broadway.

He did like cycling everywhere. Cars had always seemed a necessity that had to be endured in America. Tom hadn't driven till he was in his twenties, and he happily sold off the one and only car he had owned before leaving for his year in Oxford. Ironically enough, it had been British—a Jaguar 3.2 Barbara had bought him the year before—a reward for winning the Pulitzer Prize. There was no temptation to own "a motor" in Britain. He'd be dangerous driving on the left.

At least there's still such a thing as conversation in Britain. People didn't talk about their relatives or pets, Wall Street or moneymaking, their health, or even sport (not "sports," he reminded himself). But they talked a lot about writers, and theatre, French films, even history, and most of all politics. *Anyway, the friends you've made talked politics obsessively.* How often had he heard the quip "I have very extreme views, very weakly held"?

Think about how the few Africans and American Negroes in Oxford are treated. Pretty much like everyone else. It made them act like everyone else, instead of the all too stolid, reserved, cautious, resentful black men Tom had grown up knowing in New York. He knew that many Brits discriminated against West Indian blacks. But it was against the law, and no party would countenance discrimination. That made a difference to Tom.

Another thing he admired was the English tolerance for eccentricity, even quite extreme irregularity in styles of dress, behaviour, belief. And no one ever said a word about it. There were perfectly respectable people who employed barnyard epithets that would have banned any book in which they appeared. He had a neighbour who was never seen abroad without a large white cockatoo on her shoulder. Twice he had been invited by newly made acquaintances for naturist—nudist—weekends. And no one batted an eyelash. Irreligion was not an eccentricity at all, even among the ordained Anglican clergy dotted across the colleges.

And then there were the children. Distinctively English, preternaturally and invariably polite, but winning. Tom remembered the first time he'd met Liz's two kids, craning over his back garden gate. He had noticed from the conservatory and invited them in. They were seeking what they described as Ian's footie ball. Over cookies and milk Olivia had explained, "I think you Americans call it a soccer ball." The boy had whispered to his older sister, and she had turned to Tom. "I'm sorry—that was rude, but Ian wants to know if he may have a second biscuit." Tom replied, "Sure," and with mock sternness added, "but he must ask for himself." The next week Liz warned him Olivia would have nineteen children to a birthday party in the back garden. All Tom could hear that afternoon was "please," "thank you," "may I," "so glad you invited me." But there was enough joy and laughter to reassure him English children were perfectly human for all their reserve.

The stewardess broke into Tom's reflections, offering another martini. "Yes, please." He handed her the empty and lit another cigarette. *Now, where were you . . . lining up all the things you hate about living in Britain? Well, maybe you can put up with Blighty. It's the only way you'll ever have the chance of a life with Liz.* He knew now for the first time in his life how easily and completely love overbore every other consideration. The feeling was a palpable ache, but one to be sought and then savoured, indulged. The emotion was truly new to him. At almost forty he had finally found it, after more than a decade of marriage spent convincing himself there was no such thing.

Liz drove away from Heathrow and back into her real life. She had neglected the three hundred branches of the Abbey National for a week. Could she look in on two or three driving back to Oxford? It was only seven thirty in the morning, and she'd probably be able to drop in at Slough, High Wycombe, and Bicester before five o'clock. Slough was a new branch with trainee tellers. At Bicester the turnover was well above normal. Was it a branch manager laying hands on the girls as they stood penned in their stalls?

Having sorted both Slough and High Wycombe by eleven thirty, Liz began her drive north. By two o'clock it was still another hour up country roads to Bicester, and Liz was getting hungry. She slowed at the entry to Thane and began looking for a tea shop or a pub. There in the middle of town was an attractive, half-timbered, newly plastered public house called the Birdcage. Well, she felt rather like she'd been in a cage after two hours in the Humber sedan. After parking, she entered. No one was behind the counter, nor was anyone in the snug bar when she opened its frosted glass door. Then she looked at her watch—two fifteen in the afternoon. Of course, it was already closed for the afternoon. *Pub hours! I completely forgot! And nowhere else in the village to go.*

She walked back out into the sun, sought one of the benches, pulled over a large ashtray, and lit a cigarette. Would people in this village frown on a woman alone smoking in public? She laughed to herself. *If only they knew what I'd really been up to all week!*

The days with Tom had been intruding in her thoughts all morning. They were a pleasure she was trying hard not to relish, not this day at least. She needed to get back to thinking about work, about reality, about the here and now, not what was past or might have been. That was why she had resolutely not looked back, not even once, not even in the rear-view mirror, as she drove away from Heathrow East Terminal.

She drew on the cigarette. Now, sitting in the sun, she had to think it out, put it into words for herself. *Figure it out, Liz.* Exactly what had those days meant?

She knew. The experiment of those days had been an epiphany, a release. She said the words under her breath. *You're free, Liz, really, finally, free.*

Through the better part of two decades, she had shackled herself to an anchor to keep her from the abyss she'd climbed out of as a girl of nineteen. She'd arranged everything she could—pregnancy, marriage, children, work—to weight that anchor against a persistent temptation to pitch herself headlong back down into the darkness. All the demands, obligations, expectations she'd burdened herself with had done their work. They had filled up the days, months, and years since her breakdown. They'd made it so there wasn't time to ponder whether the demoness still prowled that void or whether the black cloud remained lurking above it. Liz had arranged her whole life as a rampart against these two, the pit and the overhanging darkness that between them had nearly consumed her almost sixteen years before.

Almost from the beginning of the four days in Dorset, Liz realized that she was suddenly, if perhaps only momentarily, free from what had haunted her. With Tom she didn't feel the need any longer of that anchor to keep her from self-destruction. Suddenly, somehow her own life mattered to her. And now, though the days with Tom were over, her life still mattered. She couldn't help smiling at the realization.

But does Tom want you? And if he does, could you make a life with him here, or anywhere for that matter? Her thoughts became practical. *The real problem is breaking with Trev. I can't lose the children.* She knew him too well. If she tried to make a break, he would do everything he could to thwart her. *The children are his trump cards. He'll certainly play them.* It was easy to put herself in Trev's shoes and see things the way he would, even if it was pretty much all self-indulgence and self-deception.

It wasn't just self-deception, though. Trevor had deceived her too. She'd only come to understand how deeply Trev had done so after they arrived in England when Ian was one and Olivia four. They had landed in Liverpool and gone straight to his family's home in Birkenhead. It was there she'd met Trev's older brother, Keith.

Liz's bond of friendship with Keith Spencer had been immediate. Perhaps it was the fact that he had a boy the same age as her daughter. Keith was very different from his younger brother. Straightforward, bluff, direct, comfortable in his working-class values, his friends, even his accent. Keith Spencer worked nights opening the doors of people who'd lost their latchkeys. His wife was a nurse, so in the daytime, childcare often fell to him.

Pushing prams side by side along the Mersey, Liz and Keith were soon telling each other things one mentions only to close friends. It was how Liz learned things about her husband she'd never known: what Trevor had been like in school before the war, why he had left Britain, what he'd actually done and not done in the war. These were truths Trevor never meant her to know.

One blustery day as they "aired" the children, Liz admitted to Keith that she really didn't understand her husband the way she needed to.

"It's simple, Liz. For Trev, everything's always been about shame. He couldn't even bear undressing in front of his friends. He always wanted his mum and dad to be proud of him. But he never seemed to have the grit to do what needed doing." Keith gestured towards the Albert Docks across the Mersey, war damage unrepaired. "But he was smart enough to see what was coming in '39." The undertone of resentment was easy to detect. They walked on in silence.

Keith began again. "Still, I'm glad Trev was able to straighten out the financial problem."

"Financial problem? What do you mean?"

"Replacing the money."

Liz brought her pram to a stop. "I'm sorry. I don't understand. You better tell me exactly what you're talking about."

"The five-thousand-dollar escrow cheque he diverted to the stock market. Surely you knew about that."

"No." It was all Liz could say.

"When he lost it all, he tried to raise some from Mum and Dad, and me. Told us he'd had to take the risk to make enough money to pay income tax. Seemed he'd not filed for several years, and it caught up with him. So he 'borrowed' an escrow cheque from office accounts, hoping to multiply it in the stock market enough to pay some of the tax and stay out of trouble. But he lost the lot. Well, we couldn't help . . . Even if there hadn't been the postwar currency restrictions, no one's ever seen that kind of money round here." Keith turned to Liz. "Never did learn how he did it."

"Did what? Find the money?"

Keith nodded.

Liz could only reply, "I have no idea."

She hadn't confronted Trevor with her knowledge, not then, not later. It had festered now for more than a half-dozen years. But it enabled her to understand why they'd left Toronto so precipitately. Perhaps it was why he wouldn't go back either.

Sitting in the warm sun of the pub's forecourt, Liz lit another cigarette. It struck her: did her days with Tom somehow balance the scales with Trevor? Now she had a secret to match against his. He had lied to her, probably several different lies. Well, now she had paid him back. For a moment she felt rather good about it. The thought didn't last. *Liz, you didn't spend those days with Tom just to get even. You got a good look through a window into another life, one you want to live.*

Liz put out her cigarette, got into her car, and drove away from the Birdcage pub. When she was well beyond the town, keeping her left hand on the wheel, she drew her right hand down to her thigh and slowly moved it up between her legs, taking her time as the broad sun lit fields on one side of the country road and the thick hedges on the other slipped by.

She was home by five o'clock that evening. As she put down her case, the double doors that opened to the back garden rattled open, and her children came rushing in, followed by Ifegenia. Ian reached her first. He was seven, with red hair and dimples. "Mummy, I can ride! I've learnt to pedal the two-wheeler!" The excitement in his voice broke through the English understatement he'd already learned to affect.

He was followed by his sister, ten-year-old Olivia, who announced proudly, "I taught him."

Ian was firm but quiet in his reply. "No. I did it myself."

"Ian, whether she taught you or not, Olivia was nice enough to let you use her bicycle." Liz smiled at both of them. "But tomorrow morning before the stores close, we'll go up to the Banbury Cyclery and buy you your very own." The boy hugged his mother's thighs while she reached out to tousle Olivia's thick brown hair. She looked towards Ifegenia. "Is Mr. Spencer home?"

"He was home all day till the children returned from school. Then he went out. He took his squash racket."

An hour later Liz was cooking dinner. She could hear Trevor Spencer's latchkey in the door, and then his footfalls on the stair treads as he went up to the bedroom. A few moments later he came into the kitchen. "Oh, you're home then?" It was a slight provocation. He had to have seen her car at the curb. Going directly up the stair without a word had been a demonstration of his indifference to her return.

Trevor was still in grey sweats. He evidently had not bathed after his squash game. They hadn't seen each other in five days, but there seemed no occasion for the slightest physical contact as they circled round each other in the kitchen. Who would break the silence?

It was Trevor. "They called a few times from the head office."

"Who called?"

"I told them you were away with your lover."

Liz gulped. The blood literally began to drain from her head. She was dimming out and had to grab the sink to remain standing. *Does he know? How could he? Why did he not immediately confront me?* Trevor was paying so little attention, he did not notice the consternation on her face.

"It was Beatrice Russell"—her secretary. With a breath her equilibrium returned. It had been another little jab, nothing more. "She had some messages from branches up north."

⊷

Liz was soaking in the tub when she heard Trevor go into the bedroom. With the door open, she called to him, "Kids down?"

"Yes, Ifegenia's seen to them."

She rose from the tub, dried herself, and came into the bedroom wearing nothing but a towel wrapped round her hair. Stretched across the bed with the latest *Punch* before him, Trevor looked up briefly and returned to his reading. Liz plucked a scarlet peignoir from a drawer— she had purchased it years before, in Paris, when UK clothes rationing was still in effect. Raising it above her head, she watched herself in the mirror as she lifted her arms through the nightie. She enjoyed what she saw, even if it was her own body, thirty-five years old and after two children. But it was, she knew, quite lost on her husband. *So much the better,* Liz thought. She had decided to wear the peignoir simply to go to sleep thinking about Tom.

"Trev, let's go back to North America." She had made a prediction to herself about how this conversation would go. Now she would test it.

"Back? Back to Toronto?"

"Doesn't have to be Toronto. Anywhere in Canada. Even the States."

"Not a chance. Can't go back."

Suddenly she knew why. "What do you mean 'can't go back'?"

"Just can't. There it is." Trevor looked like a small child about to stamp his feet.

She would try to be calm. She reached for a dressing gown, covered herself, and repeated his words. "Just can't? Surely there's a reason, Trev. Why ever not?"

"Ask your father." There was deep belligerence in his voice.

"My father? What's he to do with this?" *Will Trevor storm out of the room?* she wondered.

No, he was going to answer her question. "Your father told me if I came back, he'd turn me in."

"What are you talking about?" *Would he admit to Keith's disclosure, or would the shame prevent it?*

"He covered a . . . a . . . defalcation."

She had to think what the word meant. "A what? You mean a fraud, a theft?"

"Yes, my theft." There. He had said it. His look glared the thought *You deserved to hear the unpleasant truth just for provoking me.* It was too late, far too late for her to do anything about it. "You might as well know. It was the income tax. I just never kept the right records, and besides, I couldn't figure out the damn forms. I wasn't going to ask for your help with the maths. You would have made fun of me." Trevor stopped.

You're right, Liz thought, but suppressed the words.

"So I just skipped it for three years. Then they came after me. I took a bit of money from an escrow account to make enough on the stock market to pay it off." He stopped, hoping to see some understanding or acceptance on her face. Seeing none, he continued, "Should have known better . . . lost it all to a shyster broker. Your father paid it—the escrow and the taxes. Then he bought us the steamship tickets to Liverpool."

"But that was what, six, seven years ago? Why can't we go back?" Liz was reeling. Had she been exiled by her own father?

"Told me if I came back without the money, he'd press charges."

"But we haven't saved anything."

"Well, he thinks I'm putting it together. Reckons we're doing alright."

"Why?"

"Because I haven't told him the truth, and neither have you."

Well, Liz thought, standing there, *now at least you know exactly where you are.* She moved to the bed, took off the dressing gown, and slipped in between the sheets, keeping well away from Trevor's torso.

⊰⊱

The next morning when Liz arrived in the kitchen, Trevor was alone, making a cup of tea. She had begun to put together the coffee percolator when he spoke.

"I'm sorry about last night, Liz." She made no response. "I've been meaning to tell you everything for . . . for years." Liz did not express her disbelief. "I wanted to make good, to earn the money before I told you . . . then pay it back." Trevor was so close to tears Liz almost wanted to comfort him. He was trying to build a bridge, to find a modus vivendi. Would she help from her side of the divide? She decided to try.

"But then, Trev, you've got to find some other way to earn that money."

"What do you mean?"

"Look, you've been trying to sell for years now, first commercial real estate, then houses . . . now you're down to used cars. It's not working. You don't have the knack."

"I just need to make the contacts."

"Six years almost. The club dues we can't afford, standing people to drinks, squash, tennis club, Tory party dinner dances . . . you, dressing the part. I've paid for it all, along with rent, the school fees. It's not a matter of contacts. It's a matter of trust. People won't buy things from you."

"What would you have me do?"

"Drive a cab, learn a trade, get a job at the Cowley Motor Works. Anything that brings in some money. It doesn't matter . . ." She stopped for a moment. "How much do we need before we can go back to Canada?"

Trevor glared at her. "I'm never going back. And that's flat." Then he walked out.

CHAPTER SIX

Tom was sitting on the deck of the boathouse. It was a quiet late afternoon four days after his return to the United States. He was in a low-slung Adirondack chair stained to match the dark log building. The deck planking was accented by gleaming turnbuckles and white painters loosely holding a matched set of inboard Chris-Crafts to the dock. He could hear their rhythmic tapping against the deck in the wake of a passing launch. The glare of sunlight was redoubled by reflection off the polished teak prows that narrowed from each rakish windscreen. The intensity of the light forced his eyes to the north, where the shore was already an indistinct purple in the shade of the mountains surrounding the lake.

Tom knew that he would have to return to England. The question was how soon he could go. Perhaps not before October, when the Oxford Michaelmas term began. That was three months away. If he went back much sooner, Barbara would want to know why. And if she learned the truth, Trevor Spencer would soon know it too.

Behind him he suddenly detected his wife's emphatic footsteps. "Bladen told me you were down here." She bent down and gave Tom a peck somewhere between his cheek and his hairline.

"Barb, when you called you said you'd be back tomorrow."

"I wanted to surprise you." *Why does it sound more like "catch you"?* Barbara Wrought was still in her Chanel travelling suit, a narrow skirt and fitted jacket, topped by a pillbox hat. She folded her long frame into the matched chair next to his and went on, "So, after ten years of trying to get you to go camping with me, you go off alone. Very surprising, totally out of character. What possessed you?"

Tom had been trying without much luck to contrive a response to this question for days. They were interrupted by the servant carefully balancing a tray of two martini glasses. It gave Tom a little more time. Barbara glanced at him. "I asked Bladen to bring us a couple of cocktails."

Tom waited till the man had turned up the path to the main lodge. "I went into the state park for a few days because I needed time alone to think things through." It sounded more ominous than he meant it to be.

"Time alone? You were alone here. There was no one to bother you." He made no response. "What sort of things did you need to think through?"

"The future, my future, our future." *Our future? Why did he put it that way?* He almost laughed as he thought, *I don't want to provoke you, just divorce you.* But he couldn't give her the slightest hint of why. She had always been a jealous wife, interposing herself between her husband and any woman she thought might find his company agreeable. Could it have entered her head that he had already gone back to England only a week after living there for a year? It would be an easy step to the conclusion that he'd gone back for a woman.

"Barb, I've decided to go back."

"You've already decided? Can't we discuss it?"

"We can discuss it, but I have pretty well decided."

"I don't get it. You spent the whole year complaining about the tight little island—the class system, the cold, the rain, the meanness of life. What's happened to change your mind?"

"Barb, I can't work in the States."

"You don't need to work. You haven't needed to since we got married. Besides, with the Pulitzer you'll get a hefty advance for your next book."

"It's not the money."

"You liked being an Oxford don?" Her tone was dismissive. "How will you like it living on a don's salary?"

"Like you said, Barb. With an advance on my next book, perhaps I'll be able to."

Barbara rose. "Tom, I don't think you'll really go back. It won't be me that holds you. I know that. In Britain you'd be too far away to contribute anything to the Negro civil rights movement."

"You're wrong, Barb. I'll be able to do just what I've been doing all along." She looked at him quizzically. "I don't have to be in America to write things. In fact, that history of Negro education in the South I wrote for the *Brown v Board of Ed* case back in '54, I didn't even claim authorship." Tom's paper had been cited in the famous desegregation case, but they'd asked him to be anonymous. The blacklist again. Tom had realized that his usefulness to the cause would be limited till the Red Scare was over.

Barbara shrugged her shoulders. "I'm going to shower and change for dinner." She finished the drink and slowly unfolded her long body out of the deck chair.

<hr />

Coming back into the house, Tom passed his desk. Next to the Olivetti 22 portable typewriter was his US passport, lying open, facedown. Had he left it that way? Had Barbara leafed through the pages, checking the dates? Surely she would have confronted him if she had noticed the latest stamps. Quietly he slipped it into a pocket. Now, where could he hide it?

If Tom was going back to Oxford, he'd need money, and the only source was an advance from his publisher on a new book. He'd need a subject and an outline, and it would take several days to put one together. One had been kicking around in his head ever since the morning he had driven back to Heathrow with Liz: a book about the New Deal's almost comprehensive compromise with Southern racism. So, Tom spent most afternoons the next week at the Saranac Lake Public Library, reading spools of *New York Times* and *Herald Tribune* microfilm. Undisturbed in the mornings, he'd sit at the portable typewriter trying to turn ten or fifteen years of congressional politics into a story that people would want to read. He needed characters. The ones that emerged were villains—Southern senators like Bilbo and Thurmond playing the race card to win votes from poor whites while personally enriching themselves. There was only so much he could write about Eleanor Roosevelt's fight for an antilynching bill. He knew who his heroes had been, the anonymous men and women he'd known as a student. They had come out of the South and gone back to organize sharecroppers—white and black. And too many had been Communists.

When he was finished, he went to the public stenographer in the St. Regis Hotel, who typed a fair copy of the eight-page outline. Then he mailed it off to his New York publisher.

⟞⟝

That was the night he realized he'd have to leave sooner rather than later. Barbara had been back for nearly ten days, and they had not had intercourse once. When it came to sex she was clinical, and that's what she called it—intercourse. A dry spell this long was unusual, and unthinkable after a separation such as they'd experienced when Barbara had gone to California.

Sex had kept their marriage a going concern for almost a dozen years. It had repeatedly and reliably expunged the bitterness their occasional infidelities had induced in each other. Tom could always tell when Barbara wanted or expected sex. He'd come into the bedroom and find her in underclothes available only from Frederick's of Hollywood. This was a mail-order business whose packages really did arrive in plain brown wrappers with a post office box for the return address.

It was a warm night, but Barbara was lying across the bed wearing mesh stockings, whose seams ran right up to black lace tops. Each was held by a pair of black garters snaking down from a dark-purple garter belt around her waist. Below the belt there were no panties at all. Across her back was a single band without a clasp and two straps, both off her shoulders. The bra was one that opened in the front that she knew he particularly liked.

Barbara dropped the book she had been reading on the floor and twisted her head over her right shoulder. Tom noticed the title, *Anatomy of a Murder*. It had been on the *New York Times* bestseller lists for three months, but had not yet been available in Britain. Smiling ruefully, he took off his clothes, a pair of chino ducks and a plain white T-shirt. When he was down to his boxers, he threw himself on the bed next to Barbara. She turned towards him, proffering a leg so that he could roll the stocking off. Obediently he did so, and then repeated the process, moving his hands slowly down the other long leg. As he finished, he began to worry. He was not as yet even slightly aroused. Barbara had not noticed, and clambering over his prostrate body, she was soon astride him, looking down at herself and his torso.

Suddenly she stopped. He was not ready. This had never happened in more than a decade of marriage. Never, not once. She had to know what it meant. She moved off his body, and then casting her eye from his head downwards towards his groin, she finally spoke. "Well, you certainly aren't finding me attractive tonight, dear. What's the matter? Preoccupied? Can't focus on the sex?"

"No." His denial was weak. *What excuse do men give when they can't get it up?* he wondered. "Maybe I'm catching something. Can't figure out what's come over me."

"If I didn't know better, I'd say it was love . . . and for someone else."

"Why's that?" Was she reading his mind? It wasn't a cause of impotence he'd ever heard of. Men famously fucked almost anything anytime. *Having to be in love in order to be aroused was something for women,* he'd always thought. Now he knew differently. At least this man at this time couldn't service this woman for that very reason. He was in love with someone else. And it was the last thing he could admit to.

Tom rose from the bed and walked into the bathroom to wash his face. Opening the medicine cabinet, he noticed her diaphragm kit open, with the diaphragm still inside. So, she had tried to seduce him without protection. This was as unheard of between them as his own failure. She was trying to become pregnant without his consent.

Now he had to factor in the unanticipated strength of Barbara's interest in keeping him with her. It was evidently strong enough to make his wife willing to have a child. Barbara Wrought had never been drawn to parenthood. Like Tom, she had been an only child, she out of her own parents' choice and he owing to the early widowhood of his mother. He'd expected to have children, looked forwards to them, wanted them. But once they'd been married a few years, Barbara told Tom she was having too much fun to follow their friends into the postwar baby boom. By then he'd recognized his marriage was very possibly a mistake, so he didn't argue. Now Barbara was almost forty. Without children to have borne or tended, she looked far younger. Could she still have children? Of course. Was she willing to use a child as a pawn in a struggle to keep her husband from leaving her? Evidently.

Several weeks later, on an unseasonably cold and rainy day in late July, Tom sat in the cone of light cast by a standing lamp, smoking cigarettes, sipping coffee, and reading. Even in the late morning, one could still see the lights in the lodges that dotted the lakeshore. The only boats to be seen were utility craft carrying supplies to estates with no road connection to the town.

Barbara came in with the mail, sat down at the dining table, and put a thick envelope before her. "Tom, will you please come here." She indicated the seat at right angles to hers. Wordlessly he rose and carried his book to the table, put his cigarette in the ashtray, and faced her. "I had my lawyers draw up these papers." She removed them from the envelope. "They protect my property in any divorce proceeding." He did not interrupt. "They told me if you contested a property settlement, you'd have to be served papers. But they said if it were uncontested, you'd only have to have your signature witnessed. Bladen can do it." Still Tom said nothing.

"I have to protect myself and my assets. If you go back to Britain, I'll sue for divorce." They both knew each of them had grounds. Almost from the beginning Barbara had been unfaithful, in ways so casual Tom couldn't take them seriously. It was the fact that he had not felt any jealousy that made him realize he had ceased to love her, if he ever had to begin with. There was a line in one of those wonderful British novels he always remembered: "I wore my cuckold's horns like a crown of manumission." He'd had to look up the word *manumission*, only to discover it was the act of freeing one's slaves. Embarrassing. It was a word any historian of the American South should have known. Barbara's indiscretions had given him licence for his own. Now his rare lapses had provided her grounds for divorce. It didn't matter.

"Where do I sign?" He took the documents from her and began to read them through.

"Don't you understand? You'll be penniless."

"I don't actually have any money of my own now, Barbara. I live on you."

"Yes, you do. And you won't be able to live on me if I divorce you."

"I can work for a living."

"When you left Howard University, you were making six thousand dollars a year. We used up the ten thousand from your Pulitzer in Britain. You didn't even take any notice of what Trinity and the history faculty were paying you."

"Barbara, do you really want to make it plain that the only reason I should stay with you is the money? Why do you want to be married to me that badly anyway?" He hadn't meant to be so brutal. It was just the habitual pattern between them asserting itself once more. But this time she didn't snap back. As she walked away from the table, he sought to say something that might cushion the blow, spare her self-esteem. "You never really loved me." She turned back with a bitter smile. Tom spoke again. "You loved the idea of being married to me."

She glared at him. "You egoist!"

Tom's placatory aim vanished. "No, it wasn't me you wanted. Just someone like me who'd serve as a sign of your own rank. You've kept me all these years like an object gaining value. It was the prestige of having a professor for a husband, one with a slightly risqué pedigree and then a glittering prize or two." He paused. "You've always treated me like one of those minks you throw over the shoulders of a cocktail dress."

"You really think you're going back, don't you?"

"Yes, I do."

"Well, you're not." She turned and finally left the room.

What could her categorical statement mean? Tom became anxious.

<hr />

For an hour early that afternoon they moved through the house in silence, wary of each other, taking care their paths not cross. The gloom outside matched the ominous mood inside, as if both were preparing for a violent storm. About one thirty Barbara came out of the bedroom wearing the Chanel suit, white gloves, a hat with a fine mesh veil, carrying her pocketbook. To no one in particular she said, "I'm going to Plattsburgh. I'll probably be back late."

Plattsburgh? It was the nearest large town, two hours away, along narrow alpine roads. What could be in Plattsburgh? An air force base and not much else. The combination of uncertainty about what Barbara might do and her absence decided matters for Tom. Once she'd gone he found a suitcase in the storage room of the boathouse, brought it up to the lodge, and began to pack. He wouldn't be able to take much, and he would have to hide the bag. When it was packed, he took his passport from its hiding place beneath a dresser drawer and placed it on top of the Olivetti portable, snapped down the metal case, and put it and the valise in the woodshed next to the carport.

Then he called BOAC and Trans-Canada Airlines in Montreal. Suddenly he had to think about cost. It was, he ruefully admitted to himself, a new experience. Then he remembered Barb had insisted on securing a Diner's Club charge card in his name. At least he'd be able to buy the ticket on credit. Paying for it later would be another matter.

Tom was in bed feigning sleep when he heard Barbara pull in towards midnight. He was relieved. The car was essential to his plan. He needed to wake at 4:00 a.m. if he was to make his flight at Lachine, west of Montreal.

When he next looked at his watch, it was three thirty, and he felt as though he'd never gotten to sleep at all. There was no point trying to snatch that last thirty minutes. With infinite slowness he rose from the bed, lifting the covers just enough to emerge from them. In bare feet he tiptoed down the wooden stairs, each tread groaning slightly with his weight. Entering the laundry room behind the kitchen, he closed the door and then snapped on the light. There was the suit, shirt, tie, socks, and shoes he'd laid out the night before. Quickly he dressed, came out of the lodge by the back door, grabbed the suitcase from the woodshed, and made for the car. As he swung the bag into the trunk, something gnawed at him . . . what was the matter? Why did he feel as though he had forgotten something? He patted his pockets, feeling for his wallet, keys, money clip. Then it hit him . . . he had nearly ruined everything. He was about to drive off without the typewriter and passport! His body relaxed, and he tiptoed back into the woodshed for the grey metal box.

Now he sat in the car, put the key in the ignition, and began to worry about the noise the motor would make. Opening the door, he put his foot out onto the ground, then pulled the shift lever on the steering wheel column into neutral. Slowly disengaging the handbrake, he turned the key in the ignition switch to on and gave the car a push with his foot. Gently it moved away, gathering speed on the gradual descent to the main road. By the time the car was coasting into the turn of the road, he was going fast enough to slowly let in the clutch so the wheels could silently start the motor. Suddenly Tom felt the exhilaration of action. *Yes, like the last time you did this, in June!*

⟻⟼

"Show them in." Even before the men had offered their FBI badges and names, Barbara began, "I told your boss yesterday. If you waited till this morning he might be gone. Well, he is."

"Excuse me, ma'am?" The older of the two looked perplexed. He had removed his hat to reveal a crew cut that he was much too old to carry off. His two-piece gabardine suit was so wrinkled, one would be excused for thinking he had slept in it. In fact he had, on a flight from Washington, DC, and then on a long drive from Albany along narrow valley roads that had begun before dawn. In a vaguely Midwestern accent he continued, "If you told somebody something 'bout Mr. Wrought's leaving, it wasn't my boss. I report directly to the director of the FBI himself." He looked at his younger partner. "My name is

Sandusky, and this is Agent Geary." The latter looked a little more like the fresh-faced FBI agent one expected, trim, dark hair held down by something that smelled like Brylcreem, and no immediate need of a shave, unlike his older partner. Geary was wearing a seersucker suit that had travelled better in the heat, but his collar was open and tie disarrayed. Both looked like they needed refreshment.

"Gentlemen, can Bladen get you some coffee?"

Geary spoke, apparently slightly out of turn, as Sandusky's face grimaced in slight annoyance. "Glass of cold water would be fine, ma'am."

Bladen went to the kitchen and returned with two glasses tinkling with ice. Both were gratefully accepted.

By now Barbara had realized that their call had nothing to do with her trip the day before to the local FBI office in Plattsburgh. "So, what can I do for you, gentlemen?"

Sandusky spoke. "We came to see Mr. Wrought. But you say your husband is gone. How long ago did he leave?"

"Probably sometime during the night or early this morning. My car is gone too. A '58 Lincoln coupe, licence plate BF 825." She wondered if the FBI could get her car back. "Probably he's gone to Montreal for the Trans-Canada Constellation to London."

"Let me get this straight, ma'am," Geary said. "You knew he wanted to leave and tried to get the FBI to stop him? Why's that?"

Barbara was slightly flustered. *I wanted to keep my husband, that's why.* But she replied, "I know the Justice Department wants to take his passport away. I wanted to warn them he was going to leave the country."

"I see." Geary subsided, and Sandusky began again.

"Mrs. Wrought, we're not here about your husband's passport. Not directly. Do you mind if we ask you a few questions?"

"Not at all, Mr. . . . . Sandusky."

The agent removed a large billfold from his suit coat pocket and withdrew a piece of paper. It was a photostat of a newspaper article.

"We wanted to speak to Mr. Wrought about this article in a British newspaper, the *Tribune*." He handed her the photostat. "We'd like to know if Mr. Wrought wrote the article."

Barbara was perplexed. "Why not check the byline?" She began to scan the writing. It was about the atom spy case of 1951, in which a couple, Julius and Ethel Rosenberg, had been convicted of providing the Soviet Union with the trigger designs for the first nuclear weapon.

"There isn't any byline. Do you by any chance recognize it?" Geary asked.

"No. I've never been interested much in Tom's . . ." She sought the right word—*fun, avocation, hobby, writing*? It wasn't really "work," but that was the word she settled on. "Why don't you just ask the editor?"

Without suppressing the sarcasm, Sandusky replied, "Thanks for the suggestion." Then he changed the subject. "Why would your husband suddenly want to leave the country?"

"I don't know. He didn't give me a reason. It was more a matter of getting back to England than leaving the US. But I can't understand the urgency."

"So he didn't get a message or hear from anyone that made him suddenly want to leave?"

"No, nothing like that. I told you, he wasn't fleeing the US. He had decided to get back to England."

Now Geary inquired, "Did Mr. Wrought ever talk to you about his past, what he did in the war or afterwards?"

"He was a captain with a Negro service company in France and then took them into combat in Germany in the winter of '44–'45."

"And after that?"

"Oh, he once said he'd been a spy in Finland for the OSS right after the war. I suppose I can tell the FBI that, can't I?"

"We know all about that. Anything else?"

"Not that I recall . . . oh, wait, he went back to Europe, I think it was Sweden, in 1951 for three weeks. Said it was research for a book he wanted to write. But that didn't make sense. I accused him of meeting another woman."

"What did he say, if I may ask?"

"He just laughed. But he wouldn't say any more about it."

Sandusky tried once more. "So, he hadn't talked to anyone lately, someone he might have known from back in New York City, someone who might have scared him or warned him to get out of the country or anything like that?"

Barbara had become impatient. These men weren't listening. "No, no, no. He didn't want to leave this country. He just wanted to get back to England. You want to know why he left? Figure out why he'd want to go back to England right after he spent a year there. Why would he come home and go back a month later?" When the two agents said nothing, she went on, "Look, before I answer any more questions, I need to know what this is about. You didn't come for his passport. Why did you come?"

Both men rose, looked at each other, and put on their hats in unspoken agreement that it was the moment to leave. As they moved to the door, Sandusky only said, "I'm sorry, we can't discuss the matter. Good-bye."

"But thanks for the ice water, ma'am," Geary added in a tone that suggested regret for his partner's abruptness.

"What about my car?" Barbara said to no one in particular.

CHAPTER SEVEN

At the moment Tom's Super Constellation touched down at Heathrow, Liz was driving the Humber sedan down a narrow valley in the Pyrenees. It was her annual holiday from the Abbey National. The Spencers had endured a rough passage in a car ferry crossing the channel, and several tailbacks coming into and going out of Paris. Everyone had been seasick, the children carsick, and the parents cross about each other's driving and map reading. But a week later they had discovered Lescun—a small village in the high Pyrénées. As the crow flew, it was a kilometre off the road down to Spain, but three times as far in switchbacks, with a hostel and spectacular views down the valley and back towards the magnificent cirque of peaks that surrounded the village.

Saturday was market day in the *jardin publique* of Oloron-Sainte-Marie, the only town of any size near Lescun. Under the plane trees, the stalls had been doing a strong business since early that morning. Goat cheese, olives, *saucisson*, braids of garlic pegged above tables covered in thyme and tarragon, all clamoured for attention. Competing against them were endive, leeks, a half-dozen different varieties of lettuce and dried mushrooms, gigot of lamb, pig's knuckles, and fowl half-plucked to show their local provenance. At the *boulanger's* truck, baguettes were still available, but there was no more *bon pain de quatorze*—the bread of '14, what the veterans of the First World War pretended they had subsisted on in the trenches.

Walking through crowded rows, Liz's eye was drawn by one *delicattese* after another, mostly unknown on the other side of the channel. The trouble was keeping track of her children, darting from stall to stall, plucking samples and swiping treats. Ian, the younger, was struggling between keeping his mother in sight and following his more venturesome older sister. Olivia was extending her distance from her mother with each passing minute. Finally they came rushing back to her, importuning the purchase of two plastic bow and suction-cup arrow sets. After pretending to resist such an enormously expensive purchase, Liz gave in.

With two string bags full of provisions for the evening, she led the children back to the café where they had left Trevor. He was sitting on the *terrasse* sipping an *express* and trying to make sense out of *Le Monde*. But he couldn't read French. Then it came to her: Trevor was not going to be seen reading the American *Paris Herald Tribune*, even though it hung on a wooden spool from a rack on the café wall.

Liz put down her bags on an adjacent seat and handed out the bow-and-arrow sets. "Olivia, take Ian across to the park. Stay in view. Teach your brother how to use it and not to point it at anyone." The kids pulled the toys off the cardboard and rushed off. Liz picked up the litter and pulled out a chair. She was tempted to ask what Trevor had learned in *Le Monde*, but since they both knew he couldn't make out the French beyond immediate cognates, it would just have been provocative.

The waiter came up, and she ordered a *café crème*, ripped the end off a baguette, and looked round. At the boundary between the *terrasse* and the interior of the café, where prices were slightly cheaper, two men of about sixty were engaged in an argument. It started quietly enough, but within moments they were hissing at each other. Then one of them rose, picked up a glass of milky liquid—*pastis*, she would soon learn—and pitched its contents in the other's face. Walking out of the café, he turned and hurled a parting condemnation: *"Sale petite putain bourgeois connard réactionnaire."*

Perplexed, Liz turned to the only other person sitting on the terrasse. He was tall and rather dark, with short brown hair too stiff to respond to a comb. He had the weathered, tanned face of a local. With feet stretched out, the Frenchman was lounged as naturally as if he owned the café, smoking an aromatic Gauloise. Catching his eye, Liz asked, *"Excusez-moi, monsieur. Pouvez-vous expliquer ce qui se est passe?"*

"Oui, madame." He smiled, but catching her accent immediately shifted to a faultless English. "They were discussing current events."

"De Gaulle's new government?" She wanted to sound informed.

"Not that current. No, they were arguing about the war. It's still pretty current in these parts." He looked across the broad footpath between the *terrasse* and the road. "See the plaques on the trees?" She looked up and realized she had not noticed them before. "The Germans hung résistants from those trees in '43 and '44. The plaques bear their names."

"Is that what they were arguing about?"

"That's how it started. For years now the local branch of the Communist Party and the veterans of de Gaulle's anti-German resistance have been arguing about how many plaques each gets."

Trevor put down his *Le Monde*. "But why did that bloke douse the other one with . . . the drink?"

Their interlocutor smiled. "The pastis? Ah, well, the *ancient* Communist claimed that they had been the only résistants during the war. Then the other said the Communists might as well have been Nazis, the way they had started out the war collaborating with the Germans against the British."

"Too complicated for me." Trevor picked up *Le Monde* and began again to try to make something of the closely printed articles.

But Liz remained interested. "So, the Communists in France only started fighting the Nazis because the Germans attacked Russia?"

"I'm afraid so."

"What about everyone else? Wasn't everyone else in the Resistance?"

"Not quite. Mostly people just waited round to see who would win. The French were worried about food, wine, and cigarettes during the war, not politics. So, now you know what that argument was about."

Liz was grateful. "Thank you for the history lesson, monsieur. Where did you learn English so well?"

"Ah, I was what they called a 'premature antifascist.' I left France with the Free French in 1940, went to England, and returned with de Gaulle in '44. Whence my English." The words had an echo to Liz. "Premature antifascist." Where had she heard the expression? It could only have been from Tom.

Giving up the hopeless challenge presented by *Le Monde*, Trevor had begun to listen again. "So, you were with us, in the Blitz and all? Whenever I come to France, I notice how untouched by the war it seems. We still remember the austerity, even after the war. Nothing like that in Paris." The pronoun "us" in Trevor's mouth burned in Liz's ears. Then he did it again. "Most of your countrymen didn't seem to have suffered in the war the way we did." *We?* Had her husband convinced himself he had spent the war in Britain? *And why are you trying to provoke this Frenchman anyway?* Liz fumed silently.

Trevor didn't notice the anger contorting Liz's face. If the Frenchman did, no gesture of his betrayed it. "Yes, we weren't bombed, we didn't go as hungry, we didn't lose so many lives. But we lost our souls by the collaboration—and the lies we told ourselves afterwards. That's why those two old men are still at each other's throats."

Liz had to change the subject before her anger bubbled over. "Monsieur, permit me to introduce myself. Elizabeth Spencer . . . and this is my husband, Trevor."

"*Enchanté,*" he responded. "D'Alembert, Philippe D'Alembert, à *votre service.*"

Liz took his hand. It was not the French brief tug at the fingers, but a solid English grip. "On holiday here?"

"No, I'm an *agent immobilier*, an estate agent. My card . . ." He reached into a shirt pocket and proffered one. Without thinking, Liz put it in her purse. D'Alembert turned to Trevor, trying again. "So, Monsieur Spencer, we were comrades-in-arms." He extended his hand.

Trevor hesitated for a moment and replied, "Suppose so . . ." Then he accepted the hand.

Liz didn't want to hear any more dissimulation from Trevor. She interrupted. "We're at a hostel in Lescun, down the road towards Spain."

"*Quelle coïncidence.* I'm on my way there . . . to walk the GR10 to Pic d'Anie this afternoon."

"We were hoping to do it, but it seems a long tramp. Can it be done in an afternoon?" Liz looked doubtful.

"*Mais bien sur!*" D'Alembert looked towards the children, still absorbed by their new bows and arrows. "Even for children, if they are strong and the weather is fine, like today." He looked first at Liz, then decided he had better address Trevor. "It would be my pleasure to be your guide."

By now the children's plastic bows had broken. As they returned to the café disconsolately holding the broken halves of their toys, Liz rose. Without giving Trevor a chance to concur or dissent, she announced, "That would be wonderful. We accept." She turned to her children. "We're off back to the village for an adventure. Monsieur D'Alembert here is going to lead us up Pic d'Anie." As she expected, the children immediately forgot about the tragedy of broken bows and arrows.

⟢⟣

Ascending the steep track to Lescun, Liz watched D'Alembert's little yellow *Citroen Deux Chevaux* doggedly keeping up. Its canvas top flapped, and the corrugated metal sides visibly shivered. But its two little bug-eyed headlamps managed to stay in her rear-view mirror right through the thousand-metre climb from the valley floor. She would be glad to have the company of someone she liked.

⟢⟣

"How much farther?" It was Trevor's third inquiry in less than an hour. But now seeing the avalanche wall above them, D'Alembert could answer with confidence.

"*Regarde*—eh, look, do you see the avalanche marker up there? We'll be able to see the peak when we get there."

Trevor replied, breathless from the steepness of the slope, "Don't see it. What's it look like?"

D'Alembert looked at the marker high up on the right a hundred metres ahead of them. "Looks like one of those Bangalore torpedoes from the war, but striped and sticking straight up from the rocks."

Trevor replied with a tone of slight impatience, "Bangalore torpedo? Don't know what that is. I told you, I was army, not Royal Navy. Never got anywhere near the Indian Ocean either."

D'Alembert looked at the Brit closely and thought, *This compagnon de la guerre has been lying to me. Every infantryman in the British army knew a Bangalore torpedo as an explosive grenade on a long spike used to blast through barbed wire. But he thinks it was a naval weapon to be found in a landlocked Indian city 350 kilometres from the Bay of Bengal.*

D'Alembert asked himself, *Why would this man bother lying to a perfect stranger about matters fifteen years old?* Mentally, he shrugged. There was no point pursuing it, no point at all.

⟨═⟩

That evening, after a supper of omelettes and potatoes sitting along rough benches outside the hostel, all five of them, the four Spencers and D'Alembert, watched the setting sun change the colours of the rock faces from gold to rose to purple and then to grey across the vast cirque of mountains above the village. All were enjoying the wonderful lassitude of a formidable accomplishment.

The walk had been a six-hour affair, up into summer snow and through a vast scree field above a promontory that looked down past the village to the deep valley below. The three adults had all stood at the edge of the great cliff, each silently contemplating the question of why they did not simply allow themselves to drop over the edge into space. None knew that the other two were thinking the same thoughts. What they wordlessly agreed upon was the need to keep the children well away from the edge.

"Your Ian and Olivia were—how do you say?—'troupers' today. You must be proud of them." D'Alembert addressed Trevor while tousling Ian's head.

"Well, you made a hit with them. Telling them your stories along the trail. We'll have to try that." Trevor smiled his winning smile.

Their guide rose. "I must go."

The two children reached towards him. Tugging at his arms, they said simultaneously, "No, no . . ." Liz looked towards Trevor. The children had warmed to this stranger, mobbing him in a way they never did their father.

"I'm afraid I must." He looked at Liz for a moment, a little too long perhaps, but then addressed Trevor. "If you would all care to meet me in Cauterets day after tomorrow, I'll show you another wonderful trail, from the *Pont d'Espagne* to the *Refuge Wallon*."

Liz replied for her husband. "But, Philippe, don't you need to work on Monday?

"It's a holiday, *L'Assomption de Marie*. No one will be interested in real estate, certainly not me."

D'Alembert took a map from his rucksack, and they arranged a rendezvous.

※

That night the Spencers were lying in four narrow cots along the walls of the *dortoir*—the open dormitory of the hostel. The rest of the family was asleep. In fact, Trevor was snoring in a steady rhythm. Liz was *still* awake, trying to retrieve from memory the last time she had felt the look D'Alembert had given her. It was the frankly sexual glance of inquiry Tom had cast before the first time they'd kissed. Liz closed her eyes and found herself able to recall the moment over and over. *Will you ever have the experience again?* She knew then she was willing to risk all to do so. Then Liz grew warm reliving the wordless response of her own that first night Tom had kissed her. She knew how she was going to get herself off to sleep.

※

"Weren't expecting you back so soon, sir." The scout for Tom Wrought's staircase was being diplomatic, as befitted a college attendant. In fact, the Trinity staff hadn't expected Thomas Wrought back at all. When he left six weeks before, his tips had been generous, and there was a finality to his leave-taking they were familiar with from Americans eager to return to their more affluent ways of life. They would give their scouts the half-empty bottles of sherry, port, brandy, even whiskey with any luck, and leave their gowns hanging on their study doors—one more thing for a scout to pawn. Tom Wrought had done all of these things, and yet here he was, back in Oxford, and long before Michaelmas term.

"Can I get back in to my rooms, Mr. Lloyd?" In a year he hadn't been able to shake the American feeling that calling someone by his surname alone was slightly rude.

"'Fraid not yet, sir." Lloyd indicated the smock he was wearing and the paint can in his hand. "It'll be a week or more. Entire staircase is being painted, all ten rooms. You know what undergraduates get up to. Most rooms are a bloody . . . a complete shambles. Tell you what, sir, the head porter can probably find you some temporary digs in Holywell Manor."

"Thanks. I'll check with him." Tom turned and began to make his way back through the large Garden Quad. In the deep shade of the ancient oak in its centre, he decided, for the first time, to exercise the right of walking through the Fellows' Garden. Leaving the crushed stone of the footpath, he moved onto the lush, closely cropped grass. Then he looked back towards the hall and staircase XXI in the crenellated tower next to it. Once repainted, those two small rooms at the top would be his home. *For how long,* he wondered.

As he approached the porters' lodge, Tom realized he had not even searched his postbox. Perhaps there would be something from Liz. He asked for the head porter. While he waited, Tom turned to his pigeonhole, scooped up the handbills from tailors, catalogues from Blackwell's, announcements from the faculty of history, and riffled through them. Not a single first-class letter. Nothing.

Immediately he began to assuage his disappointment. She had no idea that he was coming back. He hadn't been able to communicate. She had no reason to write to him at the college.

The need to sort out digs suddenly gave way to an overwhelming urgency to make his return known to Liz. Tom stuffed the post back in his box and walked out of the college into the sun of Broad Street. He hailed a cab and gave his former address on Park Town crescent. As the cabbie turned off Banbury Road, Tom said, "Stop at the park." He knew he could stand in the green space between the two crescents relatively unobserved and watch for Liz.

He stood behind an oak for ten minutes, smoking and beginning to feel foolish and conspicuous. Then he realized her car—the Humber— was not to be seen on the street. Was she just out or at work somewhere in the country? Tom plucked up his courage, crossed the street, and walked past the houses, first his own former dwelling, then the Spencers' house. He walked round to the back gardens. There was no sign of anyone in either building.

≈━

Two days later Tom stood at 219 Baker Street before the London head-quarters of the Abbey National Bank, an impressive granite pile that rose to a great lighthouse carved above the building's lintel. Evidently this structure had been spared, or else had stoutly resisted, the German Blitz and the V-weapons.

Entering the vestibule Tom sought a commissionaire standing at a podium against the back wall. Kitted out in the standard-issue blue uniform and white hat, the man offered a brief unmilitary salute. "Can I be of service, sir?"

"Is there a directory? I have an engagement." He lied fluently and in his best Mayfair voice.

The commissionaire drew a small leather-bound volume from beneath the top of the podium. "Name?"

"Elizabeth Spencer."

"Ah yes. I'll just call through for you, sir." Tom was about to stop him but realized this would draw attention to the enquiry. The man held an old-fashioned earpiece to the side of his head, dialled the base, and leaned towards the receiver to speak. Then he looked up at Tom. "Engaged."

Tom looked at his watch. "I'm behind my time already."

"Ah well, go on up, sir. Eighth floor, room 816, Training Department."

Tom smiled. It was the air of entitlement, the accent, the dress, class that again secured deference.

Another commissionaire closed the metal gate of the elevator and opened it again with a flourish even as the car was still slowing, showing the exquisite perfection that resulted from years performing exactly the same task. It came to rest perfectly level with the eighth floor.

Tom walked down the hall reading the names in gold-edged black on the pebbled glass of the doors till he came to **816, Training Department**. He knocked and quietly entered. At the desk athwart the door, a bespectacled woman of about fifty was typing at a machine with a ledger-length platen. She loomed over the desk, suggesting great height even without standing. Her hair was a brown turning grey, pulled back in a bun. Her reading glasses looked like they were about to fall off the end of her nose. She wore a light-blue wool sweater with a fine cable knit running vertically. The woman smiled but put up a finger to indicate she was in the midst of some task. The words Mrs. Russell were engraved in a nameplate at the front edge of her desk. In the corner of the room was another desk, with nothing on it but a blotter and a telephone. A large square window gave a fine view over rooftops.

Having typed a few more strokes, the woman looked up at Tom. "Yes?"

"Good day, I'm looking for Miss Spencer."

"Mrs. Spencer. I'm afraid she's on holiday in France. Not expected in the office for a further week. Can I take your name and leave word?" She plucked a pencil from the desk and poised it above a shorthand pad.

"No, that's alright. I'll come back when she returns."

"I'm afraid she isn't ever in the office much. Her work takes her all round the country. If you want to get in touch with her, you'd better leave a name and a number or address."

"Very well. Thomas Wrought. Trinity College, Oxford." What trouble was he getting her into, he wondered.

"And the subject?"

Now he was getting in deeper. "She consulted me on a point of employment law."

"Ah yes, Mrs. Spencer has had to sack more than one person."

Relieved that his confabulation had worked, Tom moved back to the door. "Thank you. Good day."

She smiled and got back to work. His stride back down the hall was distracted. *Why had she volunteered that titbit about firing people,* Tom wondered. Slightly unprofessional. *Can I trust her to be discreet?*

The letter arrived a week later. There was an Abbey National Bank return address prominent in the upper left corner and a first-class stamp with the profile of the queen in blue, as if to announce that this was no circular.

Tom knew the etiquette. Fellows didn't read their mail at their pigeonholes. It showed far too much interest. But he couldn't resist. Opening the envelope, he took out the letter and read it with a broadening smile and a bit of puzzlement. The letterhead read TRAINING DEPARTMENT and gave the Baker Street address:

Dear Mr. Wrought:
Mrs. Spencer has returned from holiday and asked
me to invite you to visit to discuss the employment

law matter on which she wishes to consult you. Mrs. Spencer will be pleased to meet with you at 11:00 a.m. on Monday, 1 September, at this office.

Sincerely yours,

(Mrs.) Beatrice Russell

Sec't to Mrs. E. Spencer

Should he confirm the appointment and wait? Should he return to Park Town crescent and try to intercept her? Did he dare call now that she had returned? Could he hope to meet her in the Covered Market or rowing on the Cherwell? No. There was a method to this meeting, a week away and with the pretext of a business appointment.

PART III

September 1958–January 1959

Too Clever by Half

CHAPTER EIGHT

Tom was sitting in the senior common room the next evening before supper. Without undergraduates, the hall was closed, and fellows in residence took their meals in a wainscoted dining room nearby. He was in flannels, meeting a standard that would have been considered formal in America, but daringly casual in one of Britain's ancient universities, even out of term. Before him sat a gin and tonic he had nursed for a quarter of an hour and just signed for. Next to it on the leather arm of the chair was an almost empty packet of Senior Service cigarettes. How, he wondered, would he pay his *battels*—the monthly accounts of fellows and students? There were still several weeks till his New York publisher could confirm the advance he'd been promised. And three transatlantic airline tickets were languishing unpaid on his Diner's Club charge account. He fully expected the card to be withdrawn from him any day now for nonpayment.

Lindsay Keir, the master of the college, came into the common room, looked round, smiled, and lowered his girth into the chair next to Tom's. "Glad you decided to stay on, Wrought." He sounded avuncular and actually laid a hand over Tom's, patting it. "Buy you another?" He looked up at the steward, pointing to Tom's drink. "Two more please, Moore."

"Thank you, Master. Yes, I've come back to stay."

"They tell me you've been reassigned the digs on staircase XXI. Living in college then?"

"'Fraid I must, Master. Can't afford to live out of college as we did when my wife was here. Don't exactly know how I'll survive, even with college rooms."

Keir was too discreet to enquire further, or perhaps too indifferent, Tom supposed. But he was wrong. "Well, perhaps something can be done about that, Wrought. Fact is, I came in looking for you. Pryce-Jones, editor of the *TLS*, needs a review of the new Schlesinger volume on the New Deal. Told him I knew just the man. Pays twenty quid." He paused. "Interested?"

Twenty pounds was more than a month's wages for the scout on Tom's staircase. He was rather surprised at the amount. The last time he had done something for a newspaper, the pay was derisory. He had done it last spring only out of a strong interest. He needed no money then, living in Park Town crescent with Barbara.

"Very interested, Master. Just read the previous volume this summer. Actually I knew him—Pryce-Jones, the *TLS* editor—slightly, just at the end of the war, sir."

"Did you?" Keir merely smiled at the coincidence. Pryce-Jones had been a lieutenant colonel in army intelligence during the war. That Pryce-Jones and Tom were acquainted would make a difference to the master. Meant that Tom was practically top drawer. "Well, just give him a call. College secretary will give you the number." Keir rose, his gin and tonic unfinished.

Tom was left with the recollection of his first experience writing for an English paper. It had all been perfectly typical of the best and worst of

England—old boy network, establishment, eccentricity, implicit trust based on class alone, but also a radical eagerness to stir hornets' nests.

One afternoon the previous spring, a scout from the porters' lodge had appeared at the door of his college study. "Trunk call for you, sir, from London." He caught his breath. "Said I was to come get you. They're ringing back in half a tick. You can take it in the college office." There were few telephones in fellows' studies.

"Thanks. I'll go along straight away. Did they say who it was?" The man shook his head.

Five minutes later Tom was seated at a desk in the college secretary's office, from which she had discreetly removed herself, when the phone rang.

He picked up the receiver and identified himself.

"Ah, Wrought. Is that you? My name is Michael Foot—"

Tom could not help interrupting. "Not *the* Michael Foot?"

"Don't know of others, but I'm the editor of the *Tribune*, radical socialist, unilateral nuclear disarmer, and thorn in the side of Hugh Gaitskell." This was the rather moderate leader of the Labour Party, for whom Foot had little use. Tom was being treated to Foot's impish sense of humour, or perhaps being tested by it.

"What can I do for you, Mr. Foot?"

"Michael, Michael, you must call me Michael. I've got a book review that needs writing, and I thought you were the very man for it."

"What do you have in mind?"

"Well, Bertie Russell—uh, Lord Russell—has just sent me a book published in the States about the Rosenberg spy case. Malcolm Sharp, *Was Justice Done?*" The couple, Ethel and Julius, had been executed five years before for passing details of dubious value about the US atom-bomb project to the Soviets. It had been the first executions of spies in peacetime and the first execution of a woman, one with two young children, for treason ever in the history of the country.

"How long, how soon?" Tom was interested. It would be fun and a distraction from academic work. He smiled to himself. *Foot couldn't know you'd gone to university with them, could he?*

"No rush; we're prepared to print a quite lengthy piece. You can use the book as a jumping-off point. I gather you might have some scores to settle—blacklist and all that."

"You've got a deal," Tom responded. He was about to ask, *How do you know I'm on the blacklist?* but he knew the answer. *This is England, where everyone knows someone who knows something.* And besides, it was his being on the blacklist that made Foot ask him.

"Good. I'll have the book sent up tomorrow. You haven't asked how much we pay, old man. Only five pounds, I'm afraid."

"Keep it," Tom had replied.

"We will; thanks. Cheerio."

Tom worked quickly and had the review back to Foot in less than a week. He was surprised by Foot's response. Again he was brought to the phone at the college secretary's office.

"Wrought? Michael Foot here. I say, your review is bloody marvellous. But it may be too hot to handle, even for us." Tom made no reply. "Your charges against the US government go beyond anything in the book you've reviewed. Can you back them up?"

"Which ones?"

"Well, you say that the government knew the spy's wife, Ethel, was demonstrably innocent and that the wife of the chief witness against them was guilty. How ever can you know these things?"

"Look, Foot." Tom had been invited to call him Michael, but he was trying to get used to the English style of addressing even friends by their surnames. It wasn't so off-putting when you got used to it. "You know I was a member of the party in the late '30s."

"So what?"

"Well, I knew them, the Rosenbergs, knew them both before the war. And I knew—"

Foot interrupted. "That proves nothing."

"Do you want an answer to your question?" This time it was Foot's turn to be silent at the other end of the phone. "Well, Ethel Rosenberg couldn't type—not before the war, not after, never. And Ruth Greenglass could, fast and accurately. She typed my doctoral thesis."

"Well?"

"It's obvious. The charge against Ethel Rosenberg was that she typed the stuff for the Russians. But she couldn't have. Greenglass implicated Ethel Rosenberg to protect his wife. The FBI knew that and used the false charge against her to force her to testify against other spies. She refused and went to the chair for it." Tom stopped and wondered, *Did Foot know this particular Americanism from all those 1930s Edward G. Robinson/James Cagney movies?*

A sigh at the other end of the line. "Ah, the penny drops. Look, Tom." Foot was back to Christian names. "Are you prepared to back up your charges if you have to? Your FBI isn't going to like them."

"Can't you publish it anonymously?"

"Can do. Not our usual practice. Most people like their names in print."

"So do I, but I don't need any more attention to my chequered past than I already have."

"Very well. Good work, comrade." Foot chortled. *Was he joking?* "By the way, do you want the five quid after all?"

"Save it. I did the work for love of country." It was Tom's turn to laugh.

Now, six months later, living on a college fellowship, he would have taken the money—and asked for another assignment.

But it turned out that Keir was as good as his word, and within a few days, Tom had at least one solid piece of work lined up from the *Times Literary Supplement.*

———◆———

As he knocked on the pebbled glass door of 816 of the Abbey National building at the appointed hour on 1 September, Tom had still not decided on his approach. All the way from Oxford to Paddington, and even on the brief two-stop tube ride to Baker Street, he had tried on one opening after another. None had seemed right.

Let's just assume that the four days Liz and you spent in Dorset never happened.

Carrying an empty briefcase, he crossed the threshold. There at the entrance was Mrs. Russell, and at the desk in the corner, Liz Spencer. Russell had to know. *But if she did, the dissimulation between her and Liz could not have been better orchestrated,* he thought.

"Come in, Mr. Wrought." It was Russell.

Liz looked up from her desk. "Nice to see you again, Mr. Wrought. I'll be with you in a moment." She closed a diary and slipped it into an attaché case, rose, and went to a coat stand. "We can't work here without disturbing Mrs. Russell, so I thought we'd find a quiet corner at my club." Tom visibly gulped. *Your club? You've really gone native, Liz.* And it wasn't exactly what he was hoping for. He missed Liz's glance as she went on, "I'll be at the Univ. club, Beatrice, and then I'm off home. See you next week." Russell nodded with a smile and went on working.

When they reached the elevator, Liz squeezed his hand and then put her index finger to her mouth. They were soon joined by an office boy, and all three stood in silence for what seemed to Tom like an age. The descending elevator made slow progress, stopping at every floor, enabling its driver to showcase his precision and grace.

In the lobby, Liz looked round and saw the commissionaire nod to her with a salute. "Lister, a cab, please. Tell the driver University Women's Club." They followed him out and in a moment were in a cab moving down Baker Street. Five minutes later the taxi had just crossed Seymour Street. Liz leaned forwards and spoke to the driver. "Please stop here."

They were in front of a small Georgian building with a dull brass plate that announced "Ormond Hotel." Tom smiled. Seeing his smile, Liz said, "Booked it this morning." They entered, arm in arm.

There was an elderly woman at the small registration desk. Liz addressed her. "Key for room 24, please."

The woman's look turned sour, and she replied, "Sorry, no visitors."

Liz turned to Tom and looked back at her. "This is my husband."

"You booked a single, madame. Said nothing about your husband." She turned her registration book around. "You'll have to register, Mr. . . . Spencer, is it?" Her sceptical tone was not missed. "Can I see some identification?"

Liz looked at Tom. There was nothing for it but mock outrage. She hissed, "I've never been treated like this. Wait here, Tom. I'll just get my things. We'll go elsewhere." She reached for the key and hurled herself at the ascending stairs. Tom stood waiting, speechless.

The woman at the desk began muttering to herself, words he could make out. "Not a knockin' shop . . . respectable house . . . brazen hussy."

Liz returned with a small case. "Refund, please."

The woman reached into a drawer and drew out a pound note. Relishing the phrase, she replied, "With pleasure."

They stood in the street again, the comedy of their predicament overmastering their desire, at least for the moment.

"What now, Liz?"

"If we try another one of these little hotels, I'm afraid the same thing will happen again."

"Not at the Dorchester round the corner." It was a top-class hotel. "They're used to this sort of thing." Tom laughed. "But I can't afford it, not anymore."

Liz nodded. "We need to talk. Let's find a pub." She led him up one block and into a mews. The pub opened to a rear space with benches. They carried two shandies out to the unoccupied garden.

"Now I understand all of that back at the Abbey National about your club." He smiled. "Do you really have a club?"

"Yes, University Women's, about three streets from here. Just a place to hang a hat in London. Look, Tom, I think you understand the need to be . . . discreet. You put me at risk by visiting the office while I was on holiday. Russell's been my personal assistant for a few years, but we know almost nothing about each other. She's never even met Trevor. I don't know her attitude towards me or her own personal mores."

"Is that why you had her contact me? To maintain the fiction I'd worked out at the spur of the moment?"

"Yes. It was a pretty good one."

"How did I put you at risk?"

"Isn't it obvious? First, the Abbey National is a pretty conventional outfit. If management thought I was stepping out on my family, there is no telling what they'd do. What if Russell had called me at home, and God forbid, left a message for me with Trev about a Mr. Wrought? We'd be sunk. Well, I'd be sunk. If we are to carry on, you've got to be more careful."

"So, we are going to 'carry on'?"

Liz smiled, took his hand, and ran her fingers up under his French cuffs to stroke his wrists. "I did book the room for us."

Tom turned serious. "Liz, I came back to England for you, not for the sex."

"Well, you may have to settle mainly for sex till I can get my marriage sorted out."

"I think I can bear it." He leaned across the narrow table, and their lips finally met, tongues finding each other. As she had twice before, Liz joined her hands behind his neck, while his hands brushed aside her light coat and searched her blouse for her breasts. After a few moments, they both looked round again to assure themselves they were alone. "Look, Liz, I've left Barbara. And she's probably had divorce proceedings started. I'm committed. You're the only reason I came back."

It was what Liz had longed to hear. But instead she replied, "I didn't force you to leave your wife."

"No, you didn't. But it was the only way I'd ever have a chance at a life with you. I've crossed a Rubicon. So, I need to know where I am. Have you decided? Do you want to be with me?"

"There's more at stake for me." But she knew that wasn't her reason for hesitation. She wasn't ready to tell Tom that being with him had freed her, because she was still afraid to tell him what he had liberated her from.

"I gave up a great deal just to give us a chance."

"I understand that. But you certainly were impetuous doing it so soon. I'm afraid I'm more cautious."

"So, what are you telling me? That you didn't want me to leave my wife? That you won't leave your husband because of the kids, you're mortally afraid we'll be discovered, but you want to 'carry on'? Does that mean you're only interested in me for my body, Liz?" He laughed to make it clear he was not really angry.

"Well, let's say I am very interested in your body." She moved her face towards his, inviting another smouldering embrace. Then she continued, "No one has ever made love to me like you, Tom." *How many lovers have you had?* he wondered, and almost immediately she told him. "During the war, I met a lot of men, men headed for action, not like Trev. It was fun, but nothing like what we've had. Those four days in Dorset are about all I have been able to think about whenever I am alone." Her life in those years hadn't been quite like that. She dared not tell him the whole truth, but at least she'd begun.

"It's exactly the same for me." He smiled.

"It's those days we spent that make me feel I am really alive. I want more, much more, of that. I'm not sure about anything else, but I am sure about that."

"And you're willing to risk everything for it?" He gulped.

"Yes, Tom, I am. And I think we're smart enough to get away with it. At least for long enough to get my marriage sorted and keep Trevor from taking my kids."

"Well, I wouldn't say we're off to a good start." Tom was rueful. "Shall we try the Tate Gallery?" It was one museum they had missed that first day together. "Maybe they won't ask for a marriage licence."

"What about your digs in Oxford?"

"I'm living in college. I suppose they wouldn't stop us, but we're sure to be seen by people I know. There'd be titters, innuendo, talk, and Oxford is a small town."

"You're right." Liz took out her diary. "Look, the kids' school doesn't begin till end of September, just before the Oxford term starts. Trev's parents want to see the children in Birkenhead for a week. He always prefers to go without me anyway. That would give us four or five days away." She couldn't explain. She'd miss being with the kids for the week—yet *more* time away from them—but it would be best if she didn't go to Birkenhead. In his parents' home, Liz's success in work was a standing rebuke to Trevor's failure. And now she found herself seething every time she recalled Kevin's story and Trevor's admission. Seeing his brother and parents, the straitened circumstances in which they lived, would make her angrier still at the preposterousness of Trevor's asking them for money. If she went, there were sure to be scenes. She opened her diary. "Yes, I'm pretty certain we can get away." Trevor would be pleased. He'd do much to avoid an argument before his family. "So, that's 22–25 September."

"Not before? That's almost three weeks."

"Trouble is making contact even if there is a spur-of-the-moment opportunity. How can we?"

"I'm going to get a phone installed in my rooms at college. They'll think me an extravagant American, but when my advance comes in, I'll be able to afford it."

"Getting a private line will take months, Tom. Things don't happen here the way they do in North America."

He turned her diary round and began to look at the dates. "Alright, if you're willing to commit to those dates, I'll take you to Paris on the advance I'm expecting for my new book."

"I accept. As for our immediate problem, I may have a solution. Let's get the 12:45 from Paddington. My car is at Oxford railway station, and on the journey you can . . . tell me about the new book." Their smiles were conspiratorial.

⟨⟩

The train ride had been an agony in spite of the first-class compartment that this time they had paid for. It had to be shared with four tourists eager to discuss their discoveries about the quaint folk hereabouts with their fellow North Americans. After three hours of unreleased sexual arousal, Liz and Tom were without restraint when finally they were alone in the car. By the time they reached the first roundabout on the Botley Road, their hands were in each other's laps, trying to move the clothing away from between their fingers and their bodies. Liz was driving deftly with one hand, while raising her torso so that Tom could move her skirt and slip above her thighs.

"Where are we going?" Tom asked.

Between moans, she replied, "Boar's Hill. Bagley Wood, lots of footpaths, some clearings, few walkers, no tourists!"

Every time Tom turned back to look down the hill their little car was climbing, he was presented with a new picture postcard, each increasingly panoramic: the college roofs dominated by the Radcliffe Camera, dwarfing even the dome of Christ Church; above it the steeple of St.

Mary the Virgin, the university's church, looking down on the spires of All Souls' College. Tom had never seen the university town spread out below him like this. For a brief moment its grandeur swamped the erogenous demands that dominated both of them.

Finally Liz turned on to a narrow hedge-bordered lane. When it crossed a stream and began to descend back towards the town, she pulled the car onto the grass verge and stopped. "I've got a picnic blanket in the boot." She removed the red plaid cloth and a pair of leather walking shoes.

"And I brought some protection this time." Tom patted a back pocket.

They found a trailhead and entered the wood. When they had proceeded for about ten minutes, encountering no one, each began to look off to the left and right for a glade or some patch of clear ground not obviously visible from the path. Nothing seemed quite right—too exposed, too rough, wet, thorny. The image in Tom's head of being detected flagrante delicto was dimming the whole venture's allure when they came within sight of a large boulder off the trail by twenty-five yards. Liz led them round it. On the other side they found a relatively flat apron of granite, evidently levelled by ten thousand years of weather. Liz threw down the blanket, kicked off her shoes, removed her coat, and began disrobing. "Mind if I take my clothes off myself?" she teased him. Tom smiled, pulled his tie off, and stuffed it into his coat. Then he too began taking his clothes off, bundling his suit into a headrest that he placed at the top of the blanket. Still he said nothing, preferring to drink in Liz's body, her aroma, and soon, he thought, her taste. They reached complete nudity at the same moment and fell to the blanket.

<hr />

An hour later they were driving back down from Boar's Hill. "Liz, I got the impression that your secretary, Mrs. Russell, is someone you can trust."

Liz thought about it for a moment. "Maybe. But I'm not going to take the chance you're wrong."

"There may be an easy way to get her on your side."

"What's that?"

"Introduce her to Trevor."

———◆———

The next morning there was a letter in Tom's pigeonhole at the porters' lodge, with a return address marked *Tribune, Fleet Street, London, WC1.* Tom opened it and began to read as he slowly moved out of the gate into Broad Street. It was a note in bold cursive.

> *Dear Tom,*
>
> *Jungle tom-tom says you're back in Britain. Jolly good. Welcome back, comrade. I'd like to have you write a feature for us about the desegregation fiasco in the States. If you're game, call me at the number on the letterhead.*
>
> *[signed]*
>
> *Michael Foot*

Well, thought Tom, *I'll call, but I am not going to work for five quid now that I am making twenty from the TLS.* He walked back into the quad and headed for the college office to use the phone. *I've got to get my own telephone, damn it!*

———◆———

"Foot here. Is that you, Tom? Glad you called. Tell you what, we'd like to do an in-depth appreciation for our readers of the school desegregation crisis in Little Rock, Arkansas." He pronounced it R-Kansas. "Our readers can't understand how the governor can just close every school in the city and offer no public education to anyone."

"Well, it's simple, Michael. There's nothing to force any state to provide schooling in the United States. Mississippi just removed public education from its constitution altogether."

"But that's absurd."

"Absurd or not, that's how it is in America."

"Then I suppose our readers need to have that explained to them."

"Very well, how far back do you want me to go? The victory of the South after the Civil War?"

"What are you talking about, Wrought?" In his irritation Foot had given up calling him "Tom."

"Just that. The Jim Crow system that has been in place since 1876 reenslaved the Negroes under terms economically even more favourable to the whites than slavery. And the whites don't intend to lose those war gains."

"Well, don't refight the Civil War. But tell our readers why Eisenhower can't enforce the law and how the governor gets away with flouting it."

"Now that's interesting, Michael." Tom wanted to get back to first names. "First of all, why suppose Eisenhower wants to enforce the law? After all, when he was chief of staff in '48, he was opposed to integrating the US Army. Said so before a congressional hearing."

"Didn't know that." Foot was genuinely surprised.

"Hell, during the war he was against letting Negroes into combat even when he needed infantry replacements. I know because I had a unit of black soldiers that were sneaked into the fight in spite of his orders."

"Tom, that's another story. Let's stick to this one."

"Well, the other interesting angle is Orville Faubus, the governor. You'd think he might be in favour of integration. After all, he's an old-time fellow traveller, maybe even a former Communist."

Foot almost shouted down the line, "What?"

"Yup. At the start of the Depression, Faubus was student body president at Commonwealth College in a town called Mena. In Arkansas." Tom made a point of pronouncing it clearly so that Foot would not make the same mistake again. "College was supported by the party, and Faubus had no trouble with that as student body president. Like most successful politicians, he only became a racist to win elections."

"How do you know?"

"Same reason I know Ethel Rosenberg was innocent. Firsthand. I met Faubus during the war when he was an intelligence officer in the Third Army."

"I knew you were the right man for this piece, Tom. Get to it."

It is the moment to strike, Tom thought. "Just one thing. I'll want twenty-five quid for the piece. Can the *Tribune* pay that much?"

"Make it fifteen guineas, Tom."

What exactly is a guinea? Tom had lived in Britain for a year and was still too embarrassed to ask.

CHAPTER NINE

Tom met Liz at Victoria Station for the 8:15 *Fleche d'Or* express to Paris on a Monday late in September. By that time they had found the moments, hours, afternoons, even a night or two on one of Liz's branch visits to slake the ardent edge of their sexual appetites. Neither had ever realized such ravenous desires lurked beneath the identities they presented to the world, or for that matter to themselves. But it wasn't just that. They'd learned enough about each other to be sure that they were a match, they needed to be together, they completed each other.

Paris in September. Three nights, and each wanted to show their Paris to the other. The prospect dominated their thoughts and words until they were confronted with the realities of the English Channel. Leaving Folkstone they stood, arm in arm, at the rail below the captain's bridge, enjoying the breeze over the bow. By the time they arrived, both Tom and Liz were stretched prone on the hard benches of the second-class lounge, completely preoccupied by their throbbing heads and leaden, cramping stomachs. Grasping their cases, they lurched from bulkhead to bulkhead out of the lounge and down the gangplank towards the waiting French train. Curiously, they seemed cured by the time they found their reserved seats in a second-class carriage. A few minutes later, they were hungry and stopped the trolley passing through the corridor for baguettes spread with ham and Camembert, along with bottled mineral water.

They arrived in Paris at the onset of *l'heure d'affluence*—a rush hour different from any on the London Underground. They could hear the metro pull in as they came down the stair, only to be confronted by the *portillions automatique*—large grey barriers that closed to prevent anyone rushing onto the platform as a train came in. When the train pulled out, it left the strong smell of ozone each of them already associated with the Paris metro. In the second-class nonsmoking carriage, the men, and especially the women, round them looked more fashionable and more lightly dressed. No tweeds or double-breasted suits, narrower waists, lapels and ties among the men, more than one woman wearing a nylon see-through blouse revealing a lacy bra. Strangers were standing much closer together than they ever did in the crush of a London rush hour. But from even the most attractive of them, an occasional strong scent of body odour assailed Liz as they swayed against her. Then there was the endless *correspondence*—change of lines—at *Chatalet Les Halles*, a corridor at least two hundred metres long, smelling like a urinal. The passage was crowded with shoppers carrying home their evening meals, in some cases still alive, Tom noticed.

It was past six o'clock when at last they found themselves before a three-star hotel on the Rue Racine just up from the Boulevard Saint-Michel. Liz had stayed there years before. They entered, and by agreement, Liz would do the talking. "Would there be a room for three nights?" Her French was quite passable.

"*Désolé, complet*"—the young desk clerk looked up, decided on the right salutation, and went on—"*madame*. Perhaps the Hotel Moderne, at the end of the street, may have rooms." He pointed away from the Boul'Mich.

It had but one star and a small entry from which a banister, blackened by years of wear, turned its way steeply up six flights of a central opening beneath a skylight darkened with soot. A naked incandescent bulb hung down the middle of the stairwell reflected the badly painted gloss across the walls' mottled surface. "Well, more money for dinner," Tom said brightly as he dropped their bags.

A well-fed elderly lady came bustling into the foyer, her evidently hennaed hair pinned up firmly, glasses hanging from a string round her neck. *Do all hotelkeepers wear them?* Tom recalled the lady in Exeter the last time they had travelled together. It seemed so long ago now that it might have been in the previous century. As she approached the registration, the woman smiled brightly and addressed Tom, *"Combine du nuits?"*

Liz cleared her throat and answered for them, *"Trois."*

"D'accord. Vos documents, s'il vous plaît. Paiement en avance, seize francs par nuit." In return for their passports, she handed them a key. *"Quatrieme."*

"That's the fourth floor," Tom protested as he picked up the cases.

"No, it's your fifth floor, Yank," Liz corrected. "But you're paying about two bucks a night."

They ate round the corner at the Cremerie Polidor, a restaurant Tom had found when he had first come to Paris, three days after the liberation in August 1944. It was still the same fourteen years later. The tables were long, and soon Liz and Tom were being jostled in the friendliest way by students rushing in from the Sorbonne across the Boul'Mich and stagehands from the Comédie Française a street away.

Tom flourished a carnet of metro tickets at her. "Where to tomorrow?"

"Let's decide tomorrow." She became serious. "I'm afraid Beatrice, my assistant, has found us out."

"How?"

"Carelessness. Last time we were in London, I left my diary at that hotel on Bloomsbury Street, the Gresham. They very kindly called round with it."

"Ouch. What did she say?"

"Nothing. She just left it on my desk. Never said a word." She paused. "Then, when I told her on Friday, I'd be out of touch for a few days this week, she said, 'Have a nice time.'"

"My dear, she knows! She's probably smart enough to have realized it's me. If I were you, I'd bring a propitiatory gift back from Paris." He laughed.

"It's serious, Tom." She couldn't suppress a small smile. Then she turned grave. "Everything could unravel."

"Liz, what's the worst that can happen if it ever came out? I'm living in Oxford now, probably for good. If you divorce Trev, you'll get at least joint custody of the kids. You won't need to take them out of the country because we'll stay here." He smiled at the neat solution.

Liz put her knife and fork down, swallowed her last bite, and began, "I can't divorce Trev, ever."

Tom's ears pricked up. *Ever? Did I hear the word right? What are you going to tell me?*

Tom said nothing, but Liz saw the despairing look. She gulped. *You have to tell him. Now!* "I've a confession, Tom. Something happened to me during the war, before I met Trev. I didn't go to university immediately, and I didn't go to work either. I had a breakdown. No one ever knew why. It just came on. I was in a mental hospital for a year. Started out as depression . . . just couldn't get myself out of bed. Then I became manic." *How much can you tell him? About losing yourself with soldiers on leave—strangers, up against alley walls, sometimes twice or three times a night, shooting up dope outside of dives no one thought even existed in "Toronto the Good."*

Tom was still silent.

"Anyway, it got worse till my family couldn't deal with it anymore. I was out of control . . . hearing voices. What they were saying was pretty lurid. There were other experiences so real the only reason I don't believe they happened is that they're impossible. I had shock therapy. They tried insulin too, along with a lot of talking to trick cyclists."

Tom didn't understand. "Trick cyclists?"

"Oh, it's what Brits call psychiatrists." She stopped and gripped the table as though she needed to hold on to something. "I've never told anyone." She stopped. "But Trev knows."

"How did he find out?"

"Snooping. There was a copy of my case history. My mother kept it for me. Hidden away in a drawer. The week Olivia was born, Trev stayed at my parents'. One morning the next week, she noticed the file in her drawer. It had been put back carefully, but not carefully enough. All the case notes were in reverse order. The hospital envelope was put back upside down. She told me. I've never confronted him. But I'm pretty sure." She picked up her fork. "Heard enough?"

After a moment Tom spoke. "It'll take a lot more to scare me off you, Liz." He looked at her steadily. *Do I need to say more? No. She knows how I feel about her. Words won't add anything just now.* Then he reached across for her hand.

"Thank you." She smiled. "I didn't mean to tell you quite this way. I knew I had to sometime. All the years since the children came, I've worried about a relapse. So I did everything I could to cement my life into a pattern that would prevent its ever happening again." She pulled their clasped hands to her. "But now, with you, I'm certain it's over, forever. My life really matters to me again."

Tom replied, "I think I understand, at least a little. With you I feel like I've been able to start over again myself."

"But we still have the problem. I don't have any grounds for divorce. If I left him, he could threaten to sue for divorce—desertion, maybe even use the history of mental illness, adultery too. If he found out, he'd claim it was a symptom of returning schizophrenia. I'd lose any chance at custody for sure."

"But won't he sue for divorce anyway if he finds out about us?"

"I don't know. Maybe not. If we're discreet and if I can keep him comfortable, he might turn a blind eye. What he'd worry about is other people finding out—his family, his brother, our friends, the parents in the kids' school, the stuffy Dragon school for that matter. For Trev, image is everything. I think if he twigged to you and me, he'd use the threat of divorce to maintain the status quo."

"What about sex?" Tom couldn't help asking.

"Possessive, aren't you? I told you, Trev and I haven't slept together for a year."

"Finish your croissant, and I'll show you the most extraordinary thing tourists never see." Liz rose as she made the command and began looking for the bra she'd shed the night before.

They'd found their breakfast on a tray at the foot of their door, announced with a sharp rap. Tom had brought it in, and they'd taken it sitting on each side of the unmade bed. Their clothes were in heaps on the floor. The double window was open to a view of a soft blue sky rising above the Ecole du Médecine across the narrow street, drawing in the warmth of a late summer day.

"Where are you going to take me that I haven't been before in Paris?" Tom challenged.

"Not telling."

Under Liz's guidance they walked down Rue Monsieur le Prince towards the metro stop at Place de l'Odéon. More than once Tom stopped to survey the lithographs and posters in the windows of small galleries and print shops. "Go in if you like," Liz encouraged. "There's no rush where we're headed."

"I'd like to buy a couple of those Klees and Kandinskys for my college rooms. It would rather shock the tastes of the undergraduates."

"More than demure nudes by Alma-Tadema?"

They were still laughing when they reached the Odéon metro. When Tom stopped to buy a *Le Monde,* Liz immediately recalled the morning in the Pyrenees the month before when they had met that nice estate agent. *What was his name?* She had the card, she realized, somewhere at the bottom of her purse.

As the carriage lurched out of the Gare du Nord metro station, Tom leaned over to Liz. Under the noise of the wheels he said, "I know where you're taking me. The *marché aux puces* just beyond the last stop at Porte de Clingancourt." Liz nodded. Tom admitted, "Well, you're right. I've never been there." It was the vast flea market, the oldest, or at least the largest, in Europe.

She replied, "Too lowbrow for you, *Monsieur les Grandes Boulevards?*"

"Not at all. Just frightened of pickpockets." He made a show of stealth as he reached into her open handbag.

⊷

It was all they could do not to lose each other a dozen times in the next few hours. Tom found himself wandering through the history of the nineteenth century: shops full of medals, service ribbons, decorations from the Franco-Prussian War of 1870, even the Crimean War fifteen years earlier, bookstalls with complete sets of classics back to the eighteenth-century *Encyclopedia*, dozens of kiosks from which boxes of old picture postcards flooded out onto the sidewalk. In one corner he could relive the campaign of the *Dreyfusards* of 1900 and in another the defence of Verdun during the First World War. Here and there faded, fraying posters hung proclaiming the war bond drives of '14, the smiling soldier, the *Poilu,* above the slogan *Nous les aurons*—"We'll get them!" *If only they had known,* Tom groaned within. There were framed pictures of Clemenceau—the tiger of France, prime minister in 1918. Even pictures of Petain, the collaborationist leader during the German occupation. But the new president, de Gaulle, was only to be seen in ancient copies of *Paris Match*, stacks and stacks of them, from the weeks after the liberation of Paris in 1944, that no one seemed interested in.

Liz meanwhile was always no more than three shops away but in another world entirely. She moved along the racks of dresses and coats, designer suits from two decades before, rows of well-polished but equally well-worn pumps and mules, tables laden with a profusion of cloche hats that had once been chic, and then on to the glass cases of costume jewellery still glittering sixty years after they had last adorned the bosoms of *Belle Epoch* debutantes. Or perhaps these were tools of the courtesan's trade.

Escaping from the heat, they both turned into a covered arcade of "better" shops, more restrained in their display, less importuning in their solicitation of business, each item on display tagged by a small "etiquette"—a price tag to discourage haggling. Shops with almost identical Chinese vases on black pedestals and French empire chairs, newly reupholstered, seemed to glare at one another across the passageway. Beyond them were stalls selling silver plate from the time of Napoleon III, tarnish too deep in their tracery for any amount of silver polish to remove.

They emerged from the gallery to find themselves in the region of ancient toys and taxidermy. Tom drew Liz to one of the shops. "Let's find something for the children."

Liz was surprised but gratified. She'd been thinking of Ian and Olivia off and on all morning, wondering about their day with Kevin Spencer's kids in Birkenhead. Had they gone for a walk along the Mersey, or was it bleak and rainy? *If only I could be there with them for a moment or two.* "I'm afraid they take no interest in antiques."

"There's got to be something . . ." He began moving between the tables, picking up toys he'd recognized from his own childhood— windup trains, balsa wood biplane gliders, a sheet metal steamroller.

Liz gestured towards a large bright-yellow toy car, a Citroen Deux Chevaux made from Meccano parts, emblazoned with the words *République Française PTT* on each side. "The children would like that if we could bring it back. They made a fuss about one last summer in the Pyrenees." She turned the toy round in her hands, remembering the cirque of peaks surrounding the village of Lescun.

"Yes, but you'd need a jumble sale to find anything like that in England. Trev would surely ask you where it came from."

"You're right." She put the car back on the table.

Tom gazed thoughtfully at the toy for a moment and then, with some trepidation in his voice, looked up and said, "Liz, I love you, but I hate to take you away from your kids like this."

"It's not you taking me away, Tom." She shook her head. "Besides, after them, you're about the best thing in my life now. You make me better when I'm with them." She reached down and rocked the little car back and forth on its wheels. "All these years working, I've gotten used to not showing anyone how much I miss them, trying not even to feel it myself. I can't really. Sometimes I want to chuck my job . . . Just go home to them." Her eyes glistened, but Liz blinked back the tears. She looked at the toy on the counter, remembering the summer walks with Ian and Olivia. "When I feel like that, I just have to get to grips with reality." She smiled grimly. "I was with them when they were babies. But if I don't work, we can't stay afloat. I've known that for a long time. Trev'll never earn enough to support us, I'm afraid." Liz mulled a further thought and then came out with it. "If I were trapped at home, my resentment would just make life impossible for him. I don't want the kids to see that anger. In some ways it's better I'm gone so much." Her eyes brightened. "But when I get home, there's nothing more wonderful than Ian and Olivia rushing to hug me. You've never had any kids or you'd understand. You watch them grow. They're part of you, the best part, the part you want to work at to get better."

He shook his head. "I still can't help but feel to blame . . ."

Before he could continue, Liz grabbed his lapel and pulled him to her. "It's not you. I had to start working long before we met." She was still holding him to her. "Besides, without that job of mine, we would never be able to do this." She kissed him deeply, then released him. "My children mean everything to me, Tom. I can't always be there with them. But most of the time I can bear that. I just need to know they're close. So I can be there when they laugh or need to cry. I really do think you understand. I've seen you with them myself, the year we were neighbours on the crescent."

Tom picked up the little car and took it to the elderly shopkeeper, snoozing in a chair leaning up against the side of his shop. After a moment's haggling, she saw him reach into his pocket and hand over some banknotes.

When he returned with it, Liz was quizzical. "I thought you said it would be risky bringing something obviously French like that back for the children."

"I'm going to hang onto it . . . until I can . . ." Tom didn't finish the thought. Instead he stepped closer to her. "Look, Liz, if we ever get this mess sorted, I want to be with your kids too."

Warmth surged through her as he pulled her to him. For a moment Liz feared she'd collapse into tears, but then she mastered herself. Instead, there was a long and comfortable silence as they walked along holding the package between them. Finally, Tom spoke. "Does Trevor feel the same way about the children as you do?"

"I don't know. Maybe not. He wants to send them off to boarding school now that they're old enough. But I can't give them up. That's why we compromised on the Dragon. When Ian gets a little older, I may have to give in . . . if we can afford it. When I'm travelling, the au pairs've always done the childminding—breakfasts, getting them to school, collecting them afterwards, taking them to friends—along with household duties. It's one more expense, but every time I suggest getting rid of the au pair, he resists." She was about to say that Trev's work as an estate agent made it difficult to mind children. But Trevor Spencer was not even selling used cars any longer. She wouldn't lie to Tom, but she didn't want to look like a fool either.

"Why do you think he'd try to keep them in a divorce?"

"Well, there's the child support he'd get. But that's not the main thing. The kids are another badge of upper middle-class respectability. The Dragon School—these days the only social circle he wants to mix in is the school parents. His kids are going to be part of the establishment if it's the last thing his wife does for them!" She went on quickly, "It's not just that the children matter for him as symbols to other people. Sometimes I think they're part of a charade he carries on to fool himself."

Tom spat out the thought before he could modulate it. "You're saying that for Trevor having kids at the Dragon was just a way of getting into the right club?"

"I suppose so. Let's change the subject."

⟵⟶

That evening Tom and Liz sat under the sail-cover-blue canopy on the *terrasse* of la Méditerranée, a seafood restaurant across the Place de l'Odéon from the Comédie Française. This one had been Liz's choice.

As the waiter arrived with menus, she looked at Tom. *"Permitez-moi?"* He nodded. "Do you like oysters?"

He shrugged. "Don't know."

She addressed the waiter. *"Pour commence, monsieur, une douzaine du fines du claire numéro quartre."* Then she looked down the wine list and pointed to a Chablis. *"Et ca."*

"Tres bien." The waiter smiled and left.

When they'd been served and Tom selected a shell and surveyed it, Liz cautioned, "Please don't tell me what it looks like to you. Just gulp it down."

Each sipped the wine, and Liz reached for a second oyster. Tom wiped his mouth. The preparation made it evident to Liz that he was going to say something serious. "My turn to make a confession."

"You were in a psycho ward too?" She felt confident enough to make the joke.

"Worse. I was a spy."

"I don't think I'll mind—unless you were a spy for the Germans."

"Nothing like that. How much do you want to know?" Tom's question was serious.

"Probably more than you're allowed to tell me."

He smiled. "I doubt it. More cloak than dagger. First time was right at the end of the war. The OSS—Office of Strategic Service, that's what they called it—plucked me out of the army. I speak Finnish—my mother's language. So they sent me to Helsinki to organize listening posts to monitor Soviet communications."

"Was it exciting?"

"No, and I turned out to be a bit of a headache for the OSS. You see, all through the war, the FBI was doing everything it could to kill off the OSS. J. Edgar Hoover wanted to control not just spying stateside; he wanted to run all the spies the US had abroad too. But that was the OSS's job. When the war ended, he started lobbying the president to abolish the OSS and give the job to his FBI."

This history was lost on Liz. "So, where do you come into it?"

"Well, Hoover was a nut about leftists of any kind in the government. Now, right from the start, the OSS didn't have the same . . . scruples, qualms. They'd take on anybody with the right skills, no matter what their politics. They knew I'd been a member of the Communist Party as a kid, and they didn't care. But Hoover did. He got hold of a list of OSS operatives, right down to the lowest level, and combed it for people the FBI had been keeping tabs on for 'subversive' activities. I was pretty far down that list, but I was on it."

"So . . ." Liz prompted.

"So, I was one of the first casualties in the war between the OSS and the FBI. OSS got rid of me as an embarrassment. I didn't really mind. Helsinki was boring. Besides, I wanted to go back to school, and there was the GI Bill. So I took the hit and left. Hoover managed to get Truman to close down the whole OSS a year later. When the Cold War heated up, they realized their mistake and started the CIA. That was in '47."

"Is that it?" Liz was not impressed. "Fired by the OSS?"

"There's a little more—and it was more exciting. Five years later, the CIA sent me back to Finland for a week or so to help rescue some . . ." Tom's voice trailed off while his thoughts ran on, remembering what had happened and what hadn't, and the warning he'd been given. Suddenly he didn't want to talk about his life as a spy. He had to contrive a finish to the sentence without saying much more. "To help rescue some gear—decoding equipment, transmitters, that sort of stuff. Knowing Finnish when no one else does can really make you popular sometimes." He laughed at the absurdity of the notion.

"Doesn't sound like I'm in much danger knowing any of this. Can't you tell me something more exciting?"

"Maybe, when I get to know you better. Now let's order the rest of dinner. I'm in a hurry to get you into the sack." He pushed his knee against her thigh.

Liz smiled. "Can we really get to know each other any better?"

⇐═➤

The sleeper to London left the Gare du Nord at ten o'clock. Liz would be able to get a full day's work in on Friday, provided she got any sleep. She planned to get as little as she could. It was a plan Tom fell in with.

They were standing in the corridor outside their compartment, with the large window slid halfway down, smoking and watching the darkened outskirts of Paris move by. The still, cloudless sky was illuminated by a receding glow from the city and a pale but full moon. As the conductor passed, Tom stopped him and offered their tickets to be stamped. *Wise precaution,* Liz observed. They wanted no knocks on their compartment door this night. The conductor franked the tickets, asked for their passports, touched his Kepi in a French salute, and headed to his own compartment at the end of the carriage. They would not be disturbed until the train approached Victoria Station.

Watching the lights flash by, Liz lit another cigarette and said the obvious. "I wish I had a solution to our problem, Tom."

"Actually, there is a simple solution." He tried not to sound facetious. "Get rid of Trev." Liz looked at him in real horror that dissolved as Tom began to laugh. "Seriously—or, rather, not so seriously—I've been amusing myself trying to figure out how to get away with it."

"Ghoulish," she said, but she was smiling. "And what have you come up with—poison, a garrotte? You can't get a handgun in England."

Tom nodded. "Besides, you'd never get away with using a weapon. It has to look accidental."

"So, what have you contrived, Agatha Christie?"

"Best thing I've come up with is an accident in the London Underground. Bump, shove, push Trev from a crowded platform in front of an oncoming train. Walk away calmly, hoping no one in the crowd can be sure it wasn't an accident or that it was me who pushed him."

Liz's verdict was immediate. "I'll visit you in jail, Tom." They both laughed.

She flicked her cigarette to the tracks and watched the embers make a visible arc as they died away. "I'm going to change. Stay out till you're invited. The compartment is too small for two people to move round in."

"What are you going to change into? Can I have a preview?"

"Maybe some of the lingerie we bought on the Rue Bonaparte."

"But that's too expensive to rip off your body."

"Splurge."

One morning in late October there was a message for Tom from Michael Foot, the *Tribune* editor, to call his London number. By now Tom finally had an instrument—that is what the installer called it—in his rooms on stairway XXI. He wouldn't have to use a college line—finally.

"Michael Foot here."

"Ah, I thought I'd be getting a secretary. This is Tom Wrought."

"Good of you to call back. No secretaries at the *Tribune*. Can't afford 'em. Listen, I may have a juicy item for you—Pasternak's *Dr. Zhivago*." Foot paused, inviting a question Tom didn't need to ask. This novel, by an important Soviet author, had been smuggled out of Russia and published to universal acclaim in the West and deep embarrassment in Moscow. It was the talk of the senior common room at Trinity. Foot went on, "Ordinarily we don't review fiction. But the Nobel Prize announcement yesterday will cause a firestorm in Russia. The right-wing press has been trying to make Pasternak a big stick to beat the Soviets. Now it'll get worse."

Tom surprised himself by disagreeing. "Steady on. The Soviets have done themselves more damage trying to suppress Pasternak than any Western cold warrior could." *That's a switch, a Yank trying to get a Brit to calm down,* he thought.

"Still, I want to fight back a little. Pasternak is no anti-Communist. He's apolitical. The anti-Communists have no right to use him that way."

"And you want me to politicize him from the left?"

"Take any line you like; we'll print it."

"Well, I read the novel last spring, and I rather liked it. I'll have to say so."

"I'll send a copy round."

"Hello, Thomas."

Tom looked up from the Pasternak review typescript in his lap and recognized the owlish face. It was Sir Isaiah Berlin, the Chichele professor of political philosophy, who immediately set himself down into the adjacent chair and put a brace of books on the side table between them. Berlin was a frequent visitor to the Trinity senior common room and had rather taken Tom into his circle. As an American and a historian, Tom held attractions for Berlin, who had spent the war in America for the Foreign Office.

Berlin looked down at the side table, then up again at Tom. "I say, this is a coincidence."

"Nice to see you, Prof. What's the coincidence?"

"That book next to you, and the ones I just plunked down." There next to Tom's copy of *Dr. Zhivago* in English were two volumes, a hardback and a small volume, smaller even than cheap paperbacks. On the spine of each there were Cyrillic letters, Д-р Живаго. Tom looked at the two books and then blankly at Berlin.

"Of course, you don't read Russian. Silly of me. They are both *Dr. Zhivago*. Got them in Brussels at the World's Fair last week. Funny enough, in the Vatican pavilion."

Suddenly Tom was interested. "Why the Vatican pavilion?"

"Can't say. There were stacks of both, free for the taking." Berlin paused. "And lots of takers, mainly Russians. The *Russkis* are letting some of their people out—party faithful—to see the Soviet pavilion." Berlin glanced at Tom knowingly. "So, if they drop round to the Vatican exhibition, what do they find? The very book their government won't allow anyone at home to read—in Russian, and small enough to carry back in your shirt pocket if you are worried about your luggage being searched at Soviet customs."

"May I?" Tom picked up the two volumes—the large one hefty, the small one dense and pocket-size, like the Bibles that had been handed out to American soldiers before D-day. He dropped them on his lap and opened them. There was some non-Cyrillic printing on the flyleaf of each. But there was something odd: the large version was printed in Holland, the small one in France, by a different publisher. *Why,* he wondered?

Tom handed back the books. "Thanks, Shaya." Berlin had been in the United States long enough during the war to adopt the custom of "Christian names" with his American friends. His was not Isaiah, but a diminutive, "Shaya."

Berlin had been watching him look over the volumes. "I see you noticed that too." Before Tom could say, "Noticed what?" he leaned forwards and lowered his voice conspiratorially. "These books give off a smell I'd detect from OSS operations we'd hear about in the Washington embassy during the war."

"But the OSS was abolished in 1946."

"Yes, my dear boy, and the CIA was established in 1947." He smiled. "Say no more." Berlin didn't need to. Tom had found the angle for his *Tribune* review.

"Excuse me, Shaya, I have some work to do." Tom rose and carried the typescript back to his rooms.

A week later the cheque for Tom's review arrived from the *Tribune*, together with a note from Michael Foot. From the salutation he knew he was back in Foot's grace and favour.

> *Dear Tom,*
>
> *Well, you've put the cat among the canaries again. The suggestion that the CIA may have organized*

the dissemination of Russian editions back to the USSR certainly made your piece stand out.

As you saw, we published anonymously, as with your piece on the atomic spies.

But I should warn you we have received a number of calls asking for the name of the reviewer. We have refused to comply. One of the calls was from an old chum of mine, who may be in MI6. He asked me if our Zhivago reviewer was the same person who reviewed the Rosenberg book a few months ago. Such unwonted interest is slightly worrying. Please dispose of this note immediately.

Yours ever,

Michael Foot

Tom sank into the old chesterfield in his rooms, gripped the arm tightly, and began to feel the perspiration on his face. Suddenly he knew what the words *too clever by half* really meant. Someone had used him, had wanted the Americans to know the Russians knew they were behind their Zhivago predicament. He threw the letter in the bin, but the words *too clever by half* kept looping in his head.

All the rest of the day the thought kept returning, *Cui buono?* "Who gains?" *You're missing something. Who wanted you to know about the CIA and Dr. Zhivago?* It wasn't just an accident, Shaya Berlin's dropping into the armchair next to him in the senior common room at Trinity. *Work it out. Was it British foreign intelligence, their version of America's CIA? Or was it counterintelligence, their FBI? Was that MI5 or was it MI6—which was which?* He could never keep them straight. One was licensed to work only abroad, forbidden to act in Britain, like the CIA. The other was counterintelligence—catching other people's spies inside Britain, like the FBI, not allowed abroad. Then he realized, *MI5, MI6? It can't be either one.* British counterintelligence—MI5, he believed it was— had no brief to embarrass the Americans. Foreign intelligence—MI6— then? No. They were on the same side as the CIA. It could only be the Russians, it stood to reason. Turn *Dr. Zhivago* from "great" literature suppressed into just another front in the Cold War—"prove" the book to have been disseminated by the CIA. Pure propaganda. Clever. But how could they have arranged for Sir Isaiah Berlin to drop the hint?

CHAPTER TEN

It was a morning in mid-December that Liz and Tom were first spotted together by someone they knew, standing on the platform awaiting the 8:15 to London.

"Don't turn round," Liz said. "There's Mrs. Selwyn from Park Town crescent not ten feet behind you."

"What shall we do?"

"You walk down the platform away from her. I'll read my paper standing here. After a while I'll catch her eye, see if she's noticed you." Tom gave a slight nod. Liz added, "Meet me on the Circle line platform at Paddington."

***

Tom lingered in his seat when the train arrived in London, and was the last to walk down the platform. There, ahead of him, he saw Liz, practically arm in arm with a middle-aged lady. The two women walked right past the clock and down into the Circle and District line station. *What to do? If she sticks with Liz right down to the Circle line, it'll be too dangerous to follow them.* He walked over to a kiosk, purchased a

Manchester *Guardian*, and began to look for a review he had written only a few days before. He read it over twice, to calm himself and give the two women time to catch their trains. Would Liz go to work, to the hotel they'd been using, somewhere else? Did he dare approach Beatrice Russell again?

He decided to walk to Baker Street. It was not more than a mile up the Edgware Road. His pace exceeded the convoy of red double-deckers, seemingly stopping at every corner, where Londoners queued with never-diminishing patience. But for the smoke, Tom almost enjoyed the treacle sweetness of the diesel lorries' exhaust. The shafts of light they drove into the morning gloom made the roadway into a scene of cinematic mystery.

⟺

Fully a block behind Tom, walking up the Edgware Road, was another man, almost exactly Tom's height and build, wearing a coat and hat remarkably similar to his. This man had watched Tom and Liz separate on the platform at Oxford and momentarily worried that it was him they had spotted. Watching Liz go off with the next-door neighbour lady was a relief. He and his partner had been shadowing Tom off and on for the better part of a month now, with no reason to think they'd been noticed.

⟺

"I saw your Mr. Wrought just now, on the kerb across the street, when I came back from my elevenses," Liz's assistant said with a bright smile.

Play dumb! was her thought as Liz replied, "Oh, really? I'm not expecting him."

"Well, perhaps you should go along and see to him, Elizabeth." Beatrice Russell always called Liz by her full Christian name. She smiled. *Is that look conspiratorial?* Liz asked herself. *I think so.* She pulled her jacket off the back of her chair and tried to look unconcerned as she walked out of the office.

Tom saw Liz come out. Catching her eye, he walked down Baker Street to a nearby tea shop. He waited at the entry, and they found a booth.

Liz began, "Well, that was a dog's breakfast! Couldn't shake that Selwyn woman. What's more, she told me that it was you on the platform in front of me."

"What did you say?"

"I said that I had noticed the resemblance but thought it was just someone who looked rather like you. Then she stuck with me right down to the underground and on to the Circle line. She even got off at Baker Street, walked me right up to the office. I had no choice but to go in. It's worse. She made me promise to catch the train back this evening with her."

"What a limpet. Had no idea you were such friends."

"Neither did I." She sighed. "Anyway, there goes the day. And it gets worse still. My P.A., Mrs. Russell, saw you just now. Surely she's twigged to us. I don't know what it means."

"I'm sorry. I had no idea where you went, how to reach you. So I came here, hoping I'd catch you coming or going."

"Well, at least that idea worked out. But the day is shot." She squeezed his hand.

"Never mind. I'll go back to Oxford. I've plenty of work to do. Suddenly I'm the most popular book reviewer in England."

⊰⊱

When Liz came back to the training department, Beatrice Russell smiled knowingly and volunteered, "Why don't you just give Mr. Wrought our number here? I'll be glad to keep track of things for both of you." Then she put her finger to her lips to forestall any reply from Liz, who had to resist the urge to actually hug the woman. *What should I tell her? Everything? Nothing? Some of the truth? Do as she says, Liz. Beatrice doesn't want to know. She just wants to help. That's best.*

Liz was right. Beatrice Russell had worked with her for several years. They had come to the training department together. She felt badly that Liz had to travel so much but knew she was supporting two children and a husband. So Beatrice had taken the travel arrangements in hand and tried to make them simple, comfortable, and workable. It was difficult, plotting an efficient circuit round the country for Liz, but Beatrice had become good at it.

Nearly fifty, Beatrice was a widow. Like Liz, she too had once been a stranger to London. She'd come from a small fishery town on the Suffolk coast, Lowestoft, as a young woman. Her husband had been a fireman, killed in a flying bomb conflagration at almost the end of the war. She lived alone and liked it. There were no children. Instead, Beatrice Russell had two Jack Russell terriers. *Fancy that,* Liz would often think. They fended for themselves in a back garden during the workday. The only vice Beatrice allowed herself was active membership in the newly formed CND—Campaign for Nuclear Disarmament. Its iconic peace circle pin had become her only adornment. More than once she'd encouraged Liz to sign a petition, come to a rally, or make a contribution, but only in the gentlest way.

Somehow she understood what Liz was experiencing. She wouldn't judge.

⊰⊱

Liz was to visit a half-dozen branches of the Abbey National in Birmingham and its surroundings on a Wednesday, Thursday, and Friday. Tom reorganized his tutorials and was waiting for her at Magdalen Bridge when her car pulled up at 2:00 p.m. As he hefted a heavy cloth bag into the back seat, she said, "What's in the bag, burglar's tools?"

"Books. I have half a dozen to choose from for review. You'll be busy most of each day, so I thought I'd combine work and play."

"Not a bad idea." She let down the clutch, and they motored off. "Mrs. Russell has booked us into a lovely place in Warwick, at company expense this time. There's a happy thought!"

"Do you trust her?"

"No choice, really. Can't knock the knowledge out of her head. And complicity makes her an accomplice, no? I think our secret is safe with her."

After a long moment, she said, "Actually, we have other things to worry about." She paused, deciding how many of the details to report. "Light me a cigarette." She drew on it. "That biddy next door, Mrs. Selwyn, had to tell Trev all about seeing me at the train, and about you, or your double."

"Really? Why was she so interested?"

"Perhaps you made an impression on her too?" Liz squeezed his hand. "Anyway, Trev mentioned it to me. I had to cheerfully go along with the story. Oh yes, I had seen him too, did look vaguely like Wrought from a distance. But not up close, where I was standing. Anyway, that seemed an end to it."

"And then?"

"Well, this morning when I was packing my case, Trev came into the bedroom and noticed some of the lingerie we'd bought in Paris. I had laid out the half bra and the fishnet stockings on the bed. I thought I swept those up before he could be sure what they were." She puffed again. "But then he asked me, in a jokey sort of way, who I was meeting in Birmingham."

Tom spent his days writing. There were reviews, the article he'd promised Foot for the *Tribune* on the Little Rock desegregation crisis, and a profile for the Manchester *Guardian* of Martin Luther King Jr., the American Negro leader who had been the victim of an assassination attempt in New York the previous month. Tom decided on an angle unlike other articles on this last subject. He would tell the story of how a long-time peace activist named Bayard Rustin had come to Montgomery just as the famous bus boycott started, taken away King's handgun and rifles, and begun to instruct him in the effectiveness of Gandhi's nonviolent resistance.

When he finished, he began to worry. *Are you being too clever by half again, Tom? Will the* Guardian *ask about your sources? You'll have to tell them you knew Rustin when you were both in the party in New York in the '30s. Will you have to tell them he was arrested after the war for loitering round public toilets?* Maybe the whole angle was a mistake. What if papers in the United States picked it up? He asked Liz what she thought.

She told him not to worry so much. "The story is important."

———◆———

On Friday Liz drove them back into Oxford. She crossed the Magdalen Bridge and stopped just beyond, at the corner of High and Longwall Streets. The narrow lane led discreetly round New College towards Trinity.

"So, weekend with the kids?" Tom wondered aloud.

"Exactly." She beamed at the thought. "I'll take them for a Cotswolds walk tomorrow. They'll like that."

"With Trev?"

"I doubt it. He's not much for outings with the children. You?"

"I'd love to go." The thought took hold of him—a day with Liz and her kids, a small taste of normality, of real life with her . . . and them.

"Sorry, not what I meant, Tom. We can't risk it—the kids'd be sure to say something to Trevor." He could see she was right. "I meant what will you do this weekend?"

"Polish the piece we worked on a little more. There's a concert at Holywell Music Room on Sunday morning I want to go to. The local prodigy, Jacqueline du Pre, is playing the Bach cello suites."

Tom walked away up Longwall Street, its eponymous wall hiding the lush green lawns of Magdalen College. So he didn't see the small sedan that had stopped a hundred feet behind them and now came to the same corner. It hesitated, about to turn into the narrow lane after him, but then continued up the high street, its driver and his passenger agreeing there was too much risk of Tom noticing a single car moving slowly along behind him. They knew where he was going anyway.

———◆———

It rained hard the next day, Saturday. *Liz would not take the children walking on a day like this,* Tom thought. But it was a good day to spend in London. He had a dozen books reviewed and ready to sell to one or another of the used bookshops between Trafalgar Square and Oxford Street. The price they paid was not insignificant to someone on a don's fellowship, even one who wrote for the broadsheets. Perhaps he'd find a cheap matinee in the West End as well.

Tom had already placed most of the books at his usual buyer a block or so up the road from the Leister Square tube stop, and now he found himself looking in the window of Marks and Co. at 84 Charing Cross Road. As he peered in, the face of one of the customers looked familiar. Yes, it was an old friend from New York in the '40s. Lona Cohen was a striking woman, to whom he had once taken a fancy, though she was older and married. He stepped into the shop. As the woman turned to leave, Tom touched her arm and said, "Why, hello, Lona. What a surprise seeing you here!"

The woman's face seemed to show dawning recognition, but then, in a very Mayfair girls' school accent, she said, "So sorry, you've mistaken me for someone else." She drew his hand off her arm and left the store quickly.

Tom put down his last three books and asked if the proprietor was interested. He was, and Tom got a good price for them. On the point of leaving, he asked, "That lady who just left, what is her name? I am sure I've seen her somewhere before."

"Oh, that's Mrs. Kroger, Helen Kroger, antiquarian bookseller."

Could two different people look that similar? It wasn't just the looks, Tom realized. It was the smell, the same seductive scent that Lona Cohen had cast over him once in New York, which now came back with visceral force.

Sunday morning dawned cloudy but without rain. It would be fine, at least by British standards, for Liz's walk in the Cotswolds. As he prepared to leave for the du Pre cello concert, Tom thought how much he'd rather be with her and the children setting out for a Cotswolds village in search of a Rambler's footpath.

Tom's telephone rang only just after he had left for the concert, so he missed Liz's urgent call. And he had already passed through the Trinity gate into Broad Street when she tried the number at the porters' lodge. "Hello. Have you seen Mr. Wrought? Has he passed through the gate yet?"

"Haven't noticed, ma'am."

Liz thought for a moment. How to put this without creating suspicion? "If he passes, please just tell him not to go to the concert."

"Very well. Is there a name?"

"Tell him, it's . . . Mrs. Russell."

The porter at the lodge scribbled a note and placed it in Tom's pigeonhole.

The Holywell Music Room was the oldest hall purpose-built for music in Europe. Set above a low retaining wall, the building was small and unimpressive outside. But its chapel-like interior had been recognized as acoustically superb by Handel.

Almost since he had arrived at Oxford the year before, Tom had been attending Sunday morning concerts. The practice was almost an observance for nonbelievers. Walking down the Broad that early winter morning, the town was still—there wasn't a motor to be heard in the roadway. The clouds cast a sombre twilight on the sepulchral silence of Broad Street, broken only by the murmur of a brace of churchgoers pedalling down Parks Road from Keble to St. Mary's.

Just as the young cellist began the saraband of the fifth suite, Tom's eyes fell upon the familiar face in the pews of the gallery opposite. It was Trevor Spencer, staring intently at Tom. Composing his face, Tom moved his head back towards the cellist, leaned forwards, and rested his elbow on his knee. Then he cradled his face in his hand to cover it, and gazed at her intently for the remainder of the program.

But he no longer had an ear for Bach. He certainly couldn't get up and march through the row of other listeners in his pew. That would assure Trevor Spencer that he was seeing right. *What's the best strategy, Tom? Leave quickly at the end. Melt into the departing audience so that Spencer can't find you? No.* The audience in the building did not number more than 150. There simply wouldn't be a large enough crowd to get lost in. If Spencer left first, he would only have to wait till Tom emerged from the sole entryway.

No, your only strategy is to sit tight when the concert ends, then shuffle along to the exit with glacial slowness, inviting every lady in the audience to go ahead. Once in the vestibule, he'd duck into the gents' lavatory, lock a stall behind him, and wait. If he had enough patience, Spencer would eventually leave. He wouldn't come back in to search the gents, would he? He couldn't force open a toilet stall, could he?

Well, brazen it out. Don't be a fool, Tom. Hiding would only strengthen any suspicion Spencer had formed. *Behave normally.* So what if Spencer did find him? Tom would accost him like a friend unexpectedly encountered after a lengthy separation. *"Ah, Trev, so nice to see you . . . Yes, I've been back since before Michaelmas term began, living in college . . . How is Liz? And the children?"*

Could he pull it off? No, an encounter could end in disaster. *Well, then, back to the sit-tight strategy.*

Her program completed, Jacqueline du Pre returned to the platform to acknowledge the extended ovation, which then died away slowly. Reluctantly Tom had to stand to allow others to pass him on the way to the exit. But then he seated himself again and opened the program, seemingly oblivious to the fact that the concert had ended. Surreptitiously he took things in by peripheral vision. To his relief, Spencer simply rose and moved out of the hall along with the audience on his side of the hall. When Tom was the last person still in the room, he moved towards the exit. Nipping quietly into the gents' lavatory, Tom found an empty stall among the men making use of the facility and locked it behind him. And there he sat until, twenty minutes later, the custodian came in to clean the facility.

It was raining when Tom emerged into the street. There was no sign of Trevor Spencer. *Could he not have noticed you, Tom? Did he not recognize you? Perhaps he just didn't care.* Tom began to feel himself something of a fool, but a lucky one. With a spring in his step, he returned to College. Seeing the note, he understood that Liz had sought to warn him. *Well,* he said to himself, *a near miss.*

For Tom it was a near miss. For the two men who had followed Tom from Trinity and Spencer down from Park Town crescent, it was the beginning of a plan.

———✦———

By the time Liz drove home from their afternoon's walk, the children were cold, wet, and tired. Pulling up the handbrake, she turned to the back seat. "Go along inside, take off your wellies in the hall, and I'll make some tea."

She was disappointed not to see a warming flame on the gas grate in the lounge, but went through to the kitchen and reached for the kettle. There was Trev reading Sunday papers in the nook that overlooked the muddy and leafless back garden.

He put down the Sunday *Express*. "Well, it looks like the neighbour lady was right and you were wrong."

"Oh, what about?" Liz was desperate to not know.

"Come off it." The words were ominous, but the tone was casual, not at all argumentative. "About Tom Wrought."

"Really?" Could she sound just surprised enough?

"I saw him at the du Pre recital in Holywell Music Room. But I don't think he noticed me. He was alone. No Barbara Wrought. But then, she doesn't like that sort of thing as much as he does."

Liz decided silence on the matter was the best response. She busied herself with the tea, and the children came into the kitchen. "Lovely walk. We started at Stow on the Wold—such a perfect little town."

Trevor had returned to his newspaper. *It's just as well*, thought Liz.

———✦———

Trevor Spencer didn't want to be suspicious. He recognized that it was not in his interest. No use disturbing an agreeable state of affairs. It was true his wife wouldn't accommodate him in the bedroom. But after more than a decade of marriage, that was probably not so unusual. He was only rarely aroused, and neither of them wanted more children. He could live with it.

Still, it gnawed at him; it was a scratch he felt he had to itch. Despite her demur, it had troubled him to see Wrought that morning.

Twice, Trevor could recall, Tom Wrought had taken Liz to high table at Trinity. It was true that each time, Tom had invited him, but Trev had to decline. Yet it was, to say the least, unusual to take a woman, let alone another man's wife, to dine in hall. And she'd accepted with alacrity. Then there was the "misidentification" by the biddy next door and the underclothes she'd never worn before, for him at least. And now this sighting, with no apparent interest from Liz at all. Why?

Just to put the matter to rest, he'd do something. What exactly? First he'd check the lecture lists in the faculty of history. Was Wrought lecturing? Then he could ask for Wrought at Trinity. Was he living in college or out? Perhaps it was just a visit.

Then a thought struck him. *I should have a look at that clothing she never wears at home but takes along on her business trips. Yes, I'll do that.* He was about to rise, but at that moment, Liz got up from the table and announced that she needed a hot bath. *I'll wait till she's in the tub and can't surprise me rummaging through her things in the bedroom.* He looked up from his paper. "Good idea." He turned to Olivia just entering the kitchen. "Clear away the tea things and wash the cups, dear." Then back to his Sunday *Express.*

When Trevor heard the water shut off in the bath, he went into the lounge, where Ian was playing with small toy cars on the carpet. "You can turn on the telly if you want." It was a novelty Liz had provided and was strictly rationed. Now he wanted not to be disturbed, so he invited the children to watch.

Climbing the stair as noiselessly as he could, Trevor recalled the startling discovery he had made about his wife many years ago in Canada. Just killing a morning poking through his mother-in-law's desk drawers, he'd come upon the psychiatric reports on Liz. She'd never found out, of course, he was convinced. Surely she would have said something in all these years of bickering had she known. The thought that he had succeeded back then didn't just embolden Trevor; it vindicated his decision to investigate, at least a little.

He stood in the hallway, surveying the bedroom. Then he tiptoed back to the bathroom and listened. Liz was still sloshing round the tub. Quietly he retraced his steps until he stood before the rather plain bureau. Slowly he drew open the top drawer, taking care not to jam the sides against the frame. Then he drove his hands into the divided sections, panties on one side, bras on the other. Many more bras than he had imagined she would own. Finally he found himself examining a lacy black half bra, something he'd never seen but which immediately set a rush of arousal through his body. He could feel himself enlarged and hard against his trousers just fingering this lovely invitation to caress a woman's pouting breasts. He just knew that there was something not right about all this. There was no reason in the world for such a thing to be in the bureau of a married woman with two children and a husband she wasn't interested in sleeping with. Carefully he put the bra back beneath the others and turned to the other sections.

He found nothing more until he withdrew a neatly folded short dressing gown in maroon from beneath the slips and half-slips. It was, he thought, silk. Examining the label confirmed this, and its place of manufacture, Paris. He carefully refolded it, and as he did so, he felt something thin and smooth in the side pocket. He lifted it out and immediately recognized what was in his hand. Something he had not seen since his days in the Canadian army. It was a neat little envelope, about one and a quarter inches square, a flap that came down over the opening, coloured in a light blue, and with no image or name he recognized. But still completely recognizable as only one thing. It was the envelope for a safe, a sheath, a condom, a prophylactic. If he could not recognize the brand, it was presumably French. From the raft of jokes, double entendres, and bawdy songs, he knew all the North American brands—Sheik, Ramses, Trojan. Had even seen them in the forces. But the only British brand he knew of was Durex. Suddenly he asked himself, *Why did you have to do this? You want to spoil everything for yourself?* Trevor crumpled the envelope and forced it down to the bottom of his trouser pocket, closed the drawer, and crept down the stair. As he reached the bottom, Liz came out of the bath. He needed to regain his composure, to think, to calculate, to decide.

⟸⟹

Of course Wrought was back in Oxford. Of course he was lecturing at the faculty of history—twentieth-century American history. Of course he was living in college, and so without his wife. By noon on Monday morning, Trevor had satisfied himself on all these points. How much danger was he in? What if Liz divorced him? Took the children away? Ceased to support him? Made him look a fool to everyone he knew? It was like realizing that one had a problem so serious—a cancer one could no longer pretend wasn't there—that one had finally to consult a physician. And at the same time, like the suspicion of a cancer, it was a fear that you didn't want to find out about at all. That way you could continue to pretend there was nothing wrong, it would go away, resolve itself, disappear one day, with no more explanation than when one first detected it.

Trevor allowed it to gnaw at him for a day, two days. But by the end of that week, his anxiety had become all-consuming. He feared his way of life was hanging by a thread his wife could cut at any moment. He had to prepare for the worst. He had to protect himself. Where could he find a solicitor to advise him? There were one or two up the Banbury Road in Summertown, perhaps another in South Parade. But the thought of divulging secrets that close to home was as repulsive to him as disrobing in public. What if he later crossed paths with someone to whom he had revealed his situation? Even disclosure to a solicitor in St. Aldates or anywhere else in the city was too much for him to bear.

It wasn't the risk, he realized; it was the shame, the threat to his own self-image, his equanimity. It wasn't just that he couldn't bear meeting someone to whom he had confided shameful secrets. He couldn't even bear to pass the offices where he had done so, the building or the street where such disclosures were made. He knew it was silly, but he surrendered to the emotion nevertheless. He had to find a London solicitor.

When Trevor rose at ten on Friday morning, Liz was long gone, and the au pair had taken the children to school and was busy downstairs Hoovering the lounge carpet. Inconsiderate of her, Trevor thought, to wake him. Looking at the alarm clock, he realized that there were only two hours before the Oxford Library closed for lunch. There was a branch in Summertown, and all he needed was the telephone directory for London. But he just couldn't bring himself to do any of what he had to do even that close to home. If he were to meet anyone he knew . . .

An hour later, he was in the central library leafing through a commercial directory. There was no way to choose one London solicitor from another, or even to find those that specialized in domestic disputes. The only thing useful that he learned was that many of them had offices east of the Holborn tube stop, in Red Lion Square and onward towards the barristers' chambers at Grey's Inn. It was quiet in the library, and there was no one nearby. So Trevor neatly tore the page from the directory and stepped back out onto the high street. Monday he would simply take the train into London and go into the first office he encountered from the Holborn underground station. The resolve made him feel better.

The interview was brief and much to Trevor's liking.

Matters had started out badly. *Why,* Trevor asked himself, *did you go into the very first office you found on Red Lion Square?* Walking into the office, he had not even read the name carefully. V. Mishcon. Only as he sat there trying to puzzle out why a solicitor would have a Spanish name did he realize he was in the office of someone of the Hebrew persuasion. *These Jewish lawyers are well-known shysters.* Just as he decided to quietly walk out, the receptionist was standing before him.

"Mr. Mishcon has a few minutes now. He'll be happy to speak to you briefly." She led him into a wainscoted room with subdued lighting, walls decorated with eighteenth-century sporting prints. At the desk sat a grave man of about forty-five—with a long face with thinning hair, narrow lips, rather sunken cheeks—at work on a half-dozen files spread across the glass top of a large desk. He was wearing a beautiful bespoke pinstripe suit of impeccable tailoring, Trev noticed. The man looked up, smiled openly, and screwing the top on to his fountain pen, welcomed his guest. "Please sit down, Mr."—he looked at a note—"Mr. Spencer. What can I do for you?"

Trevor was so busy sizing the man up to his Semitic stereotype—largish nose, thinning hair, glasses—he did not respond immediately. But the beautiful cut of the man's suit, his clubman's tie, and even more, his reassuring smile brought Trevor back to his mission. *Perhaps this interview would be alright,* he thought.

"I contemplate a divorce, and I need some advice on where I stand."

"Well, I can give you the broad outlines of the law. But please tell me your situation." Mishcon folded his hands in his lap and leaned back slightly in his chair. The gestures were calculated to invite Trevor to relax.

Trevor was having trouble believing what he heard. The man was so smooth, so nice, and so confident, and the advice was so agreeable. *Could the Yid really have it right?*

"Let me get this straight. If she is working and I am at home not employed, the law deems me to be the children's caregiver, and she would have to continue to support me doing that in a divorce?"

"Yes, that's right."

"Who gets the property in a divorce?"

"It depends, but as the children's caregiver, you would have a fair claim on it. And if, as you say, this is a matter of adultery, the other party—your wife—would have no right of cohabitation."

"But she would have to continue to pay the rent?"

"That is correct."

"Could she force us to move to cheaper digs?"

"Well, you may be able to get a court order preventing any move, but in any case, she'd have to provide accommodation for you and the children elsewhere." The solicitor thought for a moment and then went on, "And it would have to be in the same vicinity and of equivalent size."

"One last question. What if she gets wind of a divorce action? Could she just leave Britain and take the children with her?"

"I am afraid so, unless there is a divorce proceeding in progress, in which case the court may issue an order forbidding removal of the children."

Trevor stood. "Thank you very much, Mr. Mishcon." He reached into his jacket for a billfold. "What do I owe you for this advice?"

"Oh, please, any competent attorney could have told you this. There's no charge."

Well, that was not what he expected at all. *Legal advice, gratis, from a Jew?*

If this man Mishcon was right, all he needed was proof of adultery. And that should not be so difficult to secure. Nice insurance against losing anything in a divorce. He had only to watch how his wife packed a bag for her business trips, or perhaps even how she chose her underthings on mornings she went into London.

That same day Tom was in London, and again his path very nearly crossed Trevor Spencer's. This time Tom was looking for a book instead of selling one—Orwell's *Homage to Catalonia*. He could have found it at the Bodleian. But he'd never be able to withdraw it, still less write in the margins. Not even King Charles had ever contrived to take a book out of the Bodleian Library. Blackwell's didn't have it either. Tom's search took him back to Marks and Co., the booksellers at 84 Charing Cross Road, and here happenstance turned into a little mystery.

As Tom browsed the shelves, the shop's front doorbell rang. A man entered, taking off his hat. Tom looked up and heard the clerk greet the customer. "Hello, Mr. Kroger." But it wasn't Mr. Kroger. It was Morris Cohen, husband of Lona Cohen, the woman whom he had mistakenly thought he'd recognized the very last time he had been in this very shop. Before Tom could say anything, Kroger—or Cohen, whoever he was—had taken a brief look at Tom, pulled his hat down over his face, and turned on his heels. Walking out of the shop, he called behind him, "In a hurry, Mr. Doel. Be back to collect my parcel tomorrow."

Can't be happenstance! What are Lona and Morris Cohen doing in London, and why have they changed their names? Tom looked back at the clerk. "Is he married to an antiquarian bookdealer, what's her name . . . ?"

Before Tom could recall, the clerk supplied it. "Helen Kroger? Yes, that's her husband, Peter Kroger. They own a shop together."

CHAPTER ELEVEN

Trevor knew that for a divorce, he'd need witnesses to adultery. There were investigators often hired by the rich to witness and testify to adultery. He could not afford to engage such a service, either financially or emotionally. But for his purposes, it would be enough if he knew, and Liz knew that he knew.

They were clearing up the dishes on a Wednesday evening in January when Liz turned to the au pair. "Ifegenia, I need to go to London in the morning and visit some midlands branches in the afternoon. I have to be gone till Friday evening. I know tomorrow's your evening off. Do you mind changing it to Saturday evening?"

"No," the girl replied. "Saturday will suit me better, thank you."

So, Trevor calculated, she was going to spend Thursday night away. If only he could rouse himself early enough to see what she packed, he might test his worst fears.

As he turned off the light that evening, he could feel a combination of excitement, dread, anticipation, and fear coursing through his body. Trevor was usually asleep five minutes after his head hit the pillow. That night he lay awake a long time, repeatedly looking up at the illuminated dial of the alarm clock, before sleep overtook him. When he finally slept, he would find himself suddenly awake and watching the hands on the clock creep along the path from midnight to daybreak. By 5:00 a.m. he was irrevocably awake. At five thirty Liz woke automatically. He had always wondered at her internal clock and her willpower to rise so early.

Returning from the bathroom in the still pitch-darkness, Liz quietly turned on a small lamp at her bureau. Now lying on his stomach, Trevor opened his eyes just enough to watch. Liz sorted through her underclothes drawer and then chose: black bra, black panties, a matching garter belt, and dark stockings. She sat in a chair and drew them up each leg, clipping them to the garter belt and then examining the seam running up the back. With a quick adjustment they were both straight. Then she withdrew the short silk maroon robe, crumpled it, and put it in her attaché case. But, he noticed, she did not snap the case, perhaps concerned about noise. Then she put on a dark blouse, severe in its modesty, and stepped into the skirt of a woman's suit.

He closed his eyes. Trevor heard her descend the stairs. A few moments later, he could hear the Humber start. Surely it was Wrought she was going to meet. Where? Perhaps a phone call to her office at Abbey National would help.

He had to wait till the office opened, so he decided to sleep till then.

Trevor had not spoken to Liz's personal assistant more than twice in four or five years. There would be no risk of her recognizing the voice. At the stroke of eight, he picked up the receiver, dialled the operator, and asked for a trunk call to London.

He was surprised when the phone was answered that early in the morning. "Training, Mrs. Russell."

He'd have to chance that Liz had not already arrived. "Can I speak to Elizabeth Spencer?"

"She's seeing to branches and is expected this afternoon." That was exactly the opposite of the schedule Liz had given the au pair.

Trevor replied, "This is a trunk call. When can I call back?"

After a moment came the answer. "Anytime after lunch. Who can I say called?"

"The branch manager at—" He did not finish the sentence before ringing off precipitately. There would be plenty of time before he needed to leave if he was to follow Liz to a rendezvous after work. He began to think about how to dress for London. Recalling the elegance of the solicitor he'd consulted, he decided on his pinstriped double-breasted, the only bespoke suit he owned.

⟫——⟪

Trevor Spencer was wearing his best suit when he died later that afternoon under the wheels of a Circle line underground train at the Paddington tube station. Death came to him as a complete and very briefly experienced surprise. One moment he was absorbed in his *Telegraph*; the next he was staring at Tom Wrought coming out on the platform behind him, and then he was hurtling onto the track.

⟫——⟪

It was from that moment on for the next several minutes that Tom Wrought did everything wrong. Running after the assailant, he merely called attention to himself among the horror-stricken bystanders, who would afterwards misremember the events they'd witnessed. Moving back towards the platform from the escalators and then heading for the Hammersmith line instead, distraught and dishevelled, he'd given more people a chance to remember him. But once he'd left a message for Liz to go back to Oxford, Tom calmed down and went back into the mainline station to do the same thing himself.

⟫——⟪

What Liz remembered most from that night wasn't the message waiting for her at the Gresham or the journey back home. It was the interview with the two CID detectives, Bennett and Watkins. She could recall every detail: their certainty that it was murder, the description of the assailant, the questions about Trevor's enemies, if any, his work, whether there was a private income. Then there was the odd question about the solicitor's card, and finally the reticence about the prophylactic wrapper in his pocket, the possibility of another woman and an irate husband. The worst of it was the momentary fear that Tom really had done it. It was only his voice when she had called that quieted her worst imaginings.

Sunday was spent with her children grieving. Liz grieved for them, so young to experience a loss so great. There were few words amidst the tears, but much holding of one another. At first it was hard to make the children really understand more than the words. But then their mother's feelings broke through. Afterwards there was the very painful call to Trevor's family in Birkenhead. Her brother-in-law, Keith, was a brick, listening to her and to the children, comforting, remembering, cushioning their pain.

Monday morning Liz decided that she had to take action. She woke Ifegenia, and before seven thirty she was on a train for London. By ten o'clock she'd already seen Victor Mishcon and was sitting in Alice Silverstone's tiny office, still slightly reeling from Silverstone's directness. The solicitor had asked, rather theatrically it seemed to Liz, "Am I to understand, Mrs. Spencer, that your husband has been murdered, and you want me to defend the man the police suspect must have killed him?" When Liz answered, Silverstone smiled like a Cheshire cat. "Excellent!" was all she said.

━━◆━━

Three days later Alice Silverstone still had no answers to the questions that troubled her. All that week she'd watched for some notice in the papers of the death in the tube station at Paddington, some report of Tom's arrest. There was nothing more beyond the squib in one of the tabloids. The papers were all concerned about the worst patch of pea soup fog London had ever dealt with.

The CID now knew Alice was Tom Wrought's solicitor, yet she had not been called to be present at a single interview. Liz had promised to alert Alice as soon as the police wanted to interview her. But they hadn't shown any interest in doing that either. Why not? The love triangle was obvious. But most of all, there was the coincidence that really couldn't be a coincidence. Tom was there on that platform because someone wanted him to be there when they killed Trevor Spencer. Of that Alice was certain.

Thursday, 29 January 1959, had been the worst smog and fog day in London for a decade. Visibility was nil. Everything had been brought to a standstill, as though a blizzard had dropped thirty inches of snow on the capital. Breathability was no better. Even the next afternoon, after it had lifted, making her way to Brixton Prison, Alice could feel the burn in her chest. It was, she thought, almost a relief to bear some discomfort elsewhere in her body.

Alice had spent the morning at her desk in the office. She was, in the expression she now really understood, "putting her affairs in order." She was closing cases, noting some for the office's clerk to transfer to other solicitors, toting up her accounts, leaving instructions about how much to pay clerks, notice servers, and revenue stamp agents. It would take time. Did she have enough? In just a week her demands on the morphine had detectably increased. Would she be able to deal with Tom Wrought's case? She needed a way to speed things up.

It was Tom's second meeting with his solicitor. When he arrived in the interview room, Alice Silverstone was already seated at the table with two composition books before her, dressed as fashionably as before. Tom couldn't resist remarking on it. "Miss Silverstone, so nice to see you again. But you didn't have to dress up for me." Just seeing her lifted the despond.

"Didn't do it for you. Did it for me." She said it lightly. *Cheeky.* "Tom?" Her tone turned interrogatory. "Liz told me I had to call you that. Alright?" Tom nodded, smiling, and Alice continued, "I can't let her visit. She'll probably be a witness in any trial, and the Crown will suggest connivance if there's a record of her being here."

"Could she be compelled to testify?"

"'Fraid so. Look, we don't have much time today. They won't let me stay more than thirty minutes at a time. Now, here is my theory of this case. Someone wants you in prison or perhaps hung, and they killed Trevor Spencer to accomplish that end." Silverstone laid out her reasoning and did not have to go over anything more than once. Tom saw it immediately.

"So, what are you going to do?" he asked.

"Well, I don't think a barrister will be able to do much with the witnesses, though I'll have them throw sand at the trainman's identification. If my theory is right, you were framed. And if so, there is one thread hanging loose: Why kill Trevor Spencer when whoever did it could have simply killed you and been done with it? If we can answer that question, we stand a chance."

"How are you going to do that?"

"By getting you to tell me who might have had an interest in framing you."

"I've been thinking about that most of the last three days . . . I can give you a list, but it would be pretty far-fetched."

"A list of names is no good to me, Mr. Wro—Tom." They both smiled at her correcting herself.

"That's all I can give you from in here."

"No, you can give me more, and you'll have to, if we are to stand a chance." She caught her breath and continued, "If you just make a list, you'll forget someone for sure. Besides, lacking context, I won't be able to figure out who the people on your list are or why they're on it. Look, Tom, we don't have time for endless interviews, piecing together your past so we can figure out who did this to you. But you're a historian, a writer. I need you to sit down and write out the history for me, your history—at least as far back as you think might be relevant."

"Write my autobiography, you mean? At my age, and behind bars?" Tom was momentarily amused by the thought. "Sounds pretty pretentious, counsellor."

"Maybe. But the more you write, the more people and events will come to you that you'd never recall just drawing up a list. You know how memory works. Start concentrating, and one recollection leads to another. Better to get down too much rather than too little. Let me be the judge of what's important."

"Well, I suppose it'll be something to do." But then Tom began warming to the task. Perhaps having an assignment, work to do, would displace the funk that was too often punctuated by moments of dread.

Alice slid the two composition books across the table. They were thick, quarto-size volumes, larger than American notebooks, ruled with narrower lines, Tom noticed as he opened one. Then she placed a fountain pen and ink bottle before him. "Don't just tell me who might want to frame Tom Wrought for murder. Tell me everything about what got you here, to Britain, to Oxford, to that underground platform, but from the beginning, as far back as you think matters."

━━◆━━

Liz was waiting in the gusty wind across the street from the main gate of Brixton Prison when Alice Silverstone emerged.

"How is he?" was her first question.

"A bit demoralized. It must be frightfully boring for him when he's not just scared. I gave him the assignment. I'm not certain he took it seriously. But I can't think of another way to speed things along." She looked at Liz and thought to herself, *"Speed things along"? Wrong thing to say, Alice.*

Liz didn't notice. "He's a man, an academic, a writer. He won't find composing his autobiography boring." Their laughter lifted the gloom briefly.

PART IV

1937–1957

The Confessions of Thomas Wrought

CHAPTER TWELVE

Tom sat himself as comfortably as he could, leaning against the wall behind his bunk. Carefully he put the fountain pen point in the small bottle, pulled the lever on the pen barrel, drawing ink into the pen, and then opened the first of his black-and-white marbled composition books. There was now nothing more he could do to postpone the writing. How to begin? *Historians are storytellers. They have to be to make their readers care. So tell Alice your story.*

━━◆━━

My parents came to New York a few years before I was born, at the end of a large migration from Finland. At the time it was still a province of Tsarist Russia. My name was Toomas, and Wrought is a rough translation of the Finnish name Koristeltu. Probably my ancestors were blacksmiths.

Growing up, my mother spoke only Finnish at home. So I learned. But the only time I ever felt Finnish was on Sunday afternoons, when we listened to Toscanini and the NBC symphony on the radio playing *Finlandia* by Sibelius. The music made me stand and cry. That got me mad at myself for being moved by music.

I grew up in Hell's Kitchen, a mainly Irish neighborhood in Manhattan between Broadway and the Hudson River docks. My father died in 1930, when I was ten; I had the run of the streets most days while my mother worked.

Hell's Kitchen was as rough as it sounds. Any other street but your own was a foreign territory. The east/west blocks between the avenues were narrow and long, four times the length of the north/south avenue blocks. These long cross streets were lined with six-story walk-up brownstone tenements—cold-water railroad flats. All winter the winds whistling up the Hudson would cut right through them. Summer nights were worse, each an agony of damp sleeplessness in stagnant heat. When we had one, my mother and I would both sleep on the fire escape, in spite of the smell of sewage.

I was Finnish, not Irish, so I didn't go to mass, have a first communion, or attend the local parochial school. I didn't wear its blue serge uniform and experience the daily afternoon's release from the nuns' terror. Coming out into the street uncorked a seething anger that the Irish Catholic boys took out on whomever wasn't Irish Catholic, was smaller, and was alone. All too often that was me. I couldn't understand why my mother wouldn't let me be Irish.

The smart thing was to hide the little money you carried in a sock and tie your latchkey to a string under your shirt. Otherwise a tough kid with a switchblade would turn out your pockets and make you take him up the stairs to rob you in your own home.

In the winter the only place to stay warm was the public library. My mother taught me how to read before I ever got to school. That, plus the steam heating in the library, is what saved me.

I was pretty much like most kids, really, except for one matter. The only serious thing I really cared about from the time I was very young was equality for Negroes. I don't really know why, but I can't ever remember not being angry about racialism. Maybe it started when I had pneumonia as a five-year-old; the doctor who treated me was a Negro, and later, the librarian who didn't turn me out into the winter snow was a black lady. I couldn't understand why Negroes weren't welcome by the toughs on our street. More than once when I was a kid, I'd see gangs of white kids jump a colored boy—"colored" was the polite term back then. They would take his money and leave him with enough bruises to remember not to come that way again. Cheap as the housing was, no Negro families were tolerated. I remember thinking it was a lot worse being colored than being Finnish.

The first time I got in trouble with authority was sixth grade. The teacher, my first male teacher, told us that the Civil War was fought over states' rights. Somewhere in an old library book, I'd seen the famous photograph, a daguerreotype maybe, of the old man freed from the New Orleans slave market, stripped to the waist showing the wretched cross-hatching of scars on his back. I raised my hand and said, "No. It was a war about slavery." Well, I had to come forward, put out my hand, and receive three strokes of a ruler. That was his response to my argument. After class the other kids started calling me "nigger lover." Maybe I became a Communist that morning. I certainly became interested in history and rebellion.

I went to an all-boys high school, where the kids were smart alecks. It was a long subway ride, and there was nothing much to do on the trains but talk about baseball and politics. By then the Depression was in full force. One of the older boys, Morty Sobell, was always going on about capitalist exploitation and Roosevelt's pointless attempt to save Wall Street from the coming Socialist revolution. Back then in New York, there were Communists wherever you went. They called themselves "Democrats in a hurry." Their slogan was "Communism is twentieth-century Americanism."

I lost contact with Sobell till after the war. In 1951 he was accused of being a Russian spy and convicted for passing atomic-bomb designs to the Russians along with the Rosenbergs. I knew Julius Rosenberg in university, but that's a little later in my story.

As I've said, there were no females in my high school. And that was a more serious matter than either sports or politics. But Morty Sobell mentioned that if you went to Communist Party meetings, you could meet girls, and these girls were not bourgeois. That was code. It meant they were "fast." So I went along to a meeting. He was right. There was something else different at these meetings. There were educated, sophisticated Negroes. Back then in New York, the color bar was different but still strong. People would say, "In the South they don't care how close you get, so long as you don't get too high. In the North they don't care how high you get, so long as you don't get too close." Not many Negroes got very high. But the party was the only organization that practiced complete integration and demanded outright racial equality.

The summer I graduated high school, 1937, there were still no jobs, but the Communist Party sent me south to help organize sharecropper and farm labor unions. That way at least my mother didn't have to support me.

———❖———

City College of New York was free. All I needed was the IRT subway fare from Fiftieth Street and Broadway. At about 120th Street, the train would break out on the viaduct and race above the deep ravine that divided Harlem from downtown. Back into the ground the subway would tunnel, coming into the 135th Street station. On my first day I bounded up the stairs and came out to a different world from the one I'd grown up in.

There was a steep hill up from Broadway to the college, on St. Nicholas Terrace. All the way up, there were Puerto Rican bodegas, where you could get *comidas crejoles*, and cafés where they'd make you a cappuccino if you knew how to ask for it; shops that sold only jazz records and sheet music; even boxing gyms taking inspiration from the black heavyweight champ Joe Lewis. Along the streets you'd see Latin girls in tight, low-cut rumba dresses, and high-yellow (light-skinned) Negro men in zoot suits and two-tone shoes, even at midday. And there were the down-and-out beggars, drunks, even bemedaled veterans of the Bonus Army. Here they were all brown and no threat to a white boy.

At the crest of the hill over the tenements rose the massive "Perp" English Gothic of City College, built of the granite schist excavated from subway tunnels all over the city. Its four gates staked out an island of mainly white faces in the middle of Harlem.

As I passed into the vast basement cafeteria of Shepard Hall that first morning, I had to dig into my pocket to be sure I had the ten cents for coffee and a donut, plus the five cents I'd need for the subway back home. Balancing a tray and my books, I found a long table occupied by two Negro girls and asked if they minded the company. Polite pleasantries were immediately swamped by noise. A definite disturbance had emerged in the alcoves at the arched basement windows. I turned to the girls at my table. "Can you tell me what that's about?"

One of the girls responded, "Oh, it's another case of no-enemies-on-the-left. Just a couple of the splinter groups in the Popular Front going after one another again."

The second girl looked over her shoulder. "Let's see, there's the Young People's Socialist League, not to be confused with the Young Socialist Alliance; the Socialist Workers' Party; the American Labor Party; the Communist Party; the Fourth International—that's the Trotskyites; and there's Eugene Debs's old Socialist Party too." Pleased with herself, she looked back at her friend. "Have I missed any?"

"'Fraid so. The plain old Workers' Party, for one. But the others don't have enough members to squat in an alcove from early morning to late at night." She looked at me, and in dead earnest said, "They'd camp out if they could." Then they both rose. "Excuse us; calculus class . . ."

Since I was already a member of the Young Communist League, I made my way to the alcove sheltering the CP. Two young men were arguing about the Popular Front—Stalin's strategy of protecting Russian communism by combining with noncommunist parties to fight fascism. One of them was adhering closely to the party line; the other was plainly a Trotskyite. I listened for *a while in silence. Suddenly the Stalinist turned to me. "I'm Irving Howe. Who's right here, me or Kristol?"*

It was obvious to my Stalinist orthodoxy. "Socialism in one country, of course. World revolution is fatuous. Kristol there is guilty of what Lenin called 'an infantile disorder.'" Kristol took a small notebook from his pocket and began writing. I turned to him. "Taking my name down?"

"No. I'm writing down the word *fatuous*. It's good, and I want to check the meaning." That was the beginning of my education as an intellectual.

I could follow the party line pretty well, at least when I got to college in 1937. At first I was doctrinaire as hell. I would look Kristol in the face and defend Stalin's show trials in Moscow. He had lined up all his old comrades from the revolution, men in their sixties, who had been loyal for forty years. Torture had made them denounce themselves as "wreckers" and "Trotskyite" enemies of the people. Anyone but a true believer could see what was really happening, especially when you noticed the bruises and fractures in the *Life* magazine photos. But the party could whistle up fifty of us students to swear the trials were "on the up and up."

Why did we care so much? Well, we took ideas seriously, but we also thought the times were really dangerous and that you had to take sides. From 1936 on, we knew war was coming, and we knew that only the Russians were prepared to take on the Nazis.

But the main reason I stayed in the party was its "line" on Jim Crow. That was always the most important thing for me. Only the Communist Party demanded Negro equality unequivocally, or at least it did till 1941, when Stalin's need for American trucks made its members into strike-breakers!

To me, Negroes were not just the equals of everyone else. The ones I knew were finer human beings. Maybe the best of them was a handsome young man named Bayard Rustin. He came to City College the same year I did, joined the party too. Rustin was a talented singer, professional in fact, and once introduced me to Paul Robeson. When I had any money and a date to impress, he could get me a late table at Café Society in Greenwich Village. There he performed for one of the few completely integrated audiences in the country. He left the party before I did, but we remained friends.

It was from Bayard I first learned the lyrics Billie Holiday made famous at Café Society:

Southern trees bear strange fruit,

Blood on the leaves and blood at the root,

Black bodies swinging in the southern breeze,

Strange fruit hanging from the poplar trees.

I found a job as a messenger boy for the *New Masses*, a weekly magazine that delivered the party's line on culture, literature, the movies, music, and theater all over New York. *New Masses* published Hemingway and Dreiser and Dorothy Parker, but it also published Negro writers like Ralph Ellison, Richard Wright, and Langston Hughes. These men I met. They took me to their jazz clubs, concerts at the Apollo, even their party meetings once I turned eighteen and could join the grown-ups.

The twenty-fourth of August 1939 must have been a weekday, because I remember getting up to go to work early. I was trying to get in as many hours as possible at the *New Masses* before classes started in the fall. At the subway newsstand I was about to grab my copy of the *Daily Worker* when I saw a very rare banner headline on the *New York Times*: "Germany and Russia sign ten-year nonaggression pact/Bind each other not to aid opponents in war acts/Hitler rebuffs London, Britain France mobilize."

By that afternoon, the most stalwart party members at the *New Masses* office had already adapted themselves to the new reality, denouncing the British, the French, even the poor Polish as warmongers. It got worse later. Within weeks the party started organizing strikes on the docks to prevent ships loading war materiel for England and France.

I didn't wait. That afternoon I went down to the party office at the *Daily Worker* building on Union Square and handed in my party card. Turns out I was the first member to come in that day to do so. That's what they told me.

⟢

A week later I was sitting in the Shepard Hall cafeteria as far away from the Communist Party alcove as I could get when someone sat down next to me. I recognized the face from party meetings. It was a senior electrical engineering student, Julius Rosenberg. He was owl-faced, nearsighted, with prematurely thinning hair. Thick glasses in a clear frame made his face even more featureless. There was still some adolescent acne on his chin. Like most of the engineering students, he wore white shirts and a tie, with a six-inch slide rule bouncing at the belt of his pleated pants.

"Party sent me," he began. "They want you to stay."

"Convince me." I was sincere, I think.

"You mean with reasons? Reasons are for idealists, not materialists."

"What do you mean?"

"What I mean is that Communism is on the right side of history; it's the wave of the future; it's going to happen whether we know the reasons or not. A little bend in the river is no reason to give it all up. Remember what Lenin said: two steps forward, one step back."

"So, Julie, after fighting against the Nazis inside Germany for twenty years, Communists should think of this rotten deal with Hitler as just a little stratagem?"

"Exactly. Stalin knows what he's doing."

"I'll bet he does. He's known all along, putting all those nice old Jewish guys up against a wall for being loyal party hacks. I was able to swallow that. Starving the Ukraine to get rid of the rich peasants — I stood still for that too. Killing Kirov, that didn't bother me. But this is treachery I can't take, Julie."

"The party has plans for you. Big plans."

"Like what?"

"I don't know. I'm just a foot soldier. But you're smart, and you're a WASP. You fit in places we don't." I knew what Julie Rosenberg meant by "we."

"Sorry. No sale." I didn't mean it the way it sounded, but he took offense.

"Look, Tom. It's not just carrots. The party has some sticks it can use too."

I stood up and glared at him for a moment. "Are you threatening me, Julie?"

He reached up and pulled me back down. "No, not me. Party bullyboys. You've seen them with billy clubs at protests. Well, they don't just protect people on picket lines."

"Alright, I know you're only trying to warn me. But I won't change my mind."

The next time I saw Julie Rosenberg, back in New York several years after the war, he was a Soviet agent, but I never knew.

—◆—

I graduated in 1941. But I figured I'd be drafted before I could actually settle down in any job. This was the peacetime draft before Pearl Harbor, when men were still being inducted for just one year. So in September I volunteered for the draft and was sent to Fort Dix, in New Jersey, outside of Philadelphia, for basic training. Eight weeks of physical fitness, unit marching, riflery with the M1, obstacle courses carrying sixty-pound packs, and endless boredom. I kept my head down, never revealed that I had graduated from university, still less my previous political affiliation.

I looked pretty much like all the other recruits—crew cut; no glasses; average height, weight, and strength. So the noncoms—sergeants and corporals—who trained us never learned my name, let alone found the need to abuse me. In a company of 120 guys, I managed not to screw up badly enough to come to anyone's attention.

After the last march-past in basic training, the company first sergeant called my name and those of three others and told us to fall out and report to him.

"Men, the army has established an Officer Candidate School, and each basic training company is required to identify four privates for training as second lieutenants. It's voluntary, twelve weeks in North Carolina. If you pass through the course, you get to order noncoms like me around, even get saluted." He smiled ruefully. "Questions?"

One of the others spoke up. "Why us, Sarge?"

"You kept your noses clean, and you can shoot straight. But mainly, it was your scores on the exams. Should have cheated."

Two of the men turned down the offer. Two of us accepted.

⟨⟩

Ten days later, wearing my private's uniform and carrying a large duffel bag, I came off a train in Fayetteville, North Carolina. The duty corporal pointed me toward a bus. A half hour later I had started to become a "ninety-day wonder." In fact, I had been fed into only the second OCS—Officer Candidate School—course the army had run. What's more, though we were being trained in the pines of North Carolina, the training company was "integrated." There was a handful of Negroes in the platoon of forty. They were easy to find in the long unheated barrack, bunked together in a corner cordoned off on two sides by empty bunks. I headed right toward them, dropped my duffel, and offered my hand.

"Tom Wrought. Glad to meet you."

The three men before me were obviously surprised, first a bit hesitant. They couldn't stop the smiles that had broken out on their faces. Each thrust his hand forward, and I quickly had three new friends. They were college boys from Washington, Chicago, and Boston.

"I'm Richard Wilson," said the first. "That's Richard; don't call me 'Dick.' You a Jew boy from New York?" he asked with no belligerence.

"Not guilty. But I am from New York. How'd you know?"

"'Cause you came over and chose a bunk next to us. They gonna make you pay." Then he introduced me to his friends.

⟡

The US Army had always been segregated. With thousands of colored men to be drafted and no white officers willing to command them, there was no immediate alternative to integrating the newly established Officer Candidate Schools. But the army hadn't contended with its own deeply Southern roots.

The master sergeant was from Mississippi. He was not going to be part of an army in which a colored officer would take his salute. Right from the start, all four black candidates were assigned to police the area — pick up litter, especially cigarette butts, for a hundred yards around the barrack area. No other soldiers were assigned to that job. And no one was ordered to "GI his butts" — that is, to break open the cigarette butt and let the remaining tobacco flutter to the ground and the bit of paper disappear among the blades of grass. Neatness was an army obsession, and litter round a barrack resulted in collective punishment. The four black candidates knew that the whole platoon would suffer loss of privileges and blame them. Collecting butts was demeaning. It was also time consuming. They never had a chance to study the field manuals. Within a couple of weeks, two of these men had fallen so hopelessly behind, they were washed out.

The last two, Richard Wilson and his friend Cullen, would march and eat and wait on lines with me, and I'd go over enough of what I was studying to keep them up. It wasn't doing me any good with the other candidates, but they couldn't really tell what we were always talking about.

195

I remember perfectly the weekend of the sixth and seventh of December that year, 1941. And not because of the attack on Pearl Harbor that Sunday afternoon.

We were four weeks into the school. Passes were being handed out for the weekend. But not to the Negroes and not to me.

That Friday evening I presented myself at the company first sergeant's office. I stood at attention. "Permission to speak, Sergeant?"

"Go ahead, Wrought."

"Why didn't I or the colored candidates receive a pass this weekend, Sergeant?"

"No recreational facilities in Fayetteville for Negro officer candidates, Wrought." I was about to interrupt, but the sergeant's message was obvious. "You can take it up with the chain of command if you want." He nodded in the direction of the captain's office.

It was going to be a lonesome weekend in an empty barrack. So the three of us pooled our money. Then I made my way to the camp entrance with dough for a couple of bottles of gin, found a willing soldier, and offered him a big enough bounty when he came back with the liquor to feel sure he'd do it.

On Saturday Richard Wilson brought out a rack of poker chips and two decks of cards. We began playing five-card stud while nursing the two bottles. The stakes were serious, since we'd all come to camp with money and were accumulating private first-class pay with nothing to spend it on. Wilson and Cullen were careful and experienced players. By lights out I was behind. The next morning my two friends went to Sunday service. Maybe they were Christians, or maybe they just wanted to spend some time with other Negro soldiers. There were many on the base, all engaged in menial tasks, none in combat training.

Wilson and Cullen returned from "divine service" as we called it and broke out their poker chips and cards. Cullen looked toward my bunk. "Wanna play, Mister Charlie?"—it was what they called me.

"Nope, cleaned out," I replied.

Once they began to play, a few others gathered round, and then one of the other white men asked to join. This breach of the protocol that required silent treatment of the Negroes was welcomed by looks of surprise and pleasure on their faces. Immediately space was made on the cots, and chips were bought by two white guys and then a third. It was the first time members of our platoon found themselves treating one another on terms of humanity.

By two o'clock news of the Japanese attack had spread throughout the town, and even before orders were given to return to base, almost everyone was back in the barrack. The shared recognition that we were now really at war, in it together—that we, the very men in this barrack, would be in the vanguard of the American counterattack—seemed for a moment to change the chemistry in the barrack. It had even broken through the color barrier. But that feeling didn't last more than a few hours.

With nothing to do, many had begun watching the poker game, including more than one Southern white boy already seething because he had been forced to sleep, eat, and share a toilet with a colored man for a month or more. Trouble was inevitable. One of the white players had begun to win consistently, and a few of the observers were sniggering. More than once Wilson and Cullen found themselves with straights or three of a kind beaten by a full house. Finally, Cullen looked up at the white soldier standing behind Wilson. "Hey, buddy, would you mind moving a little? You're in my light."

He replied with contempt, "Yes, I would mind, and don't you be callin' me 'buddy,' nigger."

Cullen turned to the others. "I'm afraid we're going to have to fold this game, gentlemen." He knew that watchers were colluding with players and there was nothing he could do about it. Wilson and he both rose.

"Hey, can't quit now, boy. I'm way behind." It was the fifth player, at the narrow end of the cot, a burly man from Indiana.

Wilson turned to him and made the mistake of being frank. "I'm sorry, but I won't play when folks are cheatin'."

From a cot about ten feet away, I watched the next scene unfold in what seemed like slow motion. The white player and his confederate turned on the two Negroes, shouting as they began to assault them. Cullen and Wilson both moved away from the cot, and a ring of men opened around two fights. Wilson was soon on the ground being kicked, but Cullen was holding his own. It was then that his assailant drew out a switchblade and made a weak lunge. Cullen pulled him into an armlock, and when the man tried to pull back, his blade went clean into his own midsection and out again. It clattered away as he fell to the floor. The quick ooze of blood on his shirtfront silenced the circle of watchers. Wilson's assailant turned and crouched at the wounded soldier's side. Slowly the man rose, not critically wounded, it turned out. A moment later the platoon sergeant arrived.

He surveyed the situation and then said, "Wilson, Cullen, under arrest." He looked at the man closest to him. "You, get the MPs."

I stood up. "Sarge, you've got the wrong men."

"Shut up, soldier. Or you'll join them."

As the crowd dissipated, I realized no one had sought the knife. Surreptitiously I began to look round for it. Finally I saw it, in the shadows beneath one of the cots left empty as a cordon between the rest of the unit and the Negroes (including me). Casually I ambled over to it and bent down. The handle had been broken on impact, and its two halves lay near the blade. I pulled out a handkerchief and picked them up with it. Surely the fingerprints on the Bakelite would clear Wilson, I thought.

On Monday morning I asked permission to report to company headquarters. I was surprised at the complete lassitude of the headquarters staff that morning after the Japanese attack. I asked a desk corporal about it.

"Everyone is just waiting for orders from the War Department. President is going to talk to Congress. It'll be on the radio this afternoon."

I walked into the company headquarters office. "Permission to speak to officer commanding?" That was a Major Barker, thin and worn from twenty-five years' service, and ready to retire. Now he knew that suddenly his career had many years and several promotions ahead if he played his cards right. That Monday morning, with nothing much to do while he waited to learn something of his future, Major Barker was prepared to see me.

"Officer Candidate Wrought." I came to attention and saluted.

Barker looked up, took my salute, and said nothing but, "Well?"

"Sir, I have come about the fight in barrack seven yesterday." With no response from the major I continued, "I witnessed the fight. The two soldiers accused were innocent of—"

Here Barker interrupted. "The colored officer candidates?"

I was relieved not to hear them called something worse. "Yes, sir."

His reply, however, surprised me. "Dismissed!" He ostentatiously turned back to the paperwork he had been ignoring when I entered.

Disobeying was a risk I was prepared to run. "I have proof, sir. And if you don't want it, perhaps a Negro newspaper up North will."

The major's look was sharp. "Proof? What are you talking about? It would be your word against everyone else in the platoon."

"Sir, the knife has only the fingerprints of the white soldier who was stabbed. That proves it was his knife, that only he held it, and that he attacked Private Wilson with it." Of course I couldn't be sure of all this, but I said it with supreme confidence.

"Hand it over, private." He put out his hand.

"Sorry, sir. I didn't bring it with me." Before he could say anything else, I went on, warming to my insubordination, toying with my superior officer. "I sent it registered mail to the Pittsburgh Courier. Or was it the Chicago Defender? Maybe it was the Amsterdam News in New York. I can't remember which now, sir. I sent letters to all three." These were the three largest Negro newspapers in the country. If they all published, it wouldn't be a local story. The brass in DC were sure to hear about it.

Now through his fury, Major Barker understood my threat plainly. He could put me in the stockade with Cullen and Wilson. But he was going to face a public relations nightmare just as

General Marshall in the War Department was beginning to think about where to assign its career regular army officers.

If I was going to get them out of the stockade, I needed to convince him the threat was real. "I do have the registration ticket and number, sir." I fished the slip out of my breast pocket. Meanwhile I had remained rigidly at attention.

The major sat staring at me for a long time. He was obviously overmastering himself. I thought I could see the train of thought passing across his forehead. General Marshall had given him a coveted assignment in the Officer Candidate School experiment. The spotlight was on Barker, and he was not going to lay an egg in full view. Marshall was famous for not giving people a second chance.

"Thank you, Private Wrought. Dismissed." As I left I could hear the clerk in the outer office called in. I smiled. I laughed. I relished my victory over the system. I hadn't thought the matter through far enough to realize I might as well have signed Cullen's and Wilson's death warrants.

The two men came back to the company that evening. Things didn't change for them of course. If anything, matters were worse. They knew that now they were marked not only as blacks, but as uppity ones. They'd raised a fist, knifed a white man, and gotten away with it. Nothing was said about why they had returned to the barrack, and no one would ask. I also noticed that all authority, including the top sergeant, had become wary of me.

<hr />

The Germans declared war on the United States three days after we went to war against Japan. By this point in the course, classroom work had given way to field exercises, map reading, camouflage, machine-gun and mortar tactics, and small group leadership. And everyone began to take it much more seriously. But whenever anyone else was under an order to do something, the two Negro soldiers were simply left to stand, as though they were observers. No one told them off for doing nothing, and no one assigned them anything to do. No one demanded they wake in the morning or even be present at roll call.

Since everyone knew Negro soldiers would never be allowed into combat, no one worried that this lack of training could harm troops under fire.

The second OCS class was only about twenty days from completing its training when we were sent to the live-fire obstacle course. The company, about 120 men, arrived in marching order, four abreast, with the first sergeant marching next to the company. When the company halted, the sergeant in charge of the obstacle course approached. "Sergeant, have your first squad man the machine guns. We'll run the company through the course by platoons." Then he looked over to the men. "Sorry, Sergeant. Your men are out of uniform for this exercise."

"What do you mean?" The company first sergeant followed his look.

"No helmets, Sarge. All they got is the helmet liners on." These were the much lighter Bakelite inserts on which the M1 helmets were placed. The M1 helmet was heavy, hot, and uncomfortable.

"Been on a long march this morning. Didn't want to carry them. Can't reschedule. Training'll fall behind."

"OK, Sarge, but tell your men to be extra good at eating dirt." I heard all this from where I stood at the back of the line with Cullen and Wilson.

Six machine guns had been set up in front of six twenty-yard-long ditches about two feet deep, across which five or six strings of barbed wire were stretched six inches aboveground. Our company sergeant ordered the first two squads — twelve men — to the Browning water-cooled machine guns, one to serve the ammunition belts and one to pull the trigger. The range sergeant warned them, "Check that the deflecting rings are tight." Everyone understood that unless the rings were tight, a machine gun bucking in the hands of a soldier could dip and fire too low. "At my command, fire in arcs across the range."

Then the company broke into platoons. Two staff sergeants set each platoon into six lines and led them to the long trenches. Once the men of each platoon were ready to crawl down the trenches, the order to commence firing was given, and the men began to work their ways toward the twenty-yard mark, where each lead soldier would find a flag to hold up indicating that firing should cease. This would happen when all six were hoisted.

Firing now commenced, and the men began to creep forward. It took each man about six minutes of writhing, clawing, elbow-churning, and knee-scraping to move themselves and their M1 rifles from one end of the course to the other. And since there were six squads in the three platoons of the company, the drill would take the better part of an hour.

By the time the last squad came forward, the Browning machine guns had been firing on and off for about forty-five minutes. Their barrels were too hot to touch. They steamed as water leaked out of breaks in the gaskets between the cooling hoses and the large cylinder surrounding the actual gun barrel. The guns had been vibrating hard while being swiveled back and forth by relatively inexperienced men at the triggers, and served by equally inexperienced loaders feeding belts into their firing chambers.

The last squad included Cullen, Wilson, me, and three other men. These were the least fit and most myopic, and therefore in the opinion of the company master sergeant, the most educated. We were actually surprised that the colored soldiers were being allowed to participate in this exercise at all. In the heat and the dust, I never noticed which of the officer candidates were at the machine guns. All I recall was that the two Negro soldiers were on the left side, I was in the third ditch, and the other three were to my right. We moved forward at about the same speed, all conscious of the fact that we were not wearing steel helmets as regulation required. But the trench was deep. Except for Wilson and Cullen, we'd all been through this obstacle course at least once before.

The six of us were halfway through when suddenly I heard a gut-wrenching groan and then a second one next to me. That was the first time I heard a man take a .50 caliber bullet. I couldn't look up immediately, and by the time I did, my platoon sergeant had moved everyone away from the machine guns and was checking their deflection rings. Later I asked myself if he were not tightening them back up.

I rose from my trench. No one had moved to Cullen or Wilson. I tried to work my way to the wounded men in the trenches but got hung up in the barbed wire. "Help them!" I demanded. "You've shot them. You can't leave them there."

I could see a couple of the men look toward the company first sergeant, who nodded. They ran along the ditches to where Wilson lay, now still, and pulled him out. Cullen was harder to reach because he was lying under two different strands of barbed wire. But it didn't matter. Both were dead of wounds to the head. Their helmet liners had been splintered back to front by the .50 caliber lead.

I moved to my right, scrambling through the trenches now vacated by the last three men in my squad, slowly walked up to the platoon sergeant, and said in a voice I didn't care who heard, "Why didn't you kill me too?"

The man looked at me with supreme hatred. Under his breath he spat out the words, "We've got other plans for you, nigger lover."

⟡

There was an inquiry, at which the two sergeants were reprimanded for failure to follow training regulations, the malfunction of the machine guns was attributed to inexperience by officer candidates, and the accident was described as regrettable. No records were kept, but everyone pretty well knew who had been assigned to the machine guns when Wilson and Cullen went into the trench. It was the two men they had fought in the barrack on Pearl Harbor Sunday.

⟡

In early February 1942, I was awarded the rank of second lieutenant with what I can only describe as distaste on the part of the company commander. He joined General McNair's staff and was killed along with the general in a friendly fire accident in Normandy in 1944.

I immediately received my orders to join the 609th Quartermaster Service Battalion at Camp Claiborne, Louisiana. It was an all-black unit that would never get closer to combat than the underside of a latrine. So far as the OCS brass were concerned, I was their first colored officer.

⟡

Tom's cell door clanked open. The warder looked in. "Exercise time, Wrought. Take your jacket. It's cold in the yard."

Tom was glad of the break. He'd been at it, writing for the better part of two days. He replaced the cap on his fountain pen and closed the composition book—now half-full—on the pen to keep his place. An hour later, cold but refreshed, he returned to the cell. Instantly he noticed that the pen was now on top of the copybook.

An unannounced search? That was hardly shocking.

But a screw taking an interest in his writing?

CHAPTER THIRTEEN

Tom settled himself again, reread the last paragraph, and began again.

For many of the soldiers on the bus from the New Orleans train depot to Camp Claiborne, the ride was a passage from the unfamiliar to the completely alien. My summer in the South in '37 had prepared me for some of it. But this trip back into American history made me despondent.

Sharecropper shacks, both white and black, leaned askew under corrugated metal roofs. Their broken windows were stuffed with newspaper. Through the screen doors you could see largely empty rooms. Before them were hand pumps over moss-covered troughs that overflowed brown water. No electric power lines ran to the roofs of any of these huts. Some did not seem to be accompanied even by a distant outhouse. For every dusty model T and model A Ford, there were a dozen mules hitched to wagons, buckboards, or just standing at posts swatting a cloud of horseflies. Every man seemed dressed in shirtless coveralls. The women were all in calico, bleached colorless by a generation of lye. There were differences between the races. The Negroes were visibly thinner and more careworn, but even the white women looked as though they'd posed for Dorothea Lange.

The army bus stopped twice at general stores that were happy to serve up fluted bottles of Coca-Cola, five cents each, out of large red bins on their porches. We soldiers sat sweating in the shade, grateful for the stop. Every toilet, every water cooler, bore the words WHITES ONLY, even though there was not a black face to be seen in any of the hamlets.

In the deeply shaded woods, you could reach out of the bus window and touch the Spanish moss hanging over the road. After a few miles, enjoyment of the exotic lushness gave way to feelings of claustrophobic oppression. By the time we were a hundred miles beyond New Orleans, I was expecting to see a lynched and burned body hanging from a tree by the roadside. I admit it wasn't reasonable. It was pure emotion, driven by the sheer prejudice of a northerner, the growing anxiety of a city dweller, and a deepening feeling of regret for anyone who had to live here, black or white, but especially black.

⟞⟝

When I got there, in 1942, Camp Claiborne sprawled across a hundred square miles of rural Louisiana. Past the gate and the few permanent buildings, what you saw was a vast sea of thirty-foot by thirty-foot tents in square arrays on wooden platforms. Beyond this was an even larger expanse of flat fields, dotted by an occasional tree. At the gate when I presented my orders, no one seemed to know where my unit—Company Two, 609th Quartermaster Service Battalion—was. No one seemed to have even heard of it.

I was sweating and my duffel was beginning to force my shoulder into a permanent list when I spotted a Negro soldier. He wore what looked like a prison uniform, blue denim with a sort of a pork-pie denim cap, and he was hauling a large metal trash barrel. I approached, dropped my duffel, and spoke to him. "Soldier." He stopped, but neither came to attention nor saluted. I was indifferent to military courtesies myself, and so I said nothing. I just asked for my unit. The man pointed to the end of the line of large platform tents. Without a word he went back to his work.

For another ten minutes, I walked down duckboard between the large taut lodgepole tents squared off with military precision. The walkway ended in a quagmire of ruts and tire tracks. I was confronted with about fifty pup tents, before which stood a very badly erected headquarters tent. There were a few dozen men milling around these tents, all dressed in the denim I thought of as prison garb, no unit designation of any kind.

Nothing much was happening in the company headquarters tent. I walked in, put down my duffel, and addressed the white corporal sitting at the desk but apparently not engaged in any work. He put down a well-worn copy of *Argosy* magazine, rose slowly, and made a slovenly salute.

I began, "Lieutenant Wrought. If this is the 609th Quartermaster Service Battalion, Second Company, I've been assigned to it."

"It is, sir."

"Where's the captain in charge?"

"Officers' quarters, sir."

"I see. Company first sergeant?"

"Transferred, sir. No replacement yet. Never did much anyway."

"Well, can you show me around, Corporal . . ."

"Manion, sir."

We began a tour of the pup tents pitched randomly on ground wet from winter rains. Five feet wide and seven feet long, not very waterproof to begin with, from each of them came a waft of mildew and body odor. Poking my head into an unoccupied tent, I found the basic army mummy sack, without its canvas water-resistant shell, moldering in the damp earth, surrounded by GI—government issue—detritus. A few of the men in the area rose, and one assayed a salute, which I returned. We moved on to the latrines and showers, which showed no signs of the maintenance to which so much emphasis had been placed in OSC.

"Where's the kitchen and mess for this unit, Manion?"

"I don't know, Lieutenant. I eat at the white troops' mess."

We walked back to the company command tent.

"Corporal, I am going to billet in this tent. Get a cot in here before I get back. I am going to see the captain in charge of the company. What is his name?"

"Captain Smythe, sir."

I had one and only one interview with Captain Smythe. When I finally found him in a wooden frame building near the quartermaster's stores building, he was packing his bag.

"Lieutenant Wrought reporting, sir." I saluted, and he returned the salute in a perfunctory way.

"Just in time, Wrought. I have been reassigned to another unit. White men." He said it with satisfaction.

"When will your replacement arrive, sir?"

"No idea. Nobody wants the assignment, uh . . . Wrought, is that your name? How did you draw it?"

I felt like saying, "Nigger lover." "Don't know, sir."

"Well, Wrought, it's your unit now. Maybe you'll get a captain or maybe not. Till then you're in charge."

So, a fresh second lieutenant with an entire company to command. "One more question, sir?"

"Yes, Lieutenant?"

"Who's my immediate superior?"

"Well, there's no captain, no major. Probably a light colonel somewhere in Headquarters Company of the new division being formed."

"Which one?"

"Eighty-Second Airborne."

<hr />

"Corporal, assemble the men." It was my first company order.

"How, sir?" The corporal seemed to be at a complete loss.

"You mean the unit doesn't fall in for roll call every day?"

"That's a sergeant's job. Not mine." The corporal's tone was not insubordinate. It was resigned.

Suddenly I realized that I was going to have to use everything I'd learned in OCS immediately and without any advice or practice.

I walked out of the tent and placed myself among the fifty or so pup tents behind it. In a few minutes, I was surrounded by about eighty-five men, most of them looking decidedly unmilitary, in varying states of dress, many needing a shave, and a few who were either hungover, sick, or very despondent.

"I'm your new lieutenant, men. My name is Wrought. We are going to be together for quite a while."

From somewhere in the mass of men came a Northern voice. "Does that mean a week?"

"No. I'm staying with you for the duration." There was a ripple of appreciable laughter. At least I had their attention. "The first thing this company needs is a top sergeant and four master sergeants. Hands up, everyone with a high school diploma." Nine men raised their hands. "Who's the oldest one of you?" One of the men stepped forward. "Name?"

"Private Jenkins, sir."

"First Sergeant Jenkins now. Pick four master sergeants out of the high school men and form up in squads."

Manion now spoke quietly. "You can't do that, Lieutenant. Coloreds ain't allowed to be noncoms." I thought at least he had the decency, or was it prudence, to keep his voice down.

I turned to him. "That'll be all, Private Manion. Take your gear to Headquarters Company and tell them to find you another billet. But first take the stripes off and cut the demotion order." I turned to the men, whose attention my demotion of Manion had now secured. "Anyone here type?"

"Took a typing course in school, sir." It was one of the high school grads.

"Alright, Corporal . . ." It was another instant promotion. He volunteered his name. "Simeon. You're company clerk now."

The new noncoms had no trouble forming the men up into squads and platoons. I addressed Jenkins, the new top sergeant, in words everyone could hear. "Have all the tents struck. I want them arranged by squad and platoon in military order. All bedding is to be aired. Then report to me."

I was in the company headquarters tent unpacking my gear when Jenkins arrived a few minutes later. "You gonna sleep here, sir?" His question came with a hint of incredulousness.

"Yes, Sergeant. I am. Now, what is the first thing this company needs?"

"Lieutenant, we need cots. We've been sleeping on the ground for weeks, and now the rain's comin'."

"Jenkins, cots won't fit in pup tents. Why is the company sleeping on the ground in pup tents anyway?" My question was rhetorical, and the answer was obvious. Before he could reply, I had an idea. "As soon as the tents are set up again, form up platoons one and two."

A few minutes later I had sent the first platoon to the quartermaster construction depot, with instructions to draw four gross of cinder blocks. Meanwhile I led the second platoon to the Eighty-Second Airborne Division military field hospital unit. At the command tent I asked for the medical officer in charge, hoping he would be a conscripted northerner unschooled in Southern ways. His name was Major Goldberg, MD, and he was.

"What can I do for you, Lieutenant?"

"Sir, I have a company of 120 men, all sleeping on the wet ground. Pretty soon they are going to start filling up the sick bay . . . if there is one for colored troops." He looked over my shoulder at the platoon I had brought along. "I'd like to borrow 120 field stretchers, sir. Your unit won't need them till the division leaves Claiborne. I'll sign a receipt for them and have them back to you in good order when you need them."

"What are you going to do with them, Lieutenant?"

"Open them up and rest them on cinder blocks to get my men off the ground and keep them dry."

Major Goldberg turned to his company clerk. "Corporal, take this platoon to the depot and tell the quartermaster sergeant to issue these men 120 collapsible stretchers."

That evening I began to cut new standing orders for the company: battledress fatigues at all times, no more prisoners' denims, all work details by squad or platoon only, to be approved by lieutenant commanding, unit march to mess, work detail, inspection and roll call daily. And finally, all platoons without service duties to fall in for close-order drill mornings and afternoons.

"That's pretty rough, sir. We don't even have rifles." Jenkins was shaking his head.

"Those are my orders, Sergeant." I couldn't believe I was talking like this — me, the anarchist, the subversive, the former party member.

The next day I denied several requests for fatigue parties from noncoms of white units. "Sorry, no men available for labor today," was my reply. I was counting on the fact that the white sergeants wouldn't challenge the refusal of an officer.

We began drill that morning far enough out on the drill fields so that no one noticed.

By the end of the week, I thought the men were ready to be seen by others. So, I led the company out into the middle of the parade ground, stood back with the first sergeant, and ordered the four master sergeants to drill their platoons.

We had been at it for an hour or so, with breaks, when I noticed a group of officers watching us from the edge of the platform tent area. Suddenly a runner came up to me from the group. "Report to General Bradley, Lieutenant."

My career as an officer was about to come to an end, I realized. I followed the runner back to the group from which he had been sent, came to attention in front of Bradley, and saluted. "Lieutenant Wrought reporting, sir." He returned the salute.

"Son, what are those colored boys doing out there marching without their weapons?"

"Sir, their weapons were taken away for a white unit that arrived without any."

"I see." He turned to an aide. "Take care of that, will you, Major James?"

Now another officer addressed me, a large lieutenant colonel, young for his rank, but with a paunch that began where the necktie was tucked into his shirt and lapped over his belt. His collar bore the tabs of the quartermaster corps. In a deep Southern accent he said, "Lieutenant, do I see four colored sergeants in front of me?"

"No, sir. There are five, including the company master sergeant."

The colonel looked at me. "Who promoted those"—I could see the word *niggers* forming on his lips, but he must have thought better of it—"colored boys to noncommissioned officers?"

I was silent till General Bradley added, "Answer Colonel Folsom, Lieutenant." It was a name I was to learn better.

"Sir, I did."

Here Bradley intervened. "Why did you do that, Lieutenant?"

"Sir, I am the senior officer commanding the company pending arrival of a major or a captain. The unit had lost all its white noncoms as well as its white officers before I arrived. I was told by the divisional staff not to expect any replacements. All the white officers and NCOs were needed elsewhere." I stopped for a moment. "Did I do wrong, sir?"

Instead of answering me directly the general said, "Carry on, Lieutenant." I saluted, made an about-turn, and walked off as quickly as I could.

The next morning, twenty crates, each containing a half-dozen M1 rifles, arrived at my command tent.

<hr />

I didn't stick my neck out again until one afternoon two months later, when I noticed a company of infantry packing to leave its platform tent billets. By this time I'd been in the army long enough to know that quartermasters don't really keep track of much. In a war like this, no one was encouraged to be a bean counter. I knew we couldn't move into white quarters. But I also knew that if no one were to occupy these tents for a few days or more, they would simply vanish from army records.

I watched for twenty-four hours. Then I called my sergeants together. "Tomorrow morning, I want every man to fall out into carpenters' parties; distribute hammers, saws, crowbars, and anything else you can get your hands on. Then I want the men to take down those tents and platforms and rebuild them here."

"Yes, sir." Jenkins paused for a moment. "Won't anyone stop us?"

"Stop a party of colored soldiers doing non-combat-related labor? Nothing to worry about."

———

A year later I was ordered to report to division headquarters, where I found an almost entirely new set of staff officers, who knew and cared no more about the 609th than did their predecessors. The one holdover was Folsom, the quartermaster corps lieutenant colonel who had challenged my promotions. He didn't seem to remember me when I reported and didn't bother to return my salute either. He looked up briefly from his desk, handed me a few pieces of paper, and said, "Dismissed." I saluted again, made an about-turn, walked out of the building, and read the flimsy sheets. They were pro forma division orders. The first one promoted me to first lieutenant, the second one promoted me to temporary captain, and the third one authorized me to promote a sergeant of my choice to lieutenant. I wasn't entirely surprised at these orders. A company required a captain to command it, and its usual complement of lieutenants was at least two. But no officer had arrived at the 609th since my posting.

———

"Sergeant Jenkins." I beckoned my top NCO into the company headquarters tent.

"Yes, sir." He came to attention.

"At ease, Sergeant. I have authority to promote you to lieutenant as from today." I smiled broadly and put out my hand. "Well done, Lieutenant Jenkins."

Jenkins visibly grimaced. "Is that an order, sir? 'Cause if it is, it'll be the first one of yours I'll disobey."

"I thought you'd be pleased. You earned it. First Negro officer in the unit, maybe the only one in the whole division."

"Exactly, sir. That's the trouble." Jenkins continued, "You Northerners don't understand, sir. But down here in the deep South, if I took to wearin' lieutenant's bars on my shoulders, it'd be like walking around with a bullseye on my back. Not just in town, if we ever got there, but on the base. Every cracker redneck in the division would have to salute me." He stopped, and together we shared the image. "And that would be about as bad for me as if I had been caught wolf-whistling a white girl."

"I see." Jenkins's analysis was irrefutable. I'd do him no favors enforcing my order.

⟨⟩

The 609th reached Britain in the fall of 1943. We were billeted in what the Brits called "Nissen huts" and we called Quonset huts, just outside the town of Arundel, east of Portsmouth. The town wasn't much more than a single street of whitewashed, timbered, two-story buildings. A post office, a tea shop, a millenary, dry goods, a hotel—The Swan—and a pub across the bridge over the River Arun. Beyond what passed for a high street, there were clusters of thatched-roof farm buildings and grain fields that ran down to a shingle on the English Channel.

Arundel was surrounded by vast parks of army stores, and especially motor vehicles. The 609th was responsible for readying jeeps, amphibious vehicles—DUKWs or "ducks" as they were called—and most of all, hundreds of "deuce-and-a-half" trucks for use after their shipment to Britain. These triple-axle, two-and-a-half-ton trucks were the backbone of our army, and increasingly of the Brits' and the Russian armies too. To withstand the trans-atlantic crossing, they had been drained of oil, sealed shut, and then covered in grease. It was the very dirty job of the 609th to degrease and make them ready for use. The first thing many of the men had to do was learn how to drive these trucks.

⊷

Ours was among the first American units in that part of Sussex. I still remember the stupefaction with which the men returned to the billets after their first visit to the town. There had been no off-limits signs, no colored washrooms, no separate facilities whatever. They had been served in tea rooms, welcomed in pubs, sold goods at the counters of the small shops along with everyone else. There was no colored bar in Britain, and for the first time in their lives, they were being treated as equals.

Men who went into nearby Worthing, or farther afield to Portsmouth or Southampton, reported that the US Army had begun to impose Jim Crow in these larger towns. But Arundel remained unaffected.

One afternoon a white staff sergeant led a half-dozen soldiers on a break into the Swan. He looked around at the black faces. Then in a loud voice he announced, "This pub is off limits to colored troops. As of now."

Trying not to sound provocative, one of the 609th's master sergeants—a higher rank—stepped forward to contradict him. "Sorry, Sarge, you're mistaken. If the place were off limits to anyone, there'd be a notice. You know that." Then with the slightest pause, he went on, "Buy you a drink?"

A white corporal could no longer repress himself. "Goddamn, nigger, who made you a fucking sergeant?"

The white sergeant looked at his companions and smiled. "Run these coons out of here." When the fight was over, three minutes later, the two whites still standing were permitted to help their wounded comrades out.

Three days later a squad of MPs arrived to erect an OUT OF BOUNDS FOR COLORED SOLDIERS sign in front of the Swan. It was then that the citizens of Arundel showed their mettle. No sooner had the MP squad erected the sign than a half dozen of the local women, together with a pair of elderly men, swarmed over it. With hammers and crowbars, they pulled it down.

I had nothing to do with all this, of course. But it was part of what has made life in Britain possible for me.

⟫═══

As the winter of 1944 turned to spring, it was clear that the invasion of France was approaching. By the end of May, there were hardly any trucks left in our compound, and no new ones were coming in anymore. In the first few days of June, the roads toward Portsmouth and Southampton were choked with military vehicles moving toward the embarkation points. The weather was poor—cold, rainy, with a strong chop on the channel visible from the beaches just south of Arundel. The night of the fifth, we watched the steady stream of C-47s towing gliders pass over the town heading across the channel. White men were going to fight and die, and the men in the 609th wanted to join them and do so at their sides. It's remarkable how the martial emotions obliterate reason.

The next evening I was in the Swan pub along with a dozen other men from the 609th when Eisenhower's voice came over the BBC.

"People of Western Europe: A landing was made this morning on the coast of France by troops of the Allied Expeditionary

Force. This landing is part of the concerted United Nations plan for the liberation of Europe, made in conjunction with our great Russian allies."

It was the last sentence that made me remember his words so well. Who made him add them?

The 609th had almost nothing to do for the next three months.

One morning at the very end of August, Sergeant Jenkins came into my office. "Message for you, Captain. They want you at battalion headquarters in Portsmouth, ASAP." Before I could give an order he continued, "Jeep's ready, sir."

"OK, Sarge. Have we done anything wrong?"

He shook his head.

The roads were empty now as the jeep drove to Portsmouth, but on either side one could see the detritus, the remnants, the waste of an infinitely rich nation at war. I kept thinking, *It's just the same—wasting my men and a million more like them, keeping them out of combat, tossed away like trash.*

Upon my arrival in Portsmouth, I found myself facing for the third time the same paunchy quartermaster colonel who had been at General Bradley's side back at Camp Claiborne when all he commanded was the Eighty-Second Airborne instead of the entire US Army in Europe. By this time I even knew the quartermaster corps officer's name, Folsom, though mine still appeared to make no impression on him. He evidently had no memory of our meeting on that parade ground in Louisiana two years before.

Folsom looked up at me from his desk, took my salute without more than a glance, and turned back to the papers. He did not ask me to sit, and he certainly showed no sign that we had met before. His accent had lost none of its Southern drawl. "Captain, how many of the . . . colored boys" —why, I wondered again, didn't he just say *niggers*— "in your company can drive a deuce and a half?" The deuce and a half was the two-and-a-half-ton truck on which my men had worked for the better part of six months.

"Every one of them, sir."

"Every last one of them?"

"Yes, sir. They all learned while setting them up for the combat troops."

"Alright." He looked up at me. "Your boys are going to France after all. Seems the First and Third Armies' breakouts from Normandy are outrunning their supplies. Supreme headquarters is organizing a convoy system from the port at Cherbourg to wherever the front is. They need drivers, and your men aren't doing anything much here in England." He handed me a file full of orders, requisitions, and authorizations. "Get on with it. Dismissed."

I saluted and turned. Every man in the Second Company of the 609th was about to find himself a lot closer to combat than we ever thought we could get.

⋙

Tom was deep enough into his recollection of the war that he did not hear the guard open his door. The man poked his head in and, seeing Tom on his cot, said, "Exercise time, Wrought."

Once the warder had turned away, Tom pulled a hair from his head, moistened its ends with bits of saliva, and pressed them carefully under the front and back covers of the composition book he had nearly filled. It was a simple trick he'd been taught by the OSS in Stockholm after the war. When he returned forty-five minutes later, everything looked untouched in the cell, but the hair was no longer over the pages. Someone, he thought, was evidently very interested in Tom Wrought's autobiography. He had come back to the cell eager to continue. But now he hesitated. The realization that his readership might not be limited to his solicitor frightened him, even though—in fact, because—he had no idea why anyone else would care what he wrote.

CHAPTER FOURTEEN

Folsom was not mistaken about how urgent the need was for the 609th in France. Within a few weeks after D-day, the US First and Third Armies were outrunning their supplies of gasoline and ammunition. So someone dreamed up a radical solution. Every spare truck on the Normandy beaches was going to be inserted into an endless conveyer belt reaching from the beaches and the port of Cherbourg right to the front and then back again. But there weren't any drivers for what they called the Red Ball Express. And that's when they thought of all those Negro service troops left back in England. Their subsequent achievement in winning the war was so important that when Hollywood came to make a movie about it in 1952, the drivers were mostly all white.

From the moment I issued the orders, the excitement of the move to France was palpable. The men packed only what one would take going into combat, including the M1 rifles General Bradley had given the unit back in Louisiana. Nothing could dampen their enthusiasm, not the seasickness of the channel, nor the cold and wet of the open trucks that took the company to Saint-Lô where the Red Ball began, nor even the prospect of a bivouac in pup tents again.

Less than four days after I got my orders, the 609th Quartermaster Service Battalion was inducted into the conveyer belt of trucks that moved around the clock for the next three months across a loop of one-way roads from the coast to the battlefield on the other side of Paris and back.

The 609th began to drive the very night we arrived, in three convoys, each led by a jeep, navigating the route through Vire, Argentan, and Dreux to Soissons on the other side of Paris. No headlights were allowed, so the trucks had to stay close just to follow in the dark. Traveling faster than the trucks were designed for, carrying ammunition and gasoline, kept every man at the wheel, and their relief drivers, on the edge all night.

I was in the lead jeep of our first convoy when the sun rose at about five fifteen on the French countryside fifty kilometers west of Soissons. There was a streak of gold across the horizon, glimmering through the leafy plane trees that lined the road. The rising sun was turning the fields from deep purple to the tawny yellow of a lioness's coat. The villages of Aisne were rousing themselves from a night probably made sleepless by the never-ending din of a thousand deuce and a halfs passing through in an endless ribbon. I was struck that la France profonde had been untouched by the war. The neat brick homes, the carefully pruned plane trees, the high fences, and even the plump cows and calmly grazing sheep testified to the wisdom of losing their 1940 war quickly and allowing others to win the 1944 war for them.

The Soissons bridgehead was a vast field of mud that morning, strewn with trucks, moving cranes, stacks of crates, fields of jerrycans and motor oil, over which men swarmed like ants tending colonies. Our trucks were being unloaded even before the drivers had climbed down from their cabs.

Walking to the drivers' billets, I watched the men unloading the several hundred trucks that had arrived with ours. Most trucks were emptied into two equal but ever-increasing stacks. I stopped and asked a soldier about it. He replied, "Not sure, sir. I think one is for First Army—Hodges, and the other is for Third—Patton. Each one suspects the other is getting more."

"Thanks, soldier. Makes sense."

I tumbled into the first cot I found free. It was in the enlisted men's tent, but no one had the heart or nerve or perhaps interest in rousing me and sending me to officer quarters. We were allowed four hours rest, and then we drove back in the daylight to Saint-Lô, not the way we came but on another one-way route that ran north of the outgoing one, 240 miles, eight hours back to Saint-Lô.

Once my unit was on the ground in Europe, the temptation to find a way into the shooting war proved overpowering. That's when I realized there might be a way to force the army to allow the 609th to fight. Back in New York, one of the most left-wing political figures was the congressman from the twentieth district on Manhattan's Upper East Side, Spanish Harlem. His name was Vito Marcantonio. Like other Communist Party members, I had worked for his American Labor Party congressional campaign in '38, and again in '40 after I had quit the party. The congressman knew me by name and had even sent me a note of congratulations when I passed through the army's second Officer Candidate School. Now, after a month in the Red Ball Express, I would ask him for a favor.

The army censors who read all V-mail would never deliver the letter I intended to write. So, I went to a French post office in Saint-Lô, bought an aerogram, wrote to my congressman, and dropped it in a French postbox. In my letter I told Marcantonio about the Red Ball and its success, the splendid work Negro soldiers were doing, their esprit de corps, and the waste of their fighting qualities by the War Department. I made it plain that, as a white officer, I was prepared to lead my Negro soldiers anywhere against the Germans. Then I asked the congressman to press the War Department to allow my unit to fight.

Be careful what you wish for.

One morning in the middle of October, I was leading a convoy of five trucks, all carrying jerrycans of gasoline. About fifty miles beyond Paris, one of the MPs who controlled traffic all along the Red Ball Highway signaled my trucks onto a side road, following signs marked CRECY-LA-CHAPELLE. I'd been dozing in the front seat of the jeep while Jenkins drove. The turn woke me. "Why'd we just turn off the Red Ball route, Sergeant?"

"Oh, happens here every few trips, especially when we're carrying gas cans, sir. MPs signal us to pull off, and they unload about half the cans here."

A half mile down the road toward Crecy, another MP came forward and signaled the convoy into a dead end between the plastered back walls of two barns that bracketed the lane. Once we came to a stop, a dozen men came forward to unload. None was a GI. Several wore the sleeveless leather vests common in the French countryside, and some had armbands with the letters FFI — *Forces Françaises de l'Intérieur*. Others wore armbands marked FTP for *Francs Tireurs et Partisans*. A few others, with British-made STEN submachine guns slung over their shoulders, watched the unloading proceed. The soldier drivers had all left their cabs and begun to stretch. Some moved well away from the trucks and lit up. Nothing seemed quite right about what was going on, so I walked over to the MP, who came to attention and saluted.

"Say, soldier, why are we unloading here, and who are these guys?" I tried to make my question conversational.

"Dunno, Captain. Maybe the brass over in that staff car can tell you." He jerked his head back down the lane to the main road. There a fastback four-door Dodge in the green paint of a US Army staff car was parked. The winged ball device on the side indicated it was a quartermaster corps vehicle. As I watched, a Frenchman in civilian clothes got out of the car, and a black Citroen Traction Avant sedan pulled up. He got in, and it drove away. As did the quartermaster's Dodge.

Was the US Army supplying the French resistance? Was it doing so this far behind the front? I thought about the armbands worn by the men unloading the trucks. The FTP, the *Francs Tireurs et Partisans*, were the Communist resistance. The others, with the FFI armbands, were the Gaullist résistance. These two organizations hated each other almost as much as they hated the Germans. Why were they working together here?

Suddenly it seemed pretty obvious that this wasn't resupply for the resistance. It was a diversion of fuel onto the French black market. I shouted out, "OK, men, saddle up, double-time. We're getting out of here, now." My unit ran back to their trucks and began backing them out of the cul-de-sac so quickly the men unloading had to jump off.

The MP reached my jeep just as we turned around and were about to drive off behind the trucks. "Sir, they haven't finished—"

"But we have." I saluted him with a wry smile. Turning to the man at the wheel, I gave the order. "Drive, Sergeant."

When we got to Soissons, I made my way to the command tents. There to my surprise was a fastback four-door Dodge staff car with the same quartermaster insignia I'd seen in Crecy-la-Chapelle. The tent flaps were open, and I could see the officers inside. There, on the telephone, in a heated conversation, was Lieutenant Colonel Folsom again, crossing my path: first, dressing me down in front of Omar Bradley on that dusty parade ground in Louisiana, then handing me a promotion to captain without even looking at me, and finally, sending us across the channel to man the Red Ball Express. Now he was the officer I'd have to report black marketeering to. This was strange, like drawing a full house three times in a row. I entered the tent and stood before the clerk. "I'd like to see Colonel Folsom, Corporal."

The man turned from his typewriter to the colonel and back to me. "Soon as he gets off the phone, Captain."

I stood there and could not help listening to the colonel's side of the sharp, loud, and obscenity-laced conversation: "What the fuck . . . Calm down and start over . . . Why did they stop unloading? . . . What do you mean, an officer ordered the trucks to leave? . . . A white officer with the colored troops? . . . I'll find out what I can . . . Yes, yes, I'll make it up to you. How much?"

I had heard quite enough. "Corporal, I don't think I'll bother the colonel after all, thanks." I tried to look casual enough not to be noticed as I left.

How long could I hide from a light colonel in my own chain of command, one that might even remember where he had seen me before, all the way back through Portsmouth to Camp Claiborne in 1942?

⟞⟝

Three days later I was leading another gasoline-heavy convoy back to Soissons. In the brightening early morning haze just at the Crecy-la-Chapelle turnoff, there was an MP, flagging us to turn off the Red Ball route again.

I leaned over to the jeep driver. "Sarge, don't stop. Go right past this MP and speed up." Then I pulled off my helmet, slipped down to the floorboards, and pulled my poncho over my head. I was counting on the fact that all black men looked alike to a white policeman. The jeep lurched forward, and after a few minutes, the driver leaned over and shook me.

"All clear, Captain. Trucks all still behind us."

When we got to the unloading area, I told the men that I was heading back immediately, and then I found an empty deuce-and-a-half truck heading back and climbed up to the running board. "Mind if I ride along in the back, soldier?"

Looking at the two bars on my helmet, the man replied, "Be my guest, Captain." Suddenly those two bars began to make me feel very conspicuous. I walked to the back of the truck, and before I climbed in, I grabbed a handful of mud and covered the bars on my helmet.

I got back to Saint-Lô late in the afternoon. Without getting much sleep bouncing around the back of the truck, I went to my tent and sacked out. Early the next morning, Sergeant Jenkins shook me awake.

"Sorry, Captain, but I need to talk to you."

I rolled over and looked up at him. "No problem, Sarge. What is it?"

"Yesterday, two MPs came to the company clerk's tent asking for you by name. I told them you were up at the bridgehead east of Paris, and I thought you wouldn't be back till tonight."

"I grabbed a truck right back after we got there this morning."

"Well, sir, I didn't like the look of them MPs. I'm pretty sure I've seen one of them detour jerrycan convoys outside of Soissons."

"And he knew my name?"

"Yes, sir. You've been a thorn in a lot of sides for a long time, Captain. I think you'd be wise to make yourself scarce the next few days."

I rose from the cot. "Good advice, Sergeant Jenkins."

"One more thing, Captain." He handed me a First Army field-orders envelope. "This came for you just after you left two days ago."

I opened it, looked at Jenkins, and asked, "Can you keep things under control for a day or two?"

He nodded and left me.

I studied the field order more carefully.

To: Wrought, T., Captain (acting), Quartermaster Corps

From: David Y. Hurwitz, Major, Office of Chief of Staff, G-2 Intelligence, Twenty-Eighth Infantry Division, First Army

Subject: Report to this officer, SHAEF Headquarters, 14:30 hours, 29 October 1944

SHAEF—Supreme Headquarters Allied Expeditionary Forces—was in Rambouillet, halfway back to Soissons, and the meeting time on the twenty-ninth was exactly eighteen hours from that moment. I showered, shaved, put on as close to a class A uniform as I could contrive, and headed for the convoy assembly area. Within an hour I found a jeep headed to SHAEF and showed my orders to the officer driving it.

"Hop in, Captain. I'm Major Faubus. What's your name?" That's how I met the future governor of Arkansas. We had a lot in common back then and found it out driving for a long day toward the war.

⟨⬩⟩

As I waited outside Eisenhower's headquarters in Rambouillet, I had to salute so many staff officers my arm and shoulder grew weary. Five minutes before the appointed time, a major in combat uniform—the first I'd seen there—arrived and began looking around. We saw each other at the same moment. I smiled and saluted.

He frowned and beckoned me over. "Wrought? I'm Major Hurwitz. Follow me, Captain."

We entered the chateau and found our way into G-2—the intelligence unit—where he took an empty desk, pulled a file from his worn map case, and pointedly did not invite me to sit. The man was gaunt and pale, with dark rings of sleeplessness round his eyes. His face was twisted into a permanent expression of worry.

"Captain, you should be court-martialed for violating the chain of command. Trying to get your pinko congressman to interfere in War Department business."

"Did it work, sir?"

"Shut up and listen." This man was not going to allow me to engage in anything like a conversation. "I'm assistant intelligence for the Twenty-Eighth Division. My division commander, General Cota, needs infantry replacements, and he'll take them anywhere he can get them. Go back to your unit. Pick out a platoon, twenty-four of your best men. Report to me at division headquarters in Aachen. Just one platoon is all. And take off those captain's bars. You have to resume the rank of first lieutenant if you want this assignment."

"Sir, you know my unit is composed of Negro soldiers only?"

"Of course I know it. But they're the only source of able-bodied men we can find for infantry replacements. You don't think the regular army wants to do this, do you?"

"Why not, sir?"

"Because they think Negroes can't follow orders, aren't smart enough to fight, and are cowards to boot."

I couldn't keep my mouth shut. "And maybe they don't have much to fight for either."

He looked up at me and sighed heavily. "Sit down, Captain . . . Lieutenant?" There was a question in the word. I nodded, agreeing to his terms. "Some of us have been trying to get colored troops into combat since we joined up. But the career army was built on generations of brass from the South, where segregation is a way of life."

"I trained in Louisiana, sir."

"Well, our division commander, Cota, he's from Massachusetts, and practically the whole staff are college men from Pennsylvania.

So, when the infantry units began scraping the bottom of the barrel, a couple of us talked him into trying out Negro soldiers."

"Isn't this against regulations, sir?"

"Absolutely. If it doesn't work, heads will roll. But the army isn't my career. If they send me home, that's fine with me. Same goes for most of us in G-2 of the Twenty-Eighth Division. And General Cota's been scorched by Ike already. He doesn't care. We need the men." He paused, lit a cigarette, offered me one, and finally seemed to relax a little. "Here's the problem. The same squads, platoons, companies, divisions have been doing all the fighting in this war practically since North Africa two years ago. No rotation." He spat the words. "Well, by now we've lost thirty percent of our men, and there aren't enough replacements coming in from the States. In the last few weeks, the Twenty-Eighth Division has had five thousand casualties fighting in the most awful place."

"So, is that where I'm headed if I can round up a platoon to come with me?"

"Yup. The Hürtgen Forest."

⟨⟩

At the beginning of November 1944, Sergeant Jenkins and I took twenty-four men into the Hürtgen Forest. Three weeks later, only eight of us came out. We were just a small part of the worst defeat the US Army suffered in the entire campaign in Europe.

The Second Battalion of the 112th Infantry Regiment, to which we were assigned, didn't have much use for two dozen black soldiers with no infantry training led by an inexperienced lieutenant. The captain commanding it left us just beyond the village of

Vossenack, well before the woods that sloped steeply down to a river called the Kall. "Dig in down at the river at the bottom of the ravine, Wrought." Then he got into his jeep and headed one kilometer back to the village.

We watched the rest of the regiment, the First and the Third Battalions, as they passed us heading down to the footbridge crossing the Kall and began moving north up along the ridge on the other side that paralleled the water. It was a narrow track that headed toward the town of Schmidt. The last noncom who passed us called back to us in a friendly way, "After we take Schmidt, we'll send back for you to serve dinner."

———◆———

The Kall River was just a stream. Looking across it and back up the ridge behind me, I made my first tactical decision. It would be suicide digging in where we'd been ordered to, on the bank of the Kall with a steep forested ridge rising behind us. We needed to be at the top of that ridge, with the town at our backs, looking down at the stream.

"Sergeant Jenkins, have the men go back up this ridge the way we came. Get them to dig in at the top, make some fires, and cook up some C-rations. Then send half of them back to the church in the town. They can bed down for the night."

It had been gray all day. The canopy of the pine trees kept us in a perpetual dusk, and the ground was a deep bed of sodden pine needles. The C-rations were warmed over the small fires, and then we rigged the shelter halves of the pup tents for the night. We could hear small arms fire, the burp of machine guns, the whoosh of mortars up ahead of us toward Schmidt. Meanwhile a steady stream of medics and aid men were bringing wounded up the narrow uphill track now churned into mud. Many of the medics had large nonregulation improvised red crosses on their helmets.

By four o'clock in the morning, the novelty of being combat troops had worn off, and every man along the ridge, including me, was rapidly becoming frightened. In my case it was cold hands and an uncontrollable tremble. Several of the men complained of stomach cramps and came back from a hastily dug latrine in as much pain as when they had left their foxholes.

"What are you doing here?" I heard myself asking no one in particular but loud enough for the man in the next foxhole to hear. The same three or four thoughts kept rotating through my consciousness. It's nice to fantasize fighting for your country. But that doesn't last a moment in combat. Oh, for a flesh wound and a ticket out. I had gone out of my way to get here, and these foolish men had eagerly followed. Now we all might as well be dead. After about an hour, I was able to calm down.

In the morning the men were relieved by the platoon I had sent back to the village church.

That next day there was nothing more to do but dig in further. We felled some trees, cut some boughs to make lean-tos against the intermittent rain, and waited.

Before sunrise on the third morning, the fourth of November, our shooting war started. Suddenly the trees above us were splintering from artillery airbursts. The first time the sound of a German 88 millimeter or a howitzer penetrates your body, you are certain that you are dying. It doesn't come in your ears. The sound wave just crumples your entire body, forcing you into the ground. You find mud in your mouth, and you are vibrating with the burst of acoustical energy. You don't even notice the limbs and branches striking your body, or the rocks and clumps of dirt rebounding from your helmet. And before you have pulled yourself together, another airburst arrives, and it starts over again. I tried to shout to the men in the line. I couldn't actually hear myself shouting. My ears weren't working.

By the previous morning we had already begun to see men from the First and Third Battalions coming back from Schmidt. They came in twos and threes—with rifles slung, quietly, not looking left or right, and not under any command. That third night the trickle turned to a stream of men. Then the shelling began.

Suddenly we found ourselves in the midst of what looked like a retreat, then a rout, and finally sheer, mass desertion. Men streaming up the track back from Schmidt, dropping weapons and ammunition at the riverbank when they saw the ridge they'd have to climb. As they came up and passed through, between the airbursts, we shouted at them to tell us what was happening down in Schmidt. All we heard was "Too much artillery," "They're coming," and "No tanks, no support." Evidently the First and Third Battalions had not been able to hold Schmidt, and their officers had lost control of their men.

In midmorning a weasel—a small, tracked vehicle—came down from the village carrying a couple of machine guns and ammunition. It reached the crest of the ridge and stopped. The corporal driving looked down at the steady stream of men coming back up the ridge from the Kall and immediately pushed the weapons and equipment off the vehicle. Then he backed up his weasel, turned it toward a large tree stump, and drove it over the obstacle until it was motionless, tracks moving in the air, listing dangerously down the slope. With his weasel now immobile, he had a good excuse and began walking back toward Vossenack with the other retreating men. That was how we finally secured some automatic weapons. Even before I had given any orders, two of the master sergeants had sent men to the weasel to strip it of anything we could use.

Frightened men who looked like combat veterans were streaming up the ridge past us, heading for the shelter of the village. But my men were staying in their foxholes. Why? Was it because they had not seen any Germans yet? Was it foolhardiness? None of them was becoming accustomed to the constant barrage of airbursts, to the cold, wet misery of a hole in the ground now four feet deep, the lack of warm food, or even the chance to relieve oneself against a tree. But they wouldn't move, except for the twelve-hour rotation Sergeant Jenkins had set up.

That fourth day we suffered our first two real casualties, both to shrapnel from an airburst. I was worried that our wounded would not be treated, but I was wrong. Two corpsmen coming up the ravine leading some walking wounded immediately found stretchers, and the men were carried to an aid station in the village.

Then the barrage lifted, and it became silent.

After about an hour of the eerie silence, through the woods to our right and north, well before we could see them, we heard the sounds of running men, their equipment jangling on their belts. Suddenly they were upon us, dozens of American soldiers, running for the track back to the village. I rose and grabbed a private by the arm. Holding tight I said, "What's your unit, soldier?"

He ripped his arm from my hold. "Second Battalion." He didn't bother with the sir or a salute. As he continued up the road, he turned. "Kraut counterattack coming." He pointed north. Before I could ask how long or how far away, he was gone.

So, I thought, we're in for it now. I returned to the line of foxholes, all facing down the ridge to the Kall, instead of north to where an attack might come. "Pass the word; keep an eye to your right. Tell the machine guns to be sure they can track up the ridgeline as well as down to the river."

But we saw no one. The retreating infantry had simply melted away from a nonexistent threat.

When Sergeant Jenkins arrived with the second squad, he dropped into my foxhole and pushed his helmet back, lit up a smoke, and reported, "It's all hell back in the village. Soldiers streamin' through in a panic. Officers stop 'em and try to set up a line. Minute they turn their back, the men they stopped are gone again."

"But we haven't seen anything here, Sarge."

"It's the shellin', sir. They can't stand it, and when it stops, they're sure it's because the Germans are comin'. They's spooked." He smiled at his use of the word. "Too many months in combat, the noncoms back there tell me."

"They talk to you?" I was surprised. "That's good."

"Yeah, some good men back there. But the Twenty-Eighth Division has been in combat now for a month, and these three regiments have already lost and replaced half their men. The new ones just can't stand it."

"How come our men are holding up?" My question was rhetorical.

But Jenkins answered it. "Maybe they don't know how bad it's gonna get."

The airbursts began again the next morning at dawn. We were no more accustomed to them than we had been four days earlier. After only a few minutes, they stopped. Then to the north, out of the mist and fog that shrouded the remaining thick pines not yet splintered by the airbursts, we saw German infantry—at first a handful and indistinct, then hundreds of them, moving quietly. But they were not moving on our line. Rather, they were flanking us on the left, where the ridge was less steep, and they were heading straight for the village of Vossenack itself, five hundred feet behind our position.

The entire squad was now aware of what was happening. These Germans would sweep into the village unless we could do something to alert the disorganized and demoralized Second Battalion and do something to distract the Germans, at least briefly.

"Alright, I'm staying with the machine gun. Sergeant Jenkins, you man the other one. Everybody else, on my signal, stay low and move back to the village. Whoever gets there first, tell them one company, possibly two companies, of German infantry are on the way up toward the north end of the town."

I gave the signal, pulled back on the firing mechanism, and looked at Jenkins.

He looked back. "Is this a good time to die, Captain?"

We began training the two .50 caliber machine guns back and forth across the ridge. Our fusillade was probably out of range, but the demonstration was enough to momentarily distract the Germans' left flank, which began heading our way. But then an officer blew his whistle, and the squad threatening Jenkins and me returned to the main unit. We continued to fire. When we had used up the ammo, I said, "Let's get out of here."

Scrambling up the track and into the eastern end of the village, we were surprised to see a line of tank destroyers spread across the field on either side of the road. The lieutenant in charge waved us toward the village. As the Germans came on up the slope, I could see the tank destroyers were readying to pull back into the woods west of town.

I stopped and approached the major in charge. "Are you pulling out, sir?"

"Yup, Lieutenant. There's no tanks for us to attack, and we're only drawing fire."

"But, sir, don't you see that you're the only armor in town, and it's helping the infantry just to know you're still with us?"

"That'll be all, Lieutenant." He climbed aboard the first vehicle and began to lead them down the road out of the village.

There were about sixty men spread out across the line in front of the village church when the Germans began their attack. We held them off for the better part of an hour, but then the threat of being outflanked led the Second Battalion commander, a captain, to order everyone to fall back to a line at the western edge of Vossenack. There we continued to hold up the German advance till nightfall.

The next morning the church became the focal point of another German artillery assault. By noon it was nothing more than a steeple and a basement, protected from direct fire by barriers of broken masonry. There fifty or so soldiers were left, waiting for another counterattack. Eight of them were members of the 609th. When the attack came, we fell back as the Germans swept through the church and almost overwhelmed our fallback line at the western end of the village. Retreating, we called artillery down on our own position. That kept the Germans at bay long enough for the handful of infantry and engineers to reform a defense along the Second Battalion headquarters outside the village. And that's how it continued for the next three days, as Germans and Americans attacked and counterattacked, exchanging ownership of the now ruined church.

After those three days, the cloud cover dissipated. Finally, the battalion command, or what was left of it, was able to call in tactical air strikes against the Germans holding the eastern end of the town. But by the tenth of November, the word came down that we would have to withdraw completely from the sector. The entire Twenty-Eighth Division was standing down from its failed advance.

It was a nighttime retreat, covered by intermittent artillery fire. We were debriefed by battalion G-2, but not very closely. The battalion didn't want to know how badly its officers had been rattled, how quickly its squads and platoons had melted away at the hint of German advance, how disorganized its responses to orders had been. There were rumors that the division commander, Cota, was on the hot seat at SHAEF. But no one much cared at the level of the 112th regiment.

When the G-2 was finished with me and my men, he looked over his notes. "Wrought? I've got a note here, says if you make it back, you're to report to division G-2, Major Hurwitz. OK?" This was the Twenty-Eighth Division intelligence officer who'd gotten me and my men into the shooting war.

"Yeah, Captain," I replied. "Right after I find my men in the field hospital and get a night's rest."

◆

I found the major in a room at a large hotel in the middle of Aachen. I knocked and entered to a broad smile from Hurwitz, who rose as I saluted, saluted back, and extended his hand. It was a greeting I had not expected. Without thinking what it meant, I reached for his hand and shook it.

"Well done, Captain. Put those bars back on your shoulders."

For a moment I did not even realize what he was talking about. My life as a captain seemed to have ended long ago and on another planet.

He went on, "Your men did well. I'm writing a report. It'll go up the chain of command, and maybe we'll get a whole new source of combat infantry." He was obviously satisfied with his achievement. But I was beginning to fume.

"Major, in your little experiment, I lost sixteen men, friends I'd spent two years with, in a pointless battle with inadequate support, poor leadership, and cowardly white soldiers."

"Wait a minute. This was your idea. I didn't write to my congressman."

I got control of myself. "Sorry, sir."

"Look, Wrought, that's not why I sent for you." He opened a file. "Evidently you are of more interest to the War Department than I expected. I am to ask if you speak Finnish."

"That's right, sir. We spoke only Finnish at home when I was growing up."

"Well, here are some travel orders, Captain Wrought." He handed them to me. "Top priority back to London, then to Stockholm, Sweden."

"Sweden? They're neutral."

"Not my business, Wrought. Dismissed." I was saluting when Hurwitz added, "I'll see to your platoon. Don't worry." He returned my salute.

That afternoon, the third one since he'd begun writing, Tom was ushered out of his cell for exercise. By this time he knew some of his fellow prisoners and was looking forwards to exchanging whispered witticisms. He rose from the bunk, and as he followed the screw out into the corridor, Tom surreptitiously tucked one copybook into the back of his trousers and the other at his front, under his prison jacket. If someone wanted to read them that badly, then there had to be a reason, and a reason not to let them do it.

CHAPTER FIFTEEN

As I climbed out of the C-47 onto the tarmac at Stockholm, I was still getting used to the scratchy wool of the civilian suit I'd been given with no explanation in London. The plane had come to a stop well away from the terminal, and no steps had been placed at the door. Instead, one of the airmen had opened it from the inside and invited the three passengers to jump down to the ground.

There was an embassy car waiting for us, but no one spoke. When we reached the chancery building, each of us went our separate ways. My orders were to report to someone named Cole. The young Swedish woman at the reception desk pointed me up the stairs. "First door on the right."

There was no name on the door, but my knock was greeted by, "Come in." A youngish man in a rumpled suit rose from a desk of papers. "Captain Wrought? I'm Taylor Cole, OSS station chief in Stockholm."

It was the first time I'd heard those words. "OSS?" My inflection carried my ignorance.

"Sit down. Smoke?" He opened a silver cigarette case and offered me one. "OSS — Office of Strategic Services. It's the War Department's intelligence unit. Spies. And now you're one."

I nodded. "So that's why no one in London knew why I had been ordered here."

"Actually, Wrought, you're not staying. You're on your way to Helsinki. You've got Finnish. Maybe the only army officer in Europe who does."

"What am I supposed to do there, sir?"

"Call me Taylor. I'll call you Tom. OK? You know Finland was a province of Russia for a hundred years. Thousands of Finnish socialists and communists went back to Russia after the revolution, right?"

"Yes, my mother told me my dad wanted to go back after the czar was overthrown."

"Do you have any idea how many did go back and settle in Karelia, between Leningrad and the Finnish border?" I gave him a chance to tell me. "The State Department thinks as many as ten thousand Finns went back from the United States alone. Anyway, it was a disaster for them once Stalin began to get a grip on the country. But they're still there, a lot of them. That's where you come in."

"What am I supposed to do?"

"The Finnish-Russian border is mostly trackless forest in the summer and blanketed white all winter. It's the best way in and out of the Soviet Union right now, and maybe for the next few years. And it's only fifty kilometers to Leningrad. The way the Russians have been behaving — not repatriating our POWs, denying landing rights for damaged bombers, liquidating the Polish resistance, industrial espionage in the United

States, pussyfooting with the Japs—Washington is worried. We need to develop agents who can move across their border That's your job."

"Taylor, if you're intelligence, you know I was a member of the US Communist Party for a couple of years in the '30s."

"So what? You aren't anymore. In fact, it's practically a job qualification for what you are going to do. A lot of these folks have become former communists, just like you. They just didn't have the luxury of telling the party where to get off like you did."

"One more question. What am I supposed to do? How do I do it? How do I find agents? How do I know I can trust them? How do I pay them?"

"Tom, that's five questions. Let's take one at a time."

⊰━⊱

I spent the dark month of January 1945 learning tradecraft from Taylor Cole. Mainly it was common sense, the generous application of money, and a bit of overpromising. And I learned the answers to my five questions.

It all involved a little recent history. The Finns had fought three wars in the space of five years. Russia had attacked Finland in 1940, when Stalin thought no one was looking. It was midwinter. At first the Finns won, since they knew how to fight in the snow and the Russians didn't. But eventually Soviet manpower overwhelmed them. When the Germans attacked Russia in '41, the Finns saw their chance to regain the lost territory. So they allied themselves with the Germans. That was the second Russo-Finnish war. When Russians swept west in '44, the Finns fought for a third time, to force the Germans out of their country. That was the war none of us ever heard about. Finland knew it had to pretty well give in to any demand the Russians made, including purging the government of anyone with a record of hostility to the Soviets. They did it. But Finnish military intelligence services secretly kept themselves intact and in contact with the west.

Taylor Cole told me that all I really had to do was make myself just visible enough in Helsinki. The Finns would find me. And that's how it turned out.

⟞⟝

It was a few weeks after I arrived. I was buying rounds for veterans of the Russo-Finnish War of 1940 in a Helsinki beer hall. The rather spartan tavern served beer at long tables to men only and closed early.

As we trudged out into the pitch darkness of midafternoon, one of my fellow drinkers leaned over to me. "Yank, we can keep drinking somewhere nicer if you're still paying." About forty, he was taller than me and strongly built, with a long face, dark hair that swept back from his forehead, and a deep cleft in the middle of his chin. I nodded at him, and we walked off together down several streets so narrow they were still banked in snow from a storm three days earlier. There was no sign announcing the much more interesting bar he brought me to, pine-paneled like a sauna, quiet and peopled by women as well as men.

We took two stools at a counter and ordered vodka. My new friend picked up his glass and pronounced, "Finnish vodka, not Russian vodka. I'm Risto Paattinen."

"I'm Toomas Wrought," I replied, using my Finnish first name. "What do you do, Risto?" My question was conversational, but his answer was not.

"Depends which side of the border I'm on."

My ears pricked up. Meeting Risto was no accident. "What do you mean?"

"Well, this side of the border I work in rural electrification. On the Soviet side, I repair tractors and trucks for cooperative farms." He looked at me knowingly. "Works out pretty well. I've also got two wives, two families, who can't really find out about each other. And plenty of excuses to travel."

"Risto, we've just met. Why are you telling me this?"

"I've got friends in the ministry of war. You're OSS, and they told me to help you." I remained silent. "I've got something you fellows can use. A dozen different ways to slip in and out of the Soviet Union."

———◆———

For the next two years, Risto made me a wildly successful OSS station chief. As the Soviets set up more and more stooge governments in the eastern European capitals, Risto was bringing out more and more information from diplomats in the USSR that could never reach the Finnish diplomatic bag.

I really had nothing much to do except serve as the postman. Risto was the cutout between me and a stable of agents in Leningrad; I never met a one. But I didn't mind; Helsinki was fun. I caught up on three years of reading, and I began to think about what I wanted to do with my life. Before I had quite decided, however, the whole matter was taken out of my hands.

One day in December of 1946, there was a knock on my door. It was a messenger from the US embassy. He asked me to sign for the letter, which I did. I opened it to find a travel warrant and a letter separating me from the OSS and from the US Army with an honorable discharge, and nothing more.

All there was to do was to leave a note for Risto in the dead drop we'd use when immediate contact was impossible. Then I packed my bag and took a train to Sweden. All night long I wondered what I had done or what might have happened. Never a reprimand, never a countermand, never a cross word from Taylor Cole in Stockholm. What had I done wrong? Without checking into a hotel, I went from the station to the embassy. Taylor was not yet in, and I cooled my heels in the lobby, shivering every time the door opened to let in another jet of the Stockholm air.

At 9:00 a.m. precisely, in he came, saw me sitting at a bench, looked again in recognition, and crooked a finger. I followed him back to the same anonymous office where I'd met him in January 1945. He didn't invite me to sit.

"You should be on your way home, Wrought." He looked around his desk and found a piece of paper. "Yup. Relieved as from immediately."

"Well, Taylor." He was calling me by my surname, but I was going to remind him of how he had addressed me the last time we'd met. "I just thought I'd stop and say good-bye. Maybe ask for a reference, given that there were no complaints about my work."

He responded to the irony in my voice. "Look, Tom, I can't say much, but you must have an idea how Washington politics operates."

"Sorry, none. I've been insulated from it since I enlisted, before Pearl Harbor." That had been almost exactly five years, I realized. "It's almost three years since I was stateside."

Taylor dropped his pen, let his chair swivel back, and pointed me at the chair in front of his desk. "Look, the OSS is trying to survive the postwar changes—Truman, Republican majorities in Congress, most of all J. Edger Hoover and the FBI. It's not even calling itself OSS anymore. We're trying to hide in the War Department—OSO, Office of Special Operations."

"What does that have to do with me?"

"Hoover has hated the OSS since the day Roosevelt created it. He'll do anything to destroy it so he can get his hands on intelligence operations outside the United States to go along with his counterintelligence operations inside."

"I repeat, what does that have to do with me?"

"Come off it, Tom; you know Hoover has been playing up Red Scares since the 1920s. What was the first thing you told me when you got here?" I couldn't remember, but he did. "That you'd been a communist as a kid. Well, OSS knew that—it was in your security check, but we didn't care, so long as you weren't a Nazi."

I smiled. "So now the OSS or whatever it's called is worried I'm a commie?"

"No, but they are worried that you are a handy stick Hoover can use to beat them up. First whispers, then leaks to congressional committees, finally headlines—'Communists in Spy Agency.' Get it?"

"I get it." There really was nothing I could do about it short of rewriting history.

"Sorry, Tom. If it's any consolation to you, I'm getting out too. Going back to my prewar job."

"What was that?"

"I was a professor. Maybe you should try it."

———⟢———

New York in the late '40s was different from the city I'd left in 1941. I was living off Broadway at 111th Street, not far south of where I'd rented in Harlem before the war. But it felt more like London. No, not London. There was no bomb damage anywhere. Riverside Drive along this part of Manhattan looked more like Paris or some other European city. When I had left six years before, Broadway had still been mainly boarded-up or vacant storefronts, nearly empty shops tended by listless owners. Now there were bookstores and bakeries, delis and florists, dressmakers and tailor shops, butchers and greengrocers with stands that spilled into the streets when the police would let them.

The crowds on the pavement were different. On the Upper West Side of New York, you could suddenly hear a dozen European languages, along with Puerto Rican Spanish and Harlem jive talk. The immigrants all seemed to be pushing baby carriages, the men walking arm in arm the way they might in Vienna. There were plenty of Americans too, men so long in the service that they seemed almost consciously to suppress a salute when they met.

Like me, most of these men were students at Columbia University. The surge of grown men in a hurry completely overwhelmed the Ivy League restraint I had sensed before the war the few times I dared to walk the mall that cut through the campus at 116th Street. Before the war there had been vast and pristine lawns, the likes of which I did not see again till Oxford. Now there were the same Quonset huts the 609th Service Battalion had known in England. Every open space from 114th Street to 123rd Street was covered with these temporary buildings — living spaces, lab spaces, classrooms.

I came back knowing what I wanted to study—history, American history, the history of slavery and reconstruction after the Civil War. And I knew whom I wanted to study it with. Richard Hofstadter had been a member of the Young Communist League and a member of the party before the war. He was about four years older than me, and when I first met him before the war, he was working on a doctorate at Columbia himself. Hofstadter had quit the party the same week as I had and for the same reason— Stalin's deal with Hitler. By the time I had returned, he was back at Columbia as a professor. The best thing about Hofstadter was that he knew nothing much about my subject. That made it easy to satisfy him, and I was able to finish a PhD in a little over four years. A record for Columbia in the '40s.

<hr />

The other reason I was able to wrap things up that quickly was my marriage. I met Barbara the second week of September 1947, in Butler Library. She was a very tall, very thin woman, long black hair, dressed with the sort of chic maturity that sorority girls at Barnard couldn't even recognize. I was standing behind her as she was checking out one of Hofstadter's books.

"You don't want to read that, miss." She was just turning around and about to respond to my cheekiness, but I went on, "I should know. He's my thesis director." For some reason she smiled. Emboldened, I went further. "I'd be glad to fill you in on the book if you'd have a drink with me at the West End." It was one of the two student bars in the neighborhood.

Barbara, it turned out, was a Barnard senior, from a place near San Francisco called Tiburon. She lived alone in a studio off West End Avenue toward the Hudson River.

We tumbled into bed that first night, began living together the next week, and married in December. I won't say any more about it beyond the fact that we were well matched, sexually and otherwise. She was looking for an academic, one who would be successful, and more than that, visible — at least in cultured circles. Whoever she picked would have to want to stay in New York. She loved New York and didn't want to go back to California. She never said so, but I suspected that the lucky man couldn't be a Jew, of which there were many in New York who otherwise fit her bill. There was one more thing she was looking for: a man who didn't want children.

I didn't know that immediately. Like most of my fellow veterans, I guess I came home from the war expecting to have kids. Barbara's time in New York led her in the opposite direction. No kids. Thanks, but no thanks. Too much trouble. I guess I should have objected a little more strongly. But we were a good match. I was too busy trying to become at least a little bit famous, famous for doing something interesting, controversial, worth arguing about. It had to be about the black-white racial question. That issue hadn't left me.

I didn't mind that Barbara had a private income. I liked the fact that she didn't want to marry a lawyer or a doctor, still less a banker or broker, even if Barbara intended to live like the wife of one. She didn't mind my politics either.

Being on the left was fashionable back then. We were still fighting the good fight, recalling Roosevelt and the New Deal, condemning Truman as a traitor to unions, workers, poor farmers. We blamed him, Churchill, and the Republicans in Congress for the beginnings of the Cold War, rallying to Henry Wallace's Progressive Party campaign in 1948. Barbara's political contributions were large enough to get us invitations to cocktail parties, to the reserved seats at rallies, and even to a dinner at which Katharine Hepburn was the guest of honor.

Meanwhile, I was being drawn into another part of the campaign, where my old friends from the Communist Party were playing active roles. The whole apparatus of the party, at least in New York City, was put at Henry Wallace's "disposal." What really happened was that the party took over his campaign. Once I began to turn up at Wallace functions, people I recognized from before the war made it clear that bygones were bygones. I was welcomed back into their crowd. The parties were fun, and Barbara liked the frisson of people with dangerous ideas.

⚬⟶

One Friday evening in the fall of 1948, I found myself alone at a party on the Lower East Side. Was it a rent party, or one to raise money to fight Truman's Taft-Hartley antiunion law? I can't remember. But there in the middle of the room I saw my old "friend" Julie Rosenberg and his wife, Ethel. The last time I'd seen him was the afternoon in September 1939 when he vaguely threatened me with a beating if I didn't rejoin the party. He was heavier now, wearing an ill-fitting double-breasted suit and a tie that even from across the room looked like it had food stains on it. Julie Rosenberg looked decidedly unprosperous.

I worked my way over to him and clinked beer bottles. "Long time, Julie."

He recognized me, thought for a moment, recovered my name, and then gave me a hug. "Tom, do you remember Ethel?" He turned to a diminutive woman with an oval face framed in dark hair. Her very red lips were pursed, and a worried look seemed permanently set on her face. Like Julie's suit, her dress was strictly "S. Klein—on the Square." "Tom and I were friends at City College before the war, Ethel."

His wife replied, "Yes, Julie, I recall your introducing us." Her smile was forced.

Julie turned back to me. "What are you doing these days, Tom?"

"I'm at Columbia, studying history. You?"

"Little of this, little of that. I was working for the army as an engineer till they fired me for having been in the party. I'd quit when the war started, but it didn't matter to them."

"Yes, I've had the problem too," I commiserated. "You quit?" I was slightly surprised.

"Ethel and I got tired of it all. We're out of politics altogether." He looked round the room and then called out, "Hey, Morty, here's Tom Wrought." He looked back at me. "Remember Morty . . . Morty Sobell?" I watched the man come across the room. After ten years he was hard to identify—glasses, longer hair, a good deal more weight. He looked altogether neater and more prosperous than Julie Rosenberg. I smiled, recognizing a really old friend, one I had ridden the subway with to high school every day for four years, the boy who introduced me to the party and, more important, to girls.

Turning to Julie I replied, "Sure, I remember Morty." By this time he had arrived, and concurring, he gripped my hand.

"So, Tom, good war?" It was the first thing Sobell said after ten years.

"Two years stateside; after that, two weeks of combat." Then I said something that must have been significant, though I couldn't know it at the time. "Spent the last two years in Helsinki." Neither man said a word. They didn't ask me what I'd done. Did they exchange glances? I couldn't be sure. But suddenly they stopped asking questions. Julie drifted away, and I asked Mort about some of the other guys we'd known in high school.

Then Julie returned, and we were joined by a rather good-looking woman. "Tom, this is Lona Cohen, friend of ours." Lona towered over Ethel Rosenberg and looked even taller with her rich brown hair pinned up over her warm, smiling face. She grasped my hand and held my gaze intensely. Was she inviting me to make a pass, I wondered. Then she noticed my wedding ring and assumed a more restrained affect.

"Hello." I smiled. "Lona is an unusual name," I remarked.

"Actually it's Leontine. Even more unusual. Julie tells me you're studying history. My husband and I have a used bookstore in the village. Lots of history on our shelves. Maybe you can lighten them." I felt a twinge when she mentioned her husband. Her warmth had been arousing.

"Love to come and browse," I replied. Lona handed me a card and drifted off.

⋄

A week later I was in Washington Square for a lecture at NYU. Afterward I headed into Greenwich Village, looking for a cup of espresso. Suddenly I found myself in front of Good Price Books and Prints, Lona's shop. I certainly had no objection to seeing her again. In fact, it might have been that thought that sent me in. At the counter was a stocky man with a thick mop of hair going gray, parted close to the middle. He was wearing heavy corduroys and a blue shirt underneath suspenders and manhandling a stack of books piled high on the counter. There was a cloud of dust behind and above him. Coughing, he pulled out a kerchief and smiled. "Can I help you?" Another spasm of coughing took him.

"Is Lona here? We met a few days ago at a party."

"Sorry, no. She's traveling. Won't be back till day after tomorrow. Are you" — he paused — "Tom? Tom Wrought? She mentioned meeting you. I'm Morris, Lona's husband." My conversation with Lona at the party had seemed to me far too brief for her to bother mentioning me to someone else, especially a husband she might have been contemplating cuckolding. I was surprised.

"Actually I came in looking for something," I lied. "George Orwell, *Homage to Catalonia*." I began to explain. "It's not published in the US. I'm looking for a British edition, Secker and Warburg, I think. She said you might have it."

He laughed. I didn't ask why, though years later I realized how transparent the lie was. Then he said, "Ah yes. Great book. I was in Spain during the civil war." He began coughing again. "Got this cough I can't shake after ten years. Didn't run into Orwell, though." He came out from behind the counter and headed to a shelf behind me, pretending to look for a book he must have known was not there. "No, sorry. If you leave me a number, I can call you if it comes in." He added portentously, "Or Lona can."

A few days later, Lona called. "Hello, Tom. I've got that book you came looking for, *Homage to Catalonia*. A copy just came in. If you can't get down here, I can bring it over."

What, I wondered, was going on? She wanted to bring me a book she knew I hadn't really asked her about at the party. What did this woman really want from me? The only way to find out was to agree to a meeting. But not at home, I decided. "I have some research to do at the Forty-Second Street Library tomorrow. Can we meet in front of the lions, say, two o'clock?"

"Great. See you then." The voice betrayed no disappointment.

———※———

Lona was waiting when I arrived. I looked for a book in her hand, but there was none. I had half thought she'd go through the motions of the pretext for the meeting. She smiled as I approached, and before I could offer my hand, she hugged me and offered her lips, mouth open, to mine. This was not quite what I was expecting, and my response — an averted face — left her looking disappointed. She cleared her throat and began, "I thought when we spoke that we . . ." She did not finish the sentence. "I guess I sized you up wrong, Tom." Still I didn't speak. "Buy me a drink, will you?" We walked down toward Grand Central Station and found a quiet bar.

When we were seated at the bar she said, "Too early for a dry martini?"

"Not at all." I spoke to the barman.

She took a long sip at the drink and then began, "Tom, you may not be interested in me, not the way I thought. Are you interested in peace?"

"Sure. Aren't we all?"

"You were in Helsinki after the war, weren't you?"

I had never said anything about Helsinki to her at the party. Had Julie Rosenberg or Mort Sobell passed every word I had spoken to Lona Cohen? If so, why? "I was there for a while in '45 and '46. You know I'm Finnish."

"Do you want to go back?"

"Can't afford it, Lona."

"If you'd like to go back for a visit, that wouldn't be a problem."

I couldn't let the conversation go on much further. "What's the catch, Lona?"

"No catch. If you want to help the cause of peace, if you want to resist the people trying to start a new war, this time against the Soviet Union, there are things you can do." I made no response. She went on, "You've been listening to Henry Wallace, haven't you?"

"Sure."

"Well, his words are not going to be enough to stop the warmongers, the men who always wanted to fight the Soviets instead of the Germans. If you want to stop them, there are things to do."

"Sorry, I can't help you." I rose and left the bar.

⸻⊰≡⊱⸻

After my conversation with Lona, I wasn't particularly shocked when the government arrested Julie Rosenberg for espionage in August 1950. But I was surprised they took Ethel too. After all, she had two little kids and wasn't a threat to anyone.

By the time they were put on trial the next year, along with Mort Sobell and Ethel's brother-in-law, David Greenglass, I was in Helsinki again. Every time I picked up a paper to read about the Rosenberg trial, I expected the Cohens to be mentioned, or at least Lona. But nothing appeared. When I got back to New York,

I went round to the bookstore. It was gone, replaced by a nice little Puerto Rican bodega selling Café Bostello espresso coffee by the bag. It had been there for a couple of years. The bookstore had folded early in 1950.

Now, here's the weird thing. Last fall I could swear I saw Lona Cohen and Morris Cohen each at Marks and Co., the booksellers on Charing Cross at Cambridge Circle. I asked the manager about them. All he could tell me was they were named Mr. and Mrs. Peter and Helen Kroger, and they owned an antiquarian bookshop in town.

⟜⟞

In the early spring of 1951, I was still at Columbia, wrapping up my thesis on the end of Reconstruction and the beginning of Jim Crow in the South. One day I got a call from the chairman of the history department at Howard University, John Hope Franklin. Howard was a Negro college, the most prestigious of them. I'd never met Franklin but knew about him and his work. He was the first Negro to finish a PhD in history at Harvard. More than that, Franklin was the most important historian writing on my subject. The fact that he called, long distance, person-to-person—a trunk call, to you Brits—instead of writing was out of the ordinary, but I didn't pick up on it at the time.

"Mr. Wrought, could you come to Washington to give a lecture on your research? We'd also like to discuss offering you a position on our faculty."

"Name your time and place, sir," I responded with enthusiasm. He seemed in a remarkable hurry. We fixed a date for two days hence.

———◆———

I arrived at Howard on a Thursday and gave my talk on the "corrupt bargain" of the 1876 presidential election, which the House of Representatives had to decide, owing to the failure of the electoral college to agree on a winner. The resulting compromise gave the Republicans the presidency in exchange for the removal of federal troops from the former Confederate States. It was the beginning of the reenslavement, as I called it, of the black agricultural proletariat. Franklin didn't approve of the heavy dose of Marxism in my analysis, but he appreciated the archival research and the census data that went into it. I returned to my hotel after a pleasant dinner, fairly certain I would not be offered the job.

As I entered the lobby, a man rose and approached. "Hello, Tom." It was Taylor Cole, my Stockholm OSS control.

"Taylor, what are you doing here?"

"It wasn't an accident."

"Nothing ever is with you fellas." I was beginning to remember the terms on which we had last seen each other. "Am I back in your good graces?"

"You were always in mine. But I don't work for the government anymore. Can we talk?"

"The bar? My room?" I looked toward the elevator.

He pointed at the walls. "Let's take the air." We walked out into the warmth of a Washington spring evening.

"The CIA asked me to get in touch with you. They need you to go back to Finland, just for a week or so."

"Wait a minute. The CIA? How did they even know I was in town?"

"They arranged it with Dr. Franklin."

"You mean there's no job at Howard? It was just a ruse to get me to Washington? Why didn't you just call me or come to New York?"

"Tom, it's not me. I left the OSS before the CIA was even created. But it's a nightmare world we're living in just now. The agency is afraid you might be under surveillance in New York."

"From whom?"

"They didn't tell me. But let's assume it's Soviet agents. You know too many of the people who've been arrested as Soviet spies lately." I nodded. "The CIA figured you wouldn't want to speak to them anyway. That's one reason they asked me to meet you."

"Spill it, Taylor."

"It's a long story, but there's another whole intelligence fiasco going on."

"You mean besides the one in New York?" I couldn't help remarking on the atom spy case.

"Yup. This one is in England. A couple of Brits turned Soviet agents have been detected by MI5, British counterintelligence, and they're on the run: names of Burgess and McLean. They were right at the top of MI6 and had access to the identities of most of the British agents in Russia. Now the Brits have to get their people out, or at least the ones who haven't been detected yet."

"How?"

"They figure that Finland is the best route out. But the Brits have no network there."

"Can't the Finns help them?"

"Tom, you were there long enough to know that won't work. The Finns are too frightened of the Russians to ever do anything overt against Soviet interests. Plus, every ministry in the Finnish government has been penetrated by Soviet agents. That's where you come in. Remember your old friend Risto Paattinen?"

"Sure. Still going strong?"

"Well, the people in the Finnish Ministry of Defense who put us on to him in '45 think he can help. But only if an American makes the contact. He can't trust a Finn, and neither will the network round Leningrad."

"So, why me? I haven't worked for the OSS in five years; I was fired for being a very ex-commie. Besides, the OSS is defunct. Can't the CIA find another messenger boy?"

"Not one who speaks Finnish like a Finn and who their military intelligence trusts. Apparently your successors were cowboys. The Finns won't work with anyone but you, and that's flat."

"So, I'm indispensable only when I am indispensable. What exactly am I supposed to do?"

"You have to go in, make contact with Risto, and help bring out the British agents."

"How soon?"

"You leave from Andrews Air Force Base tomorrow."

"But my passport? What'll I tell my wife?"

He reached into his pocket and pulled out a thick envelope. "Everything you need and enough Finnish krona to kit yourself out. They'll tell your wife something. Maybe the FBI wants to question you about atom spies; I don't know."

I couldn't help myself laughing.

I was gone for ten days. All I had to do to find Risto was go back to the bar he'd taken me to that first time in January 1945. On my second visit, a note was passed to me, telling me where to meet him, in a new town, Imatra, at the Finnish-Russian border. I had enough CIA cash simply to buy a car, and I drove through the night along empty roads north and east, into a very early morning sunrise.

As I drove by a vast paper mill on the outskirts of Imatra, a hitchhiker appeared. As I bore down on him, I recognized Risto. It was all too smooth, I thought. Someone was watching me, or maybe watching over me.

"So, Tom." He shook my hand warmly. "Keep driving north out of town and take the first right turn into the woods." As I drove, he briefed me. "We're going to bring two men and a woman out. They've been hiding for a week in Enso. The Russians renamed it Svetogorst after the Finnish government handed the town to them in '44. But it's still mainly Finns."

"A town Finland handed to the Russians in '44? No choice, I guess."

"Not unless they wanted to be crushed by the Red Army. But that's why the locals won't trust the Finnish government for a moment. You're going to have to act like an American. Don't even speak Finnish; just show wads of dollars."

"I've got even better, Risto. Gold coins."

Forty-five minutes later we stopped the car at the end of a dirt track surrounded by stunted pines. "We're going to take a walk across the border and find ourselves in Enso, uh, Svetogorst." It was a hike of about an hour through marshy ground and unmelted snowbanks. Our route was marked by long tongues of standing water, through what the Russians called *tiaga*. Then, suddenly, above us there were power lines, and I knew we were nearing the town.

"Isn't this dangerous, Risto? Just walking into Russia? If we're caught we're certain to be shot as spies."

He laughed. "Don't worry. This place is so far out of the way and so dense with Finns, the only way the Soviets will make it secure is by complete resettlement. That'll probably happen. The locals are certainly all going to leave."

"What's keeping them?"

"Well, things are not much better yet on the other side of the border. And here there's socialism. So they'll wait awhile longer."

<hr/>

It was the middle of the day in a village that looked almost completely deserted. "Where is everyone, Risto?"

"The men are in the forests probably, or down at the river. If the women are out at all, they're tending kitchen gardens. Don't worry; the MGB is a hundred kilometers away, staying dry and warm." The MGB was Russian state security. A few years later they changed their name to KGB.

By this time we had come into a clearing and were approaching a lonely ramshackle building. Risto knocked casually and spoke in Finnish. An older woman opened the door and invited us in. Then she left quietly.

There, sitting at a kitchen table sipping tea in glass cups, were two men and a woman, all of them dressed not in the rough kit of farmers and fishermen, but in the dark suits and long coats of city dwellers, but soiled and wrinkled, as if they'd been sleeping in them. They rose as we entered, breathed a collective sigh, and all began to gabble in Russian. Risto and I both put our hands up.

In Finnish he said, "I don't speak Russian," while I said the same thing in English. Suddenly all three were speaking English.

I put my hand up again. "One at a time."

The woman was about forty-five, with severe features and hair pulled back tight from her face. Evidently she spoke the best English. The other two subsided, and she began to talk. "You are American? We can't trust Finns." I nodded. "Prove it," she demanded. Slowly I withdrew my CIA-provided passport and passed it to her. She looked at it, and the date. It was only a few days old. "Too new. You are Finn or Russian." She spoke a word in Russian, and one of the men took out a small pistol.

I looked at him a little more closely. He was pudgy and hirsute, badly in need of a shave. The striped double-breasted suit he'd been living in had been fashionable in the West during the war. He certainly looked uncomfortable holding a gun.

This was my cue to get serious. I spoke slowly. "If I were Russian, you'd all be dead by now or surrounded by border security troops." She nodded in grudging agreement. "And if I am going to turn you over to the Finns, you don't have a better alternative anyway. But, as it happens, I'm not." I took the passport from her. "I'm an American spy. That's my picture but not my real name. I got the passport just for this assignment." I turned to Risto. "Can we get moving? I am not happy in the Soviet Union." I spoke in Finnish, and the woman asked me to translate. I did. She smiled, and all three rose, buttoned up and belted their coats.

As we were about to leave, Risto reminded me, "Leave the gold coins you brought on the table. It will be appreciated." I was glad to lighten my load.

By the time we were across the border and back on the road to Imatra, it was dusk. "Tom, let me off where you picked me up."

With three strange Russians in the back seat, I was not happy to part with him. We shook hands and then hugged before he stepped out of the car.

I turned to the three Russians. "Next stop Helsinki." Their silence was ominous. And it lasted through the six and a half hours it took to get to the outskirts of Helsinki.

The first time we saw a sign that read HELSINGIN KESKUSTA, the third passenger in the back sitting right behind me finally spoke. "What is that sign?"

"It says 'Helsinki City Center,'" I replied.

The man said something in Russian, to which the other two replied, nodding their heads and agreeing "Da." Suddenly the man sitting right behind me had his handkerchief around my neck, very tightly. The woman told me to pull over, and the pudgy fellow drew out his pistol. When we came to a stop, the handkerchief around my neck was loosened, and the woman began to speak. "We will not go to Helsinki. You will drive us to Turku, and then we all take the ferry to Sweden. Now! Otherwise we will shoot you."

"Seeing as I have no choice, let's go. I warn you, the crossing is rough. You'll get seasick."

They laughed, the laughter of relief.

It was four hours to Turku, and there was a sailing that night. During the twelve-hour crossing of the Baltic, none of the three would trust me alone outside the car. Each of the men left the car once for the toilet and took me with him. The woman never left the car. The farther away from Finland the ship traveled, the more relaxed the three Russians became, until in the dawn they began to feel as though they really were going to make it. It was only then that I realized that they were still frightened that the ship might turn back.

"Look, friends, perhaps you have not noticed. This is a Swedish ship. You have been under Swedish sovereignty for about nine hours, ever since we left Finnish territorial waters." I held up the ferry ticket. "See the three yellow crowns on the blue field? Swedish colors." I passed the ticket to the woman. "Now, can we go up to the second-class lounge and have some breakfast?"

⫯

We were all squeezed into a booth, sipping coffee and munching on Swedish breakfast rolls. We had even exchanged names. They were Zludmilla, Vladimir, and Boris.

Vladimir, who had handled the pistol so uncomfortably, asked, "You will bring us to British embassy? Yes?"

"If that's where you'd like to go."

They nodded vigorously.

Then Zludmilla spoke. "So, you go back for the American agents?"

I looked at her blankly. "American agents? Are there any to take out of Russia? I wasn't told about anyone but you."

She looked at the others.

Boris, the thin man who had almost garrotted me, spoke. "Yes, the American agents that were going to be rounded up along with us British ones."

"How do you know?" My question was urgent.

Boris looked at Zludmilla.

Then she spoke. "Thomas, we are MGB, communication department Leningrad. We read all the cables, telexes, messages from Moscow Center. I was on duty when the arrest orders came in." She looked at the other two. "That is how we knew that someone had betrayed the networks. It was our names and a half-dozen others in Leningrad region. I alerted Boris Ivanovitch and Vladimir Sergevitch." The patronymics momentarily confused me. "We didn't even know the others were agents until we saw the list of names. But we destroyed the message from Moscow Center and sent our MI6 control a message to get us and the American agents out."

"Why do you think they were American agents?" This wasn't my concern exactly, but I was growing anxious.

"Well, next to our names was the word *angliyskiy*, and next to the others it said *amerikanskiy*."

I had to travel back the way I had come, on military flights. It wasn't hard to arrange once I showed my passport to the embassy in Stockholm. When I arrived at Langley Air Force Base, I was met by someone who flashed CIA credentials, handed me an envelope of cash, and asked for the passport. I gave it to him and then said, "I need to be debriefed. Something happened that has to be reported." The courier asked no questions, merely nodded, and I followed him out to an unmarked car.

We drove into DC and parked at a nondescript building near the Mall. The only thing the driver ever said to me was, "OK, follow me. Don't get lost. There are no signs on the doors."

We entered the building, moved up and down stairs, along corridors, making turns through a maze of temporary structures built into the formerly open space in the closed courtyard of what was a prewar federal office building. Finally we found ourselves in front of a door and some seats. I was bidden to sit while the courier knocked and entered. A few minutes later the man came back, ushered me past secretaries in an outer room, and into an inner office. Then my courier moved behind a desk, at which a man in a three-piece suit was sitting.

The man seated at the desk looked at me from underneath bushy eyebrows. His hair was white, as was his mustache; he wore a bow tie and was chewing on a pipe, whose smoke filled the room. He did not introduce himself or otherwise betray interest in me beyond the word, "Well?"

"I'm back from an operation in Finland."

"I know that. I arranged it for the Brits. Tell me what you need to say. I'm busy."

Having not been invited to sit, I remained standing before him and repeated the last conversation I'd had with the Russians. When I finished, the two men looked at each other. Then the man at the desk looked back at me. "Sit down." He indicated a chair behind me and to my right. "Now, repeat everything you just said, and anything else you remember."

My memory is good, and the brief conversation in the buffet on the ferryboat had replayed itself enough times to make me word perfect.

The man at the desk leaned back, loosened his tie, and said to the other man, "Explains a lot, Bob."

The younger man must have been distracted, for his question — "Why didn't the Brits tell us, Mr. Dulles?" — earned a look of fierce reproof. My interrogator had evidently not wanted me to learn his name either.

The question the younger man asked was one I had pondered all the way from Stockholm. I was pretty sure I knew the right answer. And I was going to give it them, whether they wanted it or not. "It's pretty obvious. Either MI5 decided not to pass on the information, or whoever they did pass it on to here decided to sit on it. Someone in London or Washington wanted to roll up your network in Leningrad." I had said "your" instead of "our." It lost me what little welcome I had received. And my next thought made them furious. "Maybe there's a double agent here or in London who stopped you getting your people out."

The man at the desk picked up a phone. He glared at me in a rage. Then he said, "Keep that thought to yourself, or you're a dead man." Before dialing he barked, "Get him out of here."

—◆—

Now, Miss Silverstone, recall what I'd been told by Taylor Cole just before my little Finnish adventure about the two senior people in British intelligence defecting to the Soviet Union, Guy Burgess and Donald McLean. Both of them had worked in Washington during and after the war. Did either of these two have access to the names of British or American agents in the Soviet Union? Someone in MI6, British intelligence, or MI5, counterintelligence, would have known.

—◆—

When I got back it turned out that Professor Franklin did want to hire me after all. And Barbara was happy to move to Washington.

I had been at Howard for a year when serious witch-hunting began. It didn't matter how young you were when you joined the party or how long ago you'd quit. There was always someone ready to make trouble. It was a lucrative business. Finding out about someone's past and selling the information to the highest bidder was an industry that didn't need Senator McCarthy's stimulation. It became quite profitable since the Korean War got going, the Rosenbergs were found guilty, and the two Cambridge spies defected to Russia. There was likely to be a commie under every bed, and no one could sleep safely at night till they were extracted and burned at the stake.

In 1956, the Democrats regained control of the US Senate, and by seniority, the racist Senator from Mississippi, James O. Eastland, became chair of the Internal Security Subcommittee, the US Senate's version of HUAC—the House Un-American Activities Committee. It was the fixed notion of most Southern whites that the movement for racial equality was a communist conspiracy. Of course, for a long time in the '20s and '30s they had been right. That's why I had become a party member. But by the time of the Supreme Court school desegregation decision in 1954, Southern politicians were about the only ones who still thought the civil rights movement was just a communist conspiracy. Maybe they didn't really think so, but they said it often and at the top of their voices.

In the spring of 1957, Professor Franklin turned up in my office one day. He was always quite formal. "Good morning, Dr. Wrought, may I sit down?"

"Please do, sir. What can I do for you?"

"Well, Wrought, I have had some good news, but I am afraid it may not be so good for you."

"What's that?"

"I've been asked to become the chair of the history department at Brooklyn College in New York."

I smiled and then said something so funny we both laughed for a few minutes: "First Jackie Robinson, then John Hope Franklin. These things always seem to get done first in Brooklyn." Both of us knew that Franklin would be the first Negro chairman of an academic department in a "white" university. I rose and offered my hand, which he shook firmly. We both resumed our seats.

"How does it affect me, sir?" I ventured.

"Well, ever since you arrived, I've been pressured to fire you, or at least not reappoint you, by the board of trustees. I've refused. But in the last six months, since Eastland took over the Senate Internal Security Subcommittee, it's gotten a lot worse."

"Gee, I'm not that important. Why should they care about a lapsed commie in a Negro university?"

"I wish I knew. I don't know why the pressure has ratcheted up since the Democrats took control of the Senate and Eastland became chair of that committee." He rose, signaling that the meeting was over.

"It's a heads-up, Dr. Wrought. I'm leaving at the end of the spring term. If I can possibly find something for you in New York, I'll do it. Meanwhile, if I were you, I'd start looking around. We've got our share of Uncle Toms, and Howard is just too vulnerable to political ill winds."

When my contract wasn't renewed at the end of the academic year, I didn't need to ask why. But I did. I sought a meeting with the president of the university, the venerable and rather venerated Dr. Mordecai Wyatt Johnson.

I was received with cordiality but regret by the president. "I know why you have come, sir," he said, offering me a seat in his rather spare office. "You want to keep your job."

"No, actually, sir, I just want to understand exactly why I have not been renewed for the fall."

"Well, it's rather obvious, isn't it, son?" He was old enough and august enough to make the word sound natural. "In this political climate, we can't afford the controversy. Alas, we've had many white Southern donors, even some wealthy black ones, who have raised this matter over the years. But Dr. Franklin always said he'd quit if we fired you, and that was enough to protect you with the trustees. He's gone now, Dr. Franklin is." He stopped. "And I got this letter."

He slid a typewritten sheet across the desk to me. I read it quickly. It was on the letterhead of the US Senate, and below the heading in smaller letters was "Senate Judiciary Committee," and below that "Internal Security Subcommittee." It was addressed to Dr. Johnson, and it warned him that unless I was discharged by July 1, 1956, both he and I would be subpoenaed to testify before the committee staff and if necessary before the full committee in the fall session of Congress. When I got to the signature, suddenly the interest in a white assistant professor at a black college became clear. It was signed Vincent Folsom, chief investigator, assistant to Senator Eastland (D), Mississippi.

I looked up at Johnson. "Well, Mr. President, it's a small world."

"Oh, tell me."

"I know this man, the one who signed this letter. Fifteen years ago he was a lieutenant colonel in the quartermaster corps at Camp Claiborne, Louisiana. I got his attention then because

I had promoted several Negroes in my company. But I doubt he got my name or remembered it, if ever he had learned it. Then I ran into him in England, and again in France when I discovered that he was diverting fuel to the French black market. That's when he learned my name, or at least started looking for me by name. At least I think it was him looking for me. Lucky for me, I got sent into combat with a lot of my men—first Negro draftees to see combat in the infantry, I'm proud to say. Not so lucky for most of them, though." I stopped. "I guess he's finally found me. Thank you, Dr. Johnson. You've solved a mystery for me. I won't trouble you further." I took his warm but rather limp hand and, after giving it a vigorous shake, left his office.

Timing is everything. A week later the Pulitzer prizes for 1956 were announced. The winner in history was Thomas Wrought, *What If the South Had Lost the Civil War?* A few weeks later I received a letter from the master of Trinity telling me I'd been elected to a fellowship. So I had the last laugh. Barbara and I moved back to New York, spent the summer at Saranac Lake, and came to Oxford in early October 1957.

I hope this helps. Liz knows everything else that could possibly solve our problem.

Tom turned the page and wrote one more paragraph.

Alice, there's been an effort to read these composition books while I've been out of the cell for exercise. After the second time it *happened, I started to carry them with me when I went out into the exercise yard.*

—◆—

Alice had given Tom about four days to produce his "confessions." She arrived back at Brixton on a wet and cold Wednesday. Tom rose as she entered the interview room. He could almost feel her presence lifting his mood. Before he could say anything more than "Miss Silverstone," Alice began.

"I've only got a minute actually. I just came for the composition books if they are done. I have two more blank ones for you." She leaned down and drew two more marbled black-and-white books from her brief bag. But she did not sit.

Tom picked up the two thick composition books he had now filled up, opening the first one to the page on which he had written out his suspicion that the book had been examined. Then he held it before her to read without saying a word. Then, underneath the original note, Tom wrote,

Are they allowed to search the private writing of prisoners on remand? Is there a chance defendants' discussions with their solicitors are monitored? Can you be sure what we say here remains confidential?

Alice had started shaking her head almost violently before she had finished reading. She could not help herself blurting, "No, no, no. It can't happen. Absolutely not." Tom reached out a hand to her mouth and handed her his pen.

She understood and began writing furiously below his note,

What you suggest is happening would be a grave violation of law. I've never heard even of a suspicion that someone might be listening to conversations in these rooms.

Tom now spoke. "Well, good. Maybe I'm just imagining things." He looked at the two filled-in composition books she was holding, trying to convince himself she was right.

Alice swept them into her bag and turned to leave. At the door she stopped. She was categorical. "Impossible." Then she smiled. "Back on Friday for the next instalments."

Tom said no more. He decided to continue to write, but this time fiction, fables, falsehoods, and to leave the books in his cell in ways that his brief OSS training in Stockholm had taught him to detect unobtrusive searches.

PART V

January–March 1959

Brixton in Winter

CHAPTER SIXTEEN

Liz Spencer was sitting in Alice Silverstone's crowded little office. They were both smoking now, Silverstone having finally announced that she had decided to give up trying to quit, for the duration of this case anyway.

It wasn't Alice's smoking that troubled Liz, however. It was the needle marks that ran up her arm. Liz had recognized those tracks. She'd seen them close up, too close, on her own arm, before her year in a Toronto mental hospital. Was it too late to seek another solicitor? Could Silverstone control her habit? She had shown no signs of trouble yet. Liz had decided to watch and wait.

Alice hadn't noticed her interest in the marks. She had spent much of the weekend off the morphine, reading and rereading, trying to decide what steps Tom's narrative dictated. Monday morning she'd taken the notebooks to the Abbey National on Baker Street for Liz to read. Now on Tuesday they met. Some of the leads, Alice knew, would be easy to follow—for a squad of Scotland Yard detective inspectors or a Soho Mafioso with a brace of solicitors on retainer. But Tom Wrought didn't command such resources. All he had was a junior attorney . . . and Liz.

How were they to cope? Alice looked at Liz, thinking, *Defeatism is not what she wants to hear. Brazen it out, dearie!*

Squaring her shoulders, pulling down the sleeves of her silk shirtwaist dress, she adopted a confident tone. "Right. Now let's review . . . there are several things about this whole case that are perplexing." Alice paused. "We already know that the police have a very well-informed source, too well informed not to be involved, somehow, in your husband's death. The source seems to have done all the police's work for them." Liz nodded. "Now, here is the second thing. Actually it's something you observed last week when we first talked."

"What was that, Miss Silverstone?"

The solicitor frowned. "If I'm to call Mr. Wrought 'Tom,' you'd better address me as 'Alice.'" She reached across the table and squeezed Liz's hand. "Recall, you asked why whoever killed your husband didn't just kill Tom, if it was Tom they wanted to get rid of." Liz nodded. "Well, that question has bothered me all week. Then it hit me." Silverstone's sense of drama now made her pause. "Look, I don't want to sound cruel, but consider this. Trevor Spencer is pushed onto the tracks. What kind of headlines would we expect in the tabloids? Well, 'Tube Murder' and then some follow-up on Tom's arrest. The usual sordid little domestic murder story. But we didn't see that, did we? There was almost nothing in the papers." She paused.

Liz filled the silence. "So?"

"Bear with me. Now, suppose someone had pushed *Tom Wrought* onto the tracks, and he'd been killed. What would have happened?"

She waited for an answer; hearing none, she continued. "We'd expect headlines: 'Pulitzer Prize Winner Dies on Underground Track.' 'Oxford Don Killed in Tube.' 'American Author Pushed to Death in London.' 'Trinity Fellow Mystery Murder.' There would have been a lot of bylines, reporters wearing out shoe leather trying to find a story. And they'd find one—slightly famous academic, Yank at Oxford, spurned wife, secret lover, cuckolded husband, something juicy enough to keep on the front pages for a while."

"Of course." Liz now saw it. "In fact, if it had been Tom who was killed, it wouldn't have been just reporters from the tabloids out after a story. Lindsey Keir, the master of Trinity, all the editors Tom was writing for, would have started asking questions."

"Exactly. Sir Isaiah 'harrumph, harrumph' Berlin would have called up his friends in the FO—"

"FO?" Liz asked.

"Foreign Office. And they would have asked their friends in the Home Office. Who knows, Michael Foot might have gotten Dennis Healy to ask a question in Parliament."

"I see. They needed to kill someone no one would be interested in and make it look like Tom had a commonplace motive for murder—a sleazy little love triangle."

"And even then they managed to prevent the story making the papers," Alice continued. "Whoever framed Tom was also able to reach into Fleet Street and keep even the tabloids quiet."

Liz frowned. "Who's got that much power?"

"I don't know. But whoever killed Trevor did it because they wanted Tom out of the way, not just dead."

Liz looked perplexed. "What do you mean, 'Not just dead'?"

"They could just as well have killed Tom the way they killed your husband, right?" Was this, Alice wondered, a little too brutal? There just wasn't time to mince words. "They needed to discredit Tom, maybe even hang him. But they couldn't risk a thorough Scotland Yard investigation of his murder."

Liz took it in stride. "So, Tom had to be a threat to someone; I see that. But it can't be because of any of those things he did in the war, or after the war, in the States."

"Why not?" Alice asked, hoping that Liz would come to the same conclusion she'd come to. She was almost holding her breath.

"Because, if he had been a threat back then, they would have acted sooner. It must be something he's done since he got here. Something that scared someone badly enough to frame Tom for Trevor Spencer's killing."

"Exactly. Now what has he done?"

"Written a lot of disobliging articles and book reviews critical of the USA? Not enough of a reason to kill him."

"Right, but what if there is something in those articles and book reviews that has gotten someone scared, scared that Tom Wrought knows something, something very important, very dangerous, something that would make it worth trying to silence him by turning him into a common criminal and perhaps even hanging him. No one would believe anything a condemned man might say to save himself."

Liz brightened. "And that's where *The Confessions of Tom Wrought* come in? You think that somewhere in those two composition books Tom wrote is the thread we need to pull on to unravel the mystery?"

"Exactly." It wasn't very much to go on. But she felt the need to encourage Liz. "So, let's begin. There do seem to be several threads to pull on." She looked down at the two composition books.

"Too many." Liz paused. "Tom seems to have a habit of crossing people: there's the Communists who didn't want him to quit the party, the atom spies Tom knew before and after the war, the corrupt racist quartermaster he kept running into—the one who got him fired ten years after the war when Tom was at Howard University. Maybe the guy's even got the same bent military police still working with him." She stopped for a moment and then went on, "What about the officers who covered up the deaths of Cullen and Wilson, those Negro officer candidates?"

"Liz, if it's something Tom has said or done or written since coming back to England, we can exclude a lot of those people."

"Right." Liz was glad to acquiesce.

Alice went on matter-of-factly. "We can cross off the men involved in the deaths of Cullen and Wilson. Tom never made an effort to prove anything against them. And his commanding officer in OCS was killed during the war." Liz was silent. "The way I see it, there are only two or three leads it would be worth following up." She pulled a pad of scratch paper towards her and began writing. "First, we've got to read everything he's written since he got here, very carefully, with an eye both to what it says and what it doesn't say but merely suggests. Second, this American army quartermaster lieutenant colonel, Folsom, turns up too many times in Tom's life. We need to find out a lot more about him. That's going to be your job. Third, there are these interesting cases of mistaken identity, the Cohens or Krogers."

"How are we going to tackle this Folsom here in London?" Liz sounded slightly defeated.

"Let me think about that and do a little research. Meanwhile, here's a file from a clipping service. Everything Tom has written since September of last year. Take it home and read it. I'll do the same. Let's meet again day after tomorrow. I'm going to brief Tom tomorrow, and get the next two composition books."

Alice was beginning to feel some twinges. *Time for some morphine.* She rose, and Liz took the hint to leave.

⬥

The next morning Alice arrived at the law office expecting the usual grunt of a greeting from Boyle, the firm's sole clerk. Instead it was a slightly foreboding "Good morning, Miss Silverstone. Can I have a word?" Alice was the most junior of the solicitors in a practice ruled by its only clerk.

Alice stopped at his desk, put down her briefcase, and waited as he sorted some briefs before him. "Thing is, miss"—he could never call her by her name; Alice suspected it was because he couldn't bring himself to humanize a woman solicitor—"we may've had a bit of a break-in."

"Anything taken?" Alice expressed concern.

"You'll 'ave to tell me, miss, as it was mainly your office they had a look over." He nodded to her door, visibly ajar down the corridor. "May've opened the office safe"—his eyes moved to the drawers beneath his desk—"though there's nothing missin'."

"Why do you think they opened it, if nothing is missing?"

"Oh, just one of my little quirks. There's lots of little things to do so's you can tell if someone's monkeyed with a dial. But I can't tell you, or it wouldn't work. See what I mean?" Alice nodded. "Anyway, go along to your office and tell me if anything's missin', please." He looked back down at his desk.

A few minutes later Alice was back. "Can we get the lock on my door fixed, Boyle?"

"Already ordered the repair, miss. Anything irregular?"

"Can't tell. Doesn't appear anything is missing." But Alice knew what they had been looking for. Tom's suspicions had been right! The enormity of the violation of law took her breath away. Who could be so unscrupulous and so powerful as to reach into a remand prison, and then into a solicitor's office? Not the crown prosecutors, not the Home Office, never.

Who am I going to complain to about this breach? No one, no one will even believe me . . . believe us. And now she recognized finally that she had been experiencing the persistent feeling that someone was interested in her—perhaps watching her, perhaps following—ever since the moment Liz Spencer had left the office the first time they met. *Is it just my imagination, the tension of this case? Can people really sense when they're being followed? No, not when it's well done. But this is a clear signal, Alice. Watch out! Someone with the resources to open the office safe is interested in you.* And then she felt a surge of anger. *Whoever had the resources to open the office safe was much more powerful than that. They've been listening to privileged conversations between solicitor and client in the interview room of one of her Majesty's Prisons. They can do anything they like!*

Fortunately, she had kept Tom Wrought's composition books with her. But now she knew that was no wiser than leaving them in the office safe. She removed both from her case, put them in a brown envelope, and addressed it to herself at her home in St. John's Wood. No one would be foolish enough to send something that valuable by the post. Tomorrow when the envelope arrived, she'd put both books in a valise and check it at the Left Luggage in Kings Cross Station. *But, then, what should I do with the claim check? Worry about that tomorrow.* In the end, she mailed the chit to Victor Mishcon's secretary with a request that she hold it for Alice.

It was warm and sunny when Alice Silverstone next arrived at Brixton Prison. There was actually a shaft of light shining down into the interview room where she waited for Tom to arrive. As she heard the door open, Alice rose and turned. Tom came into the room and clasped her hand. "Hello, counsellor." He smiled, but she didn't notice. Instead, she was feeling the bit of paper that had been slipped into her hand. She sat down, putting the note in her jacket pocket, thanking heaven that it had pockets.

"How are you doing, Tom?"

"Look, Miss Silverstone, I am going to plead guilty. That way I may be able to avoid hanging."

Her jaw dropped. It made no sense. Alice was missing something. Was this a charade for warders or microphones? Yes, Tom was shaking his head, countermanding his words. She pulled the folded paper from her pocket as surreptitiously as she could, then reached into her brief bag as if for a file folder and slipped the note into one. Then she brought the folder up and opened the still folded note.

I fear we can't talk freely. Someone must have been listening to our interviews. My cell was searched again during my exercise periods. This time the warder made me leave the books in my cell. They didn't get anything. Everything I wrote was gibberish. Are the books I wrote for you secure?

Alice looked from the note at Tom, pressed her fingertip to her lip, and nodded her head in agreement. Pulling two new composition books from her bag, she opened one and began to write:

There's still only one theory that makes sense to me: someone wants to both discredit you and keep you behind bars or to hang for reasons that have nothing to do with Trevor Spencer.

And you're right about the spying. Someone is listening or at least being informed about our conversations. They've searched my office for the composition books. But the books are secure for the moment.

It's a good sign. It means someone is worried about what you know. If we can find out what it is, we'll have a chance.

We'll have to find a way to prevent the eavesdropping. I'll be back when I figure one out.

Tear this page from the books I hand you and give it back.

When she finished the note, she passed the two new books across the table. He pushed them back.

"Still working on the ones you gave me last week. I don't need new ones."

"I see. Well, I'll get in touch with the crown prosecutor and see if they are prepared to recommend a lesser penalty than hanging."

Tom and Alice both rose. He knocked on the door for the warder. As she opened the door, she looked back at Tom. "You'll have to call me Alice, or I'll go back to calling you Mr. Wrought."

He smiled.

CHAPTER SEVENTEEN

"Liz, I have to be frank with you. I'm worried."

"What is it?" Was Alice going to explain the track marks up her arm? Tell her she was giving up the case? Liz waited.

"All along, this has not looked like your garden-variety murder case. Now I'm getting the feeling the people who've put Tom in Brixton will start closing in on us. It won't scare me off, but you have kids to think about."

"What do you mean?"

"Whoever we're up against, they killed an innocent man to frame Tom. Then they managed to gag the tabloids when the story could have made the name of a reporter or two and sold a lot of papers." Alice stopped for a moment. "Whoever these people are, they have a lot of power. And they've even been able to pervert the course of justice."

"Pervert the course of justice? What does that mean?"

"The relations between a defendant and his solicitor are strictly protected by the courts. Anyway, they're supposed to be. But someone has reached into Tom's cell in Brixton, violated his judicial rights, and now they've broken into my office."

"What were they looking for?"

"The composition books, almost certainly. But these people won't stop there. So far, they haven't paid you any attention. But that could change."

"How about you? They've already gone after your . . . office. Why not you too?"

"I don't know. But I don't matter so much. I don't have kids. You do." That wasn't the only reason Alice was not going to be scared off. *I'm beyond their reach.* She rather relished the thought. *You can't threaten someone who's already dead.* But she wasn't prepared to tell Liz. "If they begin to think you're a threat, I don't think they'll hesitate to . . ."

Liz finished the thought that Alice could not complete. "Kill me too?" Alice said nothing, and Liz continued, "Look, Alice. I appreciate the warning, but I won't be scared off."

"You're making a decision that affects other people—two young children, Liz. Do you have that right?"

"Alice, that decision may already have been made for me by these people, whoever they are."

"Any sign you're being followed?" Alice recalled the sudden feeling, suspicion, sixth sense that had overcome her the morning after the break-in at the firm's offices.

"Not yet. But it doesn't matter, Alice. I'm in too deep already. And I want a life with Tom. My children need a father. Tom will be a fine one. There's a risk, a big one if you're right. But my kids and I'll just have to take it. We need Tom." She stopped. Did she need to tell Alice that the word *need* hadn't begun to convey the truth? She had to say aloud what she had known for months. "Having a mother without joy, or worse, would harm them, badly. Having a father who cared, well . . . that's worth almost any risk."

Alice was watching her client's—no, her friend's—face. "Very well, Liz, *contra mundum!*" Having won a smile, she went on, "It looks like you are going to have to go to America. There are leads there. We can't afford professional investigators, and in a matter like this, I wouldn't trust them anyway."

"I'll go, of course. But what am I looking for?"

"We need to know more about the name that keeps coming up in Tom's narrative—Folsom. He's a villain, and how many times does he cross Tom's path—three, four?" It was a lead Alice wanted dearly to follow to America. But she couldn't, and she couldn't tell Liz why. *Focus on the practicalities, Alice!* she silently enjoined herself. "Can you leave your kids?"

"I can send them to Birkenhead, to Trevor's brother, for a few days. He'll take good care of them."

"Your job?"

"I travel for Abbey National so much, they won't miss me if I'm gone for a week. Beatrice Russell, my assistant, is a brick."

"Have the police questioned her yet?"

"Once. She played completely dumb. Never heard the name Tom Wrought at all."

"Good. Now here is all I have about your target. Can't even be sure it's right, comes from a *Who's Who in America* I found in the solicitors' law library: Vincent Folsom, University of Mississippi, BA, 1930, law school, 1933, admitted to bar, 1934, lieutenant colonel, Mississippi National Guard, US Army, served 1941–1945, FBI, 1945–1954, staff of Senator Eastland (D) Mississippi, 1954–1957, assistant chief counsel, Senate Internal Security Subcommittee, 1957 to present. Address: Shoreham Hotel, Washington, DC." She passed a newspaper cutting across the desk. "This is a photo I got from a clipping service. It's Senator Eastland grilling a witness before his committee. The man behind him is Folsom."

Liz looked at the clipping. She thought for a moment. "I have an idea where to start. We need to find people who know Washington and who will be on Tom's side for sure. There is only one person I can think of who might fit that bill."

"Who?"

"The Negro professor who hired Tom when he lived in Washington, John Hope Franklin. If Tom is right, Franklin's in New York now. I am going to see him first. I can't think of any other way."

Alice was pleased. "It's a good start. How soon can you leave?"

"As soon as my banker gives me an overdraft to cover the flight. I'll book for day after tomorrow. The new BOAC comet jet to New York."

Alice replied, "Good. I'm going to start by talking to Tom's editors." Then she realized it wouldn't work. "But you gave in your passport, didn't you, Liz?"

"I did, my United Kingdom passport. Trev made us all get them a year after we moved here. Should have realized then it was a signal he wouldn't go back." She smiled. "But I still have my Canadian passport in the name of Jarvis."

—◈—

Fleet Street wasn't far from Red Lion Square. Alice thought she'd be able to talk to several of Tom's editors in one afternoon. As she walked down the Aldwych towards Fleet Street, she could feel the street exuded an air of authority she'd always wanted to subvert. The silent, anonymous office blocks were designed to look formidable and permanent. The proprietary air of the commissionaires at each entrance kept the gates against anyone not wearing the uniform of the ruling class—a bowler, a rolled umbrella, and most of all trousers. Looking up towards the massive columns holding up the façade of Bush House, she felt a chill. The establishment was palpable, concrete, impregnable here. *Might Tom Wrought's case be one that could subvert it, even a little?* Alice shrugged and turned left onto Fleet Street.

—◈—

The *Times Literary Supplement*, the *New Statesman*, the *Observer*, all fruitless. None of the editors particularly wanted to see a solicitor. She was fobbed on to assistants or business managers. "What exactly are you looking for, Miss Silverstone?" The assistant editors were willing enough to help. Talking to a solicitor was something to do besides proofread and fact-check. But each was equally frustrated. The conversations were all pretty much the same:

"Is there a specific question you want to put?"

"I can't tell you anything more than that we invited Wrought to review and he did."

"When you ask whether there was anything out of the ordinary about the matter, what exactly do you mean? He didn't ask for more money, he wasn't late with copy, we didn't have any trouble getting him to accept the cuts. It was business as usual. I'm afraid there's the end of it."

Of course Alice understood. She was on a fishing expedition in which she couldn't even bait the hook.

She arrived at the *Tribune* office no longer hopeful. But at least this was a chance to meet a celebrity, one she admired. She presented herself at the editorial office. "I'd like to see Michael Foot."

"Whom shall I say?" the receptionist asked.

"Alice Silverstone. Tell him I am a solicitor, and it's about Tom Wrought." She thought a minute and lied, "Tell him Victor Mishcon sent me." The solicitor was a Labour Party worthy Foot would know.

No intercom on the receptionist's desk. Just one phone line. Nothing like the massive editorial infrastructure at the other papers. The woman rose and knocked on the door marked **MR. FOOT**. After a moment, out he came, extending a hand. "Miss Silverstone, come in." He was of average height, but wiry, with a shy smile under the dark hair combed back from his forehead, his glasses sliding down his nose. The smile showed genuine pleasure. She wondered, *Was it Mishcon's name, or was it a pretty face?*

Alice had asked the same questions enough times that afternoon to know how empty they sounded. Now she decided she'd have to try something else, take a risk, play some cards. He closed the door and motioned her to a chair, then went behind his desk—a study in disarray, just as any editor's desk would look if he really ran the show. He sat down, lit a cigarette, and offered her one. She shook her head.

"Bad business Tom Wrought's got himself into. You're defending him? Seems open and shut, no?"

"Too open and shut, Mr. Foot."

"What do you mean?"

"I think he was framed. The case was watertight within hours of the murder. CID hardly had anything to do at all. Someone just filled them in on means, motive, and opportunity. I don't know who, and I don't know how."

"We don't really do crime exposés, Miss Silverstone."

"That's another thing. Apparently neither does any other paper, not when it comes to this story. Not a whisper in the press." She stopped to let Foot ponder the fact. Then she continued, "Anyway, it's the last thing we want, Mr. Foot. No, the way I see it, the worst thing that can happen for Wrought now is publicity."

"Why is that?" He leaned forwards and put his chin in his hands.

"The only way to spring him—" Foot grimaced. "Pardon the Americanism." She continued, "The only way to free him is to find out who's behind the frame-up, if there was one, and threaten to reveal it. If we get to that point, the *Tribune* would have a story, I think."

"I dare say." He nodded vigorously. "So, how can I help?"

"Well, was there anything unusual in your dealings with Tom?"

Foot thought a moment. "Now that you mention it, there was. Two things." Alice's eyes widened. "He wrote some background pieces for us on American politics. But he also wrote a couple of reviews. Both were bombshells. We published them anonymously, at Tom's request."

Anonymously? That meant Alice had not read them. "Bombshells? What do you mean?"

"They both made very controversial suggestions, things he couldn't prove or at least wasn't willing to in print. One was a guess; the other was an accusation. He had enough circumstantial evidence to claim that the CIA was behind the *Dr. Zhivago* boomlet last fall. Before that, he reviewed a book about the *Rosenberg* spy case and accused the FBI of knowing the wife, Ethel, was innocent and not caring."

"Do you have copies?" Alice clasped her hands to stop them trembling with excitement.

Foot nodded, pulled out a drawer, and riffled through some manila files till he found them. "You can have these copies." But he had more to say. "Anyway, those must have been two very good guesses, if that's what they were. And Tom must have thought he was playing with fire a bit, asking us to publish anonymously. Now here's the thing. The next week I got at least two calls from people asking who wrote the *Zhivago* review, and if it was the same person who wrote the review of the book about the *Rosenberg* case. One of them was from someone I think is former MI6, fellow named Philby."

"Philby?"

"Yes, Kim Philby. He's a journalist in Beirut for the *Observer*. Comes back to town a lot."

Alice took a note and looked up. "Anyone else?"

"Can't recall. A secretary said she was calling from the Home Office for a curious civil servant. When I asked who, she rang off. I was troubled enough to write to Wrought about the calls. Hasn't he mentioned it?"

"No, he hasn't." *Why*, she wondered, *hasn't Tom said anything about this?*

Should she tell Foot that Tom and she hadn't been able to talk freely? No. It would just make the journalist in him all the more interested in doing a story. "You've been very helpful, Mr. Foot. Thanks very much." She rose and offered her hand. Now she had something to go on. A name, someone moved enough by what Tom had written to at least make a telephone call. Who was this Philby?

Alice wended her way back to the Aldwych and retraced her steps up the Kings Way. *Philby, Philby, what sort of a name is that? Where to start?* As she passed Victor Mishcon's office, on a whim she stepped in.

She knocked on the door and entered. The receptionist looked up. "Ah, Miss Silverstone. Do you want to see Mr. Mishcon?"

"No, no. But can I use the library for a few minutes?" Mishcon had the best set of reference works outside the law library at the Inns of Court. And there was the advantage that she need not explain to anyone what she was looking for. A half hour's work turned up little more, however. Kim Philby had been a journalist, then a foreign office official in Washington throughout the war, and was now a journalist again. Just as Alice was putting the last of the fat reference books away, Victor Mishcon came into the library.

"Hello, Miss Silverstone. Find what you need? My secretary told me you were here."

"'Fraid not."

"Perhaps I can help?"

"I'm trying to find out something about a man named Philby, Kim Philby. He was in the FO during the war. That's about all I know after half an hour of searching."

Mishcon picked up a pen, dipped it in an inkwell, and scratched the name across a card. "I'll see what I can do."

⊨⇒

The next evening coming home, Alice could hear the insistent ring of her phone through the door. She was in pain and needed some relief quickly, before things became unmanageable. She fumbled for her latchkey, juggling the briefcase and a string bag with her supper. By the time she had managed to get the key in the door lock, files had tumbled out of the brief bag on to the entryway, and her dinner was hanging perilously from her wrist. But the phone was still ringing. She rushed across to the desk.

"Alice Silverstone," she announced somewhat breathlessly.

"Victor Mishcon here. Missed you at your office. Wanted to have a word about that name you gave me."

"Very kind of you, sir."

"Well, I got the strangest reaction when I mentioned the name to a well-connected friend. He wanted to know urgently who had given it to me. I told him it was a matter of legal confidentiality. He warned me not to make any inquiries about the man. But he also told me not to rely on anything this Philby says. Then he rang off. Very strange."

⊰⊱

Alice Silverstone said nothing until Tom Wrought was seated comfortably across from her in the Brixton interview room. Then she began, "The psychiatrist I have consulted about your case doesn't have time to come round, but he's suggested a diagnostic test." She withdrew two flat boards from her case. They were six inches by nine inches, grey, and covered with a piece of cellophane attached at the top. "Do you remember magic slates from your childhood?"

Tom understood immediately. "Yes, of course." He smiled at her ingenuity.

"I am going to draw a picture on my board and show it to you. You write down exactly what comes to your mind, alright?" She began to write, but Tom reached out a hand to stop her and began to write on his slate.

You don't expect anyone listening to believe this, do you?

Silverstone scribbled,

> *It doesn't matter. We need a way to communicate in writing that disappears. Whoever's been searching your cell to read the composition books searched my office too. I didn't believe you because it's a violation of the most basic principle of British justice. But it's happening, and we need to do something about it. I am going to assume that they may be listening to these conversations too. That's why we'll use the slates.*

Tom took her slate, read it, and began to write.

> *Any idea who is doing this? It can't be the screws, as least not on their own.*

Alice wrote furiously,

> *No, unless they are being paid or forced to do it. But they are letting someone violate your rights. Who? Probably the people who framed you.*

She continued writing,

> *There are many leads in the two composition books you filled out. Do you have any theories?*

She handed the slate to Tom. He looked at the pad and wrote a few words on his, passing it to her.

> *Yes. Too many. Most of them far-fetched.*

Alice took hers back, lifted the cellophane, and wrote.

> *You never told me about those two articles, anony-*
> *mous ones, you wrote for the Tribune, one last*
> *spring, the other this fall, about the Rosenbergs*
> *and the Dr. Zhivago business. But Michael Foot*
> *told me about the telephone calls he received*
> *afterwards and the letter he wrote to you. Does*
> *the name Philby mean anything to you?*

Tom replied on the pad before him and turned it towards her.

> *No.*

Then he took it back and began writing again.

> *But there was something funny that I remember*
> *about the Zhivago article. In it I speculated it was*
> *the CIA that was behind the embarrassment the*
> *whole thing caused the Russians. The way I got*
> *the idea later made me suspect that someone — the*
> *Soviets — wanted me to find out and spread the*
> *word it was a CIA plot. There was a hint, deliv-*
> *ered by an Oxford don named Berlin, who had*
> *connections everywhere — Foreign Office, intelli-*
> *gence services, maybe even the Russian embassy. I*
> *think I was being used.*

Alice nodded and wrote,

> *Philby is a journalist, worked for Foreign Office in*
> *the war, may be ex-MI6. Ring any bells?*

Tom was about to speak. Silverstone grasped his hand and pushed the slate towards him. He wrote,

No.

Why are we using two slates?

She took hers back, scribbled, and handed it back.

If they confiscate the pads and examine the backs, they won't be able to tell which of my questions your answers correspond to.

Tom nodded and wrote,

I filled the two new composition books you gave me with gibberish. Then I marked their exact locations very carefully and put a strand of hair over them. It was gone when I got back from exercise, and they'd been moved ever so slightly. They'd been examined, maybe photographed.

Alice now wrote,

Are you certain about which bookshop on Charing Cross Road you met the people you thought you knew from New York, the Cohens?

Tom scribbled,

Yes, Marks and Co., 84 Charing Cross.

She rose. "I think that's enough for today. I'll come back in a few days. Perhaps the trick cyclist will have some results."

Tom was quizzical. "Trick cyclist?"

Alice laughed. "Cockney for psychiatrist."

"Ah, yes, Liz once used the term."

⟞⟝

What to wear when "casing a joint"? Alice wondered. She loved American slang. Looking for antiquarian books might require something different from the court attire she enjoyed wearing, especially to distract opposing counsel. She could unerringly predict which barristers would come over to her and surreptitiously try looking down the cleavage in her open blouse beneath the blue serge of a tightly fitted but unbuttoned suit jacket. Once she had even been reproved for her décolletage by a "silk"—an older Queen's Counsel. But the younger barristers told her to ignore him. Would tarty be the right attire, or was it a task for Miss Marple tweeds? She decided on décolletage.

At Marks and Co., she approached the counter. "I'm looking for a copy of Orwell, *Homage to Catalonia.*"

"We've got a dozen or so on the history shelf." The clerk pointed to the room behind him.

"I'm looking for a first edition, Secker and Warburg, 1938."

"Ah, yes. We've got one—three quid."

This she did not want to hear. "A bit pricey. Can you suggest anyone else who might have one cheaper?"

"I'm prepared to bargain, miss. How much would you like to pay?"

"I'd like to shop round." She was firm. "Any suggestions?"

"Lots of shops up and down the road. Nearest one is Kroger's, behind St. Clement Danes, the church in the Aldwych."

Pay dirt! Practically under her nose. She'd passed it twice going to Fleet Street and back. "Thank you."

⟨⟩

Kroger's Antiquarian Books was a much smaller shop, where Essex Street ended at the Strand. The bell on the door rang as Alice entered. There was a very young man at the counter. If this was Peter Kroger, he could not have been more than nine when Tom Wrought knew him in New York. Alice reflected, *Looks like décolletage was the right choice.*

"Hello, I'm looking for a first edition of Orwell, *Homage to Catalonia.* Do you have one?"

"Sorry, no."

"But you haven't even looked." She smiled.

"It's a small shop, miss. I know the stock."

"Can you find me a copy?"

"Certainly." He smiled a little too eagerly. It was an opening for conversation.

"You're very young to own a bookshop like this, Mr. . . ."

"Jencks. Not the owner; it's a couple from Ruislip, the Krogers, who own it."

"Ruislip. That's a coincidence. I live in Ruislip."

"Well, then, you could collect it from Mr. Kroger without coming all the way back in to town."

"Very good. Here's a phone number you can call me on when it comes in." With a copy at Marks and Co., she wouldn't have to wait long.

⟨⟩

Indeed, she didn't. The answering service had taken the message just two days later. She could collect her book at 45 Cranley Drive, Ruislip, the next afternoon—price four guineas.

CHAPTER EIGHTEEN

Liz knew it was not the best of circumstances to be visiting New York for the first time.

She'd never flown transatlantic before, but the new BOAC Comet IV—the first turbojet in service across the Atlantic—was a revelation. Looking down at the Heathrow tarmac, Liz watched the plane come up to the Queen's terminal building like a quietly beautiful animal, gracefully and in perfect proportion. An hour later she felt the deep roar of the four jet engines as the plane accelerated into the sky, pushing her shoulders back in the seat like a gentle but insistent lover. The novelty, the smoothness, the luxury, the serenity of the view down to the clouds completely distracted her from the dubious mission she had undertaken.

She ate and dozed, drank a cocktail, and began to let her thoughts drift. She spent a long time inspecting her emotions about Tom, making sure of them again. Going over the weeks and months of the autumn had lost none of its power to arouse her. But Liz was still equally certain of what being with Tom would mean for her if he were ever freed from Brixton. These thoughts were repeatedly swamped by persistent, even relentless, longing.

Liz tried to summon up anger towards Trevor. But now she found that she could hardly remember the details of any of their repeated squabbles. The whole exercise just gave way to sadness. She had been surprised by the children's resilient response to his death. Within a week the pall it had cast was gone. Were children really so unsentimental, or had he just not been a large enough presence in their lives? It was all too early to tell.

Then the longing for Tom returned, stabbing at her gut, finally to be overwhelmed by the dark reality she faced, Tom faced. The silent but minatory voice in her head told her that conjuring a future with the man she loved would simply make her feel worse. *You've got to stop spinning fantasies, or you won't be able to continue when they come crashing to earth. Focus on your mission. What if your Professor Franklin in Brooklyn can't help? What then? You don't dare just go look up this Folsom in Washington.*

The pilot's voice came on the intercom, announcing the absence of any headwind and telling all that at present speed, they'd break the record to New York by more than an hour. And so it was. Nine hours had passed before Liz even noticed. By early evening she was walking through the *nothing to declare* gate of the customs hall at Idlewild International Airport.

She had paid for speed across the Atlantic, but now in New York, Liz would have to pinch pennies. There was a coach—Americans called it a "bus"—to Grand Central Station. She found herself queuing for the next departure, while her fellow Comet passengers standing at the taxi rank gave her a look of abject pity.

After postausterity London and white-bread Toronto, the New York that passed her by as Liz walked west from the bus stop on Forty-Second Street was exhilaration and anxiety. The pace of the pedestrians, their heterogeneity and that it seemed to go unnoticed, all were hard for Liz to accept. The serried ranks of taxicabs, among which private cars were far between, formed a bright yellow wave cresting at each traffic signal.

The brilliance of the streetlights seemed to shelter everything beneath them from the gloom of a night sky. The aggressive good humour of shoeshine boys, pushcart peddlers, the elderly women "manning" the newspaper kiosks, all these had no counterpart, she thought, in a staid London or a prim Toronto. Did she have the wiles to survive a week here?

After ten minutes' walk, Liz finally recognized something. It was the vastness of the great public library, imposing order on the intersection at Fifth Avenue. The presence of an iconic site gave her an anchor she recognized from Trafalgar Square or Queens Park in Toronto. She was not walking into anarchy after all. Then, behind Bryant Park, she could suddenly see, lit against the sky in a way nothing in London ever could be, the Empire State Building. Suddenly she was a tourist, searching the skyline for other sites, the Chrysler Building, the United Nations, St. Patrick's Cathedral, Rockefeller Center. Were any of them nearby?

Crossing Fifth Avenue she entered the west side of Manhattan. Coming to the end of another long block, Liz recognized the rolling news scrawl on the *New York Times* building at Broadway. She stopped to watch the vast face on a billboard blowing smoke rings for Lucky Strikes. Then she walked down another long street to Eighth Avenue, losing count of the movie theatres at twenty-four.

When she saw the flashing hotel sign running vertically down five stories of a small building, she decided she had seen enough for her first night in New York. It was three o'clock in the morning London time when Liz's head landed on the pillow, and she badly overslept the next morning. But she woke with a sense of mission that drove her quickly to shower and dress. Across the street from the hotel, which looked much shabbier in the morning light, was the vast picture window of a 1930s streamlined building, Horn and Hardart's Automat. *Ah, another tourist attraction,* Liz thought, *but one that will give me a quick breakfast.*

She entered, took a tray, laid some flatware on it, and began to slide it along the rails fixed at waist height to a wall that was fitted with small windowed cubicles displaying food. Liz found their little glass doors were locked against her.

With slight impatience the customer behind addressed her. "Ya needs nickels." He pointed towards a central kiosk with what looked like tellers' windows. Only then did she notice that there was a coin slot next to each of the little doors.

"Oh, thank you." Liz took her tray from the rails, put it down on a table, and went over to the teller's window. She put down a dollar and received ten nickels and two quarters. Dropping enough of these into the coin slot at one cubicle, she was able to extract a delicious slice of apple pie, still warm. Then she advanced to the large, gleaming silver coffee urns. There she plucked up a heavy mug and held it under the spout, added milk, and found her way to a solitary table.

Looking round, she spotted the bank of green phone booths with a bright enamelled white-and-blue Liberty Bell disk on each of them. There was what looked like a full set of New York telephone directories on a raised stand beside them. When she had finished her coffee, she felt for how much change remained and stepped towards the shelf of directories.

※

"Brooklyn College, extension please." The voice had the New York accent she had heard only in movies.

"I'd like to speak to Professor Franklin, in the history department."

"One moment, please."

The next voice Liz heard was chipper. "History department."

"Dr. Franklin, please."

"Won't be back till eleven thirty. He's teaching."

"Can I make an appointment to see him today? When his class is finished, if possible."

"Yes. Whom shall I say called?"

"My name is Elizabeth Spencer, and it's an urgent matter, concerning Thomas Wrought."

"I'll tell him."

"One more thing. How can I get there?"

"Well, where are you?"

"Manhattan—Eighth Avenue and Forty-Second Street."

"Easy. Shuttle to Grand Central, IRT downtown Lex express to the last stop, Flatbush Avenue. We're in Boylan, third floor."

Liz was not ashamed to ask for a translation. "Can you explain—Shuttle? Lex downtown IRT express, Flatbush?"

The voice at the other end clucked slightly. Patiently, the voice explained. Everything, Liz realized, was going to be an adventure. The first challenge would be finding somewhere that would exchange her sterling. She'd assumed it would be no more difficult to change pounds for dollars than it was to do the reverse in London. Back at the hotel, the desk clerk hadn't the slightest idea where she could do so. "Maybe Grand Central?" he offered, but he couldn't be bothered trying to find out. How much would she need, anyway? Fifteen cents for the subway each way. Well, she had that covered from the dollar she'd broken at the Automat. She kept an eye out for a *Bureau de Change* among the theatres, drugstores, bars, and cafeterias along the way to Times Square. None. *Americans must think that the dollar is the only currency in the world. Even provincial Toronto has bureaux de change.* The thought made her feel a little superior.

By eleven twenty-five Liz found herself coming out of the subway to a scene that might have been pastoral at any other season. But now, in February, across Flatbush Avenue spread a carpet of frozen winter grass leading back to a bell-towered Georgian Colonial building. It was flanked by more utilitarian office structures. One of these was Boylan Hall. It rose to the left of the steepled building on which she could see the large clock now reading eleven thirty. Liz quickened her step.

⫸

John Hope Franklin was waiting for Liz at the door to the history department office. An owlishly wise-looking man with glasses, of average height, close-cropped hair, and a bright smile beneath a black moustache, he grasped her hand firmly. His dress was formal and his manner was deliberate, but a real warmth shone in his smile.

"Come this way." He led her to an office with the name **Mr. Franklin** on it. She noticed it didn't read *Dr.* or *Professor*, just *Mr.* There was a wing chair to the left of the desk, and he invited her to sit. Then he closed the door quietly, went to his desk, and folded his hands in front of him. "So, it's about Tom Wrought? How is he?"

"In grave difficulties, I am afraid, Professor Franklin. He is in Brixton Prison, London, awaiting trial for murder."

"No! Surely I would have heard. It would have been in the papers."

It struck Liz that Franklin's voice was preternaturally calm, even as he expressed his surprise.

"There has been almost no notice taken of the matter in the London papers either. It's something that mystifies us—Tom's solicitor and me."

"But a murder and a Pulitzer Prize-winner? Doesn't stand to reason."

"He's innocent, sir." Franklin said nothing. "I know. I am the murdered man's wife. But the circumstantial evidence is compelling. Too compelling, sir. We suspect that my husband was murdered to frame Tom and silence him."

"Silence him? From saying what?"

"That's the problem. We don't know. That's why I am here."

"I don't see how I can help, Mrs. Spencer."

"I'm reluctant to tell you the theory we're working on, both because it's pretty thin and because it may make it dangerous for anyone who helps us. After all, whoever they are, they've already killed one person."

"Try me. I think I owe it to Tom at least to listen."

So Liz laid out the few bits of information that she and Alice had. She concluded, "I need to find out as much as I can about this man Folsom. He's crossed Tom's path too many times for it to be coincidence alone. You were in Washington for so many years. I thought you'd know someone there who could help me."

"I know only two people in Washington who ever had anything to do with the Senate Judiciary Committee, and I am afraid their relationship with that august body is fraught, to say the least." Liz pulled a small notepad from her purse and picked up a pen. "One is Thurgood Marshall, head of the NAACP Legal Defense Fund. He's the lawyer who won the *Brown versus Board of Education* decision. The Dixiecrats in the Senate hate him, especially Eastland, who your man Folsom works for."

"Who is the other?"

"Bayard Rustin is his name. He's close to that preacher who led the bus boycott in Montgomery, Martin Luther King Jr. The staff of the House Un-American Activities Committee has hounded him for a long time. I would expect Rustin's learned the ropes around Congress. It's the best I can do."

Where had Liz heard that name before? She replied, "It would be a start, sir. We don't have anything else to go on." And then it came to her. Rustin was mentioned in Tom's notebooks.

"I'll be glad to call them."

Liz brightened. "I'm planning to go on to Washington tomorrow. I'm booked into the Shorham Hotel, the one Folsom uses."

"Well, neither Marshall nor Rustin would be able to meet you there."

Liz looked at Franklin blankly. "Why not?"

"The Shorham is a segregated facility, Mrs. Spencer, as is most of Washington."

Liz flushed. "How stupid of me. I never thought of that."

"White people seldom do. Look, Howard University has a guest house. Let me make a call. I think you'll be more comfortable there anyway." He picked up the phone. "Leonore, get me long distance."

"Thanks." Liz sat still and listened as Franklin made three long-distance calls. When he had finished, he put down the receiver and handed her his notes.

"All arranged. We're in luck. Rustin is actually meeting with Marshall day after tomorrow—organizing protests to implement school desegregation. I've arranged for you to have a few minutes with them."

"That's wonderful. You've been so helpful." Then she thought. "One more small favour. Is there anywhere here I can cash a traveller's cheque in British pounds? I'm down to my last thirty-five cents US."

Franklin stood. Then he withdrew a billfold from inside his coat, opened it, and handed Liz a ten-dollar bill. "You'll never find currency exchange between here and the UN Building on the East River. Please take this to tide you over till you can cash one of your cheques."

"I couldn't."

He came around the desk and forced it into her hand. "I am confident you're good for it. But I do have one question, Mrs. Spencer." She nodded. "Why are you so sure Tom is innocent?"

"Because we're in love."

Franklin smiled and opened his door. "Is that really a good reason?"

———

Two days and a long Greyhound bus ride later, Liz was in the middle-class Negro neighbourhood of a still segregated city, the first one she had ever experienced—coloured washrooms, coloured drinking fountains, overdeference from the cabdriver, and the feeling of being both out of place and a bit of an honoured guest on the Howard University campus. In her room she was struck by a large framed photograph of the dedication of the Lincoln Memorial. The date on the frame was 1922. But it was clear that the audience stretching back along the mall to the Washington Monument was strictly segregated, whites to the right, blacks to the left.

⋙⋘

Liz was ushered into a large room filled with law books, in the middle of which two men were seated at a table. One was light-skinned and dressed even more formally and more elegantly than Franklin had been, down to a monogrammed French cuff at which he was tugging. Though seated, he looked tall and unapproachable. This man looked like an advocate before the US Supreme Court. He had to be Thurgood Marshall.

The other man was dressed more casually and more modishly, she thought, had a moustache and goatee, longer hair, and flashed a smile of greeting absent from Marshall. He rose. "I'm Bayard Rustin. This is Mr. Marshall. We're glad to meet you." *Somehow,* Liz thought, *Marshall doesn't seem quite as glad as Rustin does.* Quickly she discovered why. Rustin continued, "You are a friend of Tom Wrought's?" Before she could answer he went on, "I suppose Tom told you that we knew each other back in New York before the war."

"I did know that, yes." Liz recalled the first pages of Tom's *Confessions. At last,* she thought, *a coincidence that might help Tom.*

"Well, Thurgood here won't want to hear it, but we were in the Young Communist League together at City College. We used to—"

"What can we do for you, Mrs. Spencer?" Marshall interrupted, pulling out a chair and offering it. He was evidently all business, unbending in his tone. *Is it because I'm a woman, or white, or just because I'm an interruption imposed by having to do a favour for someone—Dr. Franklin?*

"I'll try to be brief." Liz sat down. By now she had a cogent narrative of Tom's predicament that didn't take more than a few minutes, one that answered obvious and immediate questions. She finished, gulped a breath, and made her request. "What I need is some help trying to track down this man, Vincent Folsom, who is on the Senate Internal Security Subcommittee staff and used to work for the FBI. Then I'll need to learn as much about him as I can." Liz didn't think she needed to add *without his finding out about my interest*. She opened her bag and pulled out the newspaper cutting with the photo of Senator Eastland and his aide. "Here is a picture." She passed it across to Marshall, who gave it a cursory glance and brushed it along to Rustin.

Rustin looked up at Liz. Very slowly he said, "I know this man."

Marshall was brusque. "Yes, I'm afraid we all know the egregious Senator Eastland."

"No, it's the other one," said Liz.

Rustin looked at Liz, turned to Marshall, and was about to speak, stopped, and looked back at Liz. "I think this is a conversation we need to have alone, Mrs. Spencer, without Mr. Marshall. We'll be done in about a quarter of an hour." He rose and went to the door, gesturing Liz into the waiting room. "Perhaps you'd care to wait out here, Mrs. Spencer." Liz took the hint.

⇒⏹⇐

Bayard Rustin and Liz Spencer were seated at a booth in a bar across the street and three blocks away from the NAACP Legal Defense Fund's offices. "One of my favourite places in DC," Ruskin began. "Hard to find a bar downtown that isn't segregated. What will you have, Mrs. Spencer?"

Liz had no idea how to answer this question. "A sherry?"

"Not sure they have any; I'll check." He rose and walked to the bar. As Liz looked round, she saw she was the only woman in the place. But it wasn't crowded, and she thought nothing much of it. Rustin turned back from the bar and shook his head. She thought for a moment, then had an idea. "Gin and tonic, please." It seemed too early, but Liz had no taste for beer.

Rustin returned with a martini for himself and a gin and tonic. "Now, Mrs. Spencer, what I have to tell you is stuff that could complicate my life even more than it is already."

"Complicate your life?"

"Make it even more difficult to do what I do for the movement—the civil rights movement. So, you can use it to trace out your leads, but don't ever expect me to confirm it publicly."

"Agreed." She nodded her head.

"Well, I think I know your Mr. Vincent Folsom, but not under that name. I only knew him under the name Vinnie. It was in the late '40s. We met in bars like this one . . ." He looked round. So did Liz, but she was evidently not seeing what Rustin had indicated by his look. He would have to explain. "You see, this is a . . . bar for men only. For homosexuals, queers, homos, the limp-wrist set . . ."

Why was he disparaging himself? she wondered. Liz had to interrupt. "I get it."

"Well, it was just after the war, '46 or '47. I was much younger and better-looking, and Vinnie was a little skinnier than he is now. It was only twice we met . . ." He paused. "The first time, he was with an Englishman I had gotten to know pretty well, Guy Burgess. He was at the British embassy here in DC. Recognize the name?" When Liz shook her head, he shrugged and went on. "Very wild Burgess was. Reckless in fact. Flouted his diplomatic immunity. Said he could do anything, and then did it, just to prove he could. Drunk and disorderly, drove a flashy car, parking it anywhere he wanted, importuning in men's rooms, cocaine along with booze. I got to know Guy Burgess well during the war." He paused, as if to ask, "Do I have to spell it out for you that Burgess and I were lovers, miss?"

Liz took out her pad and a pencil stub. Rustin gently took them from her. "No notes, please. Just commit what I am telling you to memory." He handed the pad and pencil back to her, and she returned them to her purse. "Well, one night, must have been in '46, I walked into one of these bars—can't remember which. They don't last long, get closed down by the cops pretty regularly. Anyway, there was my friend Guy Burgess, with this guy Vinnie. Not my type, I thought—too old, too Southern—but who was I to know what kind of trade Burgess liked besides me? He invites me to join them, which I did for a while." Rustin took out a packet of Newport cigarettes and offered one to Liz.

"No, thanks." She fished out a packet of Gold Leaf, took one out, and offered him the packet. "British. Try one?" He took a cigarette, lit hers, and then his. Blowing out the match, he went on.

"The next time I saw Vinnie was the last time, and I haven't forgotten. It was later in the '40s, or maybe it was 1950. I was alone in one of these places, and he came up to me, sat down, and offered me a drink, asked my name. He didn't recognize me. You know how it is, one coon looks pretty much like another to a white man." His low laugh had an edge. "I didn't like his Southern accent, the way his flesh sagged out over his pants, the way he sweated and smelled. I didn't like anything about him, right down to his suspenders and his double-breasted suit. I finished my drink and got up, thanked him, and was about to leave when he reached his arm over my shoulder and took hold of me. Then he began to talk in a whisper. 'Why don't you an' me take a little walk . . . right over to the men's room an' find us a stall . . . ' When I resisted he continued—offered me ten dollars, then twenty dollars. Finally I said no, it was illegal and we could get in trouble. That's when he grabbed me by my necktie, pulled my face down to his mouth, and said, 'Look, boy, you do what you're told, and don't be worried about the DC police. They ain't gonna touch no friend of J. Edgar Hoover's.'" Rustin decided he didn't need to tell this nice lady what happened next. Liz silently agreed.

"Well, there's just one more piece of the story that you obviously don't know." Their eyes met. "Guy Burgess made the headlines a year or so later, when he defected to the Russians along with another Brit named McLean."

Liz now drew a breath. "So, Mr. Rustin, you're telling me that a senior aide to this Senator Eastland was once an FBI agent who knew a Soviet spy, had homosexual relations with him, and claimed to be a friend of J. Edgar Hoover."

"I guess you need to know one more thing, Mrs. Spencer. It's the main reason I had to take you away from Thurgood's office to speak to you. People in the homintern around DC all know that J. Edger Hoover is queer."

"Homintern?"

"That's a little British witticism. Play on 'Comintern'—the Communist International, Stalin's subversive network of Communist parties. Us gay men are supposed to be in a secret conspiracy to undermine western civilization—the homintern." Liz laughed. "Now I am going to do one more thing. I am going to go back and ask Thurgood Marshall for a little favour. You see, like any good lawyer, Thurgood cultivates that bastard J. Edgar Hoover. That's why he can't know that Hoover is a pansy. If Hoover thought he knew, there's no telling what he'd try to get on Thurgood. Anyway, I am going to try to prevail on him to pick up the phone and call his friend J. Edgar and just casually ask him if he knows this Vincent Folsom. I've tied your Mr. Vincent Folsom to a Russian spy. Let's see if Thurgood can tie him to the head of the FBI. He might not, but it's worth a try."

"Thank you, Mr. Rustin. Thank you."

"Tom Wrought deserves it. How long are you in town?"

"I can stay a day or so longer. This country is frightfully expensive."

"Does Thurgood know where he can reach you?"

"I'm staying at the Howard University guest house."

Liz spent the next morning as a tourist. When she came back to the Howard guest house, there was a message for her. *Would it be convenient for Mr. Marshall to see you at five thirty at the guest house?* She telephoned the NAACP Legal Defense Fund office and left word to say she'd be waiting.

There he was, precisely at five thirty, soberly but elegantly dressed, with brogues—what did they call them in America? wing tips—so polished they were blinding in the afternoon light. Liz came down the stairs, and Marshall indicated the sitting room to the right of the door. They took seats on either side of a bay window, but not before Marshall pulled the drapes enough so that they could not be seen from the street, Liz noticed.

"Thank you for meeting me again, Mr. Marshall; I know you're busy."

"I must be brief, Mrs. Spencer. And I fear I can't answer any questions. But I do have something worth communicating. First, I have to say that my interests and Bayard Rustin's are broadly the same. But we differ on some important matters. One of them is the role of Communist Party members in the civil rights movement. I think it would be catastrophic to give the bigots a red-baiting stick to beat us with. Bayard disagrees. He would, given his own background."

"How does this relate to Tom, Mr. Marshall?" Liz tried hard not to sound impatient.

"Just at present I am trying to remove a Communist Party member from Dr. Martin Luther King Jr.'s inner circle." Marshall paused momentarily. Liz had no idea how to respond to this disclosure. Silence was her only recourse. She simply held his gaze and waited. Apparently gratified that she had asked no question, Marshall continued, "Well, my efforts are known to J. Edgar Hoover, and they provided a pretext to call him today. I asked him if the FBI was acquainted with this person I am trying to remove. He told me that they were." Marshall was as precise as a witness on the stand, answering his own questions. "Then I asked whether Hoover was prepared to get in touch with the Senate Internal

Security Subcommittee about this party member in Dr. King's entourage. I suggested the mere threat of forcing this man to testify might lead him to resign from Dr. King's inner circle. Hoover told me that this might be arranged. As I was hoping he might, he told me one of his best agents—a personal friend, Hoover called him—had left the bureau for Eastland's staff. Hoover said he'd see to it that the idea of subpoenaing the red in Dr. King's circle was conveyed by his friend to the senator personally. That former FBI agent must be your man, Vincent Folsom. I'm afraid I can't say any more." Marshall rose and offered her his hand. "Good luck to Mr. Wrought." Then he turned and left the building.

Liz felt slightly exultant. She had forged links in a chain that now went from the head of the FBI all the way to Soviet intelligence. And it was a chain that went right through the British foreign service. But how was this chain attached to Tom?

The next morning she boarded a Greyhound to New York. It was easy to retrace her steps east to Grand Central Station, where she found her airport bus—she wasn't calling it a "coach" any longer—to Idlewild Airport and the BOAC Comet IV back to London. This time there was a tailwind, and eight hours later the passengers were buckling their seat belts for the descent to Heathrow.

CHAPTER NINETEEN

Ruislip was a long tube ride, too long, on the Metropolitan line, almost to Uxbridge, a journey Alice had never made before. Since Harrow the train had been travelling in the open, and this gave Alice something to look at—grey clouds threatening to rain on the little back gardens of an endless line of suburban two-family villas. Hardly anyone was left in the carriage as the train pulled into Ruislip. Alice began to feel almost reluctant to alight.

Without any idea of what to expect, she had decided that paranoia was a good working hypothesis. Alice had left a note on her desk, saying exactly where she had gone, and put another one in the hands of Victor Mishcon's secretary. It would have been better to tell Liz Spencer, but Liz was already in New York. Now she was glad she'd done it.

Well before she had arrived, she had tried on and discarded half a dozen different approaches. She had very little to go on, and each one of the stratagems she tried on connected the little she knew to very far-fetched scenarios. Only one of them had any chance of helping Tom, and she was going to act on it. The Krogers were the Cohens. They'd been Russian agents in New York. Lona had to have been a courier carrying design secrets from the Manhattan Project at Los Alamos to

New York for transmission to Soviet nuclear bomb scientists. She'd tried to recruit Tom to the work. They'd left when the FBI's net had begun to close in on the Rosenbergs and were now working for the KGB in Britain. Finally, Alice recalled, Helen Kroger, as she now called herself, had been much too eager to insist that Tom had mistaken them for someone else, and Peter Kroger's retreat the instant he saw Tom was much too precipitate. She would lay it out, brook no denial. If she was right, she had a good idea of how to use the fact to help Tom.

Imagine living out here, Alice thought as she clambered up the pedestrian bridge over the tracks and then down again to the station building. She pulled out a battered *London A to Z(ed)* and made her way through a few twists and turns to 45 Cranley Drive. When she got there, it turned out to be a white stucco bungalow behind a low brick wall at the end of a street of unpainted two-storey attached villas. Prewar? Postwar? She couldn't be sure. Taking a breath, she rang the bell.

The woman who came to the door towered over Alice but smiled and invited her in. She appeared to be dressed for gardening, and the soil stain at her knees confirmed this. "I expect you've come for the Orwell. I've got it in the kitchen." Helen Kroger spoke with a decidedly London accent, nothing like the way Lona Cohen, New Yorker, would have sounded. Her hair was covered by a kerchief tied behind her head, rather the way a Russian babushka might. *Just the way a Russian spy would,* Alice couldn't help thinking. *Russian spy with Mayfair accent?* She followed the woman back to the kitchen, where Helen Kroger picked up a brown paper parcel, tied with string. "Do you want to open it and have a look?"

"Actually I don't, Mrs. Kroger, but I'd like to speak to you and your husband, if he is at home. It's rather urgent, I am afraid."

Helen Kroger looked at the young woman and decided she was serious. "Very well; I'll get him." She went to the back door and called out, "Peter, there's someone here who wants to talk to us."

A moment later Peter Kroger came in the door, also dressed for gardening. He seemed to be about fifty, with a mop of white hair parted almost in the middle. He was large enough to be a good match for his wife, but thin and rather athletic in appearance. He smiled brightly and extended his hand. Automatically Alice took it.

"Care to sit, Miss . . ." her hostess said.

"No, I'll stand, thank you." She cleared her throat. "My name is Alice Silverstone. I'm a solicitor. Thank you for the book, but that's not really why I've come." Nothing for it but to dive in. "I have reason to believe that you are not Mr. and Mrs. Peter and Helen Kroger, but that you are in fact Morris and Lona Cohen."

The woman looked at her. "I beg your pardon? Who are these people, and how did you come to mistake us for them?"

Meanwhile Peter Kroger peeled off his gardening gloves. "It's funny, young lady, but you are not the first to make that mistake. Someone addressed Mrs. Kroger that way a few months ago in town. She must have a double somewhere." He laughed at the thought.

"That was Mr. Tom Wrought, sir, who saw her . . . and you too, a few weeks later at the same bookshop." *Time to start putting some cards on the table,* Alice thought. "I believe you both know him from your days in New York, ten years ago and more."

Helen Kroger stood her ground. "Sorry, we don't know anyone of that name."

But her husband had already decided on another tack.

"Please sit down, Miss . . . Silverstone, and tell us what you came about." He pulled a chair from the kitchen table and sat down. Wordlessly Helen Kroger did the same. Alice now felt she had to take a seat as well.

When they were all sitting still at the oilskin-covered table, she began again. Alice had very few more cards to play. How well could she bluff? "As you know, Tom Wrought was arrested for murder." If they knew, it wouldn't be from newspaper stories. There had been none, really. Alice would learn something from any admission that they knew. She got none.

Helen Kroger responded, "We know no such thing. Who is this Tom Wrought? What does a murder have to do with us?"

Peter Kroger sighed. "Miss Silverstone, we are going to hear you out. But we aren't going to bother confirming or denying your innuendos. Now, pray continue."

Alice looked from Peter Kroger to Helen Kroger and back. Then she began again. "Tom Wrought has been framed for a murder. I have reason to believe that the victim was either murdered by Soviet agents or that they arranged for him to be murdered under circumstances that throw grave suspicions on Mr. Wrought."

Peter Kroger now asked, "Why would Soviet agents do this, please?" Alice watched Helen Kroger give her husband a sharp look. She must also have kicked him under the table, as he could not suppress a grimace of pain. Kroger looked back at her and repeated his question. "Why would the Russians want to make trouble for this Mr. Wrought?"

"That is something I was hoping you could help me with, Mr. and Mrs. . . ." Alice couldn't decide what to call them. Then she chose, "Cohen."

Very calmly and with all the sincere friendliness she could muster, Helen Kroger replied, "I'm sorry, Miss Silverstone, but I promise you, our names are Kroger. I think we can prove that in a court of law. And we really know nothing about Soviet agents or your Mr. Wrought. Now unless there is something else you want to tell us, we need to get back to our garden before we lose the light." She rose and began pulling on her gloves.

"Very well, Mr. and Mrs. Cohen . . . or Kroger." Alice got out of her chair. She had to raise the stakes. "I didn't expect you immediately to own up to a junior solicitor asking questions." There was only one threat to make. "So, speak to whomever your resident controller is. You may tell him that unless steps are taken to clear Mr. Wrought by revealing the real murderers, I will have no alternative but to identify you both to the CID and MI5. I should also tell you that, should I come to any harm, everything I have said today will find its way to the authorities." She put a business card on the table. "You can reach me at this number." Then Alice rose, and with all the appearance of sangfroid she could muster, walked to the front door and let herself out of the house.

⟞⟝

Alice was shivering as she walked back to the tube stop. It wasn't a very cold day, but she was walking into a stiff breeze; suddenly the shirt-waist dress under her trench coat was sodden with perspiration. It was an acrid sweat of nerves and fright that Alice had not even noticed in the Krogers' kitchen. There had been no sign of menace, but she must have picked it up without allowing the recognition of threat—especially from the woman—to penetrate her demeanour. Only at the station did she realize she had left the first edition of the Orwell and now would have nothing to distract her on the ride back to central London. And only after that did she recall that she had no particular reason to worry about threats to her life. She calmed down and cooled off quickly.

⟞⟝

It was the very next day when her intercom buzzed. "Telephone for you, a Mrs. Kroger." The office clerk was speaking.

"Very well, put her through, Mr. Boyle." Alice smiled to herself. This was indeed before time. "Alice Silverstone."

"It's Helen Kroger, Miss Silverstone. You left your copy of *Homage to Catalonia*. Can you come collect it tomorrow round eight o'clock in the evening?"

"Back up to Ruislip?"

323

"Didn't you say you live here?"

A slip! Probably harmless now, but you have to keep your wits about you dealing with spies, Alice. "Oh yes. I'm at work just now in town."

⟨———⟩

Even before Alice had rung the bell, the door was opened by Peter Kroger, whose smile seemed forced. "Come in, Miss Silverstone. Please, follow me."

This time they turned left at the hall and entered a lounge, where Helen Kroger was already seated. The chesterfield was hard, in a durable fabric, with three little buttons across the back. The matching lounge chair looked no more comfortable. In the corner were a small television and a console radio with shortwave bands on the large tuning dial. The mantelpiece over a three-filament electric fire bore no pictures, Dalton china, or figurines. It was cold in the house. The room gave the appearance of never really being used much at all. It was as if the house's occupants never wished to be seen from the street.

No longer in gardening clothes, both Krogers were dressed for an evening excursion. Neither looked as calm or confident as they had when Alice had left them. All sat down round the coffee table. Helen Kroger was glaring at her with the look of someone about to lose her husband to another, younger woman. Peter Kroger kept his eyes to the floor, looking almost sheepish. Rather like a schoolboy about to come clean about a prank he had been resolutely refusing to admit doing. The silence persisted, however, even after they had settled themselves.

Alice tried to piece the scene together. *Her look could kill; his demeanour is hangdog. None of this makes sense.*

Kroger pushed a bamboo cigarette box towards Alice, and she took one. Finally he spoke. "There is someone who wishes to meet you, Miss Silverstone. But he requires complete anonymity. And therefore we need to take some extraordinary measures."

"Such as?" Alice was more curious now than anxious.

"You will be blindfolded, and your hands will be bound, loosely, but in a way that assures you cannot pull down the blindfold."

"Would a promise on my honour not to peek suffice?"

It was a Slavic voice from another room that replied, "Nope, 'fraid not." Slavic, but obviously fluent and tinged with that Americanism "nope."

Alice stood, put her hands behind her, and allowed Helen Kroger to tie them with the sort of cord used to wrap book parcels. Then a hood was placed over her head. "I thought you said blindfolded." She was surprised. "This is rather claustrophobic."

It was Peter Kroger who replied, "With regret, our friend insists. Mrs. Kroger and I will withdraw now, Miss Silverstone, and return when your interview is over."

A few moments later, Alice heard the front door close.

"Please, tell me what you want," came the voice of the man from the other room.

Alice wanted to know at least something about the man she was dealing with. "Your English is American, isn't it? Where did you learn?"

The reply betrayed his origins. "Do not trifle with me." He hadn't lost the Russian difficulty with the English *v* for *w*, and the *th* came out as a *zed*. "Tell me what exactly you want."

"I want my client freed from jail."

"We had nothing to do with it."

"Whether or not you had anything to do with it, that's what I want. Unless I get it, your friends' names will be given to MI5."

"If that happens, Miss Silverstone, you won't live very long, and neither will Mr. Wrought, in prison or out."

"So be it."

Was the man threatening her or bluffing? She knew immediately. *Couldn't be bluffing. This meeting is an admission that the Krogers are spies.* At last she knew something for sure, something lethal. Not for her, but for Tom Wrought and Liz Spencer. It was a genie that could not be put back in the bottle without erasing their knowledge or erasing them. *This genie can kill,* she knew. *But can it grant wishes?* Alice was too scared to smile at the thought. Suddenly in the underheated lounge, Alice had begun to perspire again.

"Why do you think we had anything to do with what happened to Mr. Wrought?"

"Because he twigged to the fact that the Krogers are the Cohens." Alice had to convince, she knew. "She had tried to get him involved in espionage back in the '40s in New York. He knew immediately they were spies. They told you he'd identified them here. You couldn't kill him, because an investigation might have led back to them. So you had him framed for a murder and sold him to the CID."

"No, no, no. You're adding two and two and getting five. The Krogers never told me about meeting Wrought till yesterday. Foolish of them to have waited so long to tell me, but true. So, no one on our side had anything to do with it."

"Sorry. I'm not buying." Alice was suddenly glad the hood was hiding her slight smile. "Find a way to get him out, or he goes to British counterintelligence. As for threatening him or me, if we promise to keep our mouths shut, you'll always have to worry that we won't. But if you kill either one of us, the information is guaranteed to get to MI5."

"I'm telling you for the last time, we had nothing to do with it, so far as I know."

"Maybe you don't know everything." It was time for the card she had been holding back. She had no idea of its value. She didn't even know if it was a card in this game. "Perhaps you should ask Mr. Philby about it."

"Who?"

"Philby, Kim Philby."

There was a distinct pause, an intake of breath, almost as if her interlocutor had received an elbow in the ribcage. Then the words came, "Who is he, please?"

"Ask around." She heard the man rise, walk—no, stomp out of the room, and slam the front door. *Thank you, Kim Philby. Whoever you are, you've made everything I've said much more convincing.*

A moment later Alice heard the front door open again. The Krogers had returned. Her hood was removed and her hands unbound. Wordlessly Helen Kroger handed Alice her coat and the book, pushed her out the door, and locked it.

⸻⧫⸻

Alice walked back to the underground station. This time she felt cool and collected, happy with the way the interview had gone. Alice noticed that at least for a little while, her pain was gone, suppressed perhaps by some combination of adrenalin and whatever else made one happy. She couldn't blame the Krogers for beating a retreat, though she had no intention of blowing their cover, not immediately at any rate. But they couldn't be sure of that.

Sitting under a lamp at a bench on the open platform, she unwrapped the Orwell and began to read. She suspected that she'd hear from the Russia spy network in London even before she finished the book. She was wrong. *Homage to Catalonia* was a fast read, and the first main directorate of the KGB was a very ponderous organization.

⸻⧫⸻

A wet morning engulfed the whole southeast of England as Alice arrived at Brixton Prison. Her high-heeled pumps were sodden. The rainwater was still running off her coat and pooling round her feet by the time she'd finished filling out the prison visit forms. The walk to the interview room felt like treading on sponges. And the passageways were holding on to all the cold they had absorbed in the wintry night.

Would the authorities confiscate the magic slates? she wondered. *Were the warders really taken in by the tale about the psychiatrist? Who was so interested and so powerful that they were permitted to violate a prisoner's rights with such impunity?* Approval for that kind of illegality could only come from someone high in government—a cabinet minister or senior civil servant. Well, there was no point making an issue of it before she had found a way to free Tom Wrought. *If you live long enough to do either of those things.*

After the usual protocols, Tom and Alice faced each other and took up the psychiatric charade again as she handed him a slate.

Tom said, "Here's the next two composition books, all filled out." Alice had tried to indicate the slates, but he kept talking. Then he took a slate and wrote,

> They're filled with gibberish, but they have been examined every time I am out of the cell for exercise period. There's a long arm reaching into this prison.

Taking up her slate, she spoke a bit too loudly in case anyone was listening. "I'm afraid I didn't bring new ones."

Tom's face assumed a look of disappointment. Then he took one of the books back. "There are still some blank pages in this one. I'll finish it off, shall I?"

"Yes, of course." She handed him the slate on which she had been writing.

Krogers are spies. I visited them. It spooked them into contacting their controller. He met with me. Didn't see his face though.

My hypothesis: They alerted KGB that you could blow their cover. Their controller denies any involvement. Threatens death to you, me, if we disclose to authorities. Thoughts?

Tom read and reflected for a moment, handed the slate back, and then began writing.

Possible Krogers are gathering intelligence on British nuclear program. That would be enough to make them worth protecting. But why not just threaten to silence or kill me themselves? Another question: Does the KGB control Scotland Yard? Can it reach into a remand prison now?

He passed the slate to her. Alice wiped it clean quickly and passed it back. She had been writing at the same time that he was answering her first message.

They couldn't kill you. Thorough investigation of your death might have led the Brits right to the Krogers.

Now, if you trade Krogers to MI5 for your freedom, KGB will probably target you, me, Liz(?) anyway.

We could demand they exchange someone they are holding in Russia for you and threaten them with disclosure if they refuse.

Tom read quickly and shook his head violently.

No go. I don't want to live in Russia, and I certainly wouldn't take Liz there. How about you? Do you think the KGB will leave you here untouched?

Now it was Alice's turn to shake her head. She took up her stylus again.

There's got to be more pieces to the puzzle we're missing.

Remember the name Kim Philby I asked you about a few weeks ago? He's the one who called Michael Foot about your anonymous articles.

He thought for a moment. Then he shook his head and wrote,

Told you I don't recognize the name. Why?

She responded,

It's just a small piece of the puzzle that doesn't fit. I tried to find out anything I could about him. Then a well-connected friend warned me he was dangerous. I tried the name on the Krogers' control. He claimed not to know the name either. But he didn't act like it.

Tom picked up his slate.

I'm sorry I got you into this. Wish I could be more help. Just playing with magic slates is maddening.

Alice smiled and wrote,

Don't worry about me. Solicitors know how to protect themselves. This is the best case I've taken since I was admitted to the bar. More fun than defending Soho strippers.

Then she added,

Liz comes back from the States tomorrow morning. Let's see if she has found some more puzzle pieces.

The next morning Alice Silverstone was at her desk in Red Lion Square. She had taken *The Confessions of Tom Wrought* from the Left Luggage at Kings Cross and was rereading them for the fourth time. Alice was trying to find something she had missed or a way of connecting the episodes that would withstand the most obvious objections. What she wanted was a cigarette, but it was eight fifteen and if she took one this early, her throat would hurt, and she would have finished a packet by suppertime. *Why are you worried about smoking too much, Alice?* she demanded of herself, but could find no answer. Then the intercom rang. "A Liz Spencer for you."

"Put her through." Alice waited for the transfer. There seemed to be an extra click before she heard Liz's voice.

"I'm at Heathrow. I've got news—"

Suddenly Alice became paranoid about the extra sound she'd heard. "Can't talk now, Liz. I'm with a client."

There was a momentary silence at the other end, telling her that Liz couldn't understand why she was being put off. "I'll be there in an hour. Will you be free?"

"Yes, but let's not meet here." She thought for a moment. What was the name of Liz's administrator at the Abbey National? Yes, she had it. "Let's meet at Beatrice's desk." Would Liz understand?

"Ah . . . Yes . . . uh, good. See you then." It was clear she understood. Someone might be listening.

No need to involve Beatrice Russell. Alice would intercept Liz in the lobby of the Abbey National if she could creep in by a rear door. It would also be more fun to try to discover if she was being followed as well as bugged. She walked to the tube station at Holborn, took the underground to Leicester Square, went into the ABC movie theatre, bought a ticket, and immediately left by the rear, found a cab, and jumped in. "Edgware Road tube station, please." There she boarded a train for Baker Street. Emerging, she made her way to Siddon's Lane and entered the Abbey National building from the rear. It had taken her twenty-five minutes, cost two quid, and she didn't have the slightest idea whether anyone had followed her at all. But it had all been quite amusing. Yes, that was exactly the right word, *amusing*.

When the commissionaire approached, Alice had a ready answer. "I've a meeting with Mrs. Russell."

The man touched his white cap. "Very good, miss. Not here yet." She stood by his desk, and a few moments later he looked up. "There she is now, miss." Beatrice Russell had entered the lobby and was making for the lift. Alice moved to intercept her.

"Mrs. Russell, you don't know me. I'm a friend of Liz Spencer. If she's upstairs already, could you tell her Alice is downstairs?"

"Certainly, but I don't think she'll be there. I don't expect her at all today. She was in the West Riding of Yorkshire yesterday, visiting branches." *How nice,* Alice thought, *to have such an accomplished liar as a friend.* Russell moved along to the lifts without another word. Now, would the officious commissionaire usher Alice out of the building?

A few minutes later she saw Liz enter, carrying a small suitcase. When she was certain Liz had spotted her, Alice turned and went out the way she'd come, back into Siddons Lane. Liz followed. Up the lane they went, Alice twenty paces in front of Liz, out onto Glentworth Street and round the corner at St. Cyprian's Church. Alas, it was not open that early. But next to it, on Ivor Place, was a thoroughly uninviting tea shop, small but crowded. Alice turned to see Liz still behind her. Then she entered the café. She was seated at a small Formica table facing an empty chair when Liz got there a few seconds later, put down her case, and removed her coat.

"Sorry, I'm getting paranoid. I think the Russians are tapping my phone and following me round."

Liz didn't seem surprised. "Maybe it's the FBI." She smiled.

Alice laughed. "CIA." She couldn't help being slightly pedantic. "FBI's not allowed to operate abroad. This is CIA turf. Same rules for Brits—MI6, intelligence, operates abroad. MI5, counterintelligence, operates at home."

"Too bad. What I learned in Washington concerned only the FBI. Maybe my trip was pointless." She sighed. "Shall I tell you the gist, or give you all the details as near as I can remember them all?"

"Tell me everything and then your conclusion. That way I may notice something you didn't."

"Can I have a cup of tea first?" Alice signalled the waitress over. Then Liz began, introducing John Hope Franklin, her bus ride to Washington, DC, the NAACP Legal Defense Fund offices, Thurgood Marshall, Bayard Rustin, how they looked and sounded. Making Marshall's acquaintance was something that impressed Alice, Liz could see. Was he that much of a celebrity among lawyers? Liz conveyed as much as she could remember of the conversation in what Rustin had called a gay bar, and then Marshall's subsequent visit to the Howard University guest house.

"So, is there a theory that puts together the pieces you found, Liz?"

"Well, here's one that I toyed with most of the flight back. It was Tom's bad luck to have run-ins with Vincent Folsom in Louisiana and France during the war—just coincidence. After the war, Vincent Folsom gets a job in the FBI; maybe he even had improper relations with Hoover before he was hired. More likely, he became intimate with Hoover after joining the FBI. That's not really important. Either way, Hoover trusted Folsom, or else was being blackmailed by him." Alice nodded. "Now, Folsom was in the FBI when it was going after the atom spies in the '40s. Maybe he was even involved in the *Rosenberg* case. Could he have come across Tom at that time?"

Alice observed, "If he had, Tom would have mentioned it, no?"

"That's what I thought. Let's assume they didn't meet in New York. If they had, Folsom might have remembered looking for Tom in the war when he was on the Red Ball Express." Liz stopped to be sure Alice was following. "But then it's Folsom who writes a letter that gets Tom fired from his teaching post. Why Folsom? Just another coincidence? Can't be. And why do they want him fired from a Negro college no one in power really cares about?"

Alice suggested, "Communists in the civil rights movement?"

Liz shook her head. "No. Tom didn't have any personal contact with the civil rights movement in 1956, not that he's told us about."

"Let's assume it's Hoover who wanted Tom fired, for reasons that have nothing to do with his being a Communist, and that Hoover couldn't tell anyone about it except someone he shares other secrets with." Alice paused.

Liz asked the obvious question. "OK, but why would he want Tom fired?" Then she tried to answer her own question. "Because he doesn't want Tom in Washington, DC. For some reason J. Edgar Hoover is frightened of Tom Wrought's presence in the national capital." This didn't sound very plausible to Alice. Still, she let Liz continue. "But then, what could Tom know that would threaten Hoover? That Hoover is a pansy? No. He didn't know that. That Hoover is protecting someone who got rich selling black-market gasoline to the French during the war? No. Hoover probably doesn't even know about Folsom's war."

"Is that it?" Liz nodded. Alice took a breath. "Here's another theory. Let me tell you what I learned while you were gone." Alice recounted her journeys to Ruislip.

When she finished, Liz replied, "Your Russian spy theory is better. Protecting the Krogers gave them a motive to sideline Tom the moment he met them last fall."

"But their control said they never told him about running into Tom."

Liz pondered the objection. "Did you believe him?" Alice shrugged her shoulders. "At least we have a concrete reason why the Russians would want to frame Tom, instead of just some pretty thin speculation about a powerful man in Washington who doesn't even know Tom Wrought."

"We're missing something obvious. What is it?" Alice frowned. "There are whole parts of Tom's story that we haven't even thought about, let alone fitted together with anything we've learned so far."

Liz replied instantly, "And I can tell you what they are." She paused to let Alice catch up. Simultaneously they said the word "*Finland*," and then Alice observed, "Tom was there twice."

"Yes." Liz paused. "Two trips, years apart."

Alice pulled Tom's two composition books out of her brief bag.

Liz began again, "And there is something else, something I couldn't fit into my theory of Hoover or Folsom wanting to get Tom out of Washington." She grinned as the pieces fell together in her mind. "Rustin said that he met Folsom after the war, together with someone named Burgess, who turned out to be a Russian spy." She started to leaf through the pages of the second book and reached Tom's second trip to Finland. "Got it. Tom says he was there, in Finland, just after Burgess and the other spy, McLean, defected. Another coincidence?"

"Of course! We've got Hoover connected to a Soviet spy through Folsom, just before a lot of British and American agents in Russia were blown by that very spy—Burgess." They both paused at the thought forming in their minds. Now they had two theories to explore— Russians protecting their spies in Ruislip, or some link between Burgess, his friend in the FBI, and Tom's trips to Finland.

"I'm going home"—Liz yawned—"to call my kids in Birkenhead and take a bath." She pushed her chair back.

Alice grasped her wrist. "Look, I don't think the Soviets know anything about you, but be careful. If you think you are being followed or someone is listening to your calls, we've got to know. If you need to get in touch, use a call box, and leave the number with my clerk or the answering service if I'm not at home."

They both rose and went out of the tea shop in opposite directions.

CHAPTER TWENTY

"Walk with me, Miss Silverstone. Let's make a few turns round the square. It's not a bad day."

She'd been crossing Lincoln's Inn field on the way back to the office from the Inns of Court when the man fell in with her pace. The voice was Russian, the same one she'd listened to in Ruislip five days before. Now it was deeper, more relaxed, but still, Alice realized, betraying an English learned in America.

"My name is Feklisov, Alexandr Semyonovich Feklisov, and I'm a Russian spy." He paused for effect. "Don't worry about me, though; I have a diplomatic passport. In fact, I am the highest-ranking Soviet agent in England. You may ask about me at the Foreign Office or in the intelligence services if you know anyone there. My card." He handed her a business card embossed with heavy ink in Cyrillic and English: COMMERCIAL ATTACHÉ, SOVIET EMBASSY. Alice said nothing as she matched his pace and trajectory back round the footpath a second time. He was a marvellously nondescript specimen, she thought. You'd pass him a dozen times and still not realize you'd seen him before. He was that plain. A man of about forty-five with a somewhat oval face, no angles, rounded cheeks, salt-and-pepper hair, wearing the sort of topcoat you might purchase off the peg anywhere. The only thing that marked him out was a nice smile, one that seemed genuine when he finally turned his head and looked at her.

"I wish to repeat what I told you last week. We know nothing about the difficulties your Mr. Wrought has found himself in. But we don't intend to allow these difficulties to compromise our"—he searched for the right word—"work."

"Well, Mr. . . . . Feklisov?" Had she gotten his name right? He nodded. "What can I do for you?"

"You can tell me why you think we had any hand in Wrought's arrest and why you think we can help free him."

"I've been over that ground with the Krogers and with you. The KGB have a motive to frame Wrought, and surely you have the resources. Your denials are simply not going to change my mind."

"You mentioned a name to me up in Ruislip at the Krogers'. Philby, Kim Philby. What do you know of this man; how is he involved?"

Now Alice was much more confident. She had been followed and had her phone tapped, but had not been threatened again. Perhaps it was because of this name, Philby, that had taken Feklisov's breath away in Ruislip. If Feklisov was the most important agent in Britain, then it was this name, Philby, that had brought him to her side today. "I can only tell you this, Mr. Russian Spy, a man by that name called the editor of the *Tribune*, Mr. Michael Foot, to ask about two reviews that Wrought had anonymously written for the paper, one about the *Rosenberg* trial and the other about the *Dr. Zhivago* craze." She stopped. "Now, you tell me who Philby is."

Feklisov ignored the question completely. "Ah, Miss Silverstone, you have solved a little mystery for me. It was your Mr. Wrought who wrote those two pieces? He is a very perceptive analyst. I assume you are in touch with him."

"Yes, indeed."

"Well, ask him a personal question for me. How could he have been so sure that Ethel Rosenberg was innocent and David Greenglass's wife was guilty?"

"Why should I ask him?"

"As I said, the question is personal—just a matter of curiosity."

"I will, if you call off the shadows and the wiretap. Fair exchange?"

"I promise you, Miss Silverstone, we are doing neither."

"Then I can't help you."

"Very well; tell your Mr. Wrought that his guesses are both correct. Ethel Rosenberg was innocent, and Ruth Greenglass was guilty. And it was us trying to make Pasternak into a CIA stooge. But they started it, flooding our country with the Russian language edition of *Dr. Zhivago*. Just ask him how he found out."

"And in return?"

"I will see what I can do to help you—uh, him."

Would he really? That very much depended, Feklisov realized as he made his way back to the Soviet embassy, ensuring that there was no one very interested in his circuitous trajectory.

Alexandr Feklisov was a child of the revolution, one who had literally accepted the omniscience, if not the omnipotence, first of Lenin, then of Joseph Stalin, along with his mother's milk. He had grown to adulthood in the '30s, experiencing the visible success of socialism in one country—not just in the official statistics but in the ways his mother's life in Moscow improved from year to year. He had been a young pioneer, then a *Komsomol*, and finally a paid-up party member. Unassuming, visibly without ambition, he had been untouched by Stalin's purges. So well had he learned the catechism that by 1934 he had begun to wend his way through the alphabet of Soviet intelligence agencies—the OGPU, the NKVD, the MVD, and finally the KGB.

Trusted because he was thought to be a cipher, Alexandr Feklisov had been sent into the whirlwind of midcentury history. First Spain in its civil war, then New York in the '40s, now London. He had hardly ever managed to get back to Moscow and his mother in twenty-five years. Alas, the years abroad had ruined him with the truth. It was no longer the motherland to which he was loyal, but his people, his agents, his spies, whose trust he would not betray.

⟞⟝

"I was in the neighbourhood and thought I'd drop by, Tom." Alice tried to sound casual. "The psychiatrist said I missed a test question." She could hardly keep a straight face. "So I thought I'd pop round to make it up." She pulled the slates out of the brief bag and wrote,

> *Things are looking up. Can't discuss. Please tell me, how did you know that Ethel Rosenberg was innocent and Ruth Greenglass was guilty? That's all I need at the moment.*

Tom began writing.

> *Ethel could never type. Ruth was good at it. How do I know? Ruth typed my PhD thesis, and Ethel could never get a job that required typing. She was a singer and a filing clerk.*

Alice read the slate, pulled up the cellophane, and rose. "Thanks; that's all."

Tom looked at her quizzically, as if to say, *Can't you tell me more?* But all he said was, "Really."

It was all she could do not to scrawl that he had been right about *Dr. Zhivago* too.

⊷⊶

"Not very good at spotting a tail, are you?" It was Feklisov, catching up to her not a quarter of a mile along the Brixton Hill Road to the tube station.

"How did you do that? I was watching the whole way. Out and back." She was impressed.

"A great deal of experience." He laughed. "Actually I cheated. Since I knew where you were going, I didn't bother tailing you here once I saw you leaving your flat."

"That's a relief." Alice gave a self-deprecating laugh. "I had no idea you were so eager for an answer to your idle question."

"Not idle, just personal, Miss Silverstone. May I have the answer?"

"Tom says he knew that Ethel couldn't type and that Ruth could. In fact, he says she typed his PhD thesis. Ethel Rosenberg is dead. Why is this so important to you, Mr. Feklisov?"

"Perhaps you don't think espionage agents have feelings, Miss Silverstone. They shouldn't, but alas, they do." He paused. "I knew her husband, Julie Rosenberg, very well during the war. He was the best agent I ever ran. We were friends. So many years working together under conditions of extreme danger. You couldn't help getting to know someone. And of course his wife, Ethel. I knew her too—and the children, two small boys. I knew the older one as a baby. But Ethel didn't even know who I was, really, or what I was doing. So far as she knew, I was an immigrant garment cutter on Seventh Avenue, with a missing finger to prove it." He held up his right hand to show a ring finger that ended at the first joint.

Alice slowed their pace, then she turned to face him. "I don't see where you are going, Mr. Feklisov, besides up the Brixton Hill Road to the tube station."

He took her arm and began walking towards the bullseye **UNDERGROUND** sign they could see a street away now. "The FBI knew Ethel was innocent," he said, using her first name, "and they killed her anyway. Left two small children no one would touch—how do they say, with a barge pole? I hate those cruel men with a personal hatred, not just a professional one, Miss Silverstone. Do you understand?"

Alice turned to face him again. "Does this mean you'll help Tom?"

"I am sorry, Miss Silverstone. How can I help him? We didn't lock up your Mr. Wrought in Brixton Prison, and we can't get him out."

Alice spoke calmly and slowly. "If you don't find a way, we'll have to let the British know about the Krogers up in Ruislip."

"Would it be worth your life and Mr. Wrought's, and perhaps even mine?" He left the question hanging, climbed into a Hillman Minx parked at the tube stop, and drove away without again looking her way.

⊷

It was the lunch hour, and they were sitting in the dingy tea shop on Ivor Place.

"Can we force Feklisov to help us?" Alice wondered aloud. "He knows we can give the Krogers to MI5."

"MI5, which one is that again, Alice?" Liz just couldn't keep the labels straight.

"MI5, counterintelligence, catches spies in Britain. Like the American FBI or your Canadian Mounties. MI6 are the British spies abroad, like the CIA." Alice smiled. "Look, there is a lot we haven't told Feklisov—about Hoover and Folsom, about Burgess and what Tom did in Finland in '51, and how the CIA treated him when he got back. Maybe it adds up to something that will scare Feklisov." Then she laughed. "Or appeal to his better nature."

Liz joined in her laugh. "Well, why not tell him everything we know?"

"Why not?" Alice's voice had an edge of anger. "We don't know why, but all that information was enough to get your husband killed, and he didn't even know it!" Liz nodded. Alice pushed her cut cucumber sandwich away in disgust. "Nonetheless, we've got to tell him. We don't have a choice at this point."

"Well, Feklisov hasn't had us killed yet. Probably we can still trust him." Liz smiled weakly and dabbed her mouth with a paper napkin.

"The problem is getting in touch with him. I'm pretty certain my phone is being tapped, and I still feel as though I'm being followed . . . by Russians or by someone." She remembered his last words to her. "He said he might be risking his life if he helped us. That means he's afraid of his own side, not ours. With a diplomatic passport, MI5 can't touch him."

"Give me his embassy card. I have an idea."

Alice passed it across the table.

⟽⟾

"Soviet consulate, to whom do you wish to speak?"

Liz was surprised. The voice was English, plummy at that. She was in a call box at Victoria, with an extra earpiece that Alice was holding to her ear.

"Commercial attaché, please."

"Which one, please."

"Ah . . . Mr. Feklisov."

"Very good."

"Hello, Feklisov here."

"Ah, Mr. Feklisov. My name is Sydney Carton. I am the directress of the Sefton Park Palm House in Liverpool. As you may know, like the rest of the country, we gave up a great deal of our wrought-iron gates and fences for the war effort." She overemphasized *wrought*. Would the penny drop?

343

"Yes, how can I help?"

"Well, last month I saw a photo of the spectacular wrought-iron fence of the Mikhailovsky Gardens in Leningrad. We love wrought iron here in Liverpool, and we would like to encourage trade with the Soviet Union. So, I would like to invite you to visit Sefton Park so that we can discuss the purchase of . . . wrought . . . iron"—Liz felt like a foolish girl playing a dangerous game—"from the foundry that made those fences."

There was a period of silence on the other end of the line. "I should be pleased to come and discuss it. Let me see, Miss . . . what was your name again?"

"Carton, Sydney Carton, like the character in Dickens's *Tale of Two Cities*."

Feklisov laughed. "You mean the one who gives up his life for an innocent man?" The penny had dropped. "Well, Miss Carton—"

"It's Mrs., actually."

"I think I can get up there the day after tomorrow. Will that suit?"

"Perfectly. I'll meet you at the entrance to the Palm House in the middle of Sefton Park. Shall we say 2:00 p.m.?"

"Very good."

⟞⟝

Liz had travelled up the day before to visit her children, still in Birkenhead with Keith Spencer. Alice and Feklisov would meet her at the Sefton Park Palm House in Liverpool.

Travelling from London Alice sat in second-class, nonsmoking, just to prevent herself from doing so. She wondered if Feklisov was on the same train. When she saw him descend from first class, she decided that sharing a cab was not opportune. But then Feklisov climbed aboard the double-decker bus she had mounted. They made the briefest eye contact, and there was that warm smile again, this time not really aimed at anyone, just the look of a happy man. He left the bus two stops short of the park. Evidently he wanted her to arrive before him.

Liz was waiting, nervously smoking a cigarette, something she rarely did in public. Behind her stood the ornate white Victorian glasswork of the Sefton Park Palm House, vacant and uninviting in the winter cold.

"He's coming," Alice said as she approached.

"How shall we proceed?"

"We've agreed. Tell him everything." Alice went on, "I can't explain it, Liz, but I trust him. I even like him a little."

"Hope I will." Liz stubbed out her cigarette. She looked up to see a man in a dark overcoat enter the park and make for the Palm House.

"Mrs. Carton?" He offered his hand to Liz. Looking at Alice he said, "Glad to see you again, Miss Silverstone."

Liz interrupted. "Actually, my name is—"

"Never mind; I like the name Carton. It was a nice touch, and it's enough that Miss Silverstone and I are old friends. Shall we walk? It's always better to conduct this sort of conversation outside."

They had not been walking for more than a few minutes when Alice began, "My friend here—" She paused, and Feklisov volunteered, "Mrs. Carton?"

"Yes, my friend is the widow of the man who was pushed onto the tracks to frame Thomas Wrought. She has a good deal to tell you."

Feklisov nodded. "Begin."

"It's a long story, sir."

"We have the afternoon."

"Very well. Alice will correct me if I forget anything." She took up Tom's narrative from before the war, beginning with Julie Rosenberg, through his run-ins with Folsom, his OSS work in Finland, and his experiences in New York after the war, including the Cohen-Krogers, his brief return to Finland, and the events that led him to meet with Allen Dulles, and finally Folsom's role in his dismissal from Howard.

When she had finished, Feklisov said, "You forgot the Pulitzer Prize in history, Mrs. . . . . Carton."

Liz smiled sardonically. "That brings us to what I learned in Washington, DC, last week."

Feklisov listened impassively as they walked, the gravel crunching under their feet. He was concentrating, seemingly oblivious of passers-by. Only when she came to the name Guy Burgess did he stop her.

"Guy Burgess, the drunk and disorderly MI6 agent we owned when he was in Washington during the war? Please repeat."

Liz did so. "Mr. Rustin told me that he knew Burgess in Washington after the war and once met him together with Folsom in 1946."

"Go on, please."

Liz finished her report—Folsom's meeting with Rustin, his bluster about J. Edgar Hoover, Thurgood Marshall's report about Hoover, and Folsom's move from the FBI to the senate committee. "There it is, Mr. Feklisov."

"So, ladies." He smiled with the grin of a Cheshire cat. "I think you have everything you need to figure this out for yourselves. Tell me what you think has happened."

Liz spoke first. "Let me have a go." The three stopped and faced one another. "Remember why Tom was fired from the OSS the first time, in 1946?"

Alice answered, "Because of his party membership before the war."

"Yes, but why was that a problem for the OSS?" Feklisov sounded like a schoolmaster.

Liz answered, "Because the head of the FBI, Hoover, was trying to kill off the OSS by discrediting it."

Feklisov now chuckled. "Very good, Mrs. Carton."

"Oh, stop calling me that; my name is Elizabeth Spencer. Call me Liz." They all three laughed.

Alice now took up the thread. "So, five years later, in 1951, Hoover is still trying to get hold of American foreign intelligence, but by now it's the CIA he has to kill off. How can he do it? Well, by not sharing intelligence with the CIA, or even by working with Soviet agents to destroy CIA networks abroad." Liz and Alice both looked at Feklisov. His face was immobile. There was nothing for Alice to do but continue. "This gets a bit speculative, Mr. Feklisov. But somehow Hoover knew that British double agent Burgess had identified the CIA network in Leningrad along with the British agents there. Hoover didn't tell the CIA, and the American agents were left in the wind. Tom could have brought them out along with the British agents he went in for. He learns about the exposed American agents from the British agents he did bring out and tells the head of the CIA—Dulles—as soon as he gets back from Finland. But of course it's too late for the CIA to do anything."

Liz looked quizzical. "How could Hoover and the FBI know about MI6's operation, but the CIA not know?"

"Oh, that's not surprising, Liz." Alice looked at her brightly. "Remember about MI6, intelligence abroad, and MI5, counterintelligence in Britain?" Liz nodded. "Well, if MI5 liaises with the Americans to catch spies, who will their counterpart be? FBI, of course. MI6 operates spies in cooperation with the CIA."

Liz wasn't following. "So?"

But Feklisov was and began nodding his head.

Alice began again. "It's MI5—counterintelligence within Britain—that dealt with Burgess's defection. They warn MI6—foreign intelligence—that Burgess knows about British agents in Russia. MI6 asks for help from the CIA. But MI5 doesn't tell MI6 about the American agents whose identities Burgess also knew. They tell their American opposite number, Hoover's FBI, about the threat to American agents, assuming they'll pass it along to the CIA. But Hoover does nothing. He sits on the information and doesn't tell the CIA. End of CIA's Leningrad network."

Liz added a thought. "Maybe the beginning of the end of the CIA, Hoover hopes."

Alice took up her thread. "But then he has to worry about Burgess, late of MI6 in the States but now defected to Moscow, who may know about him or at least about his man Folsom."

Liz raised her hand as if to stop this line of argument. "Unless Hoover knew all along that Burgess was a Russian agent, in fact was his conduit to Soviet intelligence in a war both were waging against the CIA." The women both turned to Feklisov. He still said nothing.

"We'll take your silence as agreement, or at least as 'no comment.'" Alice smiled at the Russian agent.

Feklisov merely said, "Go on. Get past 1951 to the present, or at least to 1957, in Washington."

Liz began again. "Folsom leaves the FBI to work for a Southern US senator, Eastland. Then Eastland becomes head of the communist witch-hunt committee and Folsom its chief investigator. Folsom discovers Tom is in DC. It would be easy for some liberal journalist—say Drew Pearson—to find Tom and use what he knows about Folsom's black-market past to embarrass the committee and the senator who put Folsom on his staff."

"So," Alice concluded the line of reasoning, "before that could happen, Folsom had to get Tom Wrought out of Washington, and used the threat of subpoenaing the president of Howard University before the senate committee to do so."

"Right. But it still doesn't rise to the level of a reason to frame Tom for murder." Liz was firm.

Both women were silent for long enough that Feklisov felt the need to help them. "So, now we come to last year and this year. What has Thomas Wrought done to bring himself again to the attention of the CIA and the FBI?"

Alice hit her head in a gesture of mock anger. "The anonymous articles in the *Tribune*, of course. Someone saw them, presumably CIA London station, began to make enquiries, learned who wrote them. CIA Washington sends a message to the FBI asking whether they have a file on Tom Wrought. Hoover asks why, and they tell him exactly what Tom had done for them back in '51 in Finland: bringing out British agents but not American ones because the CIA didn't know they were in danger. Tom knew enough to figure out someone had betrayed the American agents. In fact, Tom even said so to the CIA when he got back." She looked at Feklisov. "Hoover realizes Tom is a mortal threat and does something about it."

"But why, Miss Silverstone? Why is Hoover suddenly afraid in 1958 that Tom Wrought knows it was him—the very head of the FBI, not some underling—who betrayed the CIA agents in 1951, that it was Hoover himself who didn't pass on what MI5 told the FBI? Mr. Wrought didn't accuse Hoover when he talked to the CIA chief in 1951."

Suddenly Alice looked like a schoolgirl just waiting to blurt out the right answer. "Because of those anonymous articles in the *Tribune*. Tom's guesses about the FBI and the CIA were too good. They frightened Hoover. Maybe he knew more. Or someone was telling him more, someone who knew enough to implicate Hoover directly. Maybe he thinks Tom wasn't even guessing at all, but using information passed along by the Russians. And he was afraid there'd be more. It was enough to make Tom Wrought worth silencing."

Feklisov looked immensely well satisfied. "You had all the pieces, Miss Silverstone. You only needed to put them together."

Liz now spoke up. "I want to be sure I get this right, Alice. It's the mathematician in me." Liz set to work on the steps as if it were a proof. "So, it starts when CIA London sees Tom's anonymous guesses in the *Tribune*—the ones about the Rosenbergs, and then the ones about *Dr. Zhivago*. They nose round and find out Tom wrote them. A report goes to CIA Washington, and they ask Hoover what the FBI has on one Thomas Wrought." Liz paused, but Alice only nodded. So she began again. "Hoover asks why, and they send him the articles Tom wrote in the *Tribune* plus the 1951 CIA file on Tom. That file will certainly have notations about his interview with Dulles, the CIA chief, when Tom told Dulles about the US assets hung out to dry at the same time he rescued the British agents. In 1951 Tom wouldn't have known enough to figure out it was the FBI, or Hoover himself, who failed to warn the CIA. But by 1958 he's in London, where it looks like Soviet intelligence is leaking titbits to Tom. Maybe they were about to leak that Hoover himself was responsible." Liz looked as though she was about to prove the Pythagorean theorem. "*Ergo* suddenly Hoover has a very strong motive to have Tom put away, perhaps hung, and certainly discredited before he writes any more anonymous articles."

Finally Feklisov spoke. "Yes, Hoover must have become convinced that your Mr. Wrought knows quite enough to destroy him."

"There's just one more loose end, Mr. Feklisov," Alice insisted. "Where does this Mr. Kim Philby fit in? That man who called Michael Foot. Could he be Hoover's man in MI5?" Alice looked towards Liz and added, "British counterintelligence." Then both women looked at Feklisov.

Feklisov stood there, deciding what to say. Finally he spoke. "Ladies, you have figured everything out, and you didn't need my help. That's good, because if I gave you any more, my life would be forfeit."

"Answer the question, Mr. Feklisov! Is Philby the FBI contact in MI5?"

"He can't be. He was MI6—a spy abroad, not MI5 working in Britain—and he hasn't been with MI6 since 1951. He was suspected of being a double agent working for us but was cleared by the prime minister, Mr. Macmillan, when he was foreign secretary, in 1955. It was in the papers."

"Look, Mr. Feklisov, we've figured out why Tom was framed. So what? We can't do a thing about it. No one will believe us. We don't have any leverage." Liz reached out and put her hand on his arm. "Isn't there anything you can do to help us?"

Then Alice spoke. "Last week you told me you hated Hoover for what he did to Ethel Rosenberg when he knew she was innocent."

"Her kids weren't the only ones who lost a parent to Hoover," Liz said. "There's mine too. Well, this is your chance to do something, and it needn't cost you your life. Give us something we can use."

"Very well. I tell you only one thing. KGB knows that the American FBI has a"—Feklisov paused and produced a Russian word, *pirs,* then found the English—"a mole in British counterintelligence. You know what it is, a mole? Give him to the British, and you may get your Mr. Tom Wrought back."

"But how do we do that?" Liz implored.

"I am afraid I cannot help you, ladies. I have already said too much. Remember, a word from either of you about the Krogers, and all three of us will be dead—four, if you include Wrought." He looked at his watch. "Now I must catch the 4:05 back to London, or I will be missed."

There was a spring in his step as he left the two women. They were resourceful. They would, he was sure, find their way to MI5. If they did, they might well force the Americans' mole there to orchestrate the release of Wrought. Unless the mole had them both killed first. No. He'd have to forbid that, or lose the Krogers. After all, the Americans' mole was his too. Still, the dividends for the KGB were considerable. Suspicion between the British services, reduced exchanges of information with the Americans, protection for Philby and for the other Soviet agents still in MI6. It was more than a fair exchange. All while protecting his friends in Ruislip, the Krogers. But it wasn't the whole reason Alexandr Semyonovich Feklisov had been prepared to risk his own position in the KGB to help the two women. He was finally surrendering to sentimentality.

Liz and Alice were seated in an otherwise empty smoking compartment on the evening train to London. They too had gone their separate ways from Sifton Park, still anxious about being followed. Liz had moved between three or four different compartments on the train just to be sure she was not shadowed. Alice had boarded just as the train pulled away. Now they felt they could breathe a little.

Liz offered Alice a cigarette, which she took gratefully and drew on deeply. "How do we get to MI5?" Liz asked.

"That's what I have been trying to figure out. I've two ideas." Alice was thinking aloud. "Who do I know who'd have contacts that deep in government? Well, there's Mr. Foot, who edits the *Tribune*. But who knows? The government may think he's a spy."

Liz added to the objection. "And there's the chance he'd try to publish any story he gets his hands on." She paused. "What's your other idea?"

"Rather a mentor of mine, Victor Mishcon. Knows everyone in the Labour Party. Can probably get us in to see the former prime minister, Atlee, or the leader of the opposition, Gaitskell."

"I think I have an idea," Liz said, brightening. "Remember Tom's friend in Oxford, Isaiah Berlin? He spent time in Washington during the war and in Russia after the war for the Foreign Office. Berlin must know people in MI5 and MI6. Anything we tell him or he tells us would be under the political radar at least."

If you could get past the porters at the gatehouse—fiercest in Oxford— All Souls College looked like no other. The perfect circle of grass at the entrance was a deep-green carpet overlain on a square of fine brown gravel immaculately raked. Liz looked up and saw the sundial, somehow unscarred by a hundred years of coal heating. The two squared-off towers closely flanking the main entrance gave the whole building the appearance of a Spanish baroque church. At the door between them, Liz found a porter dressed in what seemed to be evening clothes. Inquiring about Professor Berlin, Liz wondered what exactly a Latvian Jew was doing in a Christian college so cloistered that it didn't even admit undergraduates.

"Ah, Professor Berlin asks you meet him in the Buttery." Liz was directed to where the fellows lunched. There, in an academic gown and a three-piece suit with gold chain draped across the waistcoat, was a pudgy man with dark hair pasted down and receding from a round face. The large eyes were owlish even through thick lenses under pronounced eyebrows. His whole face beamed at her as he held out two hands. But he was quiet as he pronounced, "Mrs. Spencer, I am very happy to see you." It was evident that this man liked women, and perhaps liked to entertain them in a men's sanctum.

He led her to a table in the middle of the large domed room and pulled a chair out for her. Sitting down he said quietly, "Now, tell me what this is about. I dare say, it sounds rather cloak-and-dagger." *If that's what you think,* she thought, *why invite me to discuss it in such a public place?* He read her mind. "Always discuss delicate matters in public. That way no one suspects."

"I see," she said. "Actually it is cloak-and-dagger. You know that Tom Wrought is locked up in Brixton for murder."

Now for the first time he looked serious. "Yes, and I assume you need me to help 'spring him'—as the Americans would say."

"Not exactly, but there is something awfully important you could do to help." She waited for him to invite her to continue. He nodded. "I need advice and an introduction."

"How much can you tell me?" Before she could answer, a college servant in a white jacket approached. Berlin held up his hand imperiously. "Let's order. I suggest the sole *meuniere*." She nodded. "Aloxe-Corton?" She said nothing, and he turned to the waiter. "Two, please, Bradshaw."

"Well, I don't know how much to tell you, Professor Berlin."

"You must call me Shaya." He covered her hand briefly with his own. "What is your Christian name?" The last words came with a slight tone of mockery.

"Elizabeth, but I'm just Liz, thanks."

"I'm afraid you'll have to tell me everything if I am to help. I'm rather a Hoover when it comes to vacuuming up gossip." The last word was loud enough to be heard by anyone straining to listen. For a moment Liz misunderstood Berlin's use of "Hoover" for the FBI director instead of a vacuum cleaner.

Perhaps it was the owlish eyes betraying a benevolent wisdom. She felt she could trust him. Taking a breath, Liz began with her and Tom's affair. It was obviously the right place to start. Berlin's attention was wrapped by the *scandale*. She talked about the murder, the speed with which the police had worked, Tom's articles in the *Tribune*. "Yes, I remember those," he interrupted. When she told him what Alice had learned from Michael Foot, his eyebrows worked themselves up his brow. "Really," he said, "Philby?"

Liz paused in her narrative. "Do you know the name?"

"Yes, a journalist, that's all. Pray, continue." He poured another glass of Burgundy for himself and moved the bottle to her glass. Liz put her hand over it.

Now it would become tricky. She couldn't tell him about the Krogers or Feklisov. She couldn't tell him about Tom's suspicions—that Berlin might have been used as a conduit from the Russians, dropping hints, intentionally or not, for his *Zhivago* article in the *Tribune*. What could she tell him? Liz started with Tom's work for the OSS and then the second trip to Finland to bring out the British agents for the CIA.

"Went to see Dulles, did he? Very wise of him."

Finally she went over her mission to New York and Washington, giving him all the details. Then she stopped, feeling rather as though she were leaning over a precipice from which she could easily be pushed.

Berlin came to her rescue. "Let me guess, Miss, Mrs. . . . uh, Liz. You think that the FBI is trying to frame Tom Wrought for the murder of your husband to silence him, discredit him, perhaps even to hang him."

"How did you know?" The relief was palpable across her face.

Seeing her look, Berlin almost reached out to touch it. "What does Sherlock Holmes say? When you have eliminated the impossible, whatever remains, however improbable, must be the truth."

"Are there no other possibilities, Shaya?" Calling him that didn't feel right to her, but she needed his interest. She even contemplated reaching to his hand across the damask tablecloth.

"I think not. Suppose they just killed Tom. The first person to start asking embarrassing questions would be me." He turned portentous, as though he were addressing a malefactor set before him for punishment. "And I know whom to ask the questions of." He dabbed his mouth with a napkin. "Much of what you've told me would have come out, perhaps not in the papers, but in Whitehall, in the clubs, in the smoking room of the House." He didn't have to add that it was the House of Commons he was speaking of.

Would he now understand what Liz needed from him? "Shaya, I want to free Tom. What should I do?"

"I'm going to put a call in to an old friend named Roger Hollis. I can't tell you what he does. But he is the right man for you to talk to." She smiled and this time did cover his hand with hers. He grinned, trying hard not to show anything but a paternal interest.

Suddenly and silently, there hovering above them was the steward with two plates. Berlin smiled with relish. "Now, dear, do leave room for pudding."

—◆—

Two mornings later Liz emerged from the tube stop at Baker Street. Before she could take three steps in the direction of the Abbey National, a well-dressed young man approached her. "Mrs. Spencer, would you mind coming with me?" He pointed to a large black Daimler at the curb with a liveried driver.

Alarmed, Liz turned one way and the other for someone to come to her rescue. Before she could say anything, the young man continued, "We'll collect Miss Silverstone and take you to see Mr. Hollis." Liz recalled the name from her luncheon with Berlin and relaxed.

He held the door open, and she seated herself in the commodious back seat. The young man joined the driver in the front, and they drove north past Regent's Park towards St. John's Wood. They stopped on Hamilton Terrace at a small two-storey block of flats painted an off-white, through which streaks of fire damage still showed. The lot next to it was vacant. *A relic of the war,* Liz thought.

The young man turned to the back seat. "Would you mind coming with me to collect Miss Silverstone? It might reassure her." When Liz nodded, the young man came out from the front of the car and opened the back door for her. Together they mounted the stair, where he pressed the intercom button.

The voice came, "Yes?"

"Alice, it's Liz. I'm downstairs with a . . . friend. Please let us in."

There was an immediate buzz.

Alice just had time to put away her syringe and the morphine bottle before rolling down her sleeve and answering the door.

———◆———

Twenty minutes later, both women found themselves seated in the lounge of a detached villa in Putney, south of the Thames and well to the west of the government offices in Whitehall. There in the front room, before a silver tea set on a low, drop-leaf table, sat a man of about fifty, grey-haired, slightly beefy, well tailored. He rose as they entered.

The young man, still nameless, who had led them in left quietly, firmly closing the door to the lounge.

Without shaking their hands, the man said, "My name is Roger Hollis. Isaiah Berlin asked me to see you, Mrs. Spencer. I thought it might be useful to invite Miss Silverstone too." Alice was about to ask how he had known about her, but then decided she'd not get a straight answer anyway. "Please take a seat."

He was a kindly-looking man, with even heavier eyebrows than Berlin, Liz noticed. In a bespoke suit and a perfectly knotted club tie, Hollis looked every inch the mandarin. The poker face was pale, closely shaven, as featureless as one could want in a senior civil servant.

"Tea, ladies? I prefer Chinese. Hope you don't mind." Both women sat and nodded. Hollis looked up with a wry smile and said, "I'll play mother, shall I? Milk, sugar?"

When all three were balancing teacups on their laps, Alice spoke. "I'm sorry, sir. But what do you do exactly?"

"'Fraid the Official Secrets Act prevents me from telling you anything but my name. Still, I can assure you, you've come to the right place. Or at any rate the place Professor Berlin thinks is right for your problem, Mrs. Spencer."

Alice started to speak, but Hollis put up his hand in a peremptory way and turned back to Liz. "If what you told Professor Berlin is right, I am afraid you may be in as much trouble as Mr. Wrought, Mrs. Spencer."

Alice now began listening closely, ear cocked for the sort of innuendos or implicatures in testimony that a fine solicitor is always hunting for.

Hollis was thoughtful. Then he spoke. "We knew Mr. Wrought was behind some articles in the *Tribune* . . . but we didn't know the rest." Suddenly Alice began listening more carefully. "If it were the FBI who implicated Mr. Wrought in a murder, then given what you know of the matter, you would be in equal danger." He paused. "If, that is, the FBI were to find out what you have learned."

Alice's mind was carefully digesting everything Hollis said, turning over every word and its intonation. *Had Liz told Berlin about Tom's dealings with the* Tribune's *editor, Foot—about the anonymous articles? She would have said.* Then Alice thought, *Why did he say "if the FBI were to find out"?* She answered her question instantly. *He knows they'll find out because he is going to tell them!*

Turning to Alice, Hollis continued in a bland tone. "And if someone has been interfering with Mr. Wrought inside one of Her Majesty's prisons, then they may be powerful enough to endanger you too, Miss"—he seemed to struggle briefly over her name, and then it came out as "Silverstein."

How does he know what was happening in Brixton? Because it's his operation. Hollis is the mole! Now Alice was certain. *He's the FBI contact in MI5, maybe even the KGB contact too, playing the FBI against the CIA.*

Alice looked at Liz, frightened that she had not picked up on Hollis's slips. Liz had not even spoken yet. Now, in a voice tinged with feminine ineffectuality, she asked, "Whatever shall I do, Mr. Hollis?"

Hollis cleared his throat, smiled at Liz, and said just what Alice had expected. "Dear lady, will you leave this matter in my hands? I shall undertake a discreet enquiry. We'll get to the bottom of all this. If there's improper activity by the Americans here, we'll put a stop to it, and we'll find a way to release your Mr. Wrought."

Alice was frightened. Hollis was not going to lift a finger for Tom, and if he thought Liz and Alice could identify him as an FBI mole, and a KGB one, he'd have to accord them Tom's fate, or even Trevor's. She needed to end this interview before Hollis realized she knew. But she dared not signal Liz.

Liz spoke again, still with the innocent look and an anxious tone. "Please, Mr. Hollis, is there anything I should do to protect myself?"

"Mrs. Spencer, merely go about your business and leave everything to me." He rose, signalling that the interview was over.

"But, Mr. Hollis, for the last few weeks my business has been tracking down . . . uh, meeting with Miss Silverstone to try to help her with Mr. Wrought's case."

"Then I suggest you cease for the moment. But don't make it difficult for my people to find you. The same goes for you, Miss Silverstone." This time he got her name right.

Alice needed to conceal her suspicions. She fell in with Liz's affect. Plaintively she asked, "But what shall I tell my client?"

"Nothing, nothing at all. Just leave everything to me."

Both women were smoking as they walked up the Circular Road to the East Putney tube stop, having declined a ride back in the Daimler. As they passed into the dark, claustrophobic underpass beneath the tube tracks, Liz cringed, not for the first time. *Smoking on the footpath, do we look like a couple of hookers?* The silence between them was palpable. Neither wanted to say what she thought. Each wanted the other to explain why she was completely wrong, why Roger Hollis wasn't the mole in British counterintelligence. Finally Liz spoke. "He's it, isn't he? Right at the top of MI5."

"'Fraid so," Alice replied. "You never said anything to Isaiah Berlin about the intrusions on Tom at Brixton, did you?"

Liz shook her head. "No, and I'm certain I said nothing to Berlin about Tom's anonymous reviews in the *Tribune*. But Hollis knew. Why had he even bothered to find out?"

"Find out? He could have been the Soviet mole who planted the CIA *Zhivago* tip with Berlin for Tom to pick up." She couldn't help smiling at the connection.

But Liz was continuing. "I didn't mention your name to Berlin either. But they came for both of us. Hollis knows much more than we've told anyone."

Alice dropped her fag and ground it out. "You're in for it now. Whoever put Tom away has as much of a reason to sideline you now . . . or worse."

"What about you, Alice?"

"I've been up to my neck in it since they twigged to the composition books and began searching Tom's cell and my office." She looked at her watch as though moments mattered. "Liz, you've got a Canadian passport in another name. You can still get out. You've got kids to think about."

"I don't have Tom," Liz replied with equal force. "I've come this far . . . can't bail out now." She stopped and put a hand on Alice's arm, suddenly thinking about the track marks of syringe needles below the coat sleeve. She had noticed them again in Hollis's sitting room. Was her solicitor, now her friend, really a dope fiend? Liz wasn't going to ask. Her thoughts came back to the immediate problem. "So, what do we do now?"

"I don't think there's any use going to my Labour Party contact, Mishcon, or to Michael Foot. They'd only lead back to MI5 and Hollis."

"Still, we may not be in immediate danger, if Hollis is under KGB control." Liz stopped, hoping that Alice would confirm her conjecture.

"I suppose you're right. Feklisov is our life assurance policy. He knows if something happens to us, his spies will be blown. He'll prevent MI5 from killing us . . . if he can control Hollis."

Liz turned to Alice. "Well, then, what now?"

"I am out of ideas. I think we have to let Hollis make the next move."

CHAPTER
TWENTY-ONE

"You've just missed her," replied the manager at the Market Street, Manchester branch of the Abbey National. "Mrs. Spencer left five minutes ago."

Detective Chief Inspector Bennett began to crush the hat in his hands. "Do you know where she was going?" It had been weeks since he had brought Liz news of her husband's death. But he hadn't forgotten the face. Nor had he forgotten her answers to his questions, now apparently self-serving and probably false. He heard the manager respond, "London Road Station probably. Said she was going back to head office."

Watkins was already studying a timetable. "There's an express a few minutes after two, guv." He shared Bennett's urgency.

"Let's go." Bennett was already out the door. They'd just be able to catch it and Liz Spencer.

The men reached the station slightly breathless and bathed in perspiration despite the chill drizzle. Seeking the track number on the departure board, they turned to each other, and both said "eight" without breaking stride. Up the stairs over the tracks and then down onto the platform, they rushed through the barrier gate, flashing their CID badges at the ticket collector, and came to a stop. There was the train—conductors looking towards the engine, waiting for the signal to close the doors. Looking down the quay, they could see a few passengers still choosing their coaches—first- and second-class, smokers and nonsmokers. Bennett was about to enter the closest coach when Watkins pulled at his sleeve from behind.

"Guv. Down the platform. Look." There, headed for the stairs marked **Way Out** on the other end of the platform, two men were frog-marching a woman who was obviously struggling. One of the men was carrying a small case. The woman was turning her head to one side and the other. Her mouth was open in a shriek. But nothing could be heard at their distance over the noise of air brakes, conductors' whistles, and the clicking of wheels crossing the rail gaps. Watkins shouted again. "It's Spencer, I think!" They began to run.

For a moment the woman broke free. The two men turned, losing their hats but regaining their prisoner. As they did so, both men could see the two detectives running towards them, the younger Watkins in the lead. A brief glance at each other, and they left their prisoner, dropped her case, and headed for the **Way Out** stair up and over the tracks. Bennett stopped where Liz was standing, next to the engine, while Watkins gave chase. The pounding footfalls of three men on the old metal treads turned the heads of people still on the quay. At the top of the stair, the two men looked back, and seeing Watkins closing, they separated, one to the left, the other to the right. At the top, like Buridan's ass, Watkins stopped. After a look each way, he visibly shrugged, turned, and walked slowly down the stairs back to the quay, picking up the case.

Bennett meanwhile had taken out a pair of handcuffs, which he had attached to Liz, and then signalled the engine driver with his badge. The man seemed to understand, for the train, which had imperceptibly begun to slide out of the station, came to an equally gradual halt. Watkins reached them at the same time as a conductor.

Before the uniformed man could express his outrage at the train's delay, Bennett raised his hand to show his CID badge. "Very sorry. Let's get on this train, and I'll explain."

⟞⟡⟞

Comfortably seated in a first-class compartment of the now rapidly moving train, Bennett removed the handcuffs. "I'm sorry, Miss . . . Mrs. Spencer. I only did that for dramatic effect. We had to get them to delay the departure for us. Handcuffs usually make bystanders think matters are serious." He put them in a side coat pocket.

Liz actually found the ability to smile. "I can hardly complain. Your arrival saved me from a more serious fate."

Watkins addressed her. "Do you know who those men were?"

But before Liz could answer, Bennett spoke. "Mrs. Elizabeth Spencer, I am arresting you as an accessory after the fact in the murder of your husband, Trevor Spencer. You have a right to remain silent, but anything you say may be taken down and used in evidence." Then Bennett visibly relaxed, took out a packet of Player's, and offered them to Watkins and to Liz.

Looking at the sign on the window, Liz observed, "This is nonsmoking."

"Not for us, ma'am."

She shrugged her shoulders and took one of his Player's. It was going to be too strong, she knew, even before she began to cough. "You're arresting me," she said when she'd stopped. "But you saw those two men. They were going to kill me." As she thought about the matter, Liz's voice turned angry. How could these detectives be so thick? "They're the ones who murdered my husband. How can you arrest me after you just saved me from them?"

Bennett pushed his hat back and drew on his fag. "Look, Mrs. Spencer, I'm glad we were able to rescue you from an assault or worse. But I'm afraid it changes nothing regarding our duties."

"Those two men were dragging me away, were going to kill me, and it changes nothing?"

Watkins tried to sound reasonable. "We don't know what they were doing or why, Mrs. Spencer."

"They had guns, Detective. I saw one and could feel the other." This seemed to make an impression. The two policemen exchanged glances. But then they fell silent, perhaps sheepish about what they had to do.

In the silence Liz began asking herself, *What are they waiting for? Aren't they going to question me? Are we going to ride all the way to London in silence? This is just what Alice said happened to Tom. No interrogation, no chance for Tom to speak. I've got to do something.* "Detective Bennett, you said I have the right to remain silent. Do I have the right to talk?"

"Yes, but I advise you to wait until you have the benefit of a solicitor."

"I'll take my chances."

Watkins now made a show of taking a notepad and a pen from his jacket. They were certainly going to take down anything she did say.

Where to begin? Liz wondered. *They just don't seem interested in anything about those men except for the fact that they were armed.* She began, "Why were you on that platform? Because you were coming to Manchester for me, right?" The detectives remained impassive. "And so were those two men who were trying to take me off the platform. Do you think that was a coincidence?" Now she became emphatic, staring at each. "Two different pairs of men both after me at the same time? Like the coincidence of Tom Wrought being on the platform the moment my husband died?" Still nothing. Liz was close to tears of frustration and anger. "You never interrogated Tom Wrought, not once, never asked him anything. And now you're going to treat me the same way? A suspect has the right to remain silent. Don't they have a right to answer questions? Aren't you interested?"

The men across the compartment from her were literally looking at their shoes. But shaming them was not going to be enough.

Why aren't they interested, Liz? Because they think they already know everything. Perhaps if you show them what you know?

"You're holding me as an accessory after murder, right?" They nodded. *At least you got a couple of nods.* "You hadn't detained me before now. But then you received new information, didn't you?" Silence. "Someone told you I was in London when my husband died, that I was meeting Tom at a hotel, maybe even that he called me from a phone box near the scene of the crime, warning me to return to Oxford."

Now Bennett spoke. "Do you deny it?"

"No. Do you deny receiving this information in the last day or so without having done any police legwork to get it? Without even visiting the hotel or asking the desk clerk there about it?"

Watkins looked at his governor, who nodded permission to speak. "You were going to meet him there. You should have come forwards with this information when first questioned."

She ignored the question. Instead, she continued her argument. "But then, just a day ago, you got this anonymous tip, yes?" *No sarcasm, Liz. You need these people to believe you. It's your only chance . . . and Tom's.* Could she show them they were being manipulated, being treated as mere marionettes on strings? *Slow down, Liz. Build your case the way Alice would.*

She turned towards the senior policeman. "Detective Bennett, has it occurred to you how little actual police work you and Watkins here have had to do in order to seal up this case so convincingly?"

"What do you mean, Mrs. Spencer?" Watkins asked.

"Well, you had Tom Wrought in jail within twenty-four hours of the crime. You had witnesses, motive, evidence, all without even lifting a finger. Everything served up to you on a plate. Now you get another piece of evidence. Doubtless you've since confirmed it with the Gresham Hotel. But how did you learn of the call in the first place? Painstaking police work?"

Bennett spoke. "But you do admit that Wrought left a message for you that day?"

"Yes." Liz replied. *At least you have him questioning you now.*

Watkins asked, "What do you mean, we had everything handed to us on a plate?" They both knew perfectly well that she was right. Everything had come from anonymous tips, and everything had been confirmed by their initial enquiries.

"Someone killed my husband and framed Tom Wrought for it. Whoever did it organized the killing so that Tom would be on the platform when they pushed Trevor onto the tracks. Then they fed you all the information you needed to make the arrest. You passed it on to the crown prosecutor and remanded Tom Wrought. The police never got so many accurate tips so quickly before, right?"

Watkins looked at Bennett, who responded, "Well, however we got the information, it checked out. And now you've confirmed the tip that you were going to meet him at the Gresham."

"Gentlemen, I am going to tell you everything I know." *Careful, Liz, you can't tell them everything . . . .you can't tell them about the Krogers and Feklisov. You can't tell them anything about that. But what if it's not enough without them? It will have to be if you want to survive, if you want Tom to survive . . . and Alice.* "I think I can convince you that Tom Wrought has been framed. You've been used by the people who framed him. And you, me, Tom Wrought, we've gotten ourselves wrapped up in matters of national security, espionage, and worse. There's a foreign government interfering with the work of the police."

"That's quite a speech, Mrs. Spencer," Bennett said. He looked at Watkins, who said nothing. Liz took their silence as willingness to listen.

How far back to go, how much to tell? What can't I tell? She thought a moment, and began. "People in the American FBI and in the Russian KGB both suspect that Tom Wrought knows something, knows that they've been working together. The FBI and the KGB are both working against the American CIA, and maybe against British intelligence."

"That makes no sense." Bennett expressed annoyance. "Why would the American FBI be working with the Russians against their own CIA?"

Watkins added a question: "Why would they be working here against us?"

"It's not the whole FBI. We think—Tom's solicitor and me—that it's the director, J. Edgar Hoover. He's been trying to get control of the CIA for years. He was willing to do anything, even compromise CIA networks, just to show the CIA is incompetent so he could take it over."

"And how does Tom Wrought figure into all of this, please?" Bennett was humouring her, and Watkins was taking notes.

"Tom must have twigged to Hoover's actions. He worked for the CIA ten years ago. Then this fall he foolishly hinted at inside knowledge about the FBI and the CIA in some newspaper articles. That's what started the whole thing."

"So, why kill Trevor Spencer?"

That was an obvious question, but was it mere curiosity, or was Bennett starting to take Liz's story seriously? She couldn't tell.

"They knew Tom Wrought and I were lovers, because they had Tom under surveillance." She looked at their faces, remembering how she'd answered their questions the night the two detectives told her of Trevor's death. "They had the resources to start to follow my husband, Trevor, too. That's why they were able to kill Trevor and frame Tom. All they needed was some way to get you looking in the direction they wanted you to look. And you did."

"See here, we had solid physical evidence against Wrought, evidence no one could have manufactured—the divorce attorney's card, the prophylactic wrapper—and witnesses at the tube stop." Bennett again sounded completely unconvinced by Liz's story.

"But you would never have had Tom Wrought without a tip, one that came only hours after the crime. Without it you'd still be looking for a husband that Trevor Spencer was cuckolding." Liz was guessing now, but she had to take the chance.

Watkins broke in, asking the obvious question again. "Why kill your husband? Why not just kill Wrought?"

"Tom Wrought was 'establishment.' People knew him, influential people. There would have been questions, perhaps even questions in Parliament. Lots more than if a middle-aged husband was killed by his wife's lover who happened to be well connected." The thought immediately occurred to Liz, *If it had been Tom they killed, you lot might have worked hard enough to uncover the fact that Tom had run into both Krogers. Then you would have unravelled the Russian spy network.* It was not a thought to pursue.

"I'm sorry; you've no evidence to back up this story, Mrs. Spencer." Bennett's tone was not really regretful.

Liz persisted. "Weren't you surprised that there was nothing in the papers about my husband's death? That no one on Fleet Street cared about the arrest of a prize-winning Oxford don? You weren't even approached by a reporter from the tabloids for details about a lurid love triangle, were you? No one wanted a scoop. Wasn't that odd?" Silence from the coppers. "Why?" She answered her own question. "Someone powerful wanted the whole matter to go unnoticed." Again she asked, "Why? Could they have had some connection to whoever was feeding you all the evidence you needed?" Still nothing. She had to find something that would shake them up. "After you arrested Tom, his solicitor and I started working to try to figure out who framed him. And we must have struck pay dirt—found out why he was framed."

"Why is that?" "How do you know?" Bennett and Watkins spoke at the same time.

"Because suddenly you were sent after me. You didn't arrest me when you took Wrought in. You had them take my passport, that's all. Why the sudden interest now? Because we're on to the people who framed Tom Wrought. They gave you the tip about Tom's call to the Gresham Hotel. It's why those men came to Manchester for me." Watkins and Bennett exchanged glances, Liz noticed.

"This is preposterous, Mrs. Spencer," said Bennett. "If someone is manipulating us, why would they have sent two men up here to grab you when they knew Watkins and me was comin' up here to arrest you?" It didn't come out of his mouth as a question.

Liz, if you can answer that question, you'll have turned them to our side. "No, Inspector, it's the best evidence my theory is right! The FBI and maybe the Russians as well have been using the British security service in a war against the American CIA. They have the same mole in MI5. He found out some of what Alice Silverstone and I know about why Tom was framed. The mole had to protect himself. He had to take me out of circulation. So he told his FBI contact, and they gave him the tape to pass on to you. Then, without telling their mole in MI5, Hoover's people in London decided to send those goons out to get rid of me, probably the same ones that killed my husband. That's why they were carrying guns. They're Americans."

Bennett looked exasperated. "So, what exactly did Wrought know that made the FBI want to silence him?"

Watkins added, "And British intelligence, how is it involved?"

"I can answer both of those questions, gentlemen." Liz smiled with relief. *Do you have them on your side now?* "First, at least once— eight years ago—British intelligence passed on vital information to

Hoover's FBI that they were to give to the CIA. But the FBI withheld it, and it cost the Americans several agents in Russia. This autumn Tom figured out it was Hoover himself who betrayed the CIA." She could only hope they didn't ask her to prove this accusation. Liz went on quickly, "Second, we suspect Hoover might know that his mole in MI5 is a Russian agent too. Hoover probably knew at least one Soviet agent in our Washington embassy. Do you remember the name Guy Burgess?"

Watkins shook his head. But Bennett replied, "Burgess, yes—Burgess and McLean? The two traitors who escaped in '51?" He turned to Watkins. "Total cock-up." Then he looked towards Liz. "And what makes you think Hoover knew this man, Burgess?"

"Well, Burgess was a homosexual and had a sexual relationship with someone Hoover knew—shall we say, someone Hoover knew *well*."

"That's true," Bennett said to Watkins. "He was a queer, that Burgess." Then he looked at Liz. "But the public didn't know." He turned back to Liz. "Is there more, Mrs. Spencer?"

"Yes. Two days ago Tom's solicitor and I were taken to see the head of MI5, Roger Hollis. His people had been following us. We told him what we knew, and he told us he'd look into the matter."

Bennett looked perplexed. "You know the name of the head of MI5? That's a violation of the Official Secrets Act. Who told you?"

Liz lied. "He did."

But Bennett wasn't listening. "You spoke with Sir Roger himself two days ago?"

"Yes."

"Well, yesterday a spool of tape turned up on my desk from MI5. It was a recording of Tom Wrought's call to the Gresham Hotel, telling you to go home. That's why I decided we needed to pick you up as soon as possible." He stopped.

"Isn't it obvious where Hollis got that bit of tape? From the Americans. He couldn't have been bugging the hotel where we met.

MI5 didn't know anything about Tom and me last January. Only the FBI did. You two have been acting on tips from them fed through Hollis." Suddenly Liz felt she was talking to people who might believe her after all.

Watkins interjected, "We were told right from the start that this case had an MI5 Official Secrets Act lid on it. We were ready to stonewall the press." He paused. "But there was never any need. No one asked."

"There was no reason to question Wrought or even seek a confession," Bennett reflected. "Motive, opportunity, means—they were handed to us in neat packages and anonymous tips that all checked out. Add in the eyewitnesses locating Wrought on the platform running from the scene of the crime, and it was open and shut."

"Of course it was open and shut," Liz agreed. "The FBI had a whole team working on this in London, in Oxford, following Tom, following my husband, Trevor, tapping the Gresham Hotel phone, keeping the tabloid reporters tame." Now could she convince them of the final piece of the story? "Do you see? Roger Hollis is an FBI mole in MI5 and a Soviet double agent too. Carrying information back and forth between the Russians and Hoover's FBI in their war against the CIA."

Bennett pushed his head back, lit another cigarette, and blew a long shaft of smoke into the ceiling of the compartment. "Why should we believe you, Mrs. Spencer, and not the head of MI5, if he is our anonymous source? What if you're the Soviet agent, along with Wrought?"

Think fast, Liz. You can give them the Krogers. That would convince them. But you can't. It would be the end of all of us—Tom, Alice, me. Feklisov was very clear. Do you have anything else to give them?

She looked at Watkins and then Bennett. "Would a Soviet spy write articles in the papers drawing attention to inside information? That's what Tom Wrought did. If I were one too, would I blow my cover by involvement in a murder—of my husband, no less?" All the while there was quite a different thought running through Liz's mind. *You practically are a spy, Liz, or as close to being one as makes no difference. You won't give away the Russian agents you and Alice have uncovered.* She answered her own challenge. *I can't. Not if we're to survive.* "There is one more thing, Detective Bennett, that should make you angry about how you've been used by a foreign government."

"What's that then?" Bennett sounded almost avid.

"Someone has been reaching into Brixton Prison, either paying off the warders to spy on Tom Wrought or spying on him themselves. His personal effects have been searched when he leaves his cell. And they have tried to break into his solicitor's offices to secure documents. Alice Silverstone can give you the details."

"We don't do that sort of thing, Mrs. Spencer, not the CID!"

"I'm not accusing you. It's more evidence that someone with resources and power is interfering with British law. I think only Americans or Russians would try things like that, and only Americans would succeed."

"What exactly are we supposed to do with this information?" Bennett had surrendered to Liz's logic in spite of himself. But now he seemed at a loss.

"I'm not sure, Inspector. But to start, I think when we get to London, you had better take me off the train in handcuffs, just to discourage another attempt on my life."

Bennett agreed. "I see that. Whoever sent those men'll know you escaped in Manchester. Someone will be waiting at Kings Cross to learn if we have arrested you or not."

Liz now had a thought. "When we get there, take me to Alice Silverstone's home in St. John's Wood. She'll have an idea about how to proceed. Are you willing to do that, gentlemen?"

"I suppose so," Bennett replied with a hint of resignation.

Liz had won a round.

Darkness had fallen by the time they reached London. Liz was glad to be placed in handcuffs and frog-marched to a cab. She was gladder still to see the lights bright in Alice's windows on Hamilton Terrace in St. John's Wood.

All four were sipping tea and smoking cigarettes from the silver box on Alice's coffee table. It took only a few minutes to put Alice in the picture. Without challenge, she took charge. The other three listened as Alice summed matters up, sounding to Liz rather like an exquisitely briefed barrister in the high court. Perhaps Bennett and Watkins thought so too. They did not interrupt.

"Gentlemen"—she looked from Bennett to Watkins—"you want to catch Trevor Spencer's murderers. You also want to put a stop to a band of out-of-control Yanks making a travesty of British law. You may even want to deal with treason in MI5." The two men's tight lips and slight nods were enough for Alice. "As I see it, there is only one way to do any of those things. You have to free Tom Wrought and let Liz here go. They're the real threats, along with me, to the Americans and their mole in MI5. Then you have to watch all three of us. We'll be your bait. Once Wrought is free, they'll have to come after him—and us. When you catch whoever does"—Alice gulped—"if you catch whoever comes after us—the rogue FBI agents in London or Hoover's MI5 mole—you'll have Trevor Spencer's killers."

"Can we do that, guv?" Watkins asked.

"Spring Wrought? Only if I can get authorization from the commissioner of the Met and the Home Office." He rose, and Watkins followed his lead. "I'm going to start working on that straight away."

He turned to Liz. "Mrs. Spencer, you're to stay here. If you leave, I'll have to treat it as evidence of your guilt as an accessory after murder. Do you understand?" Then he turned to Alice. "Meet me at Brixton Prison tomorrow at two o'clock."

Alice came back from showing the two detectives out. Liz thought she looked distraught, as though she were in pain. "I don't like it. Once the mandarins in the Home Office find out about this, it will get to Roger Hollis in no time." After a moment she added, "And we can't stay here."

"But I can't leave. You heard Bennett."

"Can't be helped. People are after you. We're not safe here. Do you have Beatrice Russell's number?" Alice moved round the room turning off lights. "Give me a minute to collect some things, and then let's get out of here. Can't use the phone here anyway. We'll find a call box." Then Alice mounted the stairs to turn on bedroom lights and retrieve her morphine supply. By the time she had returned, Liz had her coat on and was waiting at the door with the small case she had been carrying from Manchester.

⟨═⟩

Bennett was already at Brixton Prison when Alice arrived. He was with Tom in an interrogation room new to Alice. Before either of them could say anything Alice began, "Do you think we can speak freely, Inspector?"

Bennett sighed. "I don't think we have much choice. But I've asked the warden to clear this corridor completely, and this is not a room used for interrogation or solicitors' visits."

"Very well. Have you explained things to Mr. Wrought?" She looked towards Tom. Everything about him was slightly different. Was he jaunty? Even sitting there he seemed taller, leaning forwards aggressively over the table. *That's it, of course,* she realized. *He's no longer anxious. Well, he still should be.*

Tom interrupted her thought. "Yes. The inspector has laid everything out pretty clearly."

"I hadn't quite finished," Bennett said. "What Mrs. Spencer told me yesterday led me to speak with the commissioner of the Metropolitan Police. The commissioner has approached the home secretary to order your temporary release, Mr. Wrought. We're waiting word now. I expect it will come shortly. Normally we would work with MI5 on a matter like this. In fact, they would simply take it over altogether. If Miss Silverstone's right, we can't do that."

"If . . . ," Alice scoffed. "You wouldn't be here if you thought it was just an 'if.'"

Bennett ignored the provocation. "If the home secretary approves, we have a plan." He looked at Tom. "But it's dangerous to you three."

"I can guess," Tom observed. "You release me. Then you watch to see if the Americans kill us—Liz, Miss Silverstone, and me—right? If they do, you will know Roger Hollis belongs to them."

Alice interrupted. "Or that Hollis is a Russian mole eager to have the FBI continue to act against the CIA."

"Or both," Tom observed coolly.

Bennett shrugged. "Scotland Yard will do everything it can to protect you. But I am afraid you will be at considerable risk."

"And the alternative?" Tom's question was rhetorical, but Bennett answered it.

"The crown prosecutor will insist on a trial, and the Official Secrets Act will prevent any of this from coming out in court. I doubt you'll hang."

Tom had already decided and was beginning to think operationally. "What will you tell Hollis about releasing me?"

Alice looked towards the detective. "They won't have to tell him. He'll find out from his people in Brixton anyway."

Bennett nodded. "Can't keep anything the Home Office does secret from counterintelligence anyway. MI5 is part of the Home Office."

"But there is one thing you can do, Inspector Bennett, to prove Hollis is bent." She paused, and then continued. "He has to find out that we know how Hoover fought his war against the CIA."

"Is there something you haven't told me, Miss Silverstone?" Bennett sounded impatient.

Alice was surprised. "Didn't Mrs. Spencer tell you about her trip to Washington?"

"Washington? She's been to Washington?" Bennett frowned. "How? We had her passport."

Alice smiled. "Not her Canadian one."

"Tell me," Bennett fairly barked.

Alice sighed and began to put Liz's trip to Washington together with Tom's experiences in Finland.

When she finished, Bennett's face assumed a tight smile. "Well, that'll seal matters once the Home Office finds out." There was almost wonderment in his voice when he continued, "So, our Hollis was using the channel to Hoover through Burgess and Folsom to attack the CIA both for the Soviets and for the head of the FBI. Chief's already livid about Hoover's agents operating on his turf. This'll complicate matters, but not much. We'll just have to brief the people watching for the Yanks to be on the lookout for Russians too."

Alice nodded. "Would it make matters easier for you if your bait, all three of us—Tom, Liz, and I—were in the same place?"

"Of course. Where do you propose the three of you go?"

"My place, in St. John's Wood." Then she addressed Bennett. "How long will you need to arrange matters?" Alice was proceeding as if Tom were not even present.

"Once we get approval, not long. Then we release Wrought and watch."

"No. Release him to me now."

Bennett shook his head. "I can't do that."

"Then I will advise my client"—she looked at Tom—"not to proceed with your scheme."

Tom interjected here, "Why, Alice? It's my only chance."

"It's not enough of one. We don't know how quickly Hollis is going to act to protect himself and his friends. I trust Inspector Bennett, but the moment he began to make arrangements, word started to spread. You may never even get to my place."

"I'm afraid she may be right." Bennett rose. "Look, I'll tell the Brixton people that I'm taking him to an identity parade at the Yard now." He looked at his watch. "I've got to see the commissioner in an hour. I can't cart you two round with me in any case. It would give the game away. You'll call me when all three of you are at your place in St. John's Wood?"

Alice nodded, then she went on, "Very well, but it won't be till it's dark this evening. I don't want to make it too easy for whoever will be coming after us."

No more than a quarter of an hour later, Tom was in the clothes he had worn when he'd arrived at Brixton. Handcuffed to Bennett, both walked out of the building to the police car in the forecourt. Alice trailed them. Bennett removed the cuffs.

"You two get in the back. When we drive off, crouch so that anyone watching won't see you in the car," Bennett warned. "I'll drop you at Clapham North." It was the next tube station after Brixton. Alice laughed as she slid down into the seat. "I fail to see the humour, Miss Silverstone?"

"Well, if anyone followed me to the prison, when I don't come out, they'll end up assuming I've been arrested . . . or that something is afoot."

"Can't be helped." Bennett started the car.

Tom was leaning against the phone box, feeling rather detached from reality suddenly standing in a tube ticket hall in civilian clothes, unsupervised for the first time in a month. *Imagine,* he thought, *if it had been the first time free after ten years or more in prison.* He reached into his coat pocket and pulled out a stale packet of cigarettes, lit one up, and watched the smoke mix with the fog of his breath in the cold air. Then he opened the call box door to listen to Alice's conversation with Liz.

She was speaking. "You understand? You're to go to Oxford and get your car at the station." She paused, evidently listening to a question. "I don't think you're in danger at the moment. If they tailed you off the train, they'll think you're still in police custody." She stopped again and then continued, "Drive directly to my office. Don't park in Red Lion Square. Park behind my firm's offices in the cul-de-sac at the end of Eagle Street. The rear door to my building will be open."

Tom was confused. He interrupted. "You told Bennett we'd be at your place."

Alice was peremptory. "Pipe down." She spoke into the phone. "Now, before you leave Oxford, figure out what time you'll be at Red Lion Square. Then call Beatrice Russell at the office from a phone box." A pause. "Yes, she'll expect your call. Ask her to come to my office at roughly the same time you arrive from Oxford. She can come in the front way." Alice thought a moment. "Do your children have their documents?" After a pause she went on, "Good. Write a note to their uncle, giving him permission to take them out of the country or send them to your parents in Canada. Post it right away." After another pause, "Right. See you this evening at my office." She rang off and came out of the box. "Let's go." She led him down the stairs to the turnstile and the long escalators of the Clapham North tube stop. The platform was crowded, and Tom felt a compulsion to stand well away from the edge.

They came up from the underground at Chancery Lane. Alice handed Tom a map she had been drawing in the train. "Wait here thirty minutes and then go to the back entrance of my office. I am going to make a stop between here and there, and then I'm going in the front way."

"What should I do here while I wait?"

"What you did for three weeks in Brixton. Keep quiet, don't look conspicuous, and don't leave before half an hour. Go back down and ride the tube if you want. No one is looking for you—not yet." Then she turned left and walked down the Holborn towards Tottenham Court Road.

Not twenty minutes later she came up the steps to her office with a bag marked "Burton, the Tailor of Taste." *Never imagined I'd actually buy something from anyone as downmarket as Sir Montague Burton,* she thought.

No one was in but the office clerk, who was readying to leave for the evening. "Messages, Boyle?" she asked without stopping as she casually moved towards her small office at the back. The clerk shook his head. "You can leave the lights on; I'll be working late." The man nodded and pulled on his coat. Once he had gone, Alice went to the rear of the building and unlocked the back door. Tom was standing there.

"Am I too early?"

She smiled but shook her head and ushered him in.

"Well, it's been two hours since you were let loose. I think we should begin to assume that Roger Hollis has gotten the word by now. Even if he hasn't yet, it's best to start acting as though he has. So, first we need to take a passport picture of you. Follow me." She picked up a box camera and led him into a darkroom with a photo enlarger. "We have to copy a lot of documents, and photostat is the simplest way. We can take pictures and develop them too. Take off your hat; straighten your tie. Stand over there against the white wall." She took three photographs while Tom did as he was told. Then she ushered him out of the door and closed it. He could hear the light switch turn off. A few minutes later she called him inside and used a set of tongs to shift three photos around their bath in the final tray of the development process. "Which one do you like?"

"They all look the same. Can you tell me what you're doing?"

"I'm making you a passport. I'll make one for Liz as soon as she gets here. You'll both need them."

"Why?"

"Because you're both leaving the country as invisibly as you can."

"I don't understand. What about the plan we made with Bennett?"

Alice gave him an exasperated glance. "I was going to wait to explain it to both of you together." She looked at her watch. "Choose a photo, would you?" When he'd made his selection, she plucked it out of its rinse. As she clipped it to a line to dry, she spoke. "To begin with, this is England. We can't expect anything to remain secret for long. We can't expect the operation that Bennett is planning to work. Most of all, we can't expect that everyone will play by the rules, even if we do. So, we're not going to play by the rules—not their rules, anyway."

"I don't follow," Tom said as she led him back into the office. He sat down and lit another of his stale cigarettes. "Start over, and go slowly."

"Look, in a couple of hours at the most, someone high up in the Home Office—whether it's the permanent secretary or the commissioner of the Metropolitan Police—is going to start using you, Liz, and me as bait in a scheme to put a stop to two foreign services operating on their turf. The last thing they'll be interested in is saving you, Liz, or me. They'll be far more interested in protecting their precious Roger Hollis, senior civil servant, a K no less . . ."

Tom interrupted, "'K no less'?"

"Oh, a knight commander of the order of St. George, a 'sir' to you." Alice assumed an arch accent. "Don't you see, old chum, he simply couldn't be the bent one." She dropped the accent. "A half-dozen mandarins in the Home Office or the FO will decide that they've known Roger Hollis too long and too well for him to be a spy. They'll have to protect him against such absurd charges. Best way to do that is to see to it that the FBI or the KGB disposes of us first. Then the police, or whoever gets the job, roll up their teams and escort them to the borders of Her Majesty's dominions."

"So, what are we to do?"

"I'll explain when Liz gets here."

At seven o'clock that evening, they heard a car drive into the alley and then a knock on the back door. Alice opened it to allow Liz in, then locked the door behind her. "Do you think you've been followed, Liz?"

"Not up to Oxford. I took some local trains. I'd have spotted people switching with me. No one followed my car out of the car park at the station." Then she saw Tom and rushed to him. Alice left the rear corridor to them and went to the front door to wait for Beatrice Russell. An age later Tom and Liz came to the office's entry hall to wait with Alice. She couldn't help noticing that they were still straightening their clothes.

"Tom has filled me in, Alice. What are we going to do?"

"Well, first we need to manufacture a passport for you, Liz. Let's get a picture." She led Liz back to the darkroom.

After a moment Liz came out, and some time later, Alice called her back in to make her selection. Once it had been clipped up to dry, both women rejoined Tom in the office.

"So, Alice, where will you get the passports for these pictures, and how do you think we're ever going to get to use them?" Tom sounded sceptical.

"Well, we are going to try to fool anyone who's looking for us that we are at my place in St. John's Wood. But in fact you two will be headed out of the country."

"How?" both Liz and Tom asked simultaneously.

"First, I am going to put on man's clothes." She pointed to the bag from Burton's lying against the wall at the entrance to her small office. "Then, I'm going home. Let's hope I'm the only one they'll want to keep track of. They saw me coming in here the front way. We've got to hope they'll assume you two are in custody at least for another few hours. When I leave here, I'll look different enough so that no one will follow me. At eight thirty I'm going to call here from St. John's Wood. You are going to pick up the phone, and we are going to have a conversation in which you say that you're at my place on Hamilton Terrace, and I will say things suggesting I am here in this office and about to leave to join you in St. John's Wood. I'm pretty certain my line is being tapped, either by the FBI or MI5, maybe even by the KGB, though I rather doubt they have the government access they would need to do that."

"But—" Liz immediately saw that this solution did not provide for Alice to escape.

Alice went on, "They will wait for me to join up with you at St. John's Wood before moving in on us. Anyway, that's my hope. But of course they'll never see me arrive, since I'll be there already. The longer they wait, the more time you'll have to escape."

"Is that where Beatrice Russell comes in?" Tom was beginning to see how this might work. Liz had fallen silent.

"Yes. She'll drive you two to Dover or Folkstone or maybe Harwich. You should be out of Britain on fake passports by the time the people watching my place in St. John's Wood lose patience and charge in."

Now both Liz and Tom spoke, each asking different questions.

Tom said, "What passports?"

Liz asked the question she had swallowed a few minutes before. "What about you?"

"Whose question first?" Alice asked as she slid behind her desk. There she opened the central drawer, from which she withdrew two

British passports. With a double-edged razor, she began removing a picture from one of them, and then using a tweezers carefully teased up the eyelet rivet holding it down to the page.

"You look like you're a professional, Alice," Liz observed.

"These are my parents' passports. They were very young when they married and still young when they died. On the *Andrea Doria* two years ago. Bodies never recovered; passports were being held by the purser of the ship." Liz and Tom needed no reminder. The Italian liner had sunk two summers before, after colliding with a Swedish ship, the *Stockholm*, in the North Atlantic. Alice set Tom's freshly dried and trimmed photo into place. "Your picture should just about have drip-dried sufficiently to move to the dryer, Liz," she said absently as she concentrated on gluing Tom's photo and resetting its eyelet rivet. "No death certificates in the United Kingdom. These passports should be good for years." She took out a bottle of India ink and an old-fashioned steel-nibbed pen. "The date stamp over the photo shouldn't be very difficult for a dab hand." She finished it and held it out the length of her arm. "Pretty good." She passed it to Tom and returned to the darkroom to move Liz's photo to the print dryer.

Now my question, Alice, thought Liz as Alice returned. "We might make it, but only because you are walking into a deathtrap for us. How are you getting out?"

"Oh, I'll have a much surer way out than you two. Remember how you introduced yourself to Feklisov, Liz, as Mrs. Carton? Well, 'It's a far, far better thing that I do . . .'" She laughed out loud. "I'm the Sydney Carton of this story, except not so heroic."

"What are you talking about?" Liz was angry. Tom was silent, trying to piece the conversations together.

"Right; you've seen my arm, Liz. Don't bother to deny it. Rather nice of you in fact never to mention that you suspect I'm some sort of dope fiend." She pulled up her sleeve for Tom, who looked at the track marks of injections. "Liz's noticed them more than once. She thinks I'm an addict." She turned to face Liz. "Well, you're right." She turned her arm, showing the tracery of veins and injection sites to Liz. "I'm dying. Inoperable uterine cancer. Detected about eighteen months ago. It's starting to give me a lot of pain. The doctors told me that would be the sign that the terminal part of the disease had begun. My GP put me on morphine—self-administered—three days before you walked into my office, Liz. This case was the best thing you could ever have done for me."

"You've been rushing round for me for weeks while you've been . . . dying? And in pain?" Tom was appalled.

Now Liz understood that first response Alice had made to her predicament: "Excellent!"

"Doing exactly what I've wanted to do. You were my last client, and I've been absorbed every minute. Just the sort of thing I love doing. It's made the time pass so quickly I've hardly needed any of the morphine the last week. I owe you two a great deal."

"For what?" Liz still sounded angry.

Alice turned and grabbed both of Liz's arms. "Try sitting round waiting to die, with no family and nothing in your life but the psychological need to work." She relented and smiled. "Then you two came along. Suddenly I wasn't feeling sorry for myself. I had an answer to the question of what I wanted to do with my last days."

The doorbell rang. Alice rose. "That must be Beatrice." As she left the office, she turned back. "I'll have the last laugh!"

Liz and Tom sat staring at each other after she'd gone. They had no words at first.

Then Tom spoke. "Do you believe her?"

Liz nodded. She went on, resignation replacing the anger in her tone. "I've seen some signs of it—along with the injection tracks. All business, she's been. No sign of interest in anything else. Besides, that's the kind of person she is. Nothing but straight talk." They rose and came out of the small office.

⊰⊱

Beatrice Russell was sitting on the small chesterfield in the waiting room of the office, with Alice across from her. Her wet mackintosh and dripping umbrella were beside her, along with a briefcase like Liz's. Russell looked up at Liz, saw Tom, smiled, and then rose. She took a step towards Tom and held out both hands. "You're Tom Wrought. I feel I know you quite well, though we've met just the once, in August or September, wasn't it?

"Yes, that's right." He held her hands while he said, "Thank you." She knew what he was thanking her for and smiled.

Alice brought everyone back to business. "I've put Beatrice in the picture. In a few minutes, I will change and go. Then you three'll go out the back. Beatrice will drive you to a channel port and then return the car to the Oxford railway station car park. Approximately where had you parked it, Liz?"

"Always the same place, under the light stanchion closest to Botley Road."

Alice looked at Beatrice Russell. "Good; see that you repark it there if you can, dear." The latter signalled her understanding. Alice picked up the bag from Burton's and headed towards her office. "Now excuse me whilst I finish Liz's passport and change." She closed the door.

The three sat in the waiting area. No one knew what to say. Liz and Tom were silently contemplating Alice Silverstone's mortality. Beatrice Russell was worried about losing Liz. Noticing an electric kettle on a sideboard, she looked at the other two and brightly said, "Tea, anyone?" Both shook their heads. "Well, I need a cup." Russell moved to the counter and busied herself with the impedimenta. By

385

the time the cup was ready to drink, an urchinlike figure in a tweed flat cap had emerged from Alice's office. He—it looked like a young man—was wearing a corduroy jacket over grey pants, men's oxfords, with a woollen tie under the collar of a blue twill shirt. Alice's hair was hidden in the cap.

Tom looked her up and down. "Newsboy? Jockey? Bookie's tout?"

"Thanks." Alice smiled briefly and passed Liz her passport. "Now, Tom, Liz, let's work out our script. Remember, you're talking from 88 Hamilton Terrace, and I am talking from Red Lion Square. I will call you, but you must answer first, as though you called me. You say something like 'Hello, is that you, Miss Silverstone? When will you get here?' I'll say, 'I'm at my office. I'll be there in thirty minutes.'"

"I understand. Shall I pass you on to Liz? That'll convince whoever is tapping the line that she is with me in St. John's Wood."

"Good idea. I'll ask to speak to you, Liz. You get on the phone, and I'll ask you to feed the cat." She looked at Liz. "There is no cat." She thought for a moment and went back to her office. Coming back out with a wad of bank notes, she handed them to Liz. "It's a fair bit of money. I won't be needing it."

Liz began to count it. "There must be five hundred pounds here." She'd never held that much cash in her hand.

"Actually six hundred and seventy-five. Wish I had more. It's going to have to tide you over for a while. You see, I won't know where you will be. I don't want to know. And I probably won't have time to get you more." Tom was about to remonstrate. But one knowing, bleak glance from Liz silenced him. "Alright. I'm on my way." She turned to Russell. "As soon as we've finished talking on the phone, Beatrice, you'll have to start driving them to the coast. You want to time your arrival to catch a ferry at the last minute. Here's a *Thomas Cook's Continental Timetable*." Alice handed Beatrice a softcover book that looked like a pocket phone directory.

She was about to open the front door of the office when the doorbell began to ring. It was a short ring. They froze. Then another, longer, insistent. Alice shrugged her shoulders and went to the door. Opening it, she saw Alexandr Feklisov standing on the step, holding an umbrella against the heavy rain, smiling.

CHAPTER
TWENTY-TWO

"Please let me in. It is important." Feklisov spoke in a calm, low voice. Alice stepped back and opened the door. He shook out his umbrella and placed it in the stand next to the door, took off his hat, and came into the middle of the vestibule. None of the others said a word.

Hearing no greeting, he began, "I have been looking for you for most of the day, Miss Silverstone. I managed to follow you to Brixton Prison. But then you never came out." He gave Alice a look of admiration.

"I never spotted you either, going there." Alice's grin was almost conspiratorial.

Feklisov bowed slightly. "I spent a long time watching the prison gate before I realized what you had done." He turned to the others. "I'm afraid you can't delay much longer. I think the Americans are already here in the quarter, uh, the neighbourhood." Then he looked at Tom, put out his hand, smiled, and said, "Mr. Wrought, I am very glad to meet you. Alexandr Feklisov, Soviet commercial attaché. We have never met, but we had mutual acquaintances back in New York City."

Tom put out his hand, and Feklisov grasped it firmly. It seemed to Tom to be an American handshake. Then he said, "Should I be glad to meet you, Mr. Feklisov?"

"Oh, yes. If you and Mrs. Spencer want to get out of here with your lives." He turned to Alice. "What was your plan?"

"Surely you don't expect me to tell you, Mr. Feklisov?" She looked surprised. "You shouldn't even want to know if you are really here to help."

"I am sorry, Miss Silverstone. But you don't understand. I am a professional at these matters. You are, what? Perhaps a gifted amateur?" Without menace he continued, "We could have rolled you up anytime we wanted, no?"

Alice wasn't going to trust him. *How much to tell?* she wondered. *Well, he's here in front of us. He can certainly track us to St. John's Wood if he wants. Maybe he's got other people in the square or in the alley with a car.* "Well, Mr. Feklisov, we're going to make everyone think we're at my place. That'll give Tom and Liz a chance to escape." She laid out her plan.

"It is ingenious, I will grant. But it probably won't work."

Alice looked at him intently. "Why not?"

"First, you are relying on the notion that the people tapping the line can't detect the direction of the vocal signals. If they can tell that you are in St. John's Wood while Mr. Wrought and Mrs. Spencer are here, the scheme will immediately collapse." The three others were silent. "Of course, you may be lucky. If it is the Americans and they are operating alone, it may work. If it is the British, at the post office telephone banks, they can probably tell the signals' directions."

Liz asked the obvious question. "Do you have a better plan?"

Feklisov ignored her question. "You have a more difficult problem." Feklisov looked at Liz. "The Brits—Hollis, MI5—know what kind of a car you drive, and they have your MOT." He looked towards Tom and explained, "The licence plate numbers. If MI5 already here or the Americans here tell them, well then, you two"—he nodded towards Liz and Tom—"will probably be stopped before you get to the coast. Even if they don't stop you, they will find your car and know where you have gone."

Tom and Liz nodded. Alice sounded resentful of his objections. "Any other problems, Mr. Feklisov?"

"Yes, actually. Your passports. You'll need them to board a ferry. You'll need them at even the meanest hotel on the Continent. If they are not detected at a channel port, MI5 will certainly be able to reach into France or Belgium, Holland, anywhere, and start tracking you from the hotel police forms."

Here Alice smiled. "We've got that covered, Mr. Feklisov."

"Good." He grinned back. "Don't tell me more."

"No fear." Alice was sarcastic. "More problems?"

"One more. And it is a very serious problem." The others were silent. "Besides the Brits and the Americans, there is a third service interested in you, Mr. Wrought, and now interested in your friends too. My service, the KGB."

"But you said you came to help us." Liz was ashen.

Alice was, however, defiant. "Besides, if you betray us, or harm us, everything about the Krogers will come out."

"True, but the Krogers are not my people's concern at all. Just now they don't even know that you have blown the Krogers' cover."

"Why not?" Alice was surprised.

"Because I have not told them." The others seemed slightly stunned. "Moscow Centre is concerned about saving its mole in MI5 and its channel to the FBI. They need them in our war against the CIA. They will certainly want to dispose of you if that will save Hollis. And by now Hollis has told the *Residentura* you are at liberty."

Beatrice Russell interrupted. "*Residentura*, what is that?"

"Oh, it's the intelligence unit at each Russian embassy," Feklisov explained. Beatrice nodded. "I am the head of the London *Residentura*, but there are several others in it."

"I don't follow, Mr. Feklisov." It was Alice again. "If we don't survive, the Krogers will certainly be blown by the records I've left. So, you'd better call off your people at least."

"But you don't understand, Miss Silverstone. As I said, the rest of the *Residentura* doesn't even know about the Krogers' problem. We've been ordered to dispose of Mr. Wrought because he knows about Hoover's alliance with us against the CIA. But if we succeed, your dead bodies—Mr. Wrought's and Miss Silverstone's—will eventually lead a good policeman to the Krogers. It is difficult to hide three bodies, especially if other people are looking for them, and the CID has many very good policemen."

"So, you're willing to betray your own service, Mr. Feklisov?" Alice asked the lawyer's obvious question. "Why?"

"The Krogers are important to me, more important to me than my service's double agent in MI5, Sir Roger Hollis. That's one reason why I want to help you get out."

Tom was listening. "Is there another?"

Feklisov wasn't listening. He was going on. Evidently he needed to talk. "I've known Peter and Helen Kroger for more than twenty years. I knew them in America when they were the Cohens. When you work with people that long, they begin to mean something to you. We were young together, in Spain before the war. Then we worked for ten years in New York. I don't want to see them in prison here. They don't want to go back to the Soviet Union. So I am going to do what it takes to keep them out of the hands of your people as well as ours."

Alice was icy. "We don't belong to MI5."

"Or the FBI," Tom added quietly.

"Which brings me to the other reason I'm going to help you, Mr. Wrought." Looking at Tom, the Russian's eyes glistened slightly.

Is he going to cry? The thought passed through Liz's mind.

Feklisov's voice quavered slightly. "You may put it down as a private gesture of revenge, Mr. Wrought. Or, if you like, a large reward for a small favour you have done me."

"What is that, Mr. Feklisov?"

"In your newspaper article, you've let the world know that J. Edgar Hoover is the killer of an innocent woman and the maker of orphans. This is my personal and private gesture of thanks to you for telling the world. I was Julie Rosenberg's control, so I knew it. Hoover knew it. Now the world may come to know it."

Tom looked suddenly world-weary. "Don't bet on it."

"It's the best I can do for their children." Then he looked at Liz. "And for yours, Mrs. Spencer."

The three others exchanged glances. Beatrice Russell searched the faces of the other two. She could see that they now believed the Russian spy. Somehow she could not yet bring herself to do so. But no one was asking her, and she decided to keep her own counsel.

"So, you're really going to help us?" Liz spoke with real warmth.

"What are you going to do?" Alice was insistent.

"Increase their chances of escape quite considerably." He looked at Tom and Liz. "That is what I am going to do, Miss Silverstone."

All three uttered the same word. "How?"

"Here is what I propose. We shall use all of your plan." He looked at Alice to reassure her. "But we shall complicate it. You will leave dressed as you are—quite fetching, actually—for St. John's Wood. When you call, Mr. Wrought and Mrs. Spencer will have that reverse conversation with you, Miss Silverstone. They will pretend to be there, in St. John's Wood, while you pretend to be here. Perhaps it will briefly delay whoever is listening. Then Mrs. Russell and I will exchange coats and hats with Mrs. Spencer and Mr. Wrought. We will leave by the front door, turning off the lights. We will walk round to the lane where Mrs. Spencer's car is parked and drive it to Oxford. Ten minutes later, you two"—he looked towards Tom and Liz—"will leave by the rear, dressed in my coat and hat and Mrs. Russell's, and find my car." He pulled out an ignition key. "It's a black Wolseley, parked two streets from here, in Jockey's Field, next to Grey's Inn. You will drive this car to whatever channel crossing you prefer." He put up a hand. "Don't tell me which." He saw a look of relief on their faces. "The car has been scrubbed by my service and cannot be traced to any actual person. When the police find it, there will be no link to me—or you." Finally, he looked round. "Agreed?"

Everyone nodded.

Alice broke the silence. "Now it's time for me to leave." It was going to be alright. Tom and Liz would make it. As the realization dawned and the uncertainty waned, Alice's emotions were being overtaken by other sensations. She could feel the burn inside spreading as her anxiety receded. She knew she had to get back to Hamilton Terrace for the morphine. Pulling down her flat cap, Alice shook Tom's hand, hugged Liz, and clasped the hands of Beatrice Russell. Finally she took Feklisov's hands in hers and said, "Thank you," adding "comrade" with an inflection of doubt. Feklisov pulled her to him with a hug that lasted several seconds. Then Alice slipped out the door.

Liz turned to the Russian. "You know?"

For the second time Feklisov blinked a glistening eye. "Enough. From following her closely for several weeks. One does not visit an oncologist alone or purchase morphine in quantity without reason."

Tom Wrought picked up the *Thomas Cook Continental Timetable* and began studying it carefully.

Twenty-five minutes later the telephone rang. Tom and Liz looked at each other. Tom picked up the phone and waited. At the other end Alice began, "Hello, Tom, did you just get there?"

"Yes, the tube up to St. John's Wood was slow tonight. We almost got off at Maida Vale and walked." Liz smiled at his creativity. "I'll put Liz on."

"Are you still at the office, Alice?" Liz began.

"Yes, just on the point of leaving," she replied. "Be there in half an hour. Please feed the cat."

"Alright. We'll have a cup of tea waiting when you get here."

"Cheers," Alice replied, and Liz immediately rung off.

In the sitting room on Hamilton Terrace, Alice put down the receiver and looked at the syringe and the three vials of morphine on a side table. *Are you sure they'll make it out? Nothing is ever sure, Alice. Can you do any more? No, I can't see how. Well, then? Isn't this the time to bow out?* She rose from the chair, swept the vials and the syringe into her hand, and mounted the stair to the bedroom. She took off the men's clothes and ran her hands over the dozen or so suits she had enjoyed wearing in court, in chambers, wherever a solicitor, but not a woman, was expected. *You know perfectly well which one you'll choose—the steel-blue one.* Once she was wearing it, standing at the full-length mirror, she knew it was right for the occasion. *Silly thing to concern yourself with!* She laughed at herself out loud. *Get on with it!*

Dispassionately she watched herself push the needle through the rubber top of the vial. She stopped to monitor her hand for a tremor—a sign that her body was rebelling or anxious or unprepared. No, the grip was steady. Then she pulled the piston up and watched the cylinder fill. She let another spasm of pain course through her. It was as good a time to go as any. Taking off the tailored jacket, she rolled up her sleeves, injected the full syringe, put the coat back on, and staggered onto the bed, where she managed to straighten the skirt just as oblivion arrived.

"Here's my coat." Beatrice Russell handed her coat and hat to Liz. As she did so, she guided Liz's hand into the pocket and closed it over a piece of paper, but held it there to prevent Liz pulling it from the pocket. She turned to the Russian. "We've got a bit of a ride to Oxford, Mr. Feklisov. Shall we make a start?" He nodded, taking the coat and hat Tom had given him and turning off the lights in the office. Both made a display of leaving by the front door, which they pretended to lock, and walked round two corners to the back lane, where Liz and Tom could see them get in the car and turn on the engine. In a moment they had driven away.

Tom looked at Liz as if to say both "what now?" and "where to?" Without answering, Liz took out the piece of paper Beatrice Russell had hidden in her coat pocket. "Tom," Liz said, "Beatrice put a note in her coat before she gave it to me." Tom pulled a match from the matchbox and lit it. Both began to read.

> Alice was right not to trust our people or the Americans. But you can't trust Feklisov either. Don't go to any channel port. My uncle, William Daven, lives in Lowestoft. He owns a herring trawler and used to smuggle liquor from Holland and France. I will call to alert him you are coming. He'll get you to the Continent safely. Go to the South Pier midjetty, the trawler Louise-Marie. Uncle William will take the Russian's car in payment and perhaps even give you something for it.
> Good luck,
> Beatrice

Tom looked up to Liz in the light of a second match. "Any idea where Lowestoft is?"

"Uh-huh. It's where Beatrice is from. There's an Abbey National branch there. But I don't think we'll give the branch a visit, do you?" She squeezed his hand, and they rose. "Let's go."

⟫—⟪

It was fifty miles of good roads from London to Oxford, but 130 much more difficult miles to Lowestoft, and after Ipswich, single-track lanes up the Suffolk Coast.

⟫—⟪

Beatrice Russell and Alexandr Feklisov were companionable but said little on their drive to Oxford and rail journey back. They parted in friendship on the Paddington quay long before Tom and Liz were even near their objective. She knew she'd have plenty of time to alert Uncle William to his unexpected passengers. Suddenly Beatrice realized, what if he were at sea? She waited while Feklisov sought the Bakerloo line. Then Beatrice found a call box that could not be seen from any stairway to the underground. Two rings, and then she heard the welcome words, "Bill Daven here."

⟫—⟪

Lowestoft was dark and quiet as Liz drove through the high street. The south pier was easy to find. It was just across the bridge from the railway station in the small harbour mouth of the Waveney River. Daven was waiting at the jetty gate when the Wolseley pulled up. Liz and Tom came out of the car, stretching and yawning, to find a thickset man in a pea jacket and a bowler hat, standing with his back to a dozen trawlers and three times as many winches rising from their bows and sterns. His silhouette was backlit by a low full moon reflecting in the iridescent current of a calm estuary.

"Captain Daven?" Tom offered his hand, but William Daven only had eyes for the car.

"Can I have the keys?" were his first words, and then, "Don't suppose you have the registration." Tom shook his head. "Well, Beatrice said I wasn't to ask any questions. Come aboard." He turned and walked up the jetty fifty yards to a pier extending out to the left. The trawlers tied alongside looked seaworthy enough, though their decks were crowded with netting and they bore an aroma strong from decades of herring catches. Showing surprising agility, the large man vaulted over the side of his trawler and reached down to help Liz aboard. Tom declined the hand and scrambled over the hemp padding at the quayside. Daven led them to the wheelhouse, where a slight young man dressed much the same as the elder one was leaning on a bulkhead. At the noise of the door opening, he stood.

Daven turned to his crewman and said, "Make ready to cast off. Quiet like." The man nodded and went forwards, slipped off the bowlines, and then headed to the stern. The captain turned a switch, and the low rumble of a diesel engine began to vibrate the entire ship. A wave of the hand from the young man at the stern, and the captain spun the wheel away from the jetty, pushing forwards the throttle at his left. The boat quietly moved away from the quay and out into the river mouth. Round the quay it bore to starboard and soon was leaving the town behind it, heading due east.

Only then did William Daven push his bowler back from his brow and appear to relax somewhat. He lit a Player's cigarette and offered the packet to Liz and Tom, who both accepted. "You both best go below. In a few minutes, you will be very seasick."

"Where are you going to land us, Captain?"

"Where would you like? Holland or Belgium?"

"We are at your disposal, sir. What do you advise?" As he spoke, Tom felt the first pangs of nausea.

"If we go into Zeebrugge, you might as well have taken the Harwich ferry. I suppose there was a reason you wanted to avoid crossing that way."

Liz nodded, but suddenly brought one hand to her mouth and grasped a bulkhead with the other.

Daven indicated the gangway from the pilothouse to below decks. "Better get to bed. Leave it to me." They did as instructed.

The berths were unmade, dishevelled heaps of coarse blankets and grey-striped uncovered pillows. Towards the stern was a head, with a door that would not close. An electric light in a wire cage above their heads was connected to no switch they could find. Tom and Liz threw themselves on the beds, becoming sicker with each passing swell. Each was now seeking oblivion, without much interest in the fate of the other, so completely seasick had they become. Despite all that had occurred that day, sleep did not come easily on the current of the North Sea. In vain they sought relief from the cramps and dizziness, first lying on their stomachs, then their sides. Finally they surrendered to the nausea, prostrate on the bunks, waiting indifferently for the voyage, or their lives, to end.

<hr />

To Tom's surprise he was woken by a shaft of sun breaking through the crack in the top of the hatch cover above their berths. He realized that he had finally found sleep. He turned to Liz and was relieved to see she too had slept. There seemed to be no particular roll in the craft, and he wondered whether he had found sea legs in a few hours sleep. Climbing back to the pilothouse he joined Daven, who was watching a fleet of similar herring trawlers, all plying a route towards a landfall on the port side.

Daven gestured. "Vlissingen, on the Scheldt. We'll come in with their trawler fleet. No one will notice." He looked up, and Tom followed his glance to the Dutch maritime flag wafting from a guy-wire. Daven withdrew a wad of bills from his pea coat. "There's some Dutch guilder and French francs there. About a hundred quid. Tell Beatrice I gave you a fair price for a hot Wolseley." He smiled. "From here there's a train into Antwerp every hour. Be on the first one this morning."

⟞✦⟝

And so they were. As the train approached the outskirts of Antwerp, Dutch customs and Belgian customs sauntered down the aisle of the second-class carriage. With world-weary nonchalance, they were asking for passports and goods to declare. It was the first test of Alice Silverstone's handiwork, and not a very severe one. Each officer—first Dutch, then Belgian—saluted with two fingers as they handed the passports back.

CHAPTER TWENTY-THREE

Sitting in the station buffet of the Antwerp railway terminal, Liz and Tom took stock.

"Let's see." Liz was laying out the British bank notes. "About eight hundred quid between what Alice gave us and what I had."

"Here's what's left from what Daven gave me for the car." Tom added the Dutch and French currency. "So, what now, my dear?" He grasped her hand and smiled warmly. Suddenly in the vastness of the glass ceiling and the arching dome above them, Tom felt free enough to think beyond the next few moments and hours.

Liz's smile turned to a laugh. She drained her café au lait. "I think I'll have another. You?" He nodded, and she raised a hand. The waiter, caparisoned in a starched apron, was instantly before them. They had already, between them, eaten two complete *petite dejeuners*, croissants, pan raisin, and tartines, along with all the butter and three little pots of jam and preserves. Without asking, he put another basket of croissants before them and glided away. The morning rush hour had subsided, and they could enjoy the view of bright polished marble floor stretching down the broad staircase all the way to the booking hall.

"Seriously, Liz, what shall we do now?" Tom was full of half-baked ideas about where to go, what to do, how to live, eager to try them on for size. But he wanted Liz to at least suggest a general direction.

She was still thinking only about the next few hours. "Very well. We are going out of this station to find the first decent hotel in the square, where we will check in. On arriving in our room, we will hand over every stitch of clothing we are wearing for washing and dry cleaning. Then we will both spend an inordinate amount of time in a bath. After that we will pass the hours awaiting our clean clothes in that room. Understood?"

"Every stitch of clothes? Does that include our hats?" Tom asked. Each smiled, and they both thought a moment about the hats they had exchanged with Beatrice Russell and Alexandr Feklisov.

Looking at Tom as they walked across the large square, Liz stopped. "Let's just stop at a chemist's before the hotel. We need a razor, a couple of toothbrushes, and a few other things before shutting ourselves away." The smile was frank.

When the bellman came to the door, Tom reached his arm out with the laundry sack and a Dutch banknote. The man could see he was wearing nothing but a towel. In French Tom apologized. "Sorry, no Belgian currency."

The man replied, "No difficulty, Monsieur Silverstone. I live in the suburbs, across the *Nederland* border." Tom almost corrected the man, till he realized that for the moment he was indeed Monsieur Silverstone.

Taking the trilingual **Do Not Disturb** sign from the inside door handle, he put it on the hallway side, double-locked the door, and padded past the double bed into the bathroom. There he sat beside the tub, watching Liz splash round the soapy water. He had not seen her body for more than a month, and he was ready to enjoy just the visual pleasure it provided him for as long as she chose to luxuriate in the warmth. She looked up at him, then down at her body with pleasure.

"Liz, where are the kids?" Tom's sudden anxiety completely displaced the relief, happiness, and pleasure that had surfeited him once the hotel room door had closed behind them. Silently, he condemned himself.

"I sent the kids to Trevor's brother in Birkenhead before I went to America. Afterwards they stayed; I wanted them out of any danger. Keith'll get them to my parents in Toronto."

"But how will you—how will we get them back?"

"As soon as we've settled down somewhere." She rose from the bath, dried, but did not cover herself. He relished the grace with which she moved across to the dressing table, picked up her purse, and moved to the window seat. Looking down three storeys to the street, she pushed the sheer drape aside and sat. As she pulled a cigarette packet from her bag, the play of muscles in her shoulder and the rise of the one breast visible to him brought desire rising in him again. She threw the packet towards him and began to look for her lighter.

Tom said, almost to himself, "Yes, but where will we get the kids back?"

Searching her hand round the inside, she felt a card at the bottom of the bag and slowly pulled it out. Unfolding and uncreasing it on her knee, she read the words,

PHILIPPE D'ALEMBERT

AGENT IMMOBILIER

OLORON-SAINTE-MARIE, BEARN

"Tom, what do you think of somewhere in the Pyrenees?

PART VI

February 1961

Pays de Bearn

CHAPTER
TWENTY-FOUR

Saturday was market day in the *jardin publique* of Oloron-Sainte-Marie. It wasn't like the summer, with the plane trees shading the stalls from the powerful sun. In fact, each tree had been severely pruned the previous fall into a neat filigree of branches. They would take the shape of an almost perfect cube when the leaves came back in April. But now the market required no protection from the weak sun and the fierce blue sky. The previous two market days had been cold and wet, so today the stalls were doing well. Some provisions were by no means seasonal: goat cheese, olives, *saucisson*, braids of garlic pegged above tables covered in thyme and tarragon, still clamouring for attention against endive, leeks, Brussels sprouts. There were only a few sorts of lettuce, no tomato worth haggling over, but the dried mushrooms, *gigot* of lamb, pig's face, and duck all showed their Béarnaise provenance.

Liz came out of the *boulangerie* with a tarte in a *boite* tied with a thin ribbon they would present to their friend Philippe D'Alembert at lunch that afternoon. Having greeted her by name, the *boulanger* repeated the salute as she left, *"A la prochaine, Mme. Silverstone."*

She began looking for the children, now fluent enough in French to make their own way through the market stalls, with their own pocket money. Eventually she saw them engaged in a pickup soccer game on the half-grass/half-barren margin of the park beyond its central fountain. There was plenty of time. She'd let them play.

Liz turned back to wander again through the market stalls, smiling nods of recognition to the other townspeople and to those merchants she favoured, until she was before the café where she had arranged to meet Tom. There he was with a manila envelope before him on the table, a broad smile on his face, and what looked like a cognac in his hands. Not like Tom to drink before noon on a Saturday morning.

Liz put down her bags on an adjacent seat. "You're beaming, Tom. Have you won the lottery?" The waiter came up, and she ordered a café crème.

"Better, I think." He passed an envelope to her. It was addressed to Mr. David Silverstone, *Poste Restante*, Oloron-Sainte-Marie, France. Liz held it before her and studied it for a moment. There was no return address, but she recognized Beatrice Russell's handwriting.

Then she opened it, and two neatly scissored newspaper cuttings floated down to the table. Before she could pick one up, Tom spoke. "Those are our tickets back to Britain, Mrs. Spencer—or will it be Mrs. Wrought?"

She began to read the first clipping. It was a small, narrow column and evidently came from a broadsheet newspaper, not a tabloid.

January 7, London. The Home Office announced today the arrest of two persons charged with being Soviet agents. Mr. and Mrs. Peter and Helen Kroger were taken into custody in their home in Ruislip, where incriminating communication equipment was also found. The Krogers have been identified as

Morris and Lona Cohen, Americans, who had previously been Soviet agents in the United States but disappeared in 1950. A Russian diplomat, Aleksandr Feklisov, Commercial Attaché at the Soviet embassy, has also been declared persona non grata and asked to leave the country immediately.

Liz picked up the second clipping. It was the "Court Circular" from the *Times*, dated 11 January. Among the list of events at Buckingham Palace, one sentence was underlined.

Tuesday:

The Queen received Sir Roger Hollis, KBE, CB, on the occasion of his retirement from the Home Office.

Liz smiled. "It would be nice to be able to go back. But I wonder if we should?"

Tom was surprised. "I thought you'd be delighted. We can go back to Oxford, put the kids in the Dragon School again, and live happily ever after."

"Well, this does free us of anxiety about the Russians. But what about MI5 and the FBI?"

"I suspect the old boy network will still want to protect Roger Hollis even after he's been sacked. But they certainly wouldn't let him harm us if we turn up in England. That would only attract the sort of attention no one in the establishment wants." Tom stopped for a minute. "As for the FBI, I think I can put something into the hands of that very same establishment to protect us. Now that Isaiah Berlin has the ear of Jack Kennedy, it wouldn't be too hard to send a message J.

Edgar Hoover might not welcome. Then there is the master of Trinity, or Alice's friend, Victor Mishcon. The threat of a word in the ear of Michael Foot should be enough to keep the Americans at bay."

"Look, Tom, I don't mind becoming Elizabeth Spencer again, or even Elizabeth Wrought." She reached over to cover his hand. "But I am not sure I want to spend my declining years in England. Not when I can live in the South of France."

Tom smiled. "Well, perhaps we can do both."

AFTERWORD: DRAMATIS PERSONAE

Many of the characters that figure in or are mentioned in this narrative were real people. The details of their lives and the chronologies of actual events in which they participated have been generally adhered to. None of them is any longer alive.

Bayard Rustin was an important peace activist who introduced Martin Luther King Jr. to nonviolence. He was an early gay rights advocate and principal organizer of the 1963 March on Washington. Thurgood Marshall, who won the *Brown v. Board of Education* US Supreme Court case that ended *de jure* (but not *de facto*) segregation in the US public school system in 1954, later became an associate justice of the Supreme Court. He was strongly opposed to allowing former members of the US Communist Party to participate in the civil rights movement. John Hope Franklin, historian of the African-American experience, was the first black Harvard history PhD and first black chair of a major American university history department—Brooklyn College, in 1956. Subsequently he was chair at the University of Chicago and from 1982 James B. Duke professor at Duke University. In 1995, Franklin was awarded the US Presidential Medal of Freedom. The US Navy declined his services as a clerk-typist when he volunteered during the Second World War. Instead, they offered to make him a mess steward. Mordecai Wyatt Johnson was president of Howard University from 1926 to 1960.

Julius Rosenberg, Morton Sobell, and David Greenglass all communicated information about the design of the first nuclear weapons to Alexandr Semyonovich Feklisov when the latter was a Soviet diplomatic officer in the United States during and immediately after the Second World War. None of their information was needed by the Soviet atomic scientists to develop their first nuclear weapon. Rosenberg and his wife were both executed in 1953 by the US government, leaving two children who at first could find no one to take them in. Decades after her execution, allegations of Ethel Rosenberg's innocence were substantiated by Greenglass. He admitted implicating her in his testimony to protect his wife, the probable real accomplice. Feklisov later worked in the United Kingdom, to which the espionage agents Lona and Morris Cohen moved after escaping the United States and spending some years in Russia. In Britain they changed their names to Kroger and operated until apprehended in 1961. The Krogers were exchanged for a British agent in 1969.

The lyricist/composer who wrote *Strange Fruit*, Abel Meeropol, published it originally in *New Masses* in 1937, then arranged it for Billie Holiday to sing at Café Society in 1939. Meeropol and his wife adopted the children of Julius and Ethel Rosenberg in the 1950s.

In the late 1930s, City College of New York was a hotbed of future Soviet agents, African-American writers, and later, civil rights activists. It was also the breeding ground for a whole generation of New York intellectuals who started off on the extreme left, some even to the left of the Communist Party. Most of them moved steadily to the centre and then to the right by the end of their lives. This group includes Daniel Bell, Seymour Martin Lipset, Irving Howe, and William Kristol, the last two of whom have minor roles here.

In 1942 Omar Bradley was the first commander of the Eighty-Second Airborne Division at Camp Claiborne, Louisiana. Like some of his superiors, including Dwight D. Eisenhower, he publicly opposed integrating the US Army immediately before President Truman ordered it in 1948. The Twenty-Eighth Division fought in the Hürtgen Forest during November 1944 under the command of General Norman Cota, who was the first to sanction and employ black combat infantry the next month during the Battle of the Bulge. David Y. Hurwitz was a major and second-in-command of G-2, Intelligence, of the Twenty-Eighth Division in the period before the Hürtgen Forest battles.

Orville Faubus had a distinguished record in the Third Army in Europe. Before the war he was student body president at Commonwealth College, a school committed to organizing farm labour and associated with the US Communist Party. As governor of Arkansas, he defied the federal government and closed the Little Rock schools to prevent their integration. Vito Anthony Marcantonio was the representative from East Harlem in the US Congress between 1934 and 1950. Frequently reelected as an American Labor Party candidate, he was sympathetic to the political line of the US Communist Party but never a member. Marcantonio was a persistent advocate of the rights of his mainly African-American constituents.

Richard Hoftstadter was a professor at Columbia University, a well-known American historian and author of *The Paranoid Style in American Politics*. Like many other intellectuals, he was a member of the Young Communist League and the Communist Party before resigning in consequence of Stalin's nonaggression pact with Hitler.

Sir David Lindsey Keir was a historian and master of an Oxford college (not Trinity) in the late '50s. Sir Isaiah Berlin, originally from Riga, Latvia, and fluent in Russian, was a fellow of All Souls College, as well as Chichle Professor of Political Philosophy. Berlin had extensive experience in British government, especially the Foreign Office, during the Second World War. He served in the United States and became acquainted with some of the "Cambridge" spies, certainly Guy Burgess, probably Donald McLean, and possibly Kim Philby, all of whom were posted to the Washington embassy at the same time as Berlin was in the United States. However, there is no reason to suppose that Bayard Rustin knew Guy Burgess during or after the war.

Michael Foot was a member of Parliament from 1945 to 1955 and again from 1976 to 1992. He was leader of the Labour Party during part of the Thatcher years. He had been an important figure in Fleet Street from the late '30s onward, and during the 1950s edited the left-wing Labour Party newspaper, the *Tribune*.

Victor Mishcon was a distinguished solicitor, chair of the London County Council, and Labour life peer. He sat on the Wolfenden Commission that recommended decriminalizing homosexuality and acted for Princess Diana in her divorce case against Prince Charles.

R. Taylor Cole was the OSS chief of station in Stockholm, Sweden, during the Second World War and later provost of Duke University. Allen Dulles was the director of the CIA in 1951. Sir Roger Hollis headed MI5, British counterintelligence, for almost a decade until his retirement in 1965, and was dogged by accusations of being a Soviet double agent throughout that period and afterwards.

J. Edgar Hoover's sexual orientation has been a matter of common knowledge for a long time.

ABOUT THE AUTHOR

Alex Rosenberg is the author of the novel *The Girl from Krakow*. He has lived in Britain and has taught at Oxford, where he made the acquaintance of some of the historical figures that play roles in *Autumn in Oxford*. Rosenberg is the R. Taylor Cole Professor of Philosophy at Duke University in North Carolina.